2-11

P9-CLI-941

SEP - 2002

By Marcus Wynne from Tom Doherty Associates

No Other Option
Warrior in the Shadows

WARRIOR
IN THE
SHADOWS

WARRIOR IN THE SHADOWS

MARCUS WYNNE

A TOM DOHERTY ASSOCIATES BOOK
NEW YORK

CHANDLER PUBLIC LIBRARY
22 S. DELAWARE
CHANDLER AZ 85225

This is a work of fiction. All the characters and events portrayed in
this novel are either fictitious or are used fictitiously.

WARRIOR IN THE SHADOWS

Copyright © 2002 by Marcus Wynne

All rights reserved, including the right to reproduce this book,
or portions thereof, in any form.

This book is printed on acid-free paper.

A Forge Book
Published by Tom Doherty Associates, LLC
175 Fifth Avenue
New York, NY 10010

www.tor.com

Forge® is a registered trademark of Tom Doherty Associates, LLC.

Library of Congress Cataloging-in-Publication Data

Wynne, Marcus.
    Warrior in the shadows / Marcus Wynne.—1st ed.
        p. cm.
    "A Tom Doherty Associates book."
    ISBN 0-765-30443-0 (alk. paper)
    1. Government investigators—Fiction. 2. Australian aborigines—Fiction. 3. Legal
photography—Fiction. 4. Murder for hire—Fiction. 5. Photographers—Fiction.
6. Cannibalism—Fiction. I. Title.

PS3623.Y66 W37 2002
813'.6—dc21

                                                                    2002069329

First Edition: September 2002

Printed in the United States of America

0 9 8 7 6 5 4 3 2 1

CHANDLER PUBLIC LIBRARY
22 S. DELAWARE
CHANDLER, AZ 85225

ACKNOWLEDGMENTS

I want to thank my agents, Ethan Ellenberg and Michael Psaltis of the Ethan Ellenberg Literary Agency and Brian Lipson of the Endeavor Talent Agency. At Tor/Forge, I want to thank my editor, Brian Callaghan; my great publicist, Elena Stokes; and the rest of the Tor/Forge crew: "Buttercup," Jennifer Marcus, Kathleen Fogarty, Linda Quinton, and Tom Doherty.

I'm indebted to the work of Percy Tresize, the great Australian artist and author whose work has brought the world of Quinkin country to life for those of us who live far away from that dark dreamland. While I've drawn on his work, any mistakes or misinterpretations are mine alone. I also owe thanks to Andrew Dineen of the Adventure Company for his help in setting up my tour of the Jowalbinna Bush Camp in Quinkin country, and to Allen and Mick, my guides to the rock art.

And of course I owe my usual great debt to my wife, Caprice. Without her support none of this would be possible.

PART 1

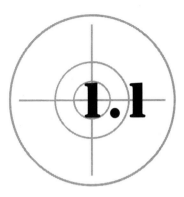

The man who would soon be eaten had enjoyed a superb supper. Broiled fresh scallops, with a hint of lemon and butter, a small filet mignon, a side of steamed vegetables—not enough to go over the strict limit of carbohydrates allowed on his diet—and a carafe of a very respectable Chilean cabernet sauvignon had left him feeling comfortably full and warm, a pleasant feeling in the chill of the late September Minneapolis night, where the hint of the bitter winter to come was still just a suggestion in the crisp cool air.

The man's name was Madison Simmons. The slightly fussy tone of his name suited him, a chubby man who seemed older than his thirty-two years, ten of which he'd spent as an international loan officer for First Bank International specializing in overseas investments in Southeast Asia and Australia. He'd been quite successful, and he was surprisingly popular with the Australian businessmen who approved of both his business seriousness and his hidden streak of fun.

While Madison enjoyed his work with the Australians, he needed time for his solitary pleasures. A bachelor who lived alone in an expensive home on the shore of Lake Harriet, his secret joy was his state-of-the-art home theater and his extensive collection of exotic pornography. His frequent visits to Southeast Asia had given him the opportunity to expand his collection into some extremely specialized areas and even, once or twice, to cast and star in a small production of his own.

He had some new videos that had been delivered to him by a discreet friend with the Australian consulate, as way of special thanks for some delicate work he had recently done. Review of those tapes would be the perfect cap to his evening.

So he walked briskly, his tailored suit coat open and flapping over the protuberance of his belly, down the wide sidewalks of Nicollet Mall to the multistory parking garage where he kept his car. There were many people out: street people jingling spare change cans, students with backpacks slung over one shoulder, couples strolling arm in arm from an early dinner.

There is a comforting buzz of background noise in a city during the hours before night becomes midnight, and Madison Simmons enjoyed those familiar sounds. He went into the corner entrance of the parking garage, paused with the caution of an urban dweller for a moment to make sure he was alone, and then went up two flights of stairs onto the level where his Lexus was parked.

"Wonk, wonk."

He stopped for a moment and looked around him, puzzled by the peculiar sound. It seemed as though it came from somewhere in the long lines of cars still parked on this level, the empty gaps between the cars like missing teeth in a grinning skull.

"Wonk, wonk."

What was that?

Madison hurried to his car, his keys jingling and ready in his hand, huddled into his overcoat, looking only straight ahead at his car gleaming under the fluorescent lights. He hit the remote unlock on his key chain and watched his car lights come on and heard the reassuring click of the doors unlocking. He paused for a moment, and looked carefully around him, even allowed himself the paranoid urge to look in the backseat of his car before he hurried in and slammed the door shut. He fumbled his keys into the ignition slot and turned them, then looked to each side and began to back out.

"Wonk, wonk."

Safely inside his car, he gripped the steering wheel so hard his knuckles stood out white against his skin. Must be damn kids, or some drunk lunatic who thought it would be funny to frighten him. He threw the car into gear, turned into the descending ramp, and squealed his tires as he went too fast for the descent to the exit gate, where a bored Sikh man, his red turban wound tight on his head, watched a miniature television set in the brightly lit glass booth.

Madison handed the attendant his validated parking ticket and said, "There's someone up on the third level, shouting, trying to scare people."

The Sikh man said nothing while he fed the parking ticket into a scanner on the cash register, printed out a receipt, and handed it back to Madison.

"Did you hear me? There's someone wandering around up there trying to frighten people," Madison said again.

The Sikh man smiled a smile that stopped at his eyes. "Thank you very much, sir. I will tell the security when they come through," he said. "Good night to you, sir."

Madison snatched the receipt and shoved it into the seat console beside him. The Lexus surged forward with his foot heavy on the gas. He pulled out onto Nicollet Avenue and drove away. Just outside the parking structure, there was a man dressed in black leather, sitting on one of those motorcycles you had to practically lie down full length on. He watched Madison drive by before he pulled out behind him. Madison looked in the rearview mirror, but he could barely see the man's figure through the glare of the motorcycle headlamp. The rider was wearing a black helmet that gleamed in the light.

The banker's enjoyment of his dinner seemed ruined by the sudden stabs of adrenaline in his belly; fear was not an emotion he'd experienced much in his adult years. This reminded him of the schoolyard bullies who'd tormented him as a boy when he was young and smart and hadn't learned the necessary lesson of keeping a low profile in the herd. But anger was something he knew how to use, and he stepped on the gas and reminded himself that in future he would park his car closer to the attendant's station.

He had to brake sharply as a stoplight hurried through yellow to red. The motorcycle rider pulled into the left-hand lane and stopped beside him. Madison stared straight ahead, but his peripheral vision was enough to give him some idea of what the rider looked like: black helmet with full face visor, long kinky hair in a ponytail hanging beneath the helmet and down his back, black leather jacket and snug black denim pants, heavy black boots and gloves.

The motorcycle rider looked over at Madison for a long moment. Madison continued to stare straight ahead. When the light changed, the rider raised his right hand from the throttle and waved at Madison, who finally looked at him before the rider put his hand back on the throttle and revved the motor, then accelerated forward and pulled a wheelie through the otherwise empty intersection and roared away. His red tail lamp disappeared around a turn in the next block, the bike at such a sharp angle in the turn it seemed as though the rider's leg would touch the pavement.

Madison drove slowly through the intersection. The light turned yellow as he passed beneath it. He took a deep breath and said, "What a weird night this is."

The rest of his drive home was uneventful. There wasn't much traffic along his normal route home to his palatial house on Lake Harriet Parkway. He drove along Forty-third Street, past the crowded sidewalk tables outside Java Jack's coffeehouse, and pulled up in front of his gated driveway. He touched the remote on his dashboard and kept the front bumper of his car right up against the opening gate, as though he meant to ram it open if it stopped.

He made sure the gate was closed behind him before he got out of the car. The driveway, the garage, and the side-door entrance were all brightly lit with movement-activated lights. He left the car in the driveway and let himself in through the side door. Madison hurried to the alarm console and punched in his code, then hung his keys on the pegboard beside the door, dropped his coat into a chair, and stepped out of his shoes.

Madison's house was his pride and joy, and he decorated and designed it as best as a wealthy Minneapolis banker could. Polished hardwood floors gleamed under track lighting, expensive Persian and Turkish rugs lay artfully arrayed, with gleaming wood and glass furniture and expensive artwork set off by carefully arranged highlight lamps. Home was his refuge and his castle, it was where he came to relax and unwind.

He needed some relaxation now.

He padded up the carpeted stairs to his bedroom suite, which had his private entertainment room adjoining it. The entertainment room was a good-sized room with a state-of-the-art digital big-screen television, DVD and videotape players, stereo equipment and the very best speakers money could buy all positioned carefully in the walls. Long racks of commercial DVD movies filled one wall, along with racks of music CDs. Classical, baroque, and early jazz predominated his music collection.

Madison's private videotape collection was locked in a discreet safe locker hidden behind wooden paneling, the keypad for the electronic lock set behind an adjoining panel. Madison spared no expense on his security, as examination of some of those hidden videotapes might cost him considerable time in a state or federal penitentiary. But he was willing to run the risk, minimal that he judged it to be. He was a slave to his tastes, like any other addict.

He undressed quickly, hanging his handmade Italian suit back in the huge closet with the rotating rack. There was a persistent squeak in the rollers that annoyed him; he'd have to call the contractor again and have them come out and adjust that for him. The system cost too much to have to put up with annoying sounds. He hated annoying sounds.

Naked, he looked at himself in a full-length mirror: pudgy, overweight, his pale skin reddish at the face, neck, and hands, pale blue indentations on his calves where his snug stockings had cut into his flesh. He wouldn't be appetizing to any woman that he knew, but then his tastes didn't run to women, or adults of any kind.

He shrugged into a thick terry-cloth robe and took a large washcloth from a stack of them just inside the closet door, then returned to the entertainment room and set the large washcloth on the arm of a large leather recliner chair that sat perfectly positioned in front of the big-screen television.

13

On an end table beside the neatly arrayed racks of CDs and DVDs he set the new VHS tape his friend from the Australian consulate had given him over lunch.

"Something special, this here, mate," the young commerce officer had said. He winked at Madison across the table.

"Really?" Madison said coolly. He looked around at the crowded tables in the bistro.

"No need to bung it on with me, mate. Nobody here's the wiser," the Australian said.

"I look forward to it. And the other thing we discussed? Have you got that, too?"

"Too right, mate. Our mutual friend likes the strip club."

"We refer to it as a 'gentlemen's club.' "

"Too right, mate. I'll expect some passes, then, for me and me mates."

"I don't go there anymore. Not a good idea for me."

"You silly old bastard. Be good for you? It would be. But just look after me and my mates, eh?"

The hearty all-men-are-equal buddy talk the Australians were most comfortable with irritated Madison, though he hid it well; he had worked too hard in his life to put social distance between him and others. He found the breezy familiarity of the Australians sometimes offensive. Of course, his straight-up ventures run through the bank were more formal. The nature of his private dealings with the contacts he'd cultivated through the consulate required him to tolerate a certain amount of offensive familiarity. The men whose money he handled expected that, and they paid well.

And then there were the perks, like this videotape.

"Wonk, wonk."

Madison froze, crouched before his VHS tape player. It sounded as though the sound had come from right outside in his driveway. He left the tape in the player slot and hurried into his bedroom. In the nightstand table was a small .38 caliber revolver that had belonged to his father. He kept it loaded, although he had never fired it, for just this sort of thing. He grabbed the revolver and went cautiously down the stairs, then peeked out the windows to see who might be there.

Nothing.

He waited, listening.

Nothing.

He started back up the stairs when there was a sudden loud thump against the side-door entrance. Madison jumped in fright. Then anger took over and he ran to the side door, brandishing his revolver. He threw open the door and shouted, "Who's there?"

There was a smear of something dark on the white paint of the side door. He looked down, then stepped back in disgust. The body of a squirrel curled limply on the step. The head was missing and blood still pulsed from the body cavity. The motion lights were all on, brightly illuminating the garage, the driveway, the side door. That was a long toss from the street, he thought.

"Who's there? I have a gun, I'm calling the police," he said.

Silence.

Emboldened by his anger, he stormed out in his bathrobe, looked on the other side of his car, and around the back of his garage. There was nothing there. He went back to the open door and slammed it shut, hurrying back upstairs. He went into the master bedroom suite and for some reason locked the door behind him. The rough fabric of his robe rubbed against his suddenly sweaty legs as he strode to the cordless phone beside his bed and picked it up.

No dial tone.

He hit the POWER button again and again.

Nothing.

Madison stared at the phone as though by willing it he could make it work. He threw the phone on the bed and went into his entertainment room, clutching the revolver like a talisman, looking for his cellular phone.

There was a motion he barely caught in the corner of his vision, a sudden dark blur, and then the revolver was snatched from his grasp, twisted out of his hand in a movement so fast he couldn't comprehend what was happening. Then he was gripped by hands stronger than he imagined a vise might be like, spun and whirled and shoved down into his recliner with such force that the heavy chair slid back a full two feet.

Directly in front of him stood a medium-sized man dressed in a heavy black leather jacket, a black sweatshirt, and dark denim pants. A black motorcycle helmet, padded gloves, and a black canvas courier's bag rested on the floor beside the big-screen television. The man's skin was the color of café au lait without enough milk, just a shade too dark, his nose broad and his heavy lips full. Long black kinky hair was pulled back into a ponytail that hung down his back. His nose was pierced at the septum and he wore some small and pale piercing there. His left ear was pierced with many small pins and rings, but his hands were bare of any ring or ornament.

"Who are you?" Madison Simmons said, wheezing. "Who are you?"

The dark man studied the revolver in his hand, then opened the cylinder with the familiarity of someone who knew how to handle a firearm, and emptied the brass cartridges into his hand.

"Bloody hell, mate," the dark man said. "When did you change the ammo last . . . Second World War?"

"Who are you?"

"Call me Alfie, mate. All me friends do."

"What do you want?"

"A little of this, a little of that, a little bit of your body fat. You got some spare, eh, mate?"

Madison squeezed the leather of the recliner armrests, his hands slick with sweat. The leather was cold against his bare legs and buttocks. He stared up at the man who stood over him. The dark man's eyes were brown with yellowed whites, sunken beneath a heavy orbital ridge slashed with thick eyebrows.

Then the dark man's face split with a huge and seemingly genuine smile.

"Take it easy, mate," he said. He dropped the revolver on the floor and scattered the handful of cartridges carelessly across the carpet, then reached into the black courier bag and pulled out an intricately carved stick, about an inch thick and two feet long, with a bulbous swell on one end that was studded with what looked to be wide nail heads. The dark man took the stick and whirled it in his hand, the blurring stick just in front of Madison's face.

. "Like my look, mate?" the dark man said, touching his chest with his free hand.

"What do you want from me?"

"Some people tell me I look like a musician, rock and roll type. What do you think?"

"I can give you money . . ."

"Money got you into this, mate."

"What?"

"I do play a couple of instruments," the dark man said. "Though I don't think you'd know a didge if I was to bring one out, me old china plate. That's Aussie for mate, mate. I do play a mean didgeridoo."

The man in black twirled his heavy club.

"And I do like to play, Madison, me boy. But not with the likes of you."

The dark man twirled the club and stepped forward, then brought the stick arcing down in an axelike swipe that put the heavy bulb end neatly into the space between Madison Simmons's left ear and temple. The club came forward so fast that it impacted before Madison's flinch reflex brought his hands up. The blow snapped the banker's head over sharply, positioning it perfectly for the second blow that came right at the nape of the neck, shattering the spine and sending bone splinters into the spinal cord and brain.

Madison Simmons's last dying vision was one of the man in black standing in what seemed to be a great nimbus of white light, slowly fading.

The dark man who called himself Alfie studied the bloody end of his club, then looked down to make sure the spray of blood and brain matter hadn't spotted his clothing.

"Not much work to see to that dag, eh?" he said to the club.

He set the club down carefully, then stepped back and removed his clothing. His body was lean and very hard, stripped a long time ago of any superfluous flesh. His arms, legs, chest, and back were carved with old scar tissue in an intricate array of forms. Some of the designs centered on old wounds, like one deep healed puncture on his right thigh that served as a starting point for a rayed pattern of incised tissue.

He took a Velcro soft roll out of the courier bag and opened it up. The soft roll held a variety of small tubes and jars with paint. He took out a tube of red ochre paint and smeared long vertical lines down his trunk, arms, and legs. He carefully drew white and yellow horizontal lines on his torso while he studied himself in the mirror beside the racked CDs. He saved his face for last: charcoal on his forehead, a white band from each eyebrow down the front of each ear and continuing down his shoulders to his arms.

Then he set his paints away and took a CD from his courier bag and studied Madison Simmons's stereo system.

"Bloody hell," he said. "Got to be a rocket scientist or a bloody banker to figure this lot out."

Finally he found the appropriate slot for his CD and started his music. The eerie high-pitched drone of the didgeridoo began to sound in the entertainment room with a hypnotic drumbeat in the background. Alfie hung his head for a moment, listening for the rhythm and letting it build in him. Then he began to shuffle his feet in rhythm and to hum deep in his throat, a guttural drone that counterpointed the drone of the recorded didgeridoo.

The dark man closed his eyes, and in his mind's eye visualized all those who watched him from the Dreamtime. He felt a tingle that began at the base of his neck and swept down through his whole body before he opened his eyes and saw, as he did each time with this ritual, as though he saw with someone else's eyes.

"Time to flash me Dover," he said out loud. He took a knife from the front pocket of his carefully folded pants. It was an Ernest Emerson Commander, a fighting folding knife with an aggressive cutting edge, a partially serrated black steel blade that folded into a titanium handle.

"Good thing you ate well tonight, Maddy, me boy," the dark man said. "My turn now."

Charley Payne made lousy coffee and he knew it. He never seemed able to find just the right balance of grounds to water, and the little pot he'd bought cheap at Target never got the water hot enough. He woke every morning to the smell of properly brewed coffee filtering up from the restaurant two floors down in the old building he lived in. His apartment was small and old: it dated back to the twenties, when most small stores had a few rooms upstairs for storage or for let. But it was cheap and the neighborhood was good, in Charley's opinion the best neighborhood in Minneapolis.

In one of his periodic attempts to be thrifty, he'd bought the coffeemaker and decided to brew his own morning mud. But he missed the friendly chat with the girls who worked the counter of the Linden Hills Diner downstairs. Charley didn't have much money to spend on coffee since he'd worked through the funds he took out of his federal retirement plan after he'd quit the government, and the little bit of money he got from his free-lance work had to go first to his rent, then to his equipment and supplies, then to groceries before luxuries like coffee, beer, and cigars. Most of the time it seemed as though he reversed those commonsense priorities, but then that kind of perverse disregard for the normality of things was one of Charley's trademarks, at least according to Bobby Lee Martaine, who was Charley's best friend.

Charley spat the brew he made into his sink, then poured the rest of the pot down the drain. He went to the window of his studio apartment and looked out over the intersection of Forty-fourth Street and

Upton, the anchor of the Linden Hills neighborhood in Minneapolis. Charley liked to be up high and have the vantage point; he liked to be able to see where he was at all times. From here he could see the tree-lined streets and sturdy homes, the lone apartment building on Forty-fourth Street, and the trees in all the yards and along the streets stretching down to the greenery around Lake Harriet.

The trees were all aflame with the colors that heralded fall in the Upper Midwest: glorious crimson, heartbreaking yellow almost butter gold. Leaves rippled when the wind passed through them, like the mad brushstrokes of Vincent van Gogh, alive with energy and life and a bit of madness.

Charley loved to see. He often felt drunk with seeing. The best description he'd ever run across that captured his love of vision was a line from a poem by Wallace Stevens: "the voluptuousness of looking." From a poem called "Sunday Morning," if he remembered correctly. He'd read that poem in college over twenty years ago, and it pleased him that he could recall it. It was a little test, one of many he gave himself each day to see just how sharp—or dull—he was becoming.

He turned away from the window reluctantly, driven by the dull headache that pounded caffeine, caffeine, caffeine behind his forehead.

He squeezed into the miniscule bathroom, not much larger than an airplane toilet, where a shower stall was wedged in the corner beside an undersized toilet stool, and a small rust-stained sink with two old-fashioned porcelain four-pronged taps sat below a cracked mirror.

Charley ran the water till he had a tepid flow from the hot water tap, then lathered his face and scraped at his gray and blond beard. He had a long face, with deep lines that ran like scars from his high cheekbones down to the corners of his mouth. His forehead had three deep furrows that ran across his brow above thin eyebrows. His eyes were a deep, dark blue, almost a light violet. Women always commented first on his eyes.

When Charley was alone, his face fell into a collection of lines, like the rigging of a sail falls into repose in the absence of wind. It took interaction with people to breathe life into the rigging of his face, and from the lines and the way his face fell, one couldn't help but wonder if all those interactions had been good ones.

Charley splashed warm water on his face, then rinsed the loose hairs down the drain. He wiped his face and got the bit of white lather that clung to one ear, then sniffed at one armpit to see if he could wring one more day out of the T-shirt he'd slept in. He decided not, took it off and tossed it into the plastic bucket he kept in the bottom of his closet. A fresh black T-shirt and patterned cotton boxers, a pair of well-worn and faded Levi's 501s (and he was pleased that he could still fit into a thirty-four-inch waist pants), a brown checkered flannel shirt and a wool baseball cap to keep the chill off his thinning head of hair, and a zip-up Patagonia fleece jacket as a final layer against the fall cool.

His room was small but carefully organized. A twin-sized bed folded out of a sofa, a small table in front of the sofa served as dining area as well as a makeshift work space. An undersized stuffed chair sat in front of the window that opened out onto the street; directly across from that was a small television with a VCR player. Books overflowed onto the floor from makeshift shelves assembled from old boards and bricks. The walls were covered in photographs, some framed, others merely tacked in place: brilliant Cibachromes of leaves, forests, wildlife, black-and-white shots of people on the street, and several candid por- traits, some of an astonishingly attractive young woman.

Charley opened up the drawer of the tiny dresser he kept beside the couch. Inside the top drawer was a Glock 30 .45 automatic pistol in a Kydex plastic holster. Two fully loaded magazines were in another Kydex holder. Loose in the drawer with the pistol and ammunition were two knives: an Ernest Emerson Perrin neck knife in a sheath dangling from black parachute cord, and another Emerson, the CQC-7 folding fighting knife. Charley tucked the CQC-7 into the right front pocket of his Levi's, where the fabric was frayed from daily carry of the fighting knife. He hung the neck knife around his neck and tucked the tiny sheath away beneath his shirt where no one would see it. He picked up the pistol and press-checked it, easing back the slide to see the brass of the chambered round, making sure it was loaded. The first round in the chamber and the next three in the magazine locked in the pistol's well were blue-tipped Glaser Safety Slugs that would blast a cantaloupe-sized hole in a man's chest. He returned the pistol to the drawer and draped a loose bandanna over the pistol and the magazines.

Beside the dresser on the floor was a battered, stained, and frayed canvas Domke camera bag. Charley knelt and opened up the bag. Two identical Nikon F-100s were tucked inside, one wearing a 35–70 2.8 zoom lens, the other one equipped with a 80–200 2.8 lens. There was a 28–200 zoom and a fixed 24mm lens placed in their slots, along with a number of film cartridges—mostly black and white, Tri-X Pan, some 3200 Kodak, along with fewer color slides, the Fuji Velvia and Sensia chromes. What he was looking for was his tiny Olympus Epic, with its astonishingly good 35mm 2.8 fixed lens, which he tucked into the breast pocket of his fleece jacket.

After all, he never knew when he might have to shoot something.

Downstairs, the young woman art student who worked mornings in the Linden Hills Diner looked up and smiled when she saw Charley come through the door.

"Hey, stranger!" she said. "Where have you been?"

Charley smiled and leaned on the counter. "Hey, Jill. I been hiding out. Had some damn woman banging on my door at three this morning."

Jill laughed and poured coffee into an oversized mug she took from a rack behind the counter. She measured three spoons of sugar and a dollop of cream into the cup and stirred it till she was satisfied with the color.

"And so? What did she want?" she said, handing Charley the cup of coffee.

"I dunno," Charley said. He sipped the coffee and closed his eyes in happiness, the lines of his face unfurling. "I finally just got up and let her out."

Jill flicked a hand towel at him. "You're so bad, Charley."

"Quit hitting on my staff, Charley," the owner said. He was lanky and cadaverous with a wry sense of humor. "Where you been? Thought we'd lost you to Sebastian Joe's." He pointed at the ice cream/coffee shop across the street, the only other place in the neighborhood you could sit outside at a table with your coffee.

"You did lose me, Neil," Charley said. "But they make worse coffee than you do, and the help is prettier over here."

"You want something to eat?" Neil said.

"I've got fresh croissants," Jill said. "Special is two croissants and butter with coffee."

"Twist my arm," Charley said.

"I'd beat you up," Jill said. She was a sunny brunette with a runner's build. She bustled around behind the counter, leaving the two other people in line looking at each other as she put together a plate for Charley.

"Here you go," she said, handing him the plate. "You sitting outside?"

"We don't get enough days like this to waste it inside," Charley said. "Is there a paper around here?"

"Take Neil's . . . just bring it back when you're done," Jill said. She handed him a *Star-Tribune*, still rolled up with the rubber band in place.

Neil shook his head and went back to the grill. "Wish I could get her to wait like that on the people who pay."

Charley laughed and slid a five-dollar bill across the counter. "Here, darling. You keep the rest. Tell Neil to stay out of the tip jar, too."

Charley took his coffee, his plate, and his newspaper, all balanced precariously, out the front door and onto one of the tables that faced out onto Upton Street and caught the full morning sun. It was warm there in the morning sun and his was the last empty table; the others had a smattering of singles and couples, and one regular morning coffee club had pushed two together and were busy dishing gossip on the neighborhood. Charley pushed one of the chairs from his table out in front of him so he could prop his feet up, then sat down. When he sat, the clip of his fighting knife clanged against the metal of the chair. Without looking he pulled his fleece jacket low to hide the clip and cushion it from the metal. He set the paper aside for the moment and took his coffee mug in both hands and sipped slowly and appreciatively from it. After a few minutes he started on the bread and found the croissants to be perfect: flaky, still warm, slightly crusty on the bottom side and deliciously soft inside.

Charley pressed his chair back against the brick wall behind him and felt the warmth of the bricks through his jacket. He enjoyed the different sensations, the sun on his face, warmth on his back, the coolness and the slight chill the early morning air played on his wrists and neck. He shut his eyes for a moment and turned his face to the sun and let the sunshine play across him, the sun dazzling him through his closed eyelids.

He finished one croissant and took his time buttering the next. The couple at the table beside him looked at him, smiled at each other as though sharing a secret, and went back to their shared newspaper. Charley smiled lazily and nodded and said nothing, as was his custom. He cultivated an ability he'd developed long ago, the ability to tune out noise and distraction to concentrate on what he was doing—and right now what he was doing was drinking the best coffee he could hope for and eating a fine croissant.

Part of that long-standing habit of concentration was the ability to immediately sort out what was important and what wasn't, and one thing that was important in his life right now was his telephone. He heard, faint and far off from above, the distinctive ring of his cordless phone that sat in its cradle beside the window while it charged. He debated for a moment whether to jog upstairs and answer it, and immediately dismissed the thought as his automatic answering service picked up the message after four rings. Anything really urgent would bring him a message on his pager.

Charley touched the spot on his belt, just front of his left hip, where he would normally carry his pager and then, to the amusement of the couple beside him, said, "Shit." He fumed for a moment and then laughed. He'd left the pager upstairs. He knew himself well enough to know that unconsciously he didn't want to be bothered this morning and that was why he'd left his electronic leash upstairs.

He swallowed the last buttered bit of his croissant and washed it down with the rich bottom of his coffee when Jill poked her head out the front door of the diner.

"Charley?" she said. "There's a phone call for you...it's your friend Bobby Lee. He said it's important."

Charley moved so quickly it startled the couple beside him. He rolled up out of the chair to his feet, scooping up his coffee cup, the crumb-filled plate, and the unread newspaper, and continued on through the open door Jill held for him.

"Is he on the phone?" Charley said.

Neil held out the cordless phone. Charley left his plate on the counter, set the newspaper back beside it, and took the phone.

"Thanks, Neil," Charley said. "Hello?"

"You got to answer your pager, man. That's what we give you that thing for," said Bobby Lee Martaine. He had a low, intense voice, and that was a good description of Charley's best friend, one of the most gifted homicide investigators in the Midwest and the quiet star of the Major Crimes Unit in the Minneapolis Police Department.

"The one morning I forget it is the morning you call," Charley said.

"I think you just don't wear it."

"There's some of that, but I found that if I left it on and set it to vibrate, it made me dangerous around women," Charley said, winking at Jill. She made a backhand feint at his head and he ducked.

"Quit fucking around and get over here," Bobby Lee said. There was none of his typical humor in his voice, and that straightened Charley up. "I'm at the intersection of West Forty-third Street and Harriet Parkway, right across the lake from you. The big house, you know which one I'm talking about. Bring all your stuff and plenty of color."

"I'm on it," Charley said. "I'll be there in about ten minutes. Can you tell me anything?"

"It's ugly and it's going to be press intensive."

Charley's face went through a subtle metamorphosis, enough for Jill to look at him twice. Charley caught that and he smoothed out the lines in his face with a good approximation of his habitual expression of wry amusement.

"I'll be there," he said. "Sorry for missing the page."

"Whatever, see you now."

Charley handed the phone back to Jill, who replaced it in the charging cradle. "Thanks, hon," he said. "I'll see you all later."

"Bye, Charley," Jill said.

Neil just waved as Charley went out the door and then button-hooked right and into the doorway next door. He opened the door and squeezed up the narrow stairwell to the short line of apartment doors and went into his. He scooped up his camera bag and went to the corner of his kitchenette. He opened the icebox and took out a plastic-wrapped brick of high-speed color film and dropped it into the Domke bag. He took out his power winder and flash unit and replaced the AA batteries with fresh ones taken from a multipack in the icebox so that all his battery-powered equipment had fresh batteries.

He went to the bedside and opened the drawer, lifted the handkerchief and looked at the Glock 30 for a moment, then replaced the handkerchief and went out the door, pulling it closed behind him.

He was ready to shoot.

26

Detective Sergeant Bobby Lee Martaine never just worked a crime scene; he prowled a crime scene, sniffing at the evidence technicians, pawing at the detritus of a room set awry by violence, staring at the witnesses and suspects like a big alley cat. He was quiet and intense, and the low growl of his voice made the guilty feel guiltier and the innocent scared to death. He was short and stocky and dark-haired and dark-eyed, with a five o'clock shadow that never seemed to go away despite his shaving twice a day. He hated ties and sport coats and suits and cultivated the look of the old football player who'd played the detective Hunter on the television series: Levi's, cowboy boots, a plain oxford shirt with the tie knotted but pulled loose under a plain sport coat, the sport coat worn a size too large to conceal the battered old Smith & Wesson Model 645 .45 automatic pistol he carried. Bobby Lee liked his battered old pistol and ignored the jibes he got from fellow officers. He had lots of experience in gunplay, and while he knew that as a detective he had little likelihood of getting in a gunfight, he liked to be well armed in case one came his way. He stayed ready for it, and a part of him occasionally longed for it, much as it had when he was a young soldier.

Bobby Lee took off his jacket and draped it over a chair, rolled up his sleeves and pulled on a pair of rubber surgical gloves. He nodded to the uniformed officers securing the scene and went in to talk to the forensics team working the gruesome mess that was the entertainment room of one Madison Simmons, a prominent bank officer with First

World Bank. Bobby Lee stood back and let the evidence technicians work while he took in the whole of the scene with a careful detective's eye. While he did so, he unconsciously rubbed the faded master parachutist wing tattoo on his left forearm.

The first thing that struck him was the blood. Blood everywhere. But there were no arterial sprays. The blood was puddled and splashed. So the victim's heart had stopped before the main action took place. And that action had taken place in and around the leather recliner chair, so soaked and coated in blood it looked as though another layer of leather had been painted onto it.

"Detective Martaine?" one of the uniformed officers said. "The photographer is outside . . . do we sign him in as a department member or what?"

"Sign him in as a contract civilian attached to forensics," Bobby Lee said without looking at the patrolman. "Tell him to come here before he starts shooting anything else."

"Right, Sarge," the uniform said. He left and a moment later ushered in Charley, who had one Nikon poised in his hands, flash unit in place.

"Jesus Christ," Charley said.

"You could throw in all the saints, too," Bobby Lee said, "I don't think any of them ever saw anything like this."

"How do you want me to shoot?" Charley said.

"I'll point and talk," Bobby Lee said. "That way you can collate the photos to my tape. Once I'm done, you take the photos that Nordstrand over there needs you to take. I don't care about any overlap . . . just make sure we get everything. We'll work this room the most, then we'll go outside and work what we found out there. Which isn't much."

"Roger that," Charley said. "You on point, me on slack."

One of the other uniforms listening snorted and said to the officer who'd brought Charley in, "Who's that guy? Press ain't supposed to be in here."

"He's not press," the other said. "He's a contract photographer the sarge brought in to work on high-profile cases. Some kind of shit-hot photographer, knew the sarge in the war."

MARCUS WYNNE

"Which war?"

"Gulf War."

"Fucking press."

"Hey, the sarge says he's okay. They're friends."

"Must be a cozy job. Wonder what he makes."

"Why don't you ask him, you want to know so much?"

Bobby Lee said, "I want an overview shot first, from the doorway, then from that other door that leads into the living room. Use wide angle and get the big picture."

Charley stepped back and changed the lens on his Nikon to a 24mm. He began to snap a series of rapid photos catching the disarray in the room: the chair spilled backward in a sea of clotted blood, smears of blood on the wall, a drawing of some kind in blood on the wall, the body hanging from one ankle held by an electrical wire that sprouted from the ceiling where a chandelier light fixture had been pulled out.

"Close up on chair, first for the setting, then close in on the seat and arms," Bobby Lee said.

The strobe light of Charley's flash brightened, then dimmed, brightened, then dimmed.

"This son of a bitch must have killed him first," Bobby Lee said. "Then propped him in the recliner while he worked on him. Cut him open there, opened the whole body cavity with a very sharp knife. See those ragged cuts? Get those. Knife had some serration on the blade. Takes out the viscera and set it aside there, on the floor. Everything but the kidneys, he sets those over here. This is what's really peculiar . . . you see how the abdominal fat was carved out in long strips? Just like bacon. Did you look in the kitchen when you came in?"

"No," Charley said. His words were muffled by his hand as he maneuvered the camera to get a better shot of Madison Simmons's body cavity. The body was suspended upside down. The left ankle had a heavy electric cable knotted around it. The cable led into the ceiling where the chandelier light fixture had been yanked out. The right ankle was tied to the left knee, making a figure four shape with the legs. The abdominal cavity was laid completely open, and bits of entrails and body fat had flowed with the blood and bodily juices down over the purple and distorted face of Madison Simmons. The dead man's eyes bulged and were a deep dark color from hemorrhages in his eyes. His arms dangled down, rigid with rigor, fingers trailing in the puddles of hardened blood beneath him.

"What's in the kitchen?" Charley asked.

"Some of the body fat and the kidneys. Part of them anyway. This guy carved it out and fried it up in the kitchen. Ate one kidney and took a few bites out of the other, left it in there," Bobby Lee said.

Charley lowered the camera and looked at his friend. "This is the sickest shit I've ever seen."

Bobby Lee mouthed a smile with no humor in it. "It's one for the books. We'll get to the kitchen later. Work the body from all the angles . . . just make sure you don't get into the blood pool."

Charley shot and shot, stopped to reload his camera with more film and replace the 35–70 lens. After a while he switched to the other camera slung round his neck and began to shoot with a 80–200 lens for close-ups.

"This is the capper, though," Bobby Lee said, waving Charley closer. They stood in front of the wall where a large painting had been hung. The painting had been taken down and carefully set to one side, as though the killer hadn't wanted to damage it. That puzzled Bobby Lee—the violence of the butchery and cannibalism done here, yet the scene was in its own way orderly, with strange things like this.

Drawn on the wall with blood and bodily juices was a figure carefully outlined in the dark red of arterial blood. There was a rounded cylinder laid sideways where the head would be, attached with no neck to a squared-off body, the edges slightly rounded. The legs angled upward as though they were to be tucked beneath the armpits. The arms were raised above the head, rounded, with four fingers to each hand. Dangling between the legs was a long penis with a thick bulbous head. After the figure had been carefully outlined, the inside had been smeared white with some substance mixed with body fat from Madison Simmons. Then carefully drawn over that with some powdery red substance was a series of interlocked squares.

"What the hell is that supposed to be?" Charley said.

MARCUS WYNNE

"I think you'd have to go to hell to find that out," Bobby Lee said in a low voice. "I have no idea." He reached out, then drew his hand back. "The lab team thinks that's some kind of paint or stain mixed with human blood."

Charley lowered his camera and looked long at the figure. "That's a painting," he said. "Somebody took their time with it. That's too carefully done to be a spur-of-the-moment thing. Who the hell is this guy?"

"The vic is a big-time banker," Bobby Lee said. "Lots of money, if you couldn't tell by the real estate. Good security system, gated house, closed circuit TV on the power gate to the garage and the front walk-in pedestrian gate—and nothing on either tape."

"Who would do something like this?" Charley said. "This isn't a contract hit, this is a goddam psychopath."

"No shit, Sherlock? You think so?" Bobby Lee said in tired amusement. He tugged at his tie. "C'mon, I got to have a smoke."

He led Charley outside, carefully stepping around the technicians working on the side door.

"Some blood there, too," Bobby Lee said. "Cut the head off a squirrel and threw it against the door."

Charley bent and took a quick photograph.

"You can come back to that," Bobby Lee said. "What do you think of that painting?"

Bobby Lee took his time lighting a cigarette, then held his light for Charley to light his. Charley inhaled greedily.

"I hate the smell of blood," Charley said.

"I don't want to talk to Max about this," Bobby Lee said. "This is one I don't want to take home. See the press over there?" he said, lifting his chin at the television news vans with their camera booms extended.

"She'll probably have the whole story off the news before you get home. I'll come over, you guys can feed me and I'll keep her amused with Charley Payne stories."

"Nicky will like that."

"How's my boy?"

"Growing like a weed. Wish you'd quit giving him those throw-away cameras. We're going broke getting them processed. An eight-year-old can find a lot of things in a short time to take pictures of."

"Be good to that boy or I'll steal him from you. He's got a good eye. He'll end up supporting you with those pictures someday."

Bobby Lee took a drag on his smoke that added a quarter inch of ash to his cigarette. He blew the smoke out hard, as though by creating that small cloud he could block out the vision of the scene inside.

"This is not how I want to spend a fall day, bud," Bobby Lee said. "I want to go get a cup of coffee at Java Jack's and sit down by the lake and watch pretty girls run by. We haven't had anything like this in a long time."

Charley studied his friend as he always did, taking in the gestalt of his words, his mannerisms, his stance to take in the meaning underneath his words.

"Yeah," Charley said. "You don't get many of these. But you've never had one, and this is something you're going to enjoy fighting."

He grinned and busied himself with his cigarette, watching his friend from the corner of his eye.

"Nothing funny about this, Charley," Bobby Lee said. "Nothing funny about this nut-job. We are going to find him. We are definitely going to find him."

"I hope it's a one off."

"Yeah."

Charley turned and looked speculatively up at the beige walls of the house. He stroked his cheek with one finger as he took a final drag off his cigarette, then dropped it, still smoldering into the driveway's gravel.

"I'll work that picture hard," he said. "There's something familiar about it. I've seen something like that before. And I'll get the rest up, too."

"Get me the prints before you start researching it. I don't need to tell you to keep it close, right?"

"I are educated, Boss Man Bobby."

"In what, I don't know. Let's go to work."

MARCUS WYNNE

Charley lay back in the bed and stared up at the patterns on the spackled ceiling. This bed, this room, this woman . . . this was so different from the rest of his life. The bed was thick and lush, with a sheepskin pad beneath pastel-patterned flannel sheets, covered with a down comforter he found too warm most nights. The bed was the centerpiece of the room, with track lighting above it and a headboard that held a remote control to adjust the lighting or the expensive stereo and television set past the foot of the bed. There was even a small chiller that would hold a bottle of champagne and two glasses.

Every inch of the walls was covered: hanging rugs, shawls and scarves, postcards from foreign countries, modern paintings, photographs—some of them Charley's, collages professionally assembled with photos cut out from magazines, even the doors were covered with inexpensive posters and small advertising bills, the kind you saw stapled up on telephone poles in a student or artist's neighborhood.

That was appropriate, since this was an artist's quarters, Charley thought. And that led him to considering the woman he lay beside. Mara Steinway was long and sleek and blond and a brilliant artist—primarily a painter but she did wonderful work in collage and sculpture as well—and she was twenty-five years old, which made her eighteen years younger than Charley, young enough to be his daughter with no great stretch of the imagination.

He rolled on his side and propped his head on one hand. Her face was turned toward him, relaxed in sleep as she lay on her back, her large breasts lolling erotically across her thin chest, the sheet bunched at her waist, one hand clutching the sheet, the other thrown up in apparent abandon at her shoulder. The brilliant green of her eyes was hidden by long lashes over closed eyes in a heart-shaped face, with disheveled blond hair cut short in a pixie cut that brought out the full erotic length of her thin neck.

For no reason at all, he thought of when he'd been training in the desert a long time ago, in a class on stress reduction when the instructor, with a good old boy grin and laugh, had announced with mock seriousness that sex was the best stress reducer there was. Charley had laughed long and hard at that, as had the other young men—some of whom were dead now—but he'd known that for a truth as soon as he'd heard it.

Release of tension and the simple desire for a warm body to lie against in the night had brought him to Mara's condo apartment in Uptown after he dropped off the prints of the shots he'd taken for Bobby Lee. He'd kept a set for himself, tucked away into the battered canvas camera bag.

When she had answered the door, she was wearing an antique Japanese kimono and no shoes. She smiled, a turning up of her lips that seemed perfectly shaped in the sweet flesh of her face, stood on tiptoe to kiss him, and without a word tugged him inside.

She stood and solemnly studied his face, watching his eyes for the nuances of expression she had begun to know.

"Are you hungry?" she said.

"Yeah."

"For food, I mean."

"Maybe later."

"Do you ever think that I might have someone here?"

"No, not really."

"I might, someday. You know?"

"Let's worry about that on that day. Get naked. I want you."

Her solemn look vanished beneath her smile. She held open her kimono.

"I already am."

MARCUS WYNNE

It was always so intense with her. Charley couldn't remember if there had ever been a time when they hadn't had sex at least three times. She never seemed to tire of him, and the taut contours of her young body always kept him aroused. He had to laugh out loud sometimes at the thought of him, solidly middle-aged, with this young and beautiful woman who seemed quite happy with him and found him just as desirable as he did her.

He'd done some of the best portraiture he'd ever done with her in a series she'd encouraged him to take. She was completely uninhibited as a model, nude or otherwise. She told him that she'd made extra money during art school both as a nude model and as a dancer at an upscale strip club. She said that she was still sometimes asked to do private shows—either to check his reaction or, as was her style, to be completely honest about herself without opening wide the doors to her private life.

The two of them led separate lives that intersected in the bed they shared, mostly hers but occasionally his, with sometime dinners at the tiny hole-in-the-wall ethnic restaurants they both favored, or brief excursions as each other's companion into the floating nightlife of the Minneapolis art world. Charley had found, much to his surprise, that he enjoyed the brief visits to art openings at the galleries in the Warehouse District and the little parties at the Loring Bar or the Walker Art Museum. Since he'd thrown away the need for secrecy that had dictated his social doings for so many years, he enjoyed playing the man of mystery in Mara's life when the two of them were among her artist friends.

"Who is he, Mara? Do tell," her friend pled. "He seems as though he might be dangerous."

"He was a war photographer," Mara said. "He doesn't like to talk about it."

And while that wasn't exactly accurate, Charley let it stand.

Charley had met Mara at a Henri Cartier-Bresson retrospective, a traveling exhibit of the wonderful photographs the old master had done, which was showing at the Walker. They met, they talked, they went to bed.

WARRIOR IN THE SHADOWS

And sometime after that they had been at the Loring Bar, having drinks after seeing a private show of local artists in which Mara had a painting. It was late in the evening, and several people were noticeably drunk, including one yuppie professional in his early thirties in an expensive suit and a handmade Italian silk tie. Charley noticed things like that, not just with a photographer's eye, but because the remnants of a previous professional life required him to note every significant and telling detail and interpret it so as to give him insight into the individual.

The insight he got was young professional, single, drunk, and horny.

The drunk came up to Mara and said, "Was that your painting, the big red one?"

"Yes," she said, holding her wineglass in front of her face to disguise her slight smile.

"Seems kind of sexy."

"That's an interesting interpretation."

"I can be interesting," he said.

Mara smiled openly at Charley, who smiled back and winked.

"Is this your boyfriend?" the drunk said.

"He's my date, yes," Mara said.

"Lucky man."

"Yeah, I think so," Charley said.

"Think what?" the drunk said.

"That I'm lucky."

"No shit you're lucky," the drunk said. He smiled in the nasty fashion of those who imagine they have power, an oily sliding of the lips past the teeth. "Why don't you share a little bit of luck with me? I'd be willing to pay."

Several of Mara's friends, who'd turned to watch the play, froze.

Charley just smiled. "Time for you to go, buddy," he said. "You're boring everyone, and that's inexcusable."

"Why don't you just..." the drunk began.

Charley positioned himself with his left foot forward putting his body at a forty-five degree angle to the drunken man. He flicked his left hand at the man's eyes. His body position blocked the view of

MARCUS WYNNE

his right hand slipping the Emerson CQC-7 out of his right pocket of his black Levi's, but the click was audible and the knife could be seen by the gasping onlookers behind him. The drunk's hands went to his face to protect his eyes from Charley's flick. Charley brought his left hand back, low, and gripped the bottom of the expensive tie. The razor edge of the CQC-7 sliced through the tie like a fresh scalpel in the hand of an impatient surgeon, and suddenly the drunk was stumbling back, his eyes wide with fear, both hands out in front of him so as to ward off Charley, who stood with the tie in one hand and the knife in the other.

"Learn some manners," Charley said in an even voice. "Get out of here." He threw the scrap of tie on the floor. "Now."

The drunk man, his face pale, turned and walked out of the bar. Through the big plate-glass windows, everyone could see him pause between two parked cars and vomit into the street.

That gave Mara's friends all sorts of things to talk about.

And their sex that night was spectacular.

Charley slid carefully from beneath the sheets and tangled comforter. The slight chill of the room raised goose bumps on his flesh. He left his shorts on the floor and slid into his Levi's, put on his socks and his flannel shirt against the cold, and went into the kitchen. The glowing Mickey Mouse figure on the clock showed 1:30 in the morning. Charley opened the refrigerator, the front covered with magnet letters spelling out poems and messages, and took out a pint carton of half and half and some roast coffee from the freezer. He ran water into a pot and prepared the Melitta drip carafe that Mara favored.

He was used to waking up in the middle of the night. After he had quit his contract operator position with the Central Intelligence Agency's elite Special Activities Staff, he'd woken up every night for three months at three in the morning, reaching for his pistol, his ears straining for the sound of footsteps or someone trying his door. His small apartment in Fairfax, Virginia, seemed to close in around him, but he stayed there because he couldn't think of anywhere else to go.

The call from Bobby Lee had saved him from going down a dark road into depression or death. Bobby had never known what Charley was doing in Virginia, and he didn't know about Charley's dramatic exit from the program. But somehow, in the strange and near psychic fashion that best friends have, especially those who have huddled together in combat, he knew that Charley needed help. And the help he came up with was an offer of a contract forensic photographer position with the Minneapolis Police Department.

And that was exactly what Charley needed.

Charley sold what little furniture he had, packed up his books, his guns, his knives, his clothes, his cameras, and his precious negatives, and drove across the country in the beat-up station wagon he'd bought for himself.

He grinned as he looked for a filter cone for the Melitta drip, thinking how he must appear to other people who didn't know his history, which was everyone in Minneapolis. He looked like a marginally employed artistic photographer working to establish a name for himself, and he fit in as a fringe dweller on the edge of the Twin Cities art world. He held his own feeling of being a hawk among sparrows closely, even though it felt as though his thoughts leaked around his cover like light around the edges of a closed door.

Mara said from close behind him, "What is it that you like to say? Chemicals, chemicals, you need chemicals?"

Charley took down another mug without looking behind him. "I was saying I need more Mara."

"You can have that anytime. But you're making a mess of that coffee. Let me do that for you."

She brushed close by him, the smells of her washing over him: clean sweat, perfume, the bleachy hint of semen, the dry smell of her kimono. She put a fresh filter cone into the carafe, carefully measured the French roast into the cone, and then poured boiling water slowly into the paper cone so that the grounds rose evenly along the lip of the carafe.

"Like this," she said. "Slowly."

Charley slipped his hands around her thin waist. "Slowly?"

"Yes," she said, leaning back against him. "Slowly."

Afterward, he went back to the kitchen and retrieved the coffee mugs and poured the still hot coffee into them.

MARCUS WYNNE

"That wasn't so slow," Mara said.

"Are you complaining?"

"No," she said, reaching for her coffee mug, then wrapping both thin hands around it. "Thank you."

Charley got back beneath the covers with her, his own mug in his hand, and propped himself up with the pillow doubled over and braced against the headboard. Stray light from the streetlamps outside the window filtered around the edges of the thick curtains into the dark room.

"You're thoughtful and tense tonight," Mara said. "What are you thinking about?"

Charley sipped his coffee, hissing when it burnt a raw spot on the inside of his lip where Mara had chewed him.

"Are you all right?" she said.

"Just thinking," he said.

"About?"

"Did you do primitive art when you were in school?"

"I experimented with it..."

"I mean classes in art history on cave art, native arts, that sort of thing."

"Yes. When I was doing textile art I studied Japanese art, but that's not really primitive at all. I did take a class in African art, body adornments, that sort of thing...fascinating. I have a few books on it...why?"

"We respect each other's privacy, right?"

"That's why we stay together, Charley."

"You've never told me that."

"It's one reason."

"I want to show you something but I don't want you to speak to anyone else about it."

"I can do that," Mara said. She drew her knees to her chest and retucked the sheet around her. "Does this have something to do with your police job?"

"Yeah."

"Then of course I won't speak of it."

Charley slid from beneath the sheets and went to his battered camera bag. He took out the package of prints he'd kept for himself and selected one that showed the wall image in its entirety.

"This," he said when he slid back beneath the sheets. "Have you ever seen anything like this?"

Mara handed Charley her coffee cup and took the photograph in both hands. She held the 4×6 print and studied it long and carefully.

"I've never seen anything exactly like it, but the proportions of the features and the inner drawing within the main figure, those are characteristic of some schools of Aboriginal art."

"Do you have a book on that?"

"I have a good one. Over there, third shelf down, it's the end book, the tall one."

Charley fetched the book from the tall oak bookcase. Mara handed him the photograph and thumbed quickly through the book. She turned to one page and pointed at a photograph of an Aboriginal man with an intricately drawn series of squares on his chest. "See?" she said. "That's not the same, but it's similar."

Charley held the photograph beside the illustration in the book. "I see what you mean."

"I know someone who could tell you for certain," Mara said, gazing wide awake at Charley over her raised knees.

"Who?"

"Kativa, Kativa Patel. She's an art historian doing an internship down at the Walker. She's a friend of mine, we met at a party there. She specializes in primitive art."

"I'd like to talk to her."

"We can do that tomorrow."

"Tomorrow's Sunday."

"She works Sundays . . . I can call her in the morning, we can go to the museum after church."

"Church?"

"I'd like you to go with me. Then we can see her, after church."

"This should make for an interesting day."

"All your days are interesting."

"There's that."

MARCUS WYNNE

"Hand me my coffee, please." Mara took the cup and cradled it, sipping lovingly at the warm brew. She held the cup on her knees.

"What do you want from me?" she said as though she were asking the time.

Charley looked up in surprise. "What do you mean?"

"I never ask you. I take you as you are. But I'm curious. What keeps you in my bed?"

Charley licked his lips, looked away, set the photograph down carefully on the headboard behind him, laid the art book down on the covers.

"I know about the sex," Mara said. "That's fine. It's good for me, too. But it feels as though there's something else. Is there?"

"I don't know," Charley said. "I don't think about that."

"Sometime you should. I see a lot of things in your face. You're very frightening sometimes, Charley. I see things in you, my friends see things in you . . . I know about your violence and that tells me something about your past. Things come up in you and you put them away. Why is that?"

Charley felt something stirring deep inside him, something that wasn't his dinner or his middle of the night coffee.

"I don't like to dwell on the past," he said. "I try to live in the present, to pay attention. But I've got history. It's my history."

"Yes," Mara said.

She set her half-finished coffee down on the headboard, then slid down beneath the covers. She turned on her side, her back to Charley. Her hip swelled, then fell into the valley of her waist before it rose to join her torso like a great wall, like the wall of mountains around Annapurna in Nepal as Charley remembered it from all those years ago.

"Good night, Charley," she said in a faint voice. "I love you, but I don't want to talk anymore."

WARRIOR IN THE SHADOWS

Bobby Lee Martaine sat in the Great Wall restaurant in splendid isolation in the back dining room. Andy Chen, the owner and a long-time friend, always put Bobby Lee and any of his cop buddies in the back dining room and closed it off to other customers if the restaurant wasn't busy. If it was, he went out of his way to make sure that Bobby got the best table. Andy was an immigrant from Mainland China who'd worked his way up from sleeping on the floor and eating rice to save every penny to the highly successful owner of three restaurants. But the Great Wall on France Avenue was the flagship restaurant, and Andy was there every day for lunch and for dinner, greeting all his old customers by name and making sure that everything was done to his hard-nosed standard.

Bobby Lee picked through the roast duck for a good piece and followed it with rice, then a sip of Tsing Tao beer. Occasionally he would reach out and tap with his free hand on the manila folder that held the crime scene photos, the autopsy report, and the case file he'd started. Every so often he would stare at the empty seat across from him and wish that he could call up his old partner, Bob Martinson. The "Bobbsey Twins" everyone had called them, the Bob and Bob show, but the two of them had racked up the best closure rate in the department and had a lot of laughs while they were doing it. Bob had retired only two months ago, but with money saved, no kids to provide for and still married to his childhood sweetheart, he was able to take off for Florida to live large in his own fashion down in St. Petes Beach. He and Margie lived on a big boat. When they got tired of being on the water, they lived in a small mobile home in a retirement village that was full of ex-cops from New York, Boston, Chicago, and other big city cold spots.

Bobby Lee had almost called him, but decided against it. For now he worked without a partner, even though he had the pick of the whole Special Investigations Unit to draw from. He'd thought of calling Charley, but looked at the time, and thought again. It was against department regs and flew in the face of common sense, but Bobby Lee only obeyed those things that made sense at the time, and what made sense was to get a different perspective on this case.

He'd bring Charley in on it. He could use that brain.

Charley had changed from their days in the Eighty Deuce. He'd been Charging Charley then, hard-core, and ready for the Special Forces Qualification Course. He'd done his best to try and talk Bobby Lee into it, but Bobby Lee had his mind on Max and a family, and so they'd gone their ways when it came time to re-up—Charley to Special Forces, Bobby Lee to Minneapolis and a job as a patrol officer. Bobby Lee had come a long way in ten years... from patrol officer to tactical officer on the ERU to detective sergeant.

So had Charley.

Even though he didn't talk much about it, Bobby Lee knew his old friend well enough, and a couple of sessions over long-neck beers had told him what he needed to know. Charley had done real well in his Q Course, and done well on the door-kicking team he was assigned to in Okinawa. But that door-kicking team had a close special relationship with the secretive Delta Force, and somebody there had dropped Charley's name when it got time for him to be short. Four years as a door kicker in Special Forces, and then Charley dropped off the map for a year, then reemerged with postcards sent to Bobby Lee and to his son Nicolas from all kinds of exotic locales: Venezuela, Honduras, El Salvador, Afghanistan, Russia, Chechnya, South Africa, Tajikistan, India, countries and cities all over the world with one thing in common—they were dirty, violent, and dangerous.

And then something happened. Bobby Lee didn't know what, but when he heard from Charley he knew something was up. That's when the forensic photographer position came up in discussion with the chief, and Bobby Lee sold them on his friend. A faxed résumé and portfolio of photographs had clinched the deal, and then Charley showed up, driving a beat-to-shit Toyota station wagon filled with some clothes, his cameras and negatives, his books, and an assortment of guns.

Bobby Lee knew about Charley's fondness for firearms, something that went back to their grunt days, but the weapons he had now all had certain things in common. Bobby Lee had expedited Charley's civilian carry permit, even though he knew Charley rarely exercised the privilege. The handguns were the choice of a seasoned professional who carried concealed for a reason, his few long guns were the choice of someone who might have to fight seriously at close quarters in an urban environment.

That and his reticence and habitual silence about what he'd done told Bobby Lee a lot.

But those snake eyes Charley got when he wanted to get in the middle of things told a lot as well.

Bobby Lee wanted to sound him out on this and hear what Charley made of it, but it was too late. Time to go, time to go home to Max and Nick, sleep and start it all over in the morning. He pushed his plate back and waved at the attentive waiter who brought him his check immediately. He paid his bill and left a healthy tip, then walked out to the parking lot with the file under his arm.

Time to go home.

As he pulled out of the lot, a motorcycle rider, crouched over his crotch rocket, zipped by him and took the turn onto Forty-fourth Street toward Lake Harriet. The rider glanced at him as he zipped by, then seemed to double take again, right before he made the turn.

Bobby Lee laughed out loud. The guy was speeding and probably saw the light panel in the back window of his unmarked squad as he was pulling out.

Everybody worried about the Pooooolice, as Bob Martinson used to say.

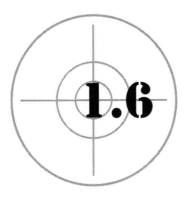

Alfie Woodard turned his jet-black Ninja motorcycle down Forty-fourth Street and slowed down after he saw the unmarked police car pull out of the restaurant parking lot. His side mirror showed him that the cop was going the other way on France Avenue, so he cranked back up the speed to the next stop sign, then zoomed again to the one after that, and then through the sole stoplight on Forty-fourth Street.

He liked riding his bike like this at night, speeding on his own, with only his thoughts to keep him company.

He took Forty-fourth all the way down to the Lake Harriet Parkway, turned right and cruised along the one-way street. Minneapolis reminded him of Cairns, in Queensland, Australia. Like Cairns, there were lots of people out at night, walking with no worries or cares, and in the day plenty of people biking, roller blading, enjoying themselves. The big difference was the weather; Alfie always felt cold here, no matter how many layers he wore. In September, when Minnesotans were running around in shorts and T-shirts, Alfie wore long underwear beneath his street clothes, a heavy shirt, and his leather jacket.

"Freeze me balls off," he said under his breath.

He followed the parkway around to Lake Calhoun Parkway, then up Hennepin for a short cruise to Calhoun Square. He parked his bike right in front of the square and went inside, leaving his helmet strapped to the seat of his bike. There was a coffee shop he favored right inside the Hennepin entrance, across from the bookstore.

"G'day, mate!" Alfie called to the young girl working the counter.

"Oh, hi, Alfie!" the girl said.

She was thin and dressed in Goth fashion: a snug-fitting black dress, black hair with black lipstick and multiple silver necklaces, bracelets, and rings.

"We're getting ready to close, do you want a coffee?" she said.

"Came all the way down here for one, mate. Do me one, will you?"

"Double shot mocha in a tall cup, right?"

"That's right, heavy on the whipping cream, me sweet tooth is acting up."

The Goth girl, Susan was her name, smiled and hurried to make Alfie his drink. Alfie turned and leaned back on the counter, both elbows propping him up as he looked over the shopping center. It was late, the shops were closed, and there was little foot traffic except that coming from the bar on the other side of the center.

"Here you are, Alfie," Susan said.

"Cheers, mate." Alfie handed her a five-dollar bill.

"It's on the house, Alfie."

He favored her with a big grin, then loosened his partial plate that hid his knocked-out right incisor, and stuck it out on his tongue at her, then clicked it back into place. She laughed out loud.

"Then fold it twice and tuck it in yer brassiere, Susan gal," he said.

"It'll buy me a beer at the Uptown," she said, doing just that.

"That's the place, then?" He pointed at the busy club across the street with a long line in front.

"I heard the Replacements might drop by and jam tonight," Susan said. "I'm going over. Want to go with?"

Alfie smiled, nodded his head vigorously, shaking his ponytail. "You're on, sheila."

Alfie cut to the front of the line and said to the bouncer, "Hey, mate! You wouldn't leave an Aussie out here in the bitter, would ya?"

The big man in the leather car coat grinned at Alfie's accent.

"We even got Foster's in there," the bouncer said. He waved Alfie and Susan through the door.

"Right, then! Thanks, mate! Ta!" Alfie ushered Susan through ahead of him.

"I can't believe you did that," Susan said.

"How's that?" Alfie said.

"He never lets anybody jump the line."

"Ah, he's all right. Let's crack a coldie, eh?"

Susan laughed and took his arm, rested her thin hand on his hard bicep. "What's that mean?"

"Get a cold one, dearie. You do drink beer, right?"

"I'll have a Foster's. What are you going to drink?"

"Susan, Foster's is piss. Really. Down under we all have a laugh with it . . . that's how you can tell the tourist from the locals when they open up calling for Foster's. I like this Sam Adams you've got here, hell even Budweiser is better than Foster's."

"Really?"

"Fair dinkum, mate."

She laughed out loud. "Then get me a beer and a bump, mate."

"Forward, aren't you?"

She bumped him with her hip. "That's American for a beer and a shot."

Alfie laughed and nodded his head in time with the bass player of the blues band jamming on the stage. "Whiskey, is it?"

"No, tequila for me."

"Oh, you're just my kind of woman." Alfie worked his way to the crowded bar. Several people looked twice at the small bone piercing his septum, and the several ear hoops in his left ear. Several other multiple-pierced Goths nodded to him. He didn't have the heavy metal piercing everywhere; just his nose and left ear. He wondered what they would think if they saw his scarification.

But then he didn't show his scars to everyone.

He ordered his drinks, handed the bartender a crisp bill from the roll he kept in his front pocket, and made his way back to where Susan stood, rocking her hips to the beat of the drums and the insistent bass line of the bass guitarist.

"Here then," he said, handing her a beer. He nodded at the band. "They're good, eh?"

"Some friends of mine are sitting over at that table. They're getting ready to leave to go to the CC Club. We can snag the table."

"Did you come to sit, darling? I came to drink and dance."

"Let's park our stuff."

Alfie led the way through the dancing crowd and the perimeter of standing people to the table she pointed out. A man and two women stood up as they got there, one of them brushing Susan's cheeks with the affectionate peck of friends who almost know each other.

"Thanks, Connie," Susan said.

Alfie nodded and smiled his big grin, then stuck his partial plate out at them. He loved the laughs that brought. He set his beer down and shrugged out of his heavy jacket and put it over the back of a chair, then turned to Susan and said, "How is it, then?" as he pulled her out onto the dance floor. They began to dance, Alfie throwing his big shoulders forward in a convulsive jerk, punctuated with a vigorous jerk of his hips again and again, his hands clenched in fists and his head thrown back, laughing out loud as he whirled around in circles. Susan laughed too as she watched the wild, uninhibited movements Alfie made, as though there were no one else on the dance floor. The other dancers made room for Alfie's wildly flailing arms and patent disregard for everyone around him. One big man, his head shaved close, with a goatee like that of a belligerent billy goat, danced with a tiny blonde with spiked blond hair who came up to his lower chest. He stopped and said to Alfie, "Make some room, man!"

Alfie ignored him.

"Make room!" the big man said.

Alfie nodded to the big man, took Susan's hand and spun her toward him once, then twirled her away. Alfie brushed against the big man, who pushed his shoulder, hard.

"Hey, mate, no worries, eh?" Alfie said, stepping back.

"I said make some room!"

MARCUS WYNNE

"No worries, everybody just wants to have a good time, right?" Alfie said. He summoned up a fierce grin, his blood already hot and moving.

The big man looked at Alfie, the thickness of his shoulders and his relaxed stance and turned away, saying, "Aw right. Cool." He turned his back to Alfie and shrugged at his date.

Alfie turned back and took Susan's hand again and said, "Let's give the bloke some room, he's a tetchy sort."

They moved through the crowd to be closer to the stage, where the sweating bass player sprinkled the crowd every time he leaped up with his guitar. The floor vibrated with the heavy rhythm of dancing feet and the music.

They finished out the set, and while the band set down their instruments and left the small stage Alfie and Susan went back to their table to finish their beers and order a couple of glasses of water to rehydrate and wipe the sweat that ran down their faces.

"Can't remember the least bit of the time I last went dancing," Alfie said. "I think I had this much fun, but there's no telling."

"That guy was such a jerk," Susan said, nodding over at a table close by, where the big goateed man held court with several of his friends.

"No need for a bloody blue when we're having fun, is there?" Alfie said. "He'll give heaps with his mouth, but why should we let him bother us?"

The bartender went to the stage and started a tape on the sound system. An old tune from the sixties started up, and Alfie began to dance by himself beside their table while he mouthed the words till it got to the chorus he liked:

"I am the god of hellfire! And I bring you ... fire! I bid you to burn!" he shouted out, to Susan's amusement.

"C'mon, let's dance," he said, tugging her back out onto the dance floor and going into his version of the twist.

"You're crazy!" Susan shouted as she joined him. "Completely out of your mind!"

"Oh, hell," he said. "You should see me when I get warmed up."

"Last call for alcohol!" the bartender shouted out. The band was breaking down and the lights came up, the too early sign of closing time. Alfie blinked rapidly as his pupils dilated to accommodate the sudden brightness.

"One for the road, Susan?" he asked.

"Not me, stick a fork in me, I'm done."

"Right then, let's hit the frog and toad?"

"What?"

"Let's hit the road."

Susan gathered up her purse and Alfie slung his jacket back on and they headed for the door. The big bruiser who'd given them a hard time earlier in the night followed them out the door. Alfie clocked him from the very moment and knew what was coming as they crossed the street to where he had his motorcycle parked and chained in front of Calhoun Square.

"Hey, Crocodile Dundee!" the bruiser called.

Alfie grinned, then let the smile drop away as he turned to see the bruiser, his girlfriend, and one other man dressed in snug leather. "Hey, mate, what can I do you for?"

"That your bike?"

"That's my trike, that's right, mate."

"You should learn the customs around here, *mate*. Like having some manners."

"No worries, mate. I'm not looking for a blue."

"A blue?"

"Any trouble," Alfie said. He noticed how the bruiser's buddy stood off at a ninety-degree angle to Alfie's right, ready to dive for him.

"Here, look," Alfie said. He reached for his pocket. "If it's any consolation I'll buy you a round, how about it?"

"I don't want your money," the big man said. He laughed. "Fucking Crocodile Dundee. I want . . ."

The time had come and Alfie was riding the crest just ahead of it, with perfect timing . . . he flicked his fingers out in a fan that struck the big man in his eyes, followed it with a quick cross square on the man's nose, then turned toward his friend, who started to close the gap, and jammed a low kick into the follower's knee, then grabbed his long hair and drove his face down into Alfie's leather-clad knee, pulping the nose, and then spun his head quickly round, just short of breaking his neck, and dumped him on his back. Back to the big man who stumbled back, his hands to his eyes, two quick stomping kicks to the outside of his right knee that brought him down, gave him the boot several times to the face and head, then onto the motorcycle with Susan clinging behind and starting it up and pulling a wheelie out and away, leaving the woman standing there screaming after him, "We're going to get you! We're going to get you!"

"Ah, bullshit," Alfie yelled back.

Susan laughed in drunken near hysteria. "That was great! You are absolutely insane!"

"Tell me where we're going, mate, 'cause I'm new in town."

"You're going to my place, Crocodile Dundee."

She was so drunk the sex was mechanical and perfunctory, which was fine with Alfie. It was all cover anyway. Her apartment just off France Avenue would be a good place to lay up for a while and spare him the exposure of a hotel room. He slipped a key off her key ring and quietly went out the door with a mumbled promise to the slumbering Susan that he'd be back.

He had a little reconnaissance to do before his next job, and Susan's place was a perfect staging point.

Time spent in reconnaissance is never time wasted. That was an ancient adage in the world of special operations, and Alfie Woodard had spent many years in that world. After a stint with the Australian Airborne, Alfie had passed the hellish selection course for the Special Air Services. He was one of the very few Aboriginals to work with the elite unit. He'd been a natural, something that the white troopers found interesting and more than slightly amusing. His performance in training and on the real world special operations deployments throughout Southeast Asia and while on secondment with the United States and other

Australian allies had made believers, albeit grudging believers, out of his fellow troopers.

But Alfie didn't like to think of those days, preferring to leave those thoughts alone and remember them as the days of preparation for his real life, the life that had begun after his military service when he met old Ralph, the Aboriginal bush doctor who'd first shown Alfie the dark ways of the old magic. He called up a ritual, a simple piece of hunting magic that called for a long, low chant and a drone through his nose, made all the more sibilant by the air blowing through his pierced septum. And while he droned, he stilled his mind, letting his body go through the mechanics of steering his fast-moving motorcycle as he made his way closer to the target, and let the picture of his prey come up in his mind. Not his enemy, no, they weren't important enough to be enemies. They were prey, the prey designated by the man who bought his time with enough money to enable Alfie to pursue his study of the lost black arts of his people.

Harold Nyquist was a former running back for the Minnesota Vikings, who'd cashed out at the top of his game and started a restaurant that he later franchised with great success. The money he'd made from his restaurants he poured into real estate, anticipating the big boom the dot-coms and other computer intensive businesses would bring.

Harold had also sunk big chunks of other people's money into the downtown Warehouse District, where fancy nightclubs and expensive restaurants mixed with cheap diners and coffeehouses. His work with foreign capital investors accounted for substantial sums in his offshore accounts resulting from his "consulting services." Among the minor services he provided were the pleasures of extremely beautiful and surgically enhanced dancers from the high-class gentlemen-only strip joint he owned through a front in downtown Minneapolis.

His activities brought him the money to build the finest house around, but it was characteristic of his Lutheran and Norwegian upbringing that he preferred to live modestly in a good home in Plymouth. While the lot and the house—custom built to his wife's specifications—cost him close to half a million dollars, it was to all appearances just one more nice house on a quiet cul-de-sac that backed onto the W&O

Rails to Trails bike path, where he could take his wife and grandchildren for walks.

Alfie needed to take a look at Harold's house.

He went for the bold drive-by first. His clothing, while completely in synch with fashion in Uptown or the artsy Warehouse District, stood out in the white, staid, and moneyed suburbs, especially at four-thirty in the morning. But he roared down the street, bearing in mind the old axiom that if you can't be discreet, be bold. He slowed when he passed Nyquist's home, mentally photographing the house, the yard, and the side yard that backed onto a low hill that rose up onto the highway's roadbed. He slowed at the end of the cul-de-sac, where a narrow walkway allowed egress for bicycles and walkers, made note of the trail, then turned around and roared away. He rode to a larger major entrance to the W&O bike trail, beside a series of shops in a strip mall. Strip mall was too plebeian a description for this collection of upscale shops and restaurants, but what appealed to Alfie was the loading zone behind the mall had plenty of nooks and crannies to hide his bike in.

He crossed the street on foot, moving fast, as the Plymouth Police Department didn't have much to do and was known to respond very quickly to calls from their rich citizens, of which there were many. He walked quickly down the trail, then paused in the shadows by the entrance that led out onto the cul-de-sac where Nyquist lived. The street was well lit, and while it was the deadest time of night, when most people were deepest in sleep, Alfie didn't want to risk making a simple walk up and across to the front door and window.

No, the back way would be best.

He continued down the bike trail for a short distance and saw that he could cut through the yard closest to the bike trail and then scale a low mesh fence to enter Nyquist's backyard. A better way would be to go down to where a small tunnel took the bike path under the highway, then cut along the sloping hill that came down from the highway pavement bed to the yards on Nyquist's street.

Alfie crouched in the bush, then slowly let himself stretch out full length on the chill ground, the weeds and sparse grass fading into brown, crisp stalks beneath him. The early morning chill seeped in around the layers of his clothing. He turned off the sensation of cold as he went inward in a way he'd learned long before his military service, in one of the many white foster homes he'd been in. He shut down his feelings and went inward, with a steady rhythmic chant in the back of his mind, and visualized the path he would take in to the target. He saw the whole line laid out in front of him, visualizing himself walking the line he hummed to himself, moving from cover to cover, hugging the shadows. He visualized so intensely that he could see an image of himself walking that path and when the image was perfect in his mind, he felt himself lifted up, as though he were leaving his body, and then his material body followed that dreamlike vision he projected forward, through the thin brush, the hiss of passing cars coming from overhead and behind him, carefully placing each foot down so cautiously, toe gingerly probing so as not to make noise, then the rest of the foot, toe, heel, toe, heel till he was crouched behind the low mesh fence and could see directly into the kitchen, illuminated dimly with lights from the oven hood and the other electric utensils there.

He could make out much of the house layout from there: kitchen, a short hall leading through into the front room, a space that was probably the dining room to one side. Alfie stilled himself even more, evened out his breathing, and let his pupils expand so that his peripheral vision might take in details that the conscious mind would miss and let the options for entry grow in his imagination. He let the stillness grow in him, and then he felt the sudden twinge that drew his attention to an important detail: on the sliding-glass door there was an unsecured security bar, but at the top corner of the door was a small square that was either a pin lock or an alarm sensor or maybe both. No sign in front alerting the passerby to an alarm system, but that didn't mean there wasn't one.

It didn't matter anyway; there wasn't a locked door in this neighborhood that could keep Alfie out. He smiled to himself, looked at the growing light in the sky, ran his teeth over his partial plate, and clicked it twice.

Time to go.

MARCUS WYNNE

Charley had slept fitfully in Mara's bed, his dreams jagged shards of light and sound, and only once could he remember a piece of his dream, and it was the image of the painting drawn in blood and body fat on the wall of Madison Simmons's entertainment room.

Mara was still and distant in the morning. The two of them dressed in silence, sat and drank coffee together in silence.

"I'm going to church," Mara announced.

"What's with this church thing?" Charley said.

"Just because you've never seen me go to church doesn't mean I don't go regularly, Charley." She looked out the window as she spoke.

"Okay, I'll go," Charley said.

"I'd rather you didn't," Mara said. "It's something special to me and I don't see the point of you going if it means nothing to you. You can stay here or go home."

"I'd like to go, look we can . . ."

"No, Charley. I prefer going alone."

And with that, she gathered up a coat and left, a hint of jasmine perfume in the air and Charley with the feeling that he'd failed some kind of test.

"Fuck," Charley said.

He drained off the last of his coffee and rinsed the cup and put it in the drying rack. He gathered up his camera bag and the crime scene prints, then went out the door and down to his car. When he got to the street he found a parking ticket on the windshield of his Camry.

"Fuck me," he said.

He sat in the car, started the engine, turned it off. He wouldn't think of her but he would. He couldn't seem to help himself. The whole thing with the two of them was crazy. She's too young for me, she's convenient, what does she mean she loves me? What the hell is that all about? What's this about church anyway? She'd said she went to the Catholic church in his own neighborhood and he'd never seen her around there and she'd never mentioned anything at all about that before.

And he hated leaving things like this.

It wasn't right. He liked resolution, clarity, a clear picture and a clean end to things. So he had to see her.

He started the car again and pulled out into the flow of traffic, holding up a middle finger for the cars that slammed on their brakes to avoid hitting him.

It surprised him that the church was so full. He didn't know why he should be so surprised, after all lots of people still went to church. He himself hadn't been to church or participated in a mass since he was in the Army, since he'd been kneeling on the airfield at Pope Air Force Base before shipping out for the Gulf. He'd never been big on religion anyway, but the seemingly pat blessing the priest had put on all the little soldiers before they went off to battle put him off even more.

There were a surprising number of devout Christians in the CIA, even in the Special Operations Division, but they seemed able to compartmentalize that part of their life from the operational demands of special operations, which called for the cunning and deceptiveness of the devil's own.

Maybe it was those thoughts and memories that contributed to his unease as he stood in the back of the church. The service had already begun and he was unsure about where to sit. There were two empty pews at the very back of the church, so Charley slipped into one with a semblance of genuflection and the hasty sketching of the sign of the cross. He remembered that much, at least.

The mass was halfway through, because the priest had ended his

58

sermon and was preparing the host for communion. Charley scanned the pews in front of him, looking for Mara, but he couldn't make her out in the crowd. He cursed himself, conscious of his blasphemy, for giving into the random compulsion to come here without a plan and for just sitting here without any idea about what he'd say to her if he did see her.

Now the ushers went to each pew, starting at the front, and indicated the celebrants should come forward for communion. Charley thought for a moment about if he would take communion, but reminded himself that he hadn't been to confession in at least ten years and to take communion at this point would be a mortal sin since he hadn't cleansed his soul through confession. Cleansed his soul. That was an interesting thought. What would he say to the priest in the confessional? Bless me, Father, for I have sinned in so many, many ways? I have killed, I have spilled blood, I have lied, I have cheated, and worst of all, Father, I have reveled in it all.

Charley felt a grin grow, just a little.

What would happen out of that?

There was a sudden commotion in the two lines leading up the center aisle to the altar. Charley heard someone cry out, and leaned out to see what was happening. An older man, well into his sixties or seventies, heavy and corpulent with the flushed features of a drinker who liked a good meal with his booze, was stopped, grasping at his chest and the arm of the woman in front of him, bringing the line to a halt. He fell, slowly and ponderously, like a great tree. The woman knelt beside him.

"Jerry! Jerry!" she cried out. "Someone help me!"

Charley was already moving. He pushed the gawkers out of the way and knelt beside him, one hand loosening the too-tight collar and the neck tie knotted there, one hand slipping to the belt buckle and loosening it, his sure eyes and hands of experience saying myocardial infarction, a heart attack and this old man was in the middle of a massive one. Charley felt for a pulse at the neck, then put his cheek beside the man's mouth, gaped wide like a fish's maw.

No heartbeat, no breath.

WARRIOR IN THE SHADOWS

"Call 911," Charley commanded. "Tell them you have someone in full cardiac arrest."

"Cardiac?" the woman companion said. "Oh, my God, he's having a heart attack, Oh, Jerry, help him, please."

Charley covered the old man's mouth with his and breathed two quick breaths, saw the chest rise, then began compressions, counting out loud, "One, two, three, four, five, breathe," then two quick breaths, then again with the compressions. Charley's heart was racing and he felt sweat pouring down his face and an inexplicable anger: why wasn't someone calling the paramedics and why did he have to be the one to help this old bastard and why did he have to have a heart attack on his watch and this wasn't his watch, it was a church and he didn't even know why he was here even while he kept up the compressions and the breathing and nothing was happening and he was furious and reared up and slammed his fist down on the man's chest and shouted, "Christ! Breathe, damn you! By the power of Christ!"

And suddenly the old man was gagging, choking, struggling to get Charley off him as Charley suddenly sat back on his heels and the ring of onlookers drew back and the priest was standing there, making the sign of the cross and everyone was looking at Charley except for the paramedics who were suddenly there, kneeling beside the man gagging and choking for air on the floor.

The woman fell to her knees in front of Charley and said, "You saved him, you saved him, oh, thank you, you saved him . . ."

Charley stood and quickly walked away, the crowd parting for him, but the priest caught his arm and held him.

"You saved a life," the priest said. He was in his sixties or seventies, too, with a thin Irish face that might be humorous on another occasion, but drawn now in intensity. "You called on the power of Christ and he moved through you. Do you know what you did just now?"

"I need air, Father," Charley said. He shrugged off the priest's hand. "Excuse me." He pushed his way through the crowd and out the door into the clean fall air. He stalked down the stairs and began to walk toward his apartment building down the street, abandoning his car in the church parking lot.

MARCUS WYNNE

"Charley!" he heard. He stopped and turned and saw Mara coming to him with that curiously awkward half trot she did when she was in a hurry.

"Charley," she said. "What did you just do?"

Charley dreamed of somewhere outdoors, in the wild, a terrain he'd never seen and yet he was seeing it now: scrub trees, like manzanita grown larger, knee-high grasses that might slice at his legs, in the distance dark hills, smoothly humped in some places, jagged and sharp in others. It was as though he glided without substance or form through this bush, and there were a series of earthen humps, each as tall as a man, in a clearing where the trees did not go. He went to the humps and there was a stirring, a movement from inside that he could sense but not see, then one of the lumps cracked open and fell apart and inside was the curled skeleton of a man, crawling with termites, giant ones, inches long, the skin drawn like leather parchment tanned almost black, the bark of the trees nearby curling up like pale hands and when he looked closely at the face of the man it was his own . . .

. . . and that image brought him fully awake in his bed, Mara gripping his arm, one hand to her mouth, saying, "Charley? Charley, are you all right?"

He was momentarily confused as he looked around his apartment and one hand went involuntarily toward the dresser drawer where he kept his .45.

"Charley!" Mara said, shaking him. "You're having a dream, a dream, look at me!"

He was in a strange state midway between dream and waking, and when he looked at her it was as if each pore on her face were a tiny whorl of spinning light that came in through the open window and fell across the narrow bed. Daylight? What time was it and where was he and why was he lying in bed?

"What time is it?" he said.

"It's almost four o'clock."

"In the day?"

"Yes, Charley," Mara said gently. "In the day. You've been napping. You had a dream."

"Dream, hell," Charley said. He swung his feet out of bed. He was fully clothed except for his shoes. He went to the sink in the kitchenette and drew a glass of water and greedily gulped it down. "That was a full-blown nightmare."

"What did you dream?"

Charley drew more water from the tap and drank two glasses in rapid succession.

"What were you dreaming, Charley?"

"I must have been tired."

"Do you remember what you did earlier today?"

Charley looked at her for the first time since waking. He remembered seeing her after the incident in the church, but he drew a blank after that.

"I remember that old man."

"You seemed as though you were a little out of your head after that, Charley. You were confused, and I came here with you. You said you had to lie down and then you fell asleep. A deep sleep. I stayed here with you."

She gestured at the file folder that held the Simmons crime scene photographs.

"I looked at the photos. I hope you don't mind."

"I must have been tired, didn't sleep well last night. Probably the excitement, the stress, something like that . . . been a long time," Charley mumbled.

"What was a long time, Charley?"

"Ah, first aid, that kind of stuff. It was hot in there."

"You don't want to talk about that, do you?"

He realized that he didn't want to talk about what happened, not with her, maybe not with anyone. The whole thing smacked of strangeness to him.

Mara nodded slowly but not unhappily. She changed the subject.

"Do you still want to meet Kativa?"

"Kativa?"

"My friend who can tell you about that image."

"Let's get coffee. I need coffee."

They went downstairs. Jill served them coffee without comment, but gave a long curious look at Mara, who'd never joined Charley in the diner before.

"So, Kativa?" Mara said after Charley drained two cups of coffee.

Charley poured the remains of his third cup into a foam to-go cup. "Yeah," he said. "Let's meet your friend Kativa."

1.8

Lieutenant Simon Oberstar was a big florid Norwegian who supervised the Special Investigations Unit. He'd been Bobby Lee's rabbi throughout his career, hovering over him all the way from patrolman to detective sergeant. Obi's wife had died from cancer five years ago, leaving Oberstar with two teenagers a year apart in private schools. They were both in college now, and the tuition was stretching Oberstar to the brink, Bobby Lee knew. They were smart kids, but lots of smart kids went to St. Olaf's in Northfield and there weren't enough scholarships to go around. Two mortgages and living as frugally as a lonely widower could was how Oberstar made it work. Maxine loved the old man who'd been a fixture in their life from day one with the PD, and she fixed him the Norwegian treats he loved and she loathed, just to see him happy when he came over, which was often.

"What you got on this Simmons thing?" Oberstar said. "What's your case file looking like? Is it thick with all kinds of leads you've run down, or skinny with all kinds of nothing?"

"I just got the autopsy back, Obi-Wan," Bobby Lee said. "The doer knew what he was doing . . . and we got a good make on the knife if we find it."

"How's that?"

"Knife was serrated halfway down, sharp as hell. Looks like this," Bobby Lee said. He reached into his front pocket and pulled out the knife Charley had given him for his birthday. He flicked it open one-handed and handed it to Oberstar.

"See?" he said.

"Jesus, Joseph, and Mary," Oberstar said. He weighed the knife in his hand, took a swipe at the air. "This is legal?"

"Oh, yeah," Bobby Lee said. He took the knife back and studied it. The chisel-pointed blade folded into a titanium handle, an elegantly designed fighting knife built for one purpose only and that was cutting up humans in a fight. He'd met the maker, Ernest Emerson, at a knife-fighting seminar sponsored by Charley's friend Rick Faye, who taught martial arts in town and was an adviser to both the FBI SWAT team and the Minneapolis Emergency Response Unit. Both Emerson and Faye were nice guys, easygoing and laid-back till you saw them in action with a knife, stick, or their bare hands. It made Bobby Lee glad they were on the side of the good guys, and taught him a whole new respect for knives. He thumbed the blade shut and slid it back into his pocket.

"Probably a blade just like that. Somebody who knew how to use it, too. We're looking into it."

"What about motive? Who benefits?" Oberstar said in his favorite pedantic voice. He scratched his nose and studied his fingernail as though looking for skin scrapings.

"Hauser and Thomas are over at his office, interviewing cowork-ers and we got a warrant for his office files. The bank is pretty coop-erative, but they're hinky about his files. He was their lead officer on a whole slew of international loans and venture capital deals . . . lots of stuff in Asia, Australia, South America."

"Was he working on any big deals?"

"Nothing out of the ordinary, according to Hauser's first pass. But we're looking into it."

"Fucking First Bank. Those sons of bitches got me by the balls with their mortgage."

"Me too," Bobby Lee said.

"Old Rollie Wheeler, used to be a mortgage officer there . . . used to be a cop, got shot back in the seventies in that big shootout down in Bloomington with the narcos. Said he'd had enough and got out. Took one in the lung and rode that disability all the way through school and then to First Bank. When Angie was still alive, old Rollie, he took care of us. He's gone now, these fuckers now . . ."

"Yeah, I know," Bobby Lee said, cutting into the tirade. "Screw them all if they can't take a joke. We'll send the Cannibal Killer after them."

"Let me know what happens, Bobby," Oberstar said. "I'll keep the assholes off your back. But make something happen soon, huh?"

"Thanks, padre. Go take a break. I got the ball."

"Dig for this boy, Bobby. Whatever you need."

"I got it. I'll let you know how it develops."

Bobby Lee watched Oberstar lumber away, hitching his baggy suit pants as though he were still wearing a patrol uniform and equipment belt. Then he turned back to his desk and flipped through the case file again, turning over the photographs as though he might now be able to see through the scramble of blood and innards strewn across his desk to the face that had to be behind it, and through that face to get some insight into the mind there.

He'd never worked a case like this before. He'd filled out the detailed questionnaire the FBI's Behavioral Sciences Unit sent to local law enforcement agencies requesting help for profiling serial offenders, but he knew what kind of backlog those harried and overworked agents had to deal with. He didn't have a serial killer yet.

Yet.

Bobby Lee's street smarts had stood him in good stead during his years on patrol, and working homicide hadn't taken the edge off that at all. He stayed tuned up and kept his senses sharp. He had a feeling about this guy, and he'd learned to trust his feelings. He was going to see this guy's work again.

But there was something about the choice of the victim. Madison Simmons wasn't right. The banker wouldn't be the usual prey of a serial offender; this smacked of a hit, someone with a grudge, business or personal. This kind of anger you sometimes saw in sex-related crimes. Gay? A hooker? Something there? There wasn't the element of disorganization you saw in a rage-induced murder, though. Simmons had been butchered, but not in a frenzy. It had been systematic and efficient, not hate-filled hacking. Madison Simmons had been taken apart the way a good hunter took apart a deer in the field, even down to preparing the kidney fat for a snack.

"That's some silly sick shit for sure," Bobby Lee said.

"You ain't kidding," said one of the uniform officers passing his desk.

"Caught me talking to myself," Bobby Lee said.

"Just don't start answering yourself," the patrolman said.

Bobby Lee laughed and went back to his pictures and his ruminations. The hunter, for that was what Bobby Lee was starting to call him, had used materials on the scene to stage it, but he'd brought his knife, and the club he'd used to kill the banker with him. The forensics team said the club was heavy, similar to a baseball bat but with a heavy bulbous head, maybe a walking stick. The blow that most likely killed him had shattered his skull and opened his brain pan. The hunter would be a strong man, strong as hell. The angle of the blow indicated that Simmons had been below and at an angle when the killing blow was delivered, probably sitting in the recliner with the hunter facing him. Everything else, the evisceration, hanging the body, that was all postmortem.

It had been messy, and it had taken time, but the scene wasn't rushed. The hunter hadn't been afraid of being discovered, or he just didn't care.

Bobby Lee felt sure that the hunter had stripped down to avoid getting blood spatter on him. Analysis of all the water traps in the showers and sinks showed that he hadn't showered or washed, at least not there. The traces of paint and minerals they'd taken from the image on the wall were still undergoing analysis.

That painting disturbed him. It was carefully drawn with its hellish palette of paints and provided a clear message about the hunter's mind if he could only translate the meaning, find some way to go where the killer's mind went. Where did all this go? What was this all about, the killing, the eating, the painting? He wracked his brains about that, but he knew he'd have to get some help elsewhere for insights into that image, and he hoped Charley, with his unconventional thinking, would take him where he needed to go.

WARRIOR IN THE SHADOWS

"Please move it to the right, Stan. Just a little," Kativa Patel said to the museum technician struggling to hold a heavy framed nineteenth-century watercolor up in the tight space she had left after laying out the exhibit.

"We're almost there . . . there," she said in satisfaction. "Let me mark that for you."

Stan was old enough to be her father and a bit slow but sweet. "I'll get it hung right for you, Miss Patel."

"I know you will, Stan. Thanks for being such a dear."

"That's why I like working with you, Miss Patel. You always take the time to get it right."

"That's the way my old dad taught me, Stan. If it's worth doing it's worth doing right."

She patted the old man on his arm and hurried back through the vaulted ceiling galleries and then the main lobby into her office, her low sensible heels clacking and resounding in the empty hallway of the administrative section. It was slow for a Sunday, but then it was late in the day. She waved to another curator working in her cubicle, and stopped to fill her coffee mug, a beautifully hand-thrown ceramic mug, a gift from an old boyfriend in Cape Town, with black French roast from the coffeepot before she went into her own office.

Her office was tiny but immaculate in its organization. Even the stacks of correspondence piled on the floor for lack of filing cabinet space were neatly set edge to edge and in the most reasonable simulation of order she could create. She kept several pieces of art from the archives in her space: a hand-rubbed copy of a spiral stone carving from Dajarra, Queensland, and a variety of prints from modern Aboriginal artists in the Cairns area, some of them originals signed by the artists she had gotten to know while doing her postgraduate work there.

She sat at her desk, leaned back in the old secretary's chair she preferred, and put her feet up on her desk, her hands cradling the hot coffee mug and slowly sipping with the delight she brought to things of the senses. She'd loved the time she'd spent in Australia, bashing around the outback in a tired 4×4 in the Laura region looking at and looking for new and old rock art in the area. Looking at the pictures reminded her of that time, and how it had been so good to be in a country that reminded her of home, yet without the fears that plagued South Africa. Cape Town was one of the most beautiful cities in the world, but the remains of apartheid, the unbelievable surge of crime after Mandela took office, and the flight of the professional class had led to her leaving, first to Australia, then to the United States, to one of the coldest states in the lower forty-eight, a fact that jarred her every time she stepped outside to enjoy the beauty of the trees surrounding the park and the Sculpture Garden across the street, the bite of the air just barely muzzled now, but ready to be bared within weeks.

She thought of Australia, and wondered if she would get the grant she'd applied for to go back and continue her research on the Laura area, to continue her interviews with old Percy Tracy, the avuncular old pilot and artist who'd done so much of the original work on the Laura rock art.

Julie, the barely twenty-one-year-old secretary, who'd celebrated her birthday with the museum staff only nights before, stuck her head around the door frame and said, "Kativa? Your friend Mara is here. Should I send her back?"

"Of course," Kativa said. She set her feet down and stood up. "Tell her to come in."

Kativa followed Julie into the hallway and saw Mara and the tall man she dated standing patiently by the reception desk. She'd first met Mara on a gallery crawl, one of those fun affairs organized by local artists that consisted of a walking tour of the local galleries downtown interspersed with stops in the local drinking establishments. South African college life and then Australian outback living had taught Kativa to enjoy a good drink, and she more than held her own with the hard-drinking Minnesotans. Mara was a painter who had some odd sources of income, and once she had seen her briefly with the man who stood there with her.

"Mara! How good to see you," Kativa said. She hugged Mara briefly, kissed her cheek, then held out her hand to the tall man and said, "Hi. I'm Kativa Patel."

He had an interesting face, this man. He was tall and almost skinny in his leanness, and his grip was gentle but hinted at great strength. The backs of his hands were webbed with dry skin, big veins, and tendons that worked like steel cable under tension. He was casually dressed in battered, baggy old khakis and a denim work shirt under a worn black leather jacket. His face was long, with three distinct grooves across his forehead, as though someone had dragged a rake across his forehead many years ago. While his face was tired, it was a sort of tired amusement, and she sensed that it was something habitual with him, rather than situational.

"I'm Charley Payne," he said.

"I'm pleased to meet you, Charley," Kativa said. "What are you two doing here? Would you like some coffee?"

"I'd love a cup, Kat. Charley?" Mara said.

"Sure," he said.

"Let me get it, Kat. Charley wants to talk to you about those pictures."

"Pictures?" Kativa said.

"The ones I told you about on the phone, the ones I think are African or Australian."

Kativa frowned, then smiled as she remembered the phone call.

"You must forgive me," she said to Charley as she led them back to her office. "I have a terrible memory."

"So do I," he said. "I'm lucky I remember to put my pants on in the morning."

He laughed and she joined him, sneaking a quick glance at Mara who just smiled and stopped at the coffee machine.

"Let me take your cup, Kat. I'll freshen this for you," Mara said.

"Thanks, darling. Come in, Charley. Take that seat and I'll fetch another chair," Kativa said, brushing past him. He smelled warm, with a not unpleasant smell of old sweat on him and just a hint of some sort of aftershave. His body was hard when she touched him. He would be quite muscley naked, she thought, then colored at the thought.

"He's a hunk, Mara," she whispered as she brushed by Mara filling the coffee cups. "Where do you find them?"

"He's a strange one, Kat. But I do like him. I think you will, too."

"Does he have a brother?"

The two women laughed, and Mara came in carefully holding three cups of coffee and Kativa followed, dragging a small chair. The three of them were quite crammed in her space, and Kativa was again struck by how big Charley Payne was. He didn't seem large till you got close to him and realized he was at least six feet three or so, and his baggy clothes hid his body definition. He dominated the space, yet was quiet, and seemed amused and interested by the artwork and her racks of books that filled up the office.

"Where is that from?" he asked, pointing to the spiral rubbing.

Kativa sat down, leaned forward, and rested her elbows on the table, her mug in her hand, quite aware that it pressed her breasts together under the low-cut cotton blouse she wore. "From the Laura River region, in Queensland, Australia. I did my postgraduate work there."

Charley took the coffee mug from Mara. "Thanks," he said to her. "Queensland is the northeast, right?"

"That's right, Charley. Queensland is the northeasternmost territory of Australia. On the Great Barrier Reef side. Have you been?"

"No, but I'd like to. I used to dive, but I haven't for a very long time. Do you dive?"

"No. I'm a poor swimmer and I don't like water over my head. Mara is a diver, aren't you?" Kativa said.

"I got my certification in Cancun a few years ago, but there's not much diving around here. I did it with my boyfriend."

"Which one?" Kativa said, laughing.

"I've forgotten him."

"Did you get your doctorate in Australia?" Charley said.

Kativa smiled. "University of Cape Town, actually."

"You're from South Africa?" Charley said.

"Kat grew up there, and left not long after Mandela came into power," Mara said. She tasted her coffee and wrinkled her nose. "This needs more sugar. I'll be back. Anybody else?"

Charley shook his head no and Kativa said, "No thank you."

"You were born in South Africa?" Charley said.

"Yes, actually in a suburb of Johannesburg called Bredell. I went to university in Pretoria, then Cape Town for my Ph.D."

"Patel, that's an Indian name, isn't it?"

"Yes. My father was of Indian descent, my mother was Portuguese."

"So you grew up under apartheid?"

"Yes. We were considered Colored."

"Ah."

"Yes," Kativa said. She looked into her coffee cup, at the fine brown café au lait that very closely matched the color of her skin. "Yes, those were hard times for everyone."

"Is your Ph.D. in Australian art?"

"Well, to be specific, it's in Australian Aboriginal art and ethnography."

"What's ethnography?"

"It's the study of Australian Aboriginal cultural heritage. It's quite fascinating. Australian Aboriginal culture is the oldest 'primitive' surviving culture we have on earth. Many of their belief systems are completely integrated in their artworks, which encompass a variety of forms. While I studied all of them, I focused on the rock art, both the engravings and the drawings. I came to that really as a fluke . . . I met a young man who worked for an outfitting company that took tourists on tours in the Laura River regions, looking at the rock art there. He introduced me to Percy Tracy, who is the foremost living authority, at least among whites, in the Laura region. Percy liked me, actually he loves all the girls, even though he's well into his eighties, and allowed me unfettered access to his notes and helped me quite a bit. That's how it came about for me."

Charley reached into the battered canvas valise he'd brought with him, then took out a dark brown manila collapsible file with the Minneapolis Police logo on it.

"Are you a policeman?" Kativa asked.

"No, but I work for the police department. I'm a crime scene photographer, and I wanted to ask you about the images in these photos."

"What do you do for them?" Kativa said.

"Nothing dangerous," Charley said. His smile seemed especially amused. "That sort of police work scares me. I just take pictures."

He handed over an 8×10 color print. Kativa took it, then picked up her glasses, large round lenses in a frame that even when pressed in place slid down onto her nose.

"This is a very high-quality photograph, Charley. Do you do your own developing?"

"No. But the shop I work with does good work and they know how to work with my stuff."

Kativa was so engrossed in the photograph she didn't notice Mara standing at the door, looking at the two of them.

"This is very familiar," Kativa said. "The design is definitely from the Laura region, I'll tell you this . . . I think I may actually have seen this before."

"What do you mean you've seen this before?" Charley said.

"Obviously not this particular painting, but the painting this is a copy of. Or rather the rock art image."

"Where?"

Mara came in silently and sat down. Charley set his coffee cup down on the edge of Kativa's desk closest to him. Kativa spun her chair around and scooted to the closest bookshelf and began running her finger across the neatly organized spines of the books.

"Here," she said with satisfaction. She pulled out a book titled

Australia's Living Heritage, then flipped quickly through the well-thumbed pages till she came to one section. She skimmed it quickly and said to herself, "Not that..." then set the book down on the floor and began looking again. She plucked out a small 6×6 bound booklet titled *Quinkan Rock Art* and said, "Ah. Here we go."

She flipped through the pages and stopped at one, then handed the booklet to Charley. "That's where. It's a copy of that image."

Charley took the booklet, pushed aside some papers on Kativa's desk, and set the booklet beside his 8×10. The three of them compared the two. The likeness was unmistakable. The photograph in the booklet was of a figure on what appeared to be a sandstone wall, outlined in red, colored white within the lines, with cross-hatching across the chest. The arms and legs angled upward, with what appeared to be a long bulbed tail dangling below.

"Is that a tail?" Charley asked.

"A penis, actually," Kativa said. "The Imjins were said to travel by bouncing on that knobbed penis, much like a kangaroo travels by bounding."

"What's an Imjin?" Mara asked.

"This is the image," Charley said. He looked at Kativa with an intensity that made her uncomfortable. The amused look was gone, replaced by a fixity of eye that reminded Kativa of her cat when she was stalking a helpless bird. "What can you tell us about it?"

"Where did this image come from?" Kativa said.

"It was drawn on the wall of a crime scene."

"That doesn't look like paint."

"It's not. There's some paint, but most of it is blood and body fluids from a murder victim."

"Oh, my God," Kativa said.

Mara touched Charley's shoulder. "Show her the other photographs."

He looked at her, then slid the manila folder across the desk at Kativa. "I'd be careful with them. They're quite ugly."

Kativa looked through the photographs and felt herself go pale when she came to the overview photograph that showed the body of

Madison Simmons hanging upside down. She forced herself to look at the photograph again and noted how the body was staged. She put the photographs down and made herself stack them neatly end to end, before she placed them on top of the manila folder and pushed it away with only her fingertips.

"I've seen enough, thank you."

"What do you think?" Charley said.

"I've seen something much like the body as well."

"Tell me," Charley said, leaning forward in his chair.

"The body, the way it was set . . . were there parts . . . missing?"

"Why do you ask that?"

"In the puri-puri ritual, in the ritual killing, some parts of the person's body are taken, sometimes eaten by the sorcerer."

Charley sat back in his chair. "The killer trimmed out portions of abdominal fat and ate it along with the victim's kidneys."

"Oh, my God," Mara said. She sat down heavily. "You didn't tell me that."

"That's another part of the ritual," Kativa said.

"You said that before. What ritual?" Charley said.

"Do you know anything at all about Australian Aboriginal culture?" Kativa said.

"If I did, I wouldn't be sitting here," Charley said.

"What I mean is the background," Kativa said.

"No."

"Australian Aboriginal culture has a very unique mythos, the Dreamtime it's called. They believe that the entire world was created by the Rainbow Serpent who made the world and everything that lives in it. Part of their belief system is what they call the Dreamtime, a reality and a time that exists concurrently with the day-to-day reality we know. Aboriginals believe they can go back and forth between the Dreamtime and the day-to-day reality through magic rituals. When in the Dreamtime, they can see the future and the past, and they can commune directly with their ancestral spirits, or the elemental forces of nature. This is a very simple explanation of a complex subject, are you following me?"

MARCUS WYNNE

"I'm with you," Charley said.

"For your purposes, there are four kinds of magic. There's hunting magic, to help the hunter find the prey, to join his spirit to the spirit of the animal they hunt. There's improvement magic, magic to improve circumstances, to call down rain, to improve health, so on. There's love magic, powerful magic to influence a young man or woman to come together with the person who wants them. And then there's puri-puri, the black magic of death. It's meant to kill someone who has wronged or alienated someone within the tribe. That's what the inversion of the body is about . . . puri-puri drawings to inflict the ritual magic always show the target of the magic upside down, an inversion or reversal of the normal order of things."

"So this image is supposed to kill the victim?"

"No, this image is not strictly speaking a puri-puri drawing," Kativa said. She took out the first book and flipped to a page, held out a drawing. "See this," she said, pointing to an image of a long black figure upside down in a gallery of right-sided red-brown figures. "That's a puri-puri drawing, meant to kill the person represented by that upside-down figure. The drawing you have is of a particular Quinkin."

"What is a Quinkin?" Charley said.

Mara set her mug down, opened her mouth as though to speak, then closed it.

"A Quinkin," Kativa began, "is a spirit being. To the Aboriginals, there were many different types of spirit and ancestral beings. Some beings were spirits of animals that inhabited certain rock shapes, some were ancestors, family members who had died in the physical realm, others were spirits that inhabited rocks but weren't of the animal world. And there were others, both malevolent and good ones. The Quinkins are particular to the Aboriginal people of the Cape York Peninsula, which is quite close to Papua, New Guinea. There in fact was a land bridge between those islands and the northernmost part of Cape York, which is the far north of Queensland.

"The Quinkins were, or are, spirit beings that live there. There are two distinct tribes, who look different and have different agendas when it comes to dealing with the Aboriginal clans of the area. I'm most familiar with those, as the Laura area was a holy area for a number of reasons, and the Quinkins were said to be especially numerous there.

"The two tribes, if you will, of Quinkins are the Timara and the Imjin. The Timara Quinkins were like the tricksters of American Indian tradition: they were generally helpful to humans, but they enjoyed playing tricks on them. They might tip you into the water, lead you astray, tease you, but they would generally not hurt a human. They were tall and thin, black stick figures that were said to live in the cracks and crevices of the rock outcroppings in the Laura area."

She took the book back from Charley, flipped it to another page, and said, "Here. See?" She offered the book, open to a page where black stick figures hid behind thin trees. "At night, in the bush, the trees all look like this. You can see how to an Aboriginal it might seem that those thin trees moved with intention at night.

"The other tribe were the Imjin Quinkins, and they were held to be evil. They looked different, they looked like that drawing, and they traveled mostly by bouncing on those knobbed penises, even though there were female Imjin, who bounced on oversized breasts. The Imjin actively hunted humans. They would snatch children, and small parties or people traveling alone. They would ambush them, or lure them away by calling out their name. That's why even today an Aboriginal in this area, especially in the Ang-Gnarra tribal region which encompasses the Laura River area, will not answer to anyone calling their name that they can't see. The Imjin Quinkin would stalk humans, sometimes drive them like animals by making sounds and herding them into an ambush.

"And the Imjin Quinkins would eat human beings." Kativa sat back. "Or so the stories are told."

"That's interesting, and maybe it's useful," Charley said. "What could you tell from this painting? The person who drew it must know all about this stuff, or have seen that drawing."

"They'd have to be fairly knowledgeable," Kativa said. "The image, they may have seen that in a book somewhere, but it's not something that is widely circulated . . . the actual ritual of ritual cannibalism, that's something that most definitely is not common knowledge. The Aboriginals don't like to mention that, as the taboo against human flesh eaters is felt today still, and it was not a common practice, only among warriors and sorcerers. I . . . I'd think that anyone practicing this would have to be quite knowledgeable about it. A student of ethnography, someone fascinated by it, maybe an artist who'd read about it somewhere . . ."

"Who would read up on that? We're a long way from Australia," Charley said.

"I don't know, Charley. The art department at the university might have some classes in Australian art, I'm sure they would have at least a section on primitive and native arts . . . the anthropology department may have someone who specializes in researching those sorts of rituals. No one here, other than me, has much interest in the primitive Australian Aboriginal work. Most of the museum and modern art critical interest is in the new work done by Aboriginal artists which derives from their ancestral customs. And you never see anything like this."

"Is there anything like an Australian expatriate community here in the Cities, like the Russians or the Asians have?" Charley said.

"No," Kativa said. "Aussies aren't clannish in that way. They'd chum around if they met someone, but it's a point of their traveling, their walkabout, to meet and mingle with as many other people as they can. They're very outgoing, very sociable, very democratic when it comes to meeting people. I'm sure I'd know if there was one in the Cities."

Charley nodded, looked back at the photograph. "A Quinkin? A spirit being. A sorcerer?"

"Yes," Kativa said. "This was done by someone who knows about and is trying to practice an ancient black magic ritual. The action of taking their kidney fat is meant to rob them in this world and the next of their ability to survive a lean time. That's one of the major time distinctions the Aboriginals use—the dry time, and the wet—the time between the monsoon rains and the monsoon rain itself. Then there are the lean times and the fat—lean times when there wasn't much food, and you lived on your body fat, and the fat times when you stored up your body fat. Taking their body fat is robbing them of the very means of survival both spiritual and physical. Hanging the body, posing it like

WARRIOR IN THE SHADOWS

this, is a ritual to kill the spirit body in the next world as well as to warn others, maybe others of the same tribe, that this was someone who offended and broke the tribal rules, or was an enemy of the tribe."

"So the painting is part of the ritual?" Mara asked.

"Normally, if you can apply that word to this or to the original intent of the magic, the painting *is* the ritual. The sorcerer, who might be hired by someone else, or be assigned the task by the head of the clan, would go and meditate and contact the spirit beings through his ritual while he stayed alone to concentrate on his task. Then he would draw the drawings on a rock, create an image that he would infuse with his energy, provide a gateway if you will into the Dreamtime where that magic was most potent, and use it to focus the killing energy onto that person who might be far distant. The drawing itself was the ritual.

"Killing someone in that fashion . . . that would be something after the fact, or it could be a stand-alone action itself. It could be part of the ritual, or it could be a complete ritual in and of itself, without the drawing happening concurrently at all. After the fact, the killer might draw a depiction of the act so as to cleanse himself spiritually, but no, the drawing normally came first."

"This definitely came after the fact," Charley said. "The victim was dead. His blood and body fluids were used along with some ochre paint we found to put this image up on the wall."

"Ochre paint?" Kativa said.

"Yes."

"That was most commonly used on the walls for the rock paintings as well as on the body of the shaman and initiated males. They would draw figures on themselves, similar to what you see on the Imjin's torso."

"That's a possible lead. We could check with art stores on that," Charley said.

"I don't think this painting was meant to be part of the ritual," Kativa said. "I think the ritual was in the killing. Do you know how he died?"

"His head was fractured with a blunt object," Charley said.

Kativa nodded, took back the big picture book, and flipped

through it. "Here," she said. She pointed to a photograph of several clubs. One had an especially large bulbous end. "This is called a nulla-nulla. It's a war club, it also looks very much like a penis, deliberately so. One of the theories about the enlarged penis the Imjin traveled on was that it was a graphic representation of a hostile tribe that used the nulla-nulla to kill."

"I'll need a copy of that," Charley said.

"You may take the book, just return it when you're through," Kativa said.

"What is the painting for, then?" Mara asked.

Kativa said, "I think it's a signature. Or it's meant to be."

"A signature?"

"Of the Quinkin, or the person who is doing this."

Charley looked at the picture, then looked at his own photograph. "Does this Quinkin have a name?"

"Yes," Kativa said. "Anurra. He's the most evil Quinkin of all."

83

PART 2

Alfie Woodard, fettered by the sheets in Susan's narrow bed, tossed and turned with his dreams. His eyes sealed with deep sleep, his body slick with sweat, he kicked at the thin blanket and worn sheets as he went back in his dreams, went back . . .

. . . to when he was a boy, naked and thin, a hard and lean mass of seven-year-old muscle running as fast as he could to escape the tribal policeman chasing him when he was suddenly brought to a halt by the hard hand gripping his tangled mane of kinky hair.

"No humbug with you!" the policeman said. His broad Aboriginal face seemed alien under the bush hat he wore as part of his khaki uniform, the same as the white policemen wore. "You're going now!"

And off he went with all the other part-white children taken from their Aboriginal parents. The new laws allowed for the removal of part-white children from their Aboriginal mothers, who were thought to be habitual drunks, idle layabouts, or general scum in the tribal lands, to be fostered with white families who out of the goodness of their Christian hearts had expressed their willingness to take in the poor heathen children of unfortunates and raise them in God's way. It was better for all parties involved, the policemen who came for the children said.

Or so that was how it was explained.

On his first night in his first home, Alfie had thrown his dinner plate to the floor and stripped off the clothes they'd forced him into and run out the door laughing while the embarrassed father chased him down and dragged him screaming back to the house. He took the first of many beatings, but he only lasted a few weeks there.

The next home was sterner yet; the father was a barber who used a razor strop from his shop with a free hand, leaving Alfie with scars that in later years he used, with an artist's precision, as starting points for his own ritual scarification. It wasn't long before that family too pled with the authorities for Alfie to be settled with someone who could handle him better.

The third home was the best. The old stockman didn't insist that Alfie be perfectly dressed.

"The boy's never worn clothes before and it'll be taking some time before he's used to it," Mr. Tokely, the head of the house, said.

He let the boy run free as long as he kept near. There were other Aboriginals working the station, herding the sheep and riding horses, who made a point of coming to the boy and telling him he was lucky with Mr. Tokely, that he was a good man and it was just the way of things how the government had taken him from his mother and sent him here.

"Make the best of a poor lot, boy," they said.

And slowly, with the caution of a wounded animal, Alfie did. He learned to wear clothes and shoes; he learned how to eat with a knife and fork. He learned how to ride a horse, under Mr. Tokely's gentle tutelage and with the help of Billy Williams, the Aboriginal foreman. He worked in the shearing house, handling sheep larger than himself, and he rode herd on the range. He took his meals in the big house with Mr. Tokely and his quiet wife. They had no children of their own, but they treated Alfie and the offspring of the station hands as though they were of their own blood. There were presents at Christmas, Easter egg hunts for the small ones, and church every Sunday. Alfie enjoyed going to church. He didn't understand why someone would let himself be crucified to save all the others, but the priest and Mr. Tokely promised him that someday he would understand.

He passed three idyllic years there. When he was eleven years old, disaster struck the station: disease wiped out much of the sheep flock, and the remaining animals had to be killed to prevent the spread of the virus. But worst of all was the fatal car accident that took Mr. and Mrs. Tokely. When the bank sent its men out to repossess the station, the buildings and the vehicles, Alfie found himself without a home and still under the control of the resettlement program.

His friends among the Aboriginal workers had offered to take him in, but that wasn't part of the resettlement program. He'd fought back tears as he stared out the back window of the beat-up government Land Rover at his friends standing, hats in hand, in the dust outside Tokely Station. That was his final memory of the good years, watching his friends fade away in the dust trail as the silent white man and woman in the front seats took him away from all that he'd learned to love to yet another new home.

The Edwards household was a way station to hell.

Their primary interest was the state stipend they received for the expenses of fostering a half white, half Aboriginal child. Their other interest was the income they could get from farming out a healthy eleven-year-old who knew his way around a sheep station to other families. Mr. Edwards had contempt for everything and everyone, including his own family. He'd especially abused his boy, Roy, who at fourteen was the oldest. But at least Roy got to sleep in the bedroom with his younger brother and his sister, while Alfie slept in a dank corner of the basement on a pile of tarps and blankets.

The first time Alfie ran off, he caught a professional beating from Mr. Edwards. Edwards had boxed in the Merchant Marine and was still handy with his fists, as the men who drank at the Quinkin Bar in Laura were quick to affirm. Edwards had spent more than his share of nights in the primitive barred enclosure that served as the Laura jail. The first night Edwards beat Alfie into unconsciousness, then dragged him into the basement and chained his leg to a support beam and left him there without water, food, or a toilet for three days.

"That'll teach you to run off," Mr. Edwards said. "Next time I'll break your bloody legs."

And the next time he did.

The doctor wasn't sympathetic or enthusiastic about patching up an Aboriginal child, but the state paid the bills, and the doctor and Edwards had a wink and nod agreement over how the billing should be presented to the proper authorities.

Over time they worked out a system that worked to both their benefits.

Worse than the beatings was Mr. Edwards taste for some sexual activity that his wife wanted no part of. A young Aboriginal boy provided an outlet for those tensions, something that Edwards found convenient and enjoyable. Roy Edwards, who'd been the recipient of some of those attentions from his father, was relieved; he welcomed the opportunity to direct some of his own deep-seated anger onto the defenseless target that Alfie provided.

Six years it went like that, until Alfie was seventeen by the state's count. The duly timed paperwork had him reporting to a bureaucrat who informed him that he would be on his own in a year. Alfie left the office, his hat in his hand, studying the floor in a state of confusion, looking round for Mr. Edwards who'd dropped him off for the meeting. In the lobby of the courthouse a military recruiter had set up a table. He was a staff sergeant in the Airborne Regiment, his maroon beret set at a cocky angle, and he hid his distaste for the bushy-headed young man in ragged clothing who stood before him but would not meet his eyes.

The recruiter looked Alfie up and down and said, "It's a fine life for the ones who can take it, mate. Think you got what it takes?"

"What does it take?" Alfie said.

"Got to be able to take punishment, go without sleep or eating and still be able to fight, do all that lot and then some, take it all with a grin."

Alfie looked up from his battered boots to meet the Airborne sergeant's eyes for just a moment, then lowered his eyes and felt a thin smile come onto his mouth.

"That's the lot, then?" Alfie said.

"Easier said than done, son."

"Show me the paperwork."

Later at home, when Alfie showed him the papers, Mr. Edwards

90

laughed out loud and cuffed him. Alfie took the blow, but said, "Will you sign or not?"

Both Edwards and his oldest boy laughed at the thought of Alfie as a paratrooper. The rest of the family carefully ignored the exchange, careful not to draw fire in the unending battle that had played out for years in the house.

"Oh, I'll be signing these papers...one of these days," Edwards said. He threw the early enlistment papers down on the table. "One of these days. In the meantime it's back to work for you."

Alfie went back to work.

Later that night, he signed the papers himself in a fair approximation of Edwards hand, gained after long practice on canceled checks. He took a check from the ledger checkbook for himself as well and lay down early to sleep. He had work to do.

Early the next morning, when Mr. Edwards went out to the pens for his morning look around, he stumbled and fell and hit his head against a shovel so hard it cracked his skull.

Or that was how Alfie told it to the constable and the doctor. Roy Edwards thought differently, but he choked to death while drinking alone the day of his father's funeral. People commented on the double tragedy and noted how the young Aborigine foster rose to the occasion and helped set things right around the station before he took off for the Army.

And Alfie Woodard showed up at the Army recruiter's office in the first set of new clothes he'd ever owned with a signed early enlistment form in his hand.

Lieutenant Oberstar held out one big hand to Charley, who perched uncomfortably on a too-small chair beside Bobby Lee's desk.

"Simon Oberstar," the lieutenant said. "I raised your friend here from a pup. You probably knew he was a son of a bitch, but he's my son of a bitch and that's the way I like it. You guys were Army together, Airborne, right?"

"That's right," Charley said.

"I did my bit a long time ago," Oberstar said. "Don't miss it one bit. You're too young for the Southeast Asia tour, eh?"

"Yeah, not me," Charley said. "You?"

"Yeah," Oberstar said.

"History," Charley said.

"There it is," Oberstar said, nodding. "So tell me what Australian Aborigines have to do with Madison Simmons?"

"Charley worked out an angle on the crime scene and that leads us to a connection with Australia," Bobby Lee said. "Simmons helped broker a complex series of loans and real estate acquisitions in Minnesota for some Australian companies. He's been known to have frequent visitors from the Australian Economic Development Council and the Australian embassy. I've got people running those leads down. On the surface there's nothing shady about those deals; they were straight-up loans with matching funds from the interested parties for real estate here."

"The Australians're buying us up now?" Charley said in surprise. "Not just the Japanese?"

"They've got lots of interest in what we've got," Bobby Lee said. "Lumber, minerals, high tech, deep-water port up there on Lake Superior . . . even with the shitty exchange rate we got stuff they want. Some of their big buck operators can play in any major league they want and some of them want Minnesota property."

Oberstar nodded sagely. "Lakeshore cabins, resorts, that sort of thing?"

"There's some of that," Bobby Lee said. "Some speculation on resort properties on the North Shore, but most of it's in the Twin Cities. My guy is getting a breakdown of specifics, but apparently they own some big pieces of downtown."

"Get me that list, Bobby," Oberstar said. "I know some old-timers in the property companies here, I get them on the phone I can save us some time." He paused and rubbed his full belly speculatively. "What's your gut telling you?"

"We're on to something here," Bobby Lee said. "We'll run this Australian thing down, it's the best thing we've got so far, thanks to Charley."

Oberstar arched backward, then slowly forward. "My back is killing me." He nodded to Charley and said, "All right. Keep me in the loop." He walked back to his office and shut the door behind him.

"That's one mean old dog," Charley observed.

"He's a good man," Bobby Lee said. "He's not off the mark when he said he taught me all I know when I was in the bag and on the street. He's had it rough the last couple of years. His wife died, and he's got a couple of kids just into college."

"So what now?"

"Not much. You shoot that homicide Myers is working on the North Side?"

"Got it on the run coming up here. That Myers is a funny son of a bitch."

"I rode with him for a while when I was in Third Precinct," Bobby Lee said. "He's crazy."

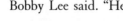

MARCUS WYNNE

"I took good care of him."

"I got nothing else for you, buddy. You want to come by the house tonight for a couple of beers, see Max and Nicky?"

"Hell yeah," Charley said. "Six, six-thirty?"

"I'll tell Max. Don't be bringing Nicky any more presents. You're spoiling that kid and he'll get to be hard to handle."

"You don't need to be a hard-ass with that kid. He's good all through."

"Easy for you to say, you get to hand him back at the end of the night."

Charley laughed. "There is that. I'll see you later."

Charley let himself out of the Major Investigations Unit, holding the keypad secured door open for a couple of uniforms he knew, then went out into the street. His beat-up Camry station wagon was parked in the center median of the street, lined up with the squad cars arrayed for the next shift change. He slid into his car, took the sign that said OFFICIAL POLICE BUSINESS and slid it under the seat, then drove down Hennepin to Calhoun and around to Upton and the Linden Hills neighborhood. He parked his car on Forty-third Street and went in the back way to his apartment. He went up the stairs and let himself into his apartment, setting the camera bag down beside the door. He stood there for a few minutes, looking at the wall where the photograph of the Anurra drawing was tacked up. He'd moved some of his photographs to make room, some of the old black-and-whites he'd taken in his early years as a photographer, the time when he was so enamored of Cartier-Bresson's theory of the decisive moment.

The decisive moment.

Charley sat slowly down in his battered armchair, took a deep breath and let himself relax, watched the room focus become soft with the only thing in sharp focus the photograph of the drawing. There was deliberation in the making of that image, each line the width of a fingertip, time taken in the making and in the deliberate pressing and stroking with that same fingertip. Not drawn from a copy, drawn from memory, a re-creation of an image seared into the memory with life. It was an image imbued with something fierce and magical in its making.

The making of it had been a decisive moment for the maker. Kativa had said it best, "The making of the image, not the image itself, that's the important thing."

Charley understood at the visceral level the decisive moment of making an image. Cartier-Bresson's theory appealed to the warrior that Charley kept concealed inside; the theory of being in tune with your equipment, in tune with your vision of the world, so that you recognized a moment in the moment before it came to be and you were there with the picture already framed as it took place in front of you. That was the shooter's Zen heaven.

Both the world of the gun and the world of the camera called for the same discipline, which was one of the many things about photography that appealed to Charley. Frame the target in your vision, take aim, press the trigger, follow through—even the mechanics were the same. So was the need to keep distance between the shooter and the other, a vital requirement to keep one's sanity in the face of the consequences of action.

Moving his photos and putting up the image of Anurra, that was a decisive moment. Charley stroked his chin, took out a cigarette and lit it up, and stared at the photograph. For no good reason he took out his Glock .45 from the drawer, unloaded it, checked the chamber, then reloaded it and replaced it in his drawer, leaving it uncovered and handy.

Why? He wasn't going after this guy. That wasn't his job anymore, to go after the bad guy, to hunt down evil men. He'd had enough of that, that's what drove him to quit the Special Activities Staff. He'd quit when he could no longer tell the difference between the good men and the evil men. Were bureaucrats evil? Men who sent other men out to do dark things in the name of national security? Men who justified everything from the invasion of privacy to the casual murder of innocents as expedient in the face of a threat to national security? Charley didn't know anymore. What had frightened him was when he found that he didn't care anymore. He was just going through the motions, and that made him dangerous by default, and he could no longer bear being responsible for the young and idealistic operators working for him. He left that part of his life behind and went from being the actor to being the man removed, the man behind the lens, the observer rather than the operator, and until now, that suited him.

But he recognized something about this killer he was documenting; there was something about him that didn't ring criminal, it rang professional, and in the way one professional recognizes another, Charley knew there was someone highly trained doing this for a specific reason or reasons. And if he could just find out what those reasons were, he'd find this man.

So what kind of man would kill someone in this fashion and then draw a picture like this? This was no gangland hit—despite the public's belief in efficient hit men, they were actually few and far between. An organized crime hit would be fast and hard and efficient. They wouldn't have spent as much time on the scene as this.

Charley was reminded of an operation he'd been told about by one of the old-timers in the Special Activities Staff, a deceptive good old boy who'd been around since the seventies. In Beirut, the CIA Chief of Station had been kidnapped and tortured to death by a Hezbollah action cell. Despite the best efforts of the Outfit's operators, they hadn't been able to get William Buckley back. But when the Soviets had one of their own taken, they snatched the son of a Hezbollah higher up. They sent the Hezbollah leader his son's testicles. The Soviet hostage was released.

There was something to speaking in the language people understood.

And there was something to this. If this was to be a message, who was it to? Not the police, not the investigators . . . someone else who would hear about it, or see it, find out about it in some way. It was front page news and of course lurid descriptions of the crime scene would leak out to reporters.

So who would be getting the message?

Charley picked up his phone and called Bobby Lee.

Bobby Lee answered, "Martaine."

"Bobby, it's me. Did you consider that maybe this was meant to send a message to somebody working with Simmons? I just thought of that. You may want to look at it that way."

"You mean a coworker?"

"Or somebody close to him."

"That's a hell of a message."

"Yeah it is. Look at the people working the Australia deals. I got a feeling there's something to that."

"There's another interesting little twist," Bobby Lee said. "You remember those videotapes, the ones he had so many of?"

"Sure. Porno, right?"

"Of the expensive custom kind. Simmons is in some of them with very young girls."

Charley tapped his nail against the phone he held to his ear and was silent for a moment. "That's a whole other angle," he said. "Maybe the killer is sending a message about the porno. Worth running that down, too."

"You think pretty good for a photographer."

Charley laughed. "You want me to bring anything later?"

"No. Good ideas, buddy. I'll get onto it. See you later."

Charley replaced the phone in the cradle and slid down in his chair so that his head was fully supported.

So Anurra, he thought. Where are you now?

Alfie and Susan sat in the crowded outside patio of a restaurant that specialized in vegetarian cuisine in the heart of the Lyn-Lake District, one of the most alternative and counterculture neighborhoods in the Twin Cities. He was dressed in his habitual black T-shirt, black sweat-shirt, black Levi's, and heavy Doc Marten boots, his black biker jacket draped over the back of his chair. He was catching glances from other patrons, some of whom were almost as extravagantly pierced, for his heavily muscled arms—incongruous in a man of otherwise medium build—the small bone in his nose, as well as the multiple piercings in his ear.

"You don't sleep well," Susan said. She sipped her coffee and looked round at the other tables, where people looked back at her and Alfie with curiosity. "You toss and turn and twitch just like a dreaming dog."

"It's the weight of my past, old dear. Living it over."

Susan paused as though to say something, then said, "Your scars are incredible."

"Can't see them, though, can you?" Alfie said.

"I can see the line of some of them under the sweatshirt around your neck," Susan said. "They're amazing."

"Part of my people's initiation," Alfie said. "We're not allowed to talk to women about it."

"Really? Why?"

Alfie leaned back in his chair, cupped his coffee mug in both hands, and said, "There's a place called Jowalbinna, in tropical North Queensland. That's where I'm from. It's the spiritual center, a holy place, for the Ang-Gnarra tribal group. The people who lived there, well, they're mostly dead. Killed by white settlers or disease or just forced out. But Jowalbinna has always been a holy place, for tens of thousands of years. There's lots of caves there, the sandstone in the hills has fallen and made caves all about. One cave in particular was a place of initiation for the young boys of the tribe.

"For us Aboriginals, there's different kinds of magic. Initiation is about learning from one kind of magic. There's men's magic and then there's women's magic. You can never mix the two because it will kill you. If you're a woman, you're not equipped to deal with men's magic, any more than a man is equipped to deal with women's magic.

"In the initiation cave, the boys crawled through this dark, narrow, twisting cave from one end to the other. And one time, a long time ago, a woman had her son going through initiation. She was afraid for him, so she hid herself near the site to see how he was doing. And one of the shaman, the senior magic man in charge of the ritual, he saw her."

"What happened to her?" Susan said, leaning forward in her seat.

"They killed her, mate," Alfie said. He sipped from his coffee. "That's what happens to people who stick their noses where they don't belong. Stoned her to death, then buried her upside down so that her spirit would never be able to find its way home again. In that initiation cave, there's a drawing of that on the wall. And they tell that story as a warning to all the young boys after they've gone through the first stage of initiation magic. That's when they get circumcised."

He held up one hand as though it held a knife and made a cutting motion.

"I guess that means I shouldn't ask you about those things," Susan said. She flushed a little on her neck. "It's just so interesting, I could listen to you all day."

"Ah, I'm just bending your ear, Suzie gal." He winked at a couple sitting at an adjoining table. "Everybody knows we Aussies like a tall tale, eh?"

MARCUS WYNNE

The couple laughed and the woman said, nodding at the remains of Alfie's vegetarian omelet, "I notice you don't eat meat. Is that the custom among Aborigines?"

"Not at all, mate," Alfie said. He paused for effect, then said, "I just eat the meat of my enemies."

All of them, the couple, Alfie, and Susan, laughed at that. Alfie turned, grinning, and began to pick at his omelet once again.

"I have to go to work soon," Susan said. "Here's a spare key," she said, handing him a single key tied with a red ribbon.

"Keys to the kingdom," Alfie said. "Can't thank you enough for putting up with me. Hotel living gets stale."

"My pleasure," Susan purred. "You can stay as long as you want. My roommate is out of town for the next month in Colorado on an exchange program."

"Many thanks, mate."

"What are you going to do today?"

"Oh, a little of this, a little of that, a little shopping, have a bit of a look around."

"I won't be back till late tonight."

"I'll wait up," Alfie said, smiling.

"Oh, whatever," Susan said. She was pleased; to hide it, she brushed at her hair with a free hand.

Alfie pulled a wad of bills from his pocket and left a twenty on the table, then they got on his motorcycle and he roared through the side streets to Hennepin and dropped Susan off in front of Calhoun Square.

He waved her good-bye and yelled, "See ya!" as he pulled away into traffic. He only rode a short distance, to Lake Calhoun, where he pulled into a parking lot, dismounted, and went to sit on a bench looking out on the water. He took out a cigarette and lit it with a plastic lighter, then blew the smoke with great contentment into the cool breeze filtering in from the water. He liked Susan, but he wouldn't be staying here much longer. One more job to do and then he had to move on.

He hoped he wouldn't have to kill her.

2.4

Kativa Patel sat hunched over her desk in her office, one leg drawn up and crossed bonelessly in her lap, her left hand holding her hair back, while her right hand wound a pencil through her hair again and again. She had only a painfully short list of notes to give Charley Payne: a brief note that the image of Anurra was from the Laura area, at Split Rock to be specific, and that it was thought to be the work of the Ang-Gnarra tribal group or possibly the Kuku-Thypan.

She set the note aside and flipped through several illustrated books of Aboriginal stories, most by Percy Tracy, who she knew and loved as a good friend and mentor. There wasn't any reference to the specific image there, but there was plenty about the Imjin. She didn't really know what else to say about the image other than what she'd told Charley. She had no idea how someone with an obviously intimate knowledge of Aboriginal ritual would come to Minneapolis to kill in the ritual fashion and put the image up on the wall.

So that's all she'd be able to tell Charley.

She wound her hair round the pencil once again. Charley. She liked that name and she liked the man, too. He had an interesting face, long and lined with good humor, but his eyes were capable of hiding things. She had the sense and intuition of all attractive women who have had to deal with the attentions, wanted or unwanted, of many men, and she had a feeling that Charley was attracted to her, just as she felt herself attracted to him. It warmed her, deep in her middle, the memory of his obviously hard body brushing against her in her small office. She chided herself for thinking that way about her friend's boy-friend and got her mind back on track.

But she still had little to tell him about Anurra.

So maybe if she took him to lunch it would make up for the paucity of her information. She picked up the phone, hesitated, then punched out his number.

"Hello?"

"Hello, Charley, this is Kativa Patel, from the museum?"

"Hello Kativa Patel from the museum."

"I have a little bit of information for you, not much I'm afraid. Would you care to meet me for lunch here at the museum? The Café is quite good for lunch and we have a very good view of the city," Kativa said.

She felt her face heating and silently cursed herself for the slight stammer in her voice.

"I'd love to have lunch with Kativa Patel from the museum," Charley said. "And the Café is just fine. I've eaten there before."

"Have you? Visiting the museum?"

"I like to take pictures in the Sculpture Garden."

"We're quite proud of that garden," Kativa chattered on. "One of the best in the country."

"Yes. Well. When?"

"How far are you?"

"Just over on Lake Harriet."

"Half an hour, then?"

"Half an hour it is."

"I'll see you shortly."

Kativa hung up the phone and twisted the cord in a knot. Should she feel guilty for not inviting Mara? No. After all, it was only lunch.

The Museum Café had ceiling-to-floor glass on the one wall that looked out over the Sculpture Garden and Loring Park. From any table in the room you could look out and see people walking in the street below, the trees in full fall bloom, the intricate maze of the carefully trimmed hedges in the Sculpture Garden punctuated with carefully arrayed pieces of art, and the twists and turns of the footbridge that crossed over Hennepin connecting the Sculpture Garden and Loring Park. Kativa and Charley sat at a table up against the glass where they could look out at the city when they weren't looking at each other.

"So you're Mara's international man of mystery," Kativa said playfully. "And you hang out in Linden Hills?"

"I like being the neighborhood oddball," Charley said.

Kativa tried to hide her laugh behind one hand. "I never know when you're serious or not."

"Either do I," Charley said. "You can laugh at me, I don't mind."

Kativa dropped her hand and laughed, then bowed her head to her salad and artfully forked the last few mouthfuls in.

"What do you think of that image now?" she said. "Now that you've thought about it for a while."

"What do you think is the question," Charley said. "You're the expert."

"We know where the original of that drawing is. This person must have knowledge of the Aboriginal artwork and history in the Laura region."

"Any idea where we'd find such a person?"

"Not here in the Cities. I checked at the University of Minnesota, but they don't have a specialty in Australian art. I have a call in to the head of ethnography degree focus, but I don't expect her to tell me anything different. I think you may have a traveler, someone who may have been there or is originally from Australia."

"That's a possibility," Charley said. He looked Kativa in the eye till she looked away. He smiled then and said, "Maybe Customs would have the latest on who's visiting from Australia."

"May I ask you a personal question?" Kativa said.

"Sure."

"You and Mara seem so . . . different together. Do you think that helps you in your relationship?"

"I don't know if I'd call what we do a 'relationship' in the sense you mean it."

"Does that mean you're just in it for the sex?"

"No," Charley said, a serious tone in his voice. "Not just that. Mara is my friend, a very good friend, an intimate. I enjoy the time I spend with her, and I think she enjoys the time she spends with me. We enjoy each other, and that makes the difference. Why do you ask?"

"I'm curious about how American men think."

"I'd think you'd have plenty of opportunity."

"Not as much as you might think."

"Why is that?"

"I'm not sure, really. What do you imagine?"

"About what?"

"About why it's hard for me to get a date here."

Charley smiled slowly, a lupine smile.

"Maybe you don't get out enough," he said.

"I am quite busy."

"Busy."

"Quite."

"Quite."

Charley laughed out loud. Heads turned at nearby tables.

"I think you're probably a bit much for your run-of-the-mill Minnesotan, Kativa Patel," he said. "They're not used to this sort of thing."

"What sort of thing would that be?"

"High-level flirtation. Around here it's more likely to be hey, how about a beer and a bratwurst and what do you think the Vikings are going to do this year? You're probably too smart for them, too exotic, too . . ."

"Too . . . ?"

"Too, too much. Do you like to walk?"

"Certainly. A turn around the garden?"

"Just what I was thinking."

They strolled slowly along the manicured paths that wound through the Sculpture Garden, both of them with their hands pressed deep into pants pockets.

"Mara tells me you are really a good photographer," Kativa said.

"I like to shoot," Charley said. He lifted his chin and inhaled greedily. "I love the fall air."

"It's the best season here," Kativa said. "Nothing like it in South Africa or Australia, that's for sure."

"Why did you leave? South Africa, I mean."

Kativa sighed. "My whole family has left. After Mandela came to office, everyone had high hopes that things would change. And they did, some of it good, but much of it bad. The crime was the worst—so much violence, and we all knew someone personally who had suffered. It was just a matter of time before something happened to us. I always knew I wanted to go. I was in Australia when the rest of my family left. My mother and father are in Canada, just outside Vancouver."

"That's a beautiful city."

"Yes it is. It's like heaven for them there, and there's a large Indian community and a fair number of South Africans there. Lots of immigrants in Vancouver. And I'm not too far away from them, here."

"What about Australia?"

"Oh, I loved it there. Loved the country, loved the people. Have you ever been?"

"No."

107

"Queensland is where I spent most of my time, out in the bush country near Laura."

"So you know this area pretty well?"

"Yes. I was there for six months, a long time."

"Is that where you learned about the magic, or was that part of your coursework in university?"

"I learned a lot in university, but it wasn't until I got out into the field that I really began to learn about the magic. Much of Aboriginal lore is held in an oral tradition and they resist having anything written down, so it's only when you hear the stories from the people themselves do you get the real insight into what makes it all come together."

Kativa crossed her arms across her chest.

"What were you just thinking?" Charley asked.

She hesitated, took a few steps, then looked sidewise at Charley.

"I had a little brush with Aboriginal magic when I was there," she said.

"Tell me about it."

She sat on a concrete bench beside a sculpture of a long-eared hare astride a bell. Charley sat beside her, both of them conscious of the warmth of their thighs brushing on the cool concrete bench.

"I'd been in the field for about three months, and besides cataloging the rock art there I was doing interviews with the women. Women would talk to me, but most of the men were uncomfortable talking about any of their rituals or ceremonies to a woman, especially a white woman. But there was one man, older, in his forties, who paid me a lot of attention. He was always trying to chat me up. Finally one of the women told me to watch out for this man, that he was trying to work love magic on me because he wanted me."

"Love magic, huh? Sounds useful."

Kativa half smiled. "It sounds silly, sitting here, but you have to be there to fully realize just how much of this Dreamtime stuff is woven into the daily life of the Aboriginals and those whites who interact with them. It wasn't long after that, that I began to have a recurring dream, a dream of an Aboriginal man with a bone in his nose, his body covered with scars."

"Like the bush men in the pictures you showed me?"

"Yes. At first I dreamed that we were outside, in the bush, and he was far away, just watching me. But then each dream, he got a little bit closer, closer and closer and he began to call my name out. It got to the point that during the day, I'd hear someone calling my name when I was working. It began to affect my work."

"What did you do then?"

"I finally brought it up to Percy, who was helping me in the work. Percy is an initiate in the tribal group there, the only white man to be accepted, and then only because of his work in conserving the rock art in Laura and helping the local Aboriginals. As soon as I told him, he immediately took it seriously. He took me to see one of his friends, a man I knew to be a shaman initiate. He spoke to me and asked me to

MARCUS WYNNE

describe the dreams to him. Once I did, he did a small ceremony for me: he and another shaman played the didgeridoo, danced out a dance, and laid hands on me so that they could see for themselves what I was dreaming."

"What?"

"It sounds silly, but I felt as though they could see what I'd seen when they touched me. They told me that the other man was working love magic on me and they cast a counterspell to defeat it. They said that I was connected to Laura in ways that I didn't know and that I would come back there again. They gave me a small cloth bag and told me to wear it. Inside was a small bone and a piece of crystal. Once I put it on, I stopped having the dream. That night."

"What happened to the cloth bag?"

"They took it back after a couple of months. They assured me I would never be bothered by that man again."

"What happened to the man who was casting the love magic?"

"This is the frightening part," Kativa said. "He died. Heart attack, one night after he'd been up drinking. Or so it was said."

Charley nodded, and Kativa saw that he was taking it all seriously.

"So you have it firsthand," Charley said.

"It's hard to explain in the light of day here in Minnesota," Kativa said. "But the rituals and magic are very real in bush Australia. And once you've been there, seen the paintings, felt what it's like at night when all those thousands of years of habitation are pressing on you, then it's much easier to believe in the potency of those images. Like that image you've taken of Anurra."

"Do you ever have dreams of that time?"

"Not since then."

Charley nodded. "You can sense something about that image," he said. "There's a sense of power in it. Somebody took their time making it and it's the making of the image that's important. That's what I see. And whoever made it sees the same thing."

"It's quite evil," Kativa said.

"Yes it is," Charley said. "Yes it is."

2.5

The Gentlemen Only was the classiest and most expensive strip club in town. It had the best lunch buffet special in the downtown district—if you found naked women with your roast beef appetizing—which accounted for the herds of overfed businessmen looking to mix business with pleasure on their expense accounts. The interior was done up in a red rococo motif that was supposed to suggest New Orleans or the Moulin Rouge in Paris, and the bartenders all dressed up like riverboat gamblers. What Bobby Lee liked about the club is that the customers never paid any attention to the other customers. He could come in here, savor the lovelies while he had a good meal, and not be bothered or distracted unless he wanted to be. It didn't hurt that it was a short walk from Police Headquarters.

Bobby Lee saw the head of security for the club standing against a wall, watching him. Dave Nyser was a huge half black, half white man with piercing green eyes who'd done a term for manslaughter, got out, went to school, and gotten his rights restored. He'd graduated from throwing drunks out of the rough workingclass bars on the North Side to working here in a business suit, with a calm and diplomatic way of dealing with rich drunks who thought that buying a lap dance entitled them to something more at the end of the song. Nyser was a silent man, but he heard everything from a variety of sources in his quiet float around the club. He had been Bobby Lee's best source for information about the gray world between legitimate business and the street since Bobby Lee had put in a good word for him when he was getting his rights restored.

He waved the big man over.

"How are you, David?"

"I'm very well, Mr. Martaine. Yourself?"

"What do you hear these days?"

"Many things, Mr. Martaine. Many things. Yourself?"

"What do you think about this cannibal thing with the banker?"

Nyser checked the buttons on his expensive suit jacket, then crossed his hands at the belt line.

"I think," he said, pitching his voice softly, "that someone may have been angry with Mr. Simmons."

"You knew the guy?"

"Mr. Simmons came here occasionally. Never alone, always in the company of several other men."

"You know any of these men?"

"They were not regulars."

"What do you remember about them?"

"Some of them were from Australia, business types, very well dressed, good manners, loud but behaving themselves."

"Australia?"

"Yes. On several occasions. Mostly different men, but one man twice."

"What about the one man who came twice?"

"Young, late twenties, very well dressed. A diplomat of some sort."

"How could you tell?"

"The way he spoke. And he mentioned the Australian consulate in Chicago as his place of work to one of the girls."

"Which girl?"

"Josie, dances as Josephine. She's no longer with us. Very popular dancer when she was."

"Josie, dances as Josephine. Okay, we'll come back to her. Have you seen any of these others or this Australian guy since then?"

"No, sir."

"Think you could work up a better description of the Australian for me? The diplomat?"

"Not too much more . . . just under six feet, sandy blond hair parted on the left, longish to the collar, brown eyes. Lean build, like a swimmer."

"You remember anything else?"

Nyser paused and took his time looking over the club. "Yes, Detective Martaine. Several times I think Mr. Simmons was accompanied by police officers."

"Cops?"

"Yes."

"You know any of them?"

"No, sir. They refused to give up their jackets when they identified themselves to the girl at the front door check. Unfortunately, I wasn't here, as it's my policy to personally inspect law enforcement credentials myself."

"Could the girl tell me?"

"Unfortunately not. We've had a change in that position, due in large part to that incident."

"What's that girl's name?"

"That would be Josephine."

"I thought she was a dancer."

"She didn't want to dance anymore, so she took the door check job."

Nyser went away for a few minutes. When he returned, he handed Bobby Lee a small slip of paper with the name Josie Royale, 140 N. Emerson Street, 555-4988 on it.

"Her last address and phone number, Detective Martaine."

"Thanks, Dave," Bobby Lee said. He took out a twenty from his wallet and began to fold it.

"That's not necessary," Nyser said.

Bobby Lee paused, then replaced the twenty. "Favors in the bank, Dave." He reached out and shook the big man's hand.

"Thank you, Mr. Martaine. Always a pleasure speaking with you."

The big man walked away, quietly nodding to the burly members of his staff, pausing by the buffet table to see how lunch was holding up, and nodding to the girls working the tables, making sure they were moving quickly from customer to customer.

Bobby Lee sat back and thought. Cops? Cops with Simmons? What the hell was that about? Australian diplomats? He was going to have to shake that tree till it fell down. There were going to be complications in this case. He took out his cell phone and dialed the Major Crimes Unit.

"Janine?" he said to the secretary who answered. "Do me a big favor and forward this to Oberstar's desk, will you?"

"Sure thing, Bobby Lee. Where are you?" she said.

"Gentlemen Only, on pussy patrol."

"The mouth on you," she said, laughing. "Here's Oberstar's phone. Don't work too hard, you hear me?"

The phone rang and rang, and then the answering machine kicked in.

"This is Lieutenant Oberstar. I'm not at my desk right now. Please leave me a message and I'll get back to you as soon as I can."

Bobby Lee left his cell phone number on the tape and hung up. He pushed away his unfinished chef salad and side order of breadsticks, his appetite diminished by the thought of cops being involved in this. What the hell was a hoity-toity downtown banker doing in The Gentlemen Only with plainclothes cops? Something smelled dirty here, and it was going to take more juice than he had to get it sussed out.

His cell phone chimed.

"Bobby Lee?" Oberstar said.

"Yeah, Obi Wan. Look, I need to talk to you."

"Where are you?"

"In The Gentlemen Only, down the street. Can you meet me here?"

"I was just taking a piss. I don't want to go in that dive."

"It's no dive and the scenery is better here than down the street."

"I don't go in that place. Bugs me to see all those girls young enough to be my daughters."

Bobby Lee laughed. "I can see if I can find you a nice wrinkled grandma."

"What's the problem?"

"Look, let's go for a ride. You want to go for a ride? I want to talk to you about something but I don't want to talk about it there."

"Why the mystery?"

"Something on this Simmons case. I got something I don't like."

Oberstar was silent for a moment, then said, "What don't you like?"

"We're not going to talk about it on the phone, Obi."

"You betcha," Oberstar said. "Then we're not going to talk about it there, either. I'll pull a squad and pick you up on the corner. I'll be there in ten minutes."

It was ten minutes exactly when Oberstar pulled up to the corner in an unmarked squad car. Bobby Lee had barely shut the door when Oberstar accelerated away into the traffic and said, "What do you got?"

"Slow down, Obi, before you hit somebody."

"I want to get over to Bertolucci's, get some sausage, before it gets too crowded."

"The kids coming home this weekend?"

"Yeah, and I gotta get a sandwich. I'm starving."

"You should of come in, ate the buffet."

"I told you, I don't like that place. That asshole Amerikahas that owns it, he's as dirty as the day is long."

"That's old news."

"It's good reason not to go in there. You think he don't like having cops in there all the time?"

"I got something along those lines."

"Whaddya mean?"

"One of the employees saw cops in there with Simmons. Simmons went in there sometimes with some Australians. We got a solid lead on that, but it bothers me about a cop with Simmons."

"How do they know it was a cop?" Oberstar said. "He in uniform, what?"

"No, plainclothes. Had the look, kept his coat, badged one of the girls but she's not there anymore. You know how they make everybody lose their jackets. Only cops keep them."

Oberstar wound through traffic, jockeying for a position at the light. "Son of a bitch," he said. "I don't like where this is taking us, Bobby Lee."

"Tell me about it. I'll have to get our financial guys to go through the records and see if any cops' names fall out."

"I got a good guy can do that, keep it quiet."

"What?"

"You think that if you send somebody to start cross-checking cops' names against Simmons's contacts and the bank that you ain't gonna come up with a bunch? First Bank holds mortgages, you got guys with checking and savings accounts, we might have a hell of a list. And then everybody will know about it, including any cop that might have his hand in the till. We use my guy, he's retired, we can have him do it on the QT, keep it quiet till we got something solid."

"For an old dog almost out to pasture, you think pretty good, Obi-Wan," Bobby Lee said. "Let's get those sausages, I can still eat."

"You can do that, you're still young and got your life ahead of you. Rot your stomach, you'll enjoy it."

116

Getting the combination to Harold Nyquist's home security system was simple. Alfie lay in the long grass behind the fence in back of Nyquist's home, with a 24-power spotting scope on a small tripod he'd purchased in a sporting goods store. He zoomed the scope in at maximum magnification on the keypad in the kitchen beside the kitchen door. There were four numbers and a symbol written on a Post-it note beside the keypad. When Nyquist came home, he drove his car into the garage, then came in through the kitchen and punched in his entry sequence before the alarm was activated. The keypad was mounted at a slight angle, just enough so that Nyquist's body didn't block Alfie's view. Like most busy people, he didn't want to think too much when he came home, so the code was simple: 1, 2, 3, 4, then hit the # sign. Just like the Post-it note said.

Dead easy, that.

Alfie watched Nyquist go about his business. His wife arrived not long after him, and he helped her unload groceries from her car into the kitchen. Since his home backed onto the long stretch of land that rose up into the bed of the highway, Nyquist rarely bothered to close the curtains or shutters at the rear of the house. He liked to look out, at the expanse of marshy land that dried out as it rose up to the highway roadbed. The hum of passing cars and the steady stream of red lights one way and white lights the other must be quite attractive from inside.

Once inside, Alfie found it to be so.

2.7

The younger of the two patrolmen stationed on the sidewalk outside Harold Nyquist's home said, "What does exsanguinate mean?"

His field training officer, a gray-haired rotund Irishman with eyes that had seen too much and didn't much care who knew, said, "Means to drain all the blood out."

"How do you know that?"

"I had to look it up for the crossword once."

"What does this guy do with it? Does he really drink it?"

"Don't know, don't much care. I'll tell you this for true, though . . . I ever get anywhere near this sick bastard I'll shoot him till he's very dead."

"The lieutenant didn't look so good when he came out."

"Go stick your head in there, see if you come out looking good."

"You don't mind?"

"This is what an FTO is for, kiddo. Go ahead, get your first sniff of stone crazy. Better you get used to it now."

Charley eavesdropped on the conversation with the ease of long practice. He stood outside smoking a cigarette to help him get the stench of rotten blood out of his nostrils. He'd shot six rolls already and probably had everything he needed except for the exterior shots of the house with its alarmed doors and windows that hadn't kept the killer out nor alarmed once through a long night of terror and pain.

Nyquist had been surprised in his bed. His wife had died there, a thin stiletto-type blade inserted into her brain through the eye socket.

The killer had spent time with Harold Nyquist. The realtor had been strapped to a chair with long lengths of duct tape. Lengthy strips of flesh had been skinned from his chest in a series of zigzagging stripes, and much of his pudgy waistline had been removed in long fatty strips and cooked while he was still alive, or so the medical examiner thought. They wouldn't know for sure until after the autopsy.

The ME had found fresh needle tracks on the inside of Nyquist's arm. He might have been shot up with drugs during the torture, since there was nothing in the house to indicate he had a drug habit.

It hurt Charley's head to try to make sense of it. He drew furiously on his cigarette, as though he could suck the poison out of the pictures in his mind and exhale them like smoke, watch them crumble into ashes that he could grind underfoot like the glowing butt of his cigarette.

Nyquist had been tortured before he died, unlike Madison Simmons. More than likely he'd died when his skull was crushed in the same way Simmons's was, but the needle marks might have been a cause of death and the club merely gratuitous violence after the fact.

But Charley didn't think so.

Nothing this guy did was gratuitous. What Kativa had told him made him see the scene with new eyes. There was purpose to this, purpose hidden under the guise of madness . . . but maybe it was just their response to all this that made it seem like madness. To the killer it all made perfect sense. Only in the orderly scheme of daylight and the crisp air of a Midwestern early fall morning did the inside of Nyquist's house scream of madness in the language of the crime scene.

The picture on the wall was the same. This one took up almost the entire panel wall in Nyquist's study, where the torture and ultimate killing took place. The killer had taken time to cook himself his favorite treat and then return. The remains of his meal were on a fine china plate set neatly out of the blood flow in a corner of the room.

Nyquist's state-of-the-art computer, set in a corner hutch in his study, had its drive completely overwritten, then initialized, wiping out any data that had been on the drive. The forensics people had boxed up the machine after Charley took his photos, but Charley thought they were optimistic: anyone who knew enough to overwrite a disk before initializing it wasn't going to be dull enough to leave them any sectors to work with. They couldn't find any backup disks to go with the Zip drive in the machine, leaving them to speculate that the killer had taken them with him.

The coroner figured that Nyquist had finally died around 4:00 A.M. No one had come to the house till late morning, when Nyquist's secretary came by to see why no one was answering the phone or her repeated pages. What she saw through the window on the side of the house sent her reeling away to vomit in the bushes and fumble out her cell phone to call for the police and an ambulance. A hasty entry by the responding officers ensured that there was no one left alive, and so they buttoned up the scene and waited for the detectives.

Bobby Lee and Lieutenant Oberstar came out of the home together, Oberstar talking fast and furious in a low tone, "We got to get something for the press, Bobby, the mayor's office, they want a bone and we've got to give it to them."

"We don't have anything to toss them," Bobby Lee said. "I got the Bureau flying in a profiler from Quantico on a special priority for us. Maybe they can come up with something."

Bobby Lee looked tired, Charley thought, and he didn't like to see that look on his friend.

"Want a smoke, Bobby?" Charley said. He nodded to Oberstar. "Lieutenant."

Oberstar pushed the air with his hand to keep distance between him and Charley. Bobby Lee took the cigarette Charley lit for him and sucked greedily on it.

"So," Charley said.

"No shit," Bobby Lee said.

"So what?" Oberstar said, confused.

"It's an old thing," Bobby Lee said. "You gonna stay out here, Obi?"

"I've had enough crazy shit for the day, and I've still got to go back and deal with more," Oberstar said in a voice rich with disgust and barely contained frustration. "You see those news crews over there?" he said, pointing at the television vans with their camera booms directed at the Nyquist home. "They're going to want to know everything about what we're doing, which is fuck all, and a Public Affairs Officer is going to be climbing up their asses kissing all the way and the only PAO around here is one I used to sleep with and she's still pissed at me for not calling her," Oberstar sputtered.

Charley slowly turned to look at Bobby Lee who gawked in open-mouthed surprise at Oberstar.

"You mean you've actually had some, Obi?" Bobby Lee said.

Oberstar, beet red, burst into belated laughter. Charley and Bobby Lee joined him in loud belly laughter, surprising the patrol officers who stood nearby.

"I think the loot has gone nuts," said the old Irishman FTO. His younger partner, his face pale after peeking in at the crime scene, shook his head in disagreement.

"I think they're all nuts," he said. "That in there is enough to drive anybody nuts."

At a table in the back of the Uptown Bar, Alfie held court with a group of Susan's young friends.

"But why the Army, Alfie?" said one of the boys, his nose pierced in three places and a single silver bomb weight protruding from his chin. "Didn't you hate people telling you what to do twenty-four/ seven?"

"Where do you go where someone isn't telling you what to do?" Alfie said. "Until you can do that, nothing much you can do about it, so you pick your fights. That's all well and good when you've got a place to go. Remember, I didn't have a thing, no family left to me. I had to have somewhere to go and it taught me to work through me fears. Jumping out of an airplane, that teaches you a lot about facing fears. The fear of falling is the greatest ingrained fear in us. Little tots, they're naturally afraid of heights, it's down deep in the brain. So if you can overcome that fear, that loosens up all the other fears you carry around with you.

"They have you practice leaping off a tower, but that doesn't come close to what it's like to be standing in the open door of an airplane at fifteen hundred feet, looking down and realizing that all that stands between you and the ground is a bit of air beneath a nylon panel. And then to make yourself go . . . mate, I'll tell you it's terribly frightening, but it's bloody amazing at the same time."

"I want to do it," Susan announced. "I want to jump out of a plane."

"Me too," several of the others said. "There's a parachute club out in Eden Prairie, we could go there. How about it, Alfie?"

"That's the brew talking now," Alfie said, pointing at the almost empty pitcher of beer. "We'll see if you still think it's a good idea after the beer's worn off. In the meantime, who's up for another cold one?"

Alfie waved for the waitress to bring them another pitcher of beer. He pushed himself back from the table and kicked his long legs out in front of him, crossed his booted feet at the ankles, lowered his eyelids in a sleepy squint, and watched Susan and her friends talking eagerly among themselves. The silent observer that catalogued everything in his head took it all in, and he felt a pang at the genuine friendship and interest from this group of youngsters. Even though they were all in their twenties, they felt so much younger than him. At thirty-six he was ten years older than any of them. Their lives in the arts, acting, painting, writing, and in the service industries of coffee shops and restaurants that supported them until they made their "big break" seemed like life from another planet to Alfie. When he was twenty-six he'd been a senior sergeant in the Australian Special Air Services, working alongside American Special Forces in the jungles of Indonesia and the Philippines, mounting covert actions against the fundamentalist Muslims funded by Iran, intent on destabilizing the fragile governments there.

He was surprised by how much he enjoyed talking with Susan and her friends about things like fear and metaphysics, things he thought a lot about to himself, and he grinned and then laughed out loud at the difference between his work here and his life at home.

"What are you laughing at?" Susan asked.

"A little of this and a little of that," Alfie said. "Just enjoying the company."

Susan looked at the plate in front of him with a barely picked over omelet. "You didn't eat much."

"Ah," Alfie said. "I had a big meal last night."

"When you were out in the middle of the night?"

"It's a bit of insomnia. I don't sleep well."

She laughed and her girlfriends giggled. "I know. I guess I'm not doing a good enough job of wearing you out."

MARCUS WYNNE

Alfie laughed. "That's not it at all, mate." He winked at the men. "Right, lads?"

He rose to general laughter and went through the thin crowd toward the back rest rooms. He heard one of the girls say to her boyfriend, "Alfie's so cool."

So cool. He laughed again while he urinated, staring at his face in the mirror above the urinal. His face was genial when relaxed, the broad face and the deep lines softened by lack of tension. He looked over his shoulder to make sure he was alone, then stared in the mirror for a moment and let the chant of the ritual that played softly in the back of his mind all the time rise up in volume—just for a moment. He watched the darkness rise in his eyes, and the grubby bathroom seemed to go soft in focus as though it might disappear if he let it go on, and then he brought himself back, pleased with how he responded. He walked between two worlds and he enjoyed reminding himself of that. What he saw in the mirror satisfied him.

He came out of the rest room wearing his genial smile for anyone who cared to notice, and stopped at the jukebox to see what sort of music he might get with his pocket full of change. He looked up as the front door to the bar opened and let a sudden flare of midday light into the dark room. Framed in the lighted doorway was a woman. He stared at her, his eyes squinting against the brightness. All he could see was an outline, a figure of a woman rich in the breasts and hips, her hair pulled back in a knot at the back of her head.

Something about her drew him.

He dumped his change back in his pocket, and slowly made his way toward her as she entered, blinking in the darkness as her eyes began to adjust and she sat at a vacant spot at the bar. Alfie stood beside a support pillar and watched her sit. She was beautiful, with olive skin. She brushed a few stray hairs that had worked loose of her braid away from her face. She set a satchel on the stool beside her. The satchel tipped, spilling several large books and one small one. From where he stood, Alfie saw several art books.

The smallest book was titled *Rock Art of the Laura Area*.

He froze for a moment, unaccustomed fear rising in him. He felt a sudden chill come up his spine and his skin pimpled as though cold. Australian rock art of the Laura area? Who was this woman? He watched her load the books back into her satchel. She hadn't seen him. This felt like trickster energy, he thought. The hands of the ancestors were all in this and he felt himself slipping into the dreamy unfocused state that presaged his own communion with the voices that came to him sometimes.

Stay clear of her, the voice urged. *She walks with the Timara.*

Alfie stalked to the table where Susan and her friends sat, and picked up his leather jacket.

"Gotta go, mate," he said, pitching his voice low.

"Where are you going?" Susan said.

"I've got to get to the cyber café, check me mail from home," he said. "Later, all," he said to the table.

A chorus of voices bid him good-bye, and he was careful to keep his back to the bar as he hurried out the side door, glancing once over his shoulder at the woman at the bar who sat with her back to him.

We'll see her again, the voice within promised.

He straddled his motorcycle, taking his time fitting his helmet in place over his mane of hair drawn back in a ponytail. He marveled for a moment at how the ancestors moved things even in the light of day. Who'd have thought he'd run into a woman reading about the Laura rock art? There'd been no pictures in the papers of the images he'd so painstakingly drawn as part of the ritual. The ancestors moved in strange ways and he wondered what it meant. Connections and connecting, that was the lesson of the elders: we're all more connected than we know how, tiny points of light connected with bright strands to make the mosaic that was the world of the Dreamtime. He turned his ignition key and gunned his motorcycle into life, then pulled into the traffic and sped toward the intersection of Lyndale and Lake, where his favorite Internet café was located. He parked his bike and went inside, waving a greeting at the girl sitting at the front counter.

"Got a machine for me, mate?" he said.

The girl brushed back her hair and smiled. "I'll start the clock for you," she said, pointing at an Apple I-Mac.

MARCUS WYNNE

Alfie sat down and logged on, then sent the browser to Hotmail and entered his account name: NullaNulla@hotmail.com. There were two messages: one a maintenance message from Hotmail and the other a Highest Priority message from Surferdude.

Alfie clicked on the tab and opened up the message.

"There's been some fallout over the last two deals," the message began. "Someone whose job it is to look into these things is closer than we'd like. The person responsible for looking out for that is getting cold feet. You'll get some more information shortly, but be prepared to meet and deal with both of those parties. I'd bring you back now, but this may need your special attention. When I have more, I'll let you know. Then we can sweep up and you can come home. The surf is good and the beer is cold."

Alfie drummed his fingers and stared at the screen. The circumlocution in the language rendered the message innocuous to anyone else, but he got the message clearly: someone was close to uncovering his connection to the killings. A cop? Not too likely. The ritual demanded a certain precision, but the same precision lent itself to confusing contradictions in any analysis of the crime scene. He'd studied with professional interest the work of the behavioral profilers at the FBI and made it a point to be familiar with their techniques. They'd be looking for connection between the victims, victimology, and yes there was connection but not necessarily in the sense they were looking for. Alfie had no overt connection to the business deals that contributed to their tasty demise.

And even if they pieced together the bad bit of work those two naughty boys had cooked up to rip Alfie's boss off for a significant portion of the take from his real estate investments, including that classy little strip club, there was no way to tie it to an Australian wanderer just passing through. Tying it to him would be a long stretch, but Alfie hadn't lived as long as he had by being careless.

He'd have to look into this, read the papers a little more closely. He generally didn't stick around long enough to follow the aftermath of his operations, but his boss wanted to be sure that the other players got the message clearly: stealing from his boss wasn't allowed. Surferdude pointed him, he went, and it wasn't so much for the money anymore as it was for the increasing sense of power he felt gathering in him each time he took down a target and ingested something of their life force.

His boss would be working his extensive connections, including the one he had in the police department here, to make sure that Alfie's back trail would be covered. If there was a problem, he'd sweep it up himself to be sure.

But one thing nagged at him: the strange synchronicity of the woman in the bar and the sense that something else was moving in the Dreamtime with him. He needed to spend some time alone and work on his ritual, tap into the special seeing that came with his private ritual to see what was happening in the Dream around him. He'd need someplace private; he didn't want Susan to stumble across him. A hotel might be in order, a nice clean hotel room with a DO NOT DISTURB sign would suit him just fine. He wondered what the woman he'd seen in the bar would think if she saw him doing the ritual. He'd seen her for a reason and the spirit ancestors were great tricksters . . . who knew what part she was going to play?

He tapped out a short response to the E-mail, his stubby fingers slow on the small keyboard: "Will sweep up once you let me know where to clean. Then home on the next plane. Ta, Alfie."

He sent the message, logged off, and went to the counter to pay his two dollars.

"Here you go, mate," he said to the girl at the counter.

He went back outside and got back on his bike. He'd hate to abandon it when he left, but it didn't fit in with his life at home; besides, he could always buy another one if he wanted to. He grinned at the thought of trying to ride a crotch rocket on the rutted dirt roads where he lived as an Aborigine in Laura. No room for a motorbike in his cave there.

He cranked up his bike and took off for a ride around Lake Calhoun. Jowalbinna and the shaman cave were his other life; this was a dreaming for him, and he wanted to take the time to enjoy it.

MARCUS WYNNE

Deep in a closed-off conference room in Police Headquarters, Bobby Lee stood in silence before a white board covered with notes detailing what they knew about the killer. A KEEP OUT sign on the door didn't slow the steady traffic of detectives coming in and out to report to him, but Bobby Lee kept himself focused with long practiced concentration. The only person that would take him out of his self-imposed trance would be Oberstar, and he knew to leave him alone; Obi knew that you got nothing worthwhile from pushing a man who was already working as hard as he could. Bobby Lee had learned that it was best for him to let things sit and collect until there was a certain critical tipping point in his unconscious mind, a time and place where everything suddenly jelled and became clear to him. Oberstar had been the one to teach him to listen for the one small true voice in the cacophony of competing voices that came up in the course of an investigation, the true inner voice that did all the real work in the back of his mind and then pushed forward exactly the right solution when it was time—and no sooner.

But then Oberstar stuck his head in the conference room, looked Bobby over, and said, "You need anything? Coffee, doughnuts, blow job?"

"You got cannibal boy's home address and photo lying around?"

"I'd have a bullet into that son of a bitch already if that was the case."

"Plenty of people to help you do that."

"How's Max and Nicky doing with you gone so much?"

"Max is Max, you know. Nicky, he's just fascinated, wants to know all about what this guy does...typical eight-year-old. Keeps asking Charley for some photos, Charley got him started on taking pictures."

"This Charley, he's okay? I only talked to him a couple of times."

"Charley is as good as it gets, Obi. Me and him got history."

"All that Airborne shit during the Gulf."

"He was solid then and he's solid now."

"He do that photography stuff after?"

"More than that, Obi-Wan. He did some kind of hush-hush supersecret squirrel stuff for the CIA for a couple of years after the war."

"CIA? No shit?"

"He don't talk about it, but he got fed up with them after a couple of years, pulled the plug."

"He wasn't in long enough to get any retirement, then."

"No retirement for Charley Payne," Bobby Lee said. "That boy is a natural-born gypsy. He's happy living in his little apartment down there in Linden Hills and taking photographs...he's pretty damn good, won some prizes, sells a lot to magazines, mostly nature stuff. He does great candid portraits, we've got a bunch of them at the house. He took the best picture of Max and Nick I've ever seen. Damn sight better than what they do at the mall."

"He's pretty sharp, though?"

"He came up with the info about the pictures this freak draws on the walls."

"What about the Bureau's guy? Any use of him?"

"Some. They agree the guy is highly organized, he's older and been doing this for a long time. They're just as puzzled about the victim selection as we are, 'cause these aren't your usual serial killer vics. It's that connection that will give us something. With what Charley added to the mix, they think the guy is highly intelligent, might be a native Australian, has technical training to bypass alarms which makes him smart with experience, military, police, or private security. We've got a decent profile going, but no significant trace evidence other than the paints. If we could get a hair or something we might be able to pin his race down. He's strong and knows how to open a body and skilled with killing with that damn club; he hits home runs like a champ with that thing."

"Why kill them with a club when he's got the knife and he's going to cut them up anyway?"

"Who knows what evil lurks in the hearts of men? Not me, Obi-Wan. Now get out of here so I can work."

Oberstar gave Bobby Lee a long, thoughtful look, then shrugged and said over his shoulder as he left the room, "Talk to me later, Bobby Lee. I want to hear something good."

Didn't they all, Bobby Lee thought.

2.10

Charley sat in his apartment and drummed his fingers again and again on the worn arm of his recliner. After a while, he went to the old wooden tool stand he'd turned into a rack of flat shelves for his prints that weren't hung up on the wall. His precious negatives were enclosed in plastic sleeves and stored in binders that took up shelf after shelf in the corner of the room. The flat drawers held prints that he hadn't yet mounted, or old ones he took down to rotate up when he had new favorites.

He found an old self-portrait he'd done not long after he quit his contract with the CIA and just before the call that brought him out to Minnesota. He'd set his camera on a tripod, then sat before it with a dark curtain behind him. He'd worn a dark turtleneck that made him seem a dim, dark outline against the dark backdrop, his pale face painfully prominent, leaping from the background. He'd scanned the resulting photo on a friend's computer, then split the image down the middle, then cloned each side to make two distinct images that he then printed side by side.

It was an eerie photograph. The bilateral asymmetry that had grown in his face over the years yielded two completely different faces side by side. It was like Dr. Jekyll and Mr. Hyde, but real. He'd seen similar images and learned the technique from another photographer who was fond of New Age enthusiasms and explained it as the predominance of the two different hemispheres of the brain, each of which controlled the opposite half of the body. The image cloned from the left side of his face had a drooping set of eyelids, a pronounced downward turn of the mouth, a squint in the eye; the image cloned from the right showed a thin line to the lips, eyes slightly narrowed but somehow softer than the other image.

We all carry our doubles around with us, Charley thought. He held the picture in his hand, then sat back down with it, looked up at the image of Anurra, then back at the image in his hand, the image of his two-faced self. Anurra would be a two-faced man as well. He would be smart, and keep that dark side hidden away. The only people likely to see it would be those who saw it last among the things they saw before they died. So where would he be? What would the other images of his self show? And where would he stay?

He's still here, Charley thought, even though the smart thing to do would be to get away. He's not through yet.

Charley got up and put his self-portrait down. He was restless, with that vague nagging feeling he often got while his brain puzzled over some problem that needed solving. He went to the plastic storage tub he kept beneath his bed and took out his Gatco knife-sharpening kit. Unclipping the Emerson CQC-7 from his pants pocket, he tested the already razor-sharp edge with his thumb, then set up the fine edge diamond hone and touched up the knife till it had the requisite "snag-ability" that marked the perfect edge. Then he put the knife-sharpening kit away and took out his gun-cleaning kit, broke down his Glock and wiped and oiled the spotless weapon, then inspected each individual round before reloading them back into fresh magazines he rotated from a stock in the plastic storage tub.

He caught himself thinking dark thoughts and laughed. Old rituals are the best rituals. The old pleasing routine of making sure his weapons were in a high state of readiness, that everything was prepared—that was a useful mechanism he carried over into his life as a photographer. He looked at the Domke bag that held his cameras. It was interesting to him that he chose to work with one set of life tools to relax even though he was actually working with the other set.

He thought about the self-portrait and laughed. What are you getting ready for? He guessed that he'd know when it got to be time. Or maybe only after the fact.

But he'd be ready for whatever happened.

He wondered how Bobby Lee was doing with all this. They hadn't talked about it much when he'd dropped by the house to visit, preferring instead to keep their talk light and to play with Nicky. He loved Bobby Lee and knew his mind, but the world of police puzzled him. He recognized and respected their clannishness, the sticking together in the face of the opposition that their mere presence often fostered in the world. But he found too often that the police investigators he met had too narrow a world view, one that limited their effectiveness in seeing all the complexities the world could bring to a bad guy problem. That was one thing he was grateful to his CIA experience for: it left him no illusions about the pettiness of humans, about evil with a capital E as well as the banality of evil with a small e.

Charley had no illusions about his true nature; he was at home and comfortable with his restless self. Or so he told himself as he looked around his barren apartment. He lived as he chose and he was happy with his friends and his women. Woman. He laughed out loud in the empty apartment at that slip of his tongue and thought about his lunch with Kativa Patel. What a delightful woman she was. That was the difference between her and Mara. Mara, for all her individual delights, was a girl, a woman-girl, but Kativa was a woman. Much woman. He looked forward to seeing her again. He stroked the edge of his self-portrait and wondered what she would make of that. He wondered if she was comfortable with duality.

It was the beginning of summer in Australia and the seaside city of Cairns, gateway to the Great Barrier Reef, was bustling with foreign tourists and vacationing Australians, sunburned and loud in flip-flop sandals and open cotton shirts over brown beer bellies. Jay Burrell studied the water from his deck with the experienced eye of a long-time surfer and thought about getting out into the water again later today. He'd already been out once, early in the morning, as he had every morning since the DEA had chased him out of California and the focus of his narcotics empire shifted from Mexico and Colombia to Thailand, Burma, and the Golden Triangle. Heroin was making a comeback and business was good.

Despite the Australian government's rigid and harsh laws on narcotics trafficking, Jay found it easy to blend into a low-profile cover as an expatriate American surfing enthusiast. He didn't live large in Cairns; his bungalow-style house looked modest from the outside and belied the roomy interior that looked out over the ocean; it was a good distance away from the pricier real estate closer to town and the resort beaches. It had cost more than it looked and its security measures were as discreet as money could buy. He did have a good boat, a cigarette runner, that raised the Marine Police eyebrows, but that was more a case of serious boat envy than anything else.

Jay Burrell had no criminal record of any kind with the Australian police, or for that matter with the DEA or any American agency he knew of. Jay Burrell had actually died shortly after birth and the birth certificate had never been cross-referenced with the death certificate as it should have been. The man who had been someone else before he was Jay Burrell had paid a good price for that. He believed in paying for the best when it came to business and he kept his people loyal with large infusions of cash.

And for those who couldn't be loyal, or fell prey to the temptations that came with dealing with the large amounts of cash in his business, he had his mate Alfie. Jay leaned back in his deck chair and kicked his salt-encrusted feet up on the deck railing. He sipped his strong black Sumatran coffee and thought about the phone call he was expecting from Minneapolis today. Minneapolis. He loathed that town, having only been there during the winter, when the biting cold had left him a shivering wreck even under two layers of clothing and the best down jacket North Face made.

Inside, the phone rang.

Jay looked at his battered stainless-steel Rolex Submariner and noted with satisfaction that the caller was right on time. He walked slowly inside to the telephone he reserved for business calls and answered it.

"Hello?"

"This isn't the way to do things."

The drawn-out ooo of the northern Minnesota accent made Jay smile; it reminded him of that movie, the funny one with the pregnant woman cop in it.

"How are things there?" Jay said.

"Not good."

"Some people needed an example."

"You could have made it a private example. That wouldn't have raised all this heat."

"That's not your decision, now is it?"

"The cop that's working on this is good. He's getting the Australian connection."

"How would he get that?"

"We're not dumb asses out here, you know."

"I wasn't thinking that," said Jay, who had been thinking that exact thought. "Can you manage things?"

"What do you mean manage?"

"Keep us informed, expedite things if necessary . . ."

"Yes. Is this through?"

"For the most part," Jay said. "I need the confirmation on the final closing of the real estate . . . that's not a problem for you, is it? Getting those records?"

"With enough money there's no such thing as a problem. But we don't need any more of the other. That just raises the heat and brings people looking where they shouldn't be looking. We don't need that at all."

"I'll take that under consideration and get back to you. Anything else?"

"I think I should meet who you've got out here working that end of the business."

Jay thought for a moment, then said, "That's not possible. My associate prefers to work alone."

"Your associate is raising a profile that isn't going to go away."

"He'll never be in Minneapolis again."

"I don't think . . ."

"How are *your* needs?" Jay interrupted smoothly. "Are they all being met? Everything work out, money show up in your account as we agreed?"

"Yes, but . . ."

"That's all we have to talk about, then," Jay said. "Let's talk again, day after tomorrow, same time."

"I . . . all right, but . . ."

"Thank you. Check your account this time tomorrow for another installment."

Jay hung up the phone and stared at it for a long moment, his fingers resting on the handset. He tapped the phone lightly, then went to his desk and sat down in front of an expensive Apple Macintosh computer with a large flat panel display. He powered up the machine, then clicked on the America Online icon and opened his e-mail account. He thought for a moment, then tapped out a short message for NullaNulla@hotmail.com. It only took a few minutes for him to outline what he wanted done, and where Alfie would find the information he needed to finish up. He sent the message, shut down the machine, and looked critically at the surf. So much for today's business. Let Alfie deal with it. He was going surfing.

2.12

Bobby Lee sat in his front room at home, reclined in his easy chair and surrounded by neat stacks of investigator reports. One of them he looked at, put down, and then picked up again to reread it for the third time. It was from the cybercops in the Computer and Financial Crime Unit, who'd been busily working on the files from Madison Simmons's and Harold Nyquist's home and office computers.

Simmons and Nyquist were way dirty.

Simmons had been cautiously maneuvering large sums of money wired from various Southeast Asian banks—Singapore, Malaysia, Australia—and running it through a series of real estate transactions, effectively laundering them. He'd been skimming off some of the margin between currency exchange rates as well as a percentage off each transaction.

Nyquist was the real estate man, and he'd been getting his share of the skim as well. He'd created a series of front companies that were headquartered in Aruba, Venezuela, and the Isle of Man, and used the fronts to buy interest in various going concerns in Minneapolis: bars and restaurants, body shops, and one strip club—The Gentlemen Only. All the businesses had one thing in common: there was lots of cash going in and out of them, which provided plenty of opportunity for creative bookkeeping to launder money.

This was the tip of an iceberg called big-time narcotics.

There wasn't any overt connection, at least not yet, to any of the major narcotics operations in the Twin Cities, but it looked like and smelled like high-level narcotics. That was the only illicit activity that generated that kind of cash flow. Bobby Lee penciled a note on a Post-it and stuck it on the page, a reminder to touch base again with DEA and see if they had anything somewhere on Simmons or Nyquist. Those two weren't low-level mopes and they had no criminal history to speak of, which made them perfect for this kind of laundering operation.

But what about the Australia connection? Could the money be originating there? Why take the risk of laundering it in the States? He didn't know enough about how that worked to say. And he was leery of talking to anyone else about it just yet. He had to build a murder case, not a money-laundering case.

So what did he have?

Two murder victims linked by computer evidence to possible money laundering with the funds originating somewhere offshore, possibly Australia, definitely Southeast Asia. That meant it was probably heroin proceeds, not cocaine. Both vics killed in a fashion that on the surface looked like the work of a lunatic, but professionally executed with entry past sophisticated alarm systems and without leaving any trace evidence to speak of. The posed crime scenes turn out to be linked to some kind of Australian ritual magic, and the best they could do with the evidence they had was that the killer might be Australian or a student of Australian Aboriginal art, was very strong and handy with a knife and a club. Other than the staged scene and the painting on the wall, the killer had left no significant trace: fingerprints wiped clean, no hairs, no fibers. This was a pro hitter, a real pro. Maybe this whole ritual killing thing was meant to throw off the investigators, get them to think it was a nut job at work.

Now that he'd looked at it, he had more than he thought. But now that he had a better handle on the doer, how did he find him? He jotted down notes on Post-its. Use the press? That was too risky, especially when casting a wide net, and they always wanted too much. Forget about that. This Australian connection and what he'd learned at the strip club, those were good leads, good basic police work. He'd have to go back and work that a bit more, chase down that little stripper who'd talked to the Australian. Max would just love that idea, for sure.

MARCUS WYNNE

He looked up the stairwell at the thought of his wife, who'd gone to bed early, pleading a headache. He'd put his son to bed himself. Nicky was fighting a cold and had a headache, too. Bobby Lee put his paperwork down and went upstairs and peeked into the room where Nicky lay sprawled in the boneless sleep of a child, completely abandoned to the movements of his dreams. Bobby Lee crept silently into the room, then tucked the covers round his boy and just lightly touched the hair on his head, then went out silently and closed the door carefully behind him.

In their bedroom, Maxine was curled across the bed like an elongated question mark, hugging his pillow to her chest, her long black hair spread like dark water across her pillow and the sheet. He stood over her for a while, and watched his wife sleep. Then he went back downstairs to his paperwork and the trouble there that kept him awake while his family slept safe.

143

2.13

Kativa tossed and turned in her dreams. Images from her past, pictures from the Laura rock art, strange meetings with men she almost recognized, and laughter blended with a weird cacophony of shrill voices, singsong chants, and the unmistakable drone of a didgeridoo. Then with a strange lucidity she felt herself fall into a familiar dream, one she hadn't had in many years:

. . . She was running, driven by a strange sound to run through thorny brush, branches raking long cuts on her naked skin, vulnerable in her nakedness she felt as though there was a great eye watching her, red and rimmed with yellow, watching her with amusement as it drove her to and fro . . . she felt a presence behind her, steadily gaining distance and she ran even harder, crying out for help though no one was there . . .

. . . but there was someone else now, someone, a man, running toward her from the front, not away from the sound but toward it, the dreadful wonk wonk wonk pushing her into the deepest part of the brush as though she might hide, trembling like a kangaroo pursued by a dingo pack . . . she looked at the man, tall and thin and naked and black, black as the space between rocks in the dark of the night, and he was someone . . .

She came awake then, her T-shirt and boxers drenched in sweat, balled and knotted like her sheets were. She lay there blinking rapidly as the images faded, then she rolled out of bed and went into her bathroom, where she splashed cold water on her face and looked at the haggard, lined face gazing back at her out of the mirror. She looked at the clock and it was after five in the morning. Going back to sleep was no option, so she showered and made herself eat breakfast and down the better part of a big pot of coffee. But even that didn't help, and she found herself grouchy and owly for most of the morning at the museum.

She spent the morning cataloguing a series of Japanese ink prints the museum had recently acquired. One of them was quite striking, an ink brush painting of a blade-thin samurai with a wild, white face dominated by two glaring black eyes, his sword held ready to chop over his head. For some reason it reminded her of Charley Payne. He always seemed ready for something to happen, some sort of violence that he was prepared for, and the feeling he left her with was an intriguing blend of apprehension and absolute safety. She put her mind back to the work at hand. Charley Payne was off-limits. She didn't poach from her friends. But it was almost time for lunch, and she'd been meaning to call Mara sometime, so she went to her office and called her.

"Mara?" she said. "Would you like to come by the museum and have lunch?"

"Hi Kat," Mara said. "I'd love to. I'm on my way out . . . is now too soon?"

"No, it would be perfect. Meet you in the Café? I'll get a table, it gets crowded in there at lunch."

"Perfect. Give me twenty minutes."

Kativa straightened her office, then went upstairs to the Museum Café and got the same table she'd had when she met Charley for lunch. She wondered if her choice was deliberate or just another one of the freakish coincidences she'd noticed lately. She decided that her dreams had left her tired, and ordered a coffee black from the waitress and sipped it thoughtfully while she looked out the big pane of glass at the garden and the city.

She saw Mara before Mara saw her and felt a little pang; Mara looked drawn under her normal serenity. Kativa waved her to the table, and Mara gratefully dropped her big coat and scarf into an empty chair and slid across from Kativa.

"Is that coffee?" Mara said. "I would really like some."

Kativa waved the waitress over and ordered another cup; the waitress set two menus down on the table and went away.

"So how are you?" Kativa said.

"I'm preoccupied with difficult men," Mara said. "Which is the whole species as far as I'm concerned."

"Charley?"

Mara took her cup of coffee from the waitress and went through a slow and deliberate dressing of the cup with Equal and two creamers before she said, "You're attracted to him, aren't you?"

Kativa was nonplussed for a moment, then laughed and said, "Yes. Who wouldn't be? I just envy you. It's so hard to meet good men and the good ones all seem to be taken."

"Charley's not taken," Mara said. She sipped her coffee slowly and studied Kativa over the rim. "Charley Payne couldn't be taken by anyone, he loves his freedom more than anything else. He's like a big alley cat: he's so used to rambling around that any sense of stability is a threat to him. He can get any woman he wants. It's the sticking around that gets to him."

"Why do you say that? Did the two of you fight?"

"Not really. I just know him. I'm a Pisces, I know things about people and I know about him. A big part of being with Charley is knowing I can't hold him, so I have to work on letting him go. The harder I want to cling to him, the more it drives him away."

"What's his sign?"

"He's total Scorpio."

"That's a dark and twisty one."

"He's dark and twisty," Mara said. "Is that why you want to go out with him?"

Kativa forced a laugh. "I'm not poaching, Mara."

"I'm taking a time out with Charley, Kat," Mara said, setting her coffee cup down on the table and leaning forward on her forearms. "I've been trying to work on nonattachment in my life and Charley is the perfect karmic problem for me to work through. I've never felt more attached to someone at the spiritual level, but he's just a visitor in my life. I suspect sometimes that he's just a visitor in his own life, no matter how hard he clings to it...I always have this sense that Minneapolis is just some kind of hiatus for him, a stopping-off place in some dark and twisted journey he's on."

"You make him sound bad."

"He's not bad. I know that. But he's dark and he's got a history he doesn't share with anyone. He's always got those knives on him, have you seen those? And he keeps loaded guns in his apartment. It seems so strange. He has these beautiful photographs on the wall—he's fabulous on the street as a photographer, he has an incredible eye—then he keeps these loaded guns right next to his bed. It's all very strange."

Mara picked up her coffee and blew on it. "You met him for lunch, didn't you?"

"Yes, I hope that was okay."

"Of course it is. Like I said, I have to work on my issues around attachment. This is a good opportunity. I wouldn't be surprised if he calls you again; he likes you a lot, I could tell that when we were together. There's some old strong karmic energy between the two of you, I could sense it."

"Do you believe that?"

"Yes."

"I wonder what that's about," Kativa said.

"He'll probably tell you when it's time," Mara said. "He believes there's a perfect moment for every action, we just have to see it when it's there and act only when it's appropriate and the right time."

"Like Cartier-Bresson said. No wonder he likes him so much." Kativa paused, then said, "And what about you, Mara?"

Mara picked up her menu and lowered her face. "So much that's good," she said. "Shall we order?"

2.14

William "Skunk" White, also known as Willy White, was a coal-black, blade-thin, skull cap and baggy jeans-clad gangster who ran an enterprising crew of crack dealers on the North Side. He was also one of the smartest gangsters on the street and Bobby Lee's prize street snitch. Bobby Lee liked to conduct his interviews under the guise of stopping and harassing Willy for matters connected to his dope dealing. He sat in the front seat of his unmarked squad car with Willy twisting uncomfortably in the front passenger seat and said, "So run it through for me one more time. Once more, with vigor."

"They's cops getting free pussy from dancers at the club," Willy said, tugging at his skull cap. "Some of them getting something else from somebody else, I don't know what and I don't know what from. That's what I knows."

"What kind of cop, Willy? Plainclothes, uniforms, patrol, crack team, narco, ERU . . . what kind of cop? You make a fine distinction among the police in everything else you do, make a distinction here for me."

"I don't know no distinction."

"What flavor cop, Willy?"

"I hear they's plainclothes, supervisors. Maybe narcs, maybe SIU, I don't know. I know some of them girls complain, couple of those guys treat them like shit. One of them is some old fucker."

"Some old fucker? What do you mean, old as in old? How old is old?"

"I don't know how old is old. You're old, you figure it out."

"Good one, Willy," Bobby Lee said. "What does the management get by giving pussy away? There something going on there?"

Willy twisted and turned away from Bobby Lee, his body language eloquent in its denial.

"Oh, we got something here, don't we, Willy?" Bobby Lee said. "You got a taste for something going on there."

"I could get killed 'cause of this. I could get got for talking to you and somebody find out."

"You could get killed for your stash, Willy. You know how to play the game. What's going on there?"

"It's the green," Willy blurted out. He looked around in the car at the streets outside. "Money. They laundering money in the club. I don't know whose money, but it's big numbers, some of them girls know."

"You got the names of the girls that know?"

"One of them, she lives down Lyndale, her dance name is Typhaney. I don't know her real name, she's a sister."

"Black female dances at the club now under the name of Typhaney?"

"That's right."

"Later, Willy," Bobby Lee said. "You got yourself a big pass— don't waste it on the small stuff."

"Later, Officer Martaine."

Willy slid out of the car and did his step and slide back to the corner where his crew waited to tap his fist and slap his hand and congratulate him on getting one over on the five-o.

Bobby Lee watched him go and for a moment longed for the simplicity of street work. That was a world, even with its strange nuances and dangerous complications, that seemed brutally simple and easy to him right now. He didn't want to put his mind around the possibility that there were brother officers involved in this—and the whole thing was shaping up to be much, much more than a homicide investigation.

He pulled away from the curb and drove back downtown and caught Fourth Street over to The Gentlemen Only. He parked in the

NO PARKING zone and jogged up the stairs and was met just inside by the looming presence of Dave Nyser.

"Detective Martaine," Nyser said. "How can I help you today, sir?"

"Josie and Typhaney," Bobby Lee said. "They work together, same shift?"

Nyser thought for a moment, then said, "Yes."

"Typhaney still work here?"

"Yes."

"I need to talk to her."

"She's working now. If you'd like to come in and take a seat, I can have her come to your table . . . there won't be anyone else around."

"That'll do for a start."

Bobby Lee followed the big man into the dark, cool interior of the club. It seemed warmer close to the T-shaped runway the girls danced on, and most of the occupied tables were within easy distance of the lunch buffet hot tables. Bobby Lee took a corner table far away from everyone else. Nyser returned a few minutes later with a tall lavishly endowed black woman in her early twenties. Her body was sleek and sculpted, and her breasts jutted straight out, defying gravity, and her sleek buttocks molded into legs almost too heavily muscled for a dancer. She reminded him of a professional ice skater he'd dated once upon a time, who had the same build, much stronger and thicker in the legs than most dancers.

"You want a dance?" she said. She leaned down and whispered in Bobby Lee's ear. "If you want to talk to me about anything, you'll have to have the dance."

"I don't want the dance. I want you to sit down here and tell me something."

"It don't look right," Typhaney complained.

"Let me worry about that."

"That's what you cops always say, let me worry about it. It's me that catches the heat, not you."

"Tell me about the other cops."

The girl visibly stiffened, looked resentfully up at the looming figure of Nyser, then back at Bobby Lee. "What other cops?"

At some other time, Bobby Lee might have laughed at her arch look of injured innocence.

"The other cops you see in here and at home sometimes, Typhaney."

"I don't know nothing about no cops and I don't want to know nothing about no cops. You all are trouble."

"I know you've been sleeping with some of them. I want to know who they are. If they're using you, I can make that go away."

Typhaney wouldn't meet his eyes. She stared off into space.

"You got feelings for these guys?" Bobby Lee said. "Is that what the problem is?"

"I gots no feeling for any man especially no policeman," Typhaney said. "They's only one thing they want from me and they make trouble for me if they don't get it. And they say they gonna hurt me if I tell anybody about it."

"Who's to know you said anything. Lots of people in here see you talking to cops, give them a dance for free, no big thing. What you do outside the club and with who, that's your business. I respect that. This doesn't have anything to do with you. I just want to know who it is, so I can talk to them about something else, something you got nothing to do with."

"Is this about that Crocodile Dundee they was bringing around? I hate that motherfucker," Typhaney spat.

"They brought in an Australian guy?" Bobby Lee said. "Who brought in the Australian guy?"

"I don't know his name, some Crocodile Dundee don't like sisters, don't like brothers, don't like anything black," she said.

"Who brought him in?"

"Don't gots to put up with no prejudiced motherfucker, plenty of white men put their money on me."

"The cops," Bobby Lee said. "Tell me about the cops."

"They both out of the bag, they working plainclothes, think they bad. One name Jerry, the other name Kirkendall. He tell everybody to call him Captain Kirk."

Bobby Lee sighed heavily. He knew both of them, long-timers in Vice and Organized Crime.

"Who else?" he said.

"Some old guy, he like that white chick Josie."

"Josie?"

"She trick for him outside of here."

"Josie. The one that don't work here no more?"

"She didn't want to dance no more, so she work the door and them cops get her in trouble. They don't care a girl got to eat."

"They're not going to know where it came from, but something is going to drop on their head from a great distance, Typhaney. I'm going to screw them over just like they tried with you," Bobby Lee promised.

"Captain Kirk, he's okay. He's a little freaky but he don't treat me bad. That Jerry I don't want no part of, he don't like women, I can tell, he's that kind."

"Tell me about the old guy, Typhaney. How many times you seen him?"

"Just once. He look like somebody's grandpa. He always looking around, nervous. He nervous but he like that young pussy, that why he like that Josie so much, she give it to him for rent money. She say he good to her. She never say his name 'cause he told her not to, and he take good care of her."

"Okay, Typhaney." Bobby Lee slid a folded twenty across the table and into her hand. "For your time."

"You okay, Detective," she said. She stood up and said, "I can go now?"

"I'll take care of that thing for you."

"Thank you," she said, almost bashfully, before she pranced off, tucking the twenty inside the seam of her thong.

Bobby Lee pulled out two twenties and slid it at Nyser, who ignored the money and said, "That's not necessary, Detective."

"Go ahead."

"Rendering of courtesy is a necessary thing in both our businesses."

"That's true," Bobby Lee said. He put the money back in his billfold. "I didn't mean you any disrespect."

"None intended, none taken."

"Josie?"

"At the address I gave you previously. I hear that she may be working at a coffee shop in Calhoun Square. This time of day might be a good time to stop for an espresso, if you like them."

"That's a good idea. Maybe we should get an espresso together."

"Thank you for the thought. Can I help you with anything else?"

"One thing, Dave . . ."

"And that would be . . ."

"Do you know how much money they launder through this place on a monthly basis?"

The big black man stood silent for what seemed to be a full minute. To Bobby Lee it seemed as though the gleam on Nyser's shaven head took on an extra layer of sweat.

"I don't know anything about that, Detective. And even if I did, it wouldn't be something I could discuss. You understand that."

Bobby Lee nodded, carefully watching the big man's hands.

"I understand that," he said. "I want you to know up front that I'm looking for a killer that may have a connection to the cops. I'm looking for that white Australian guy. I don't do dope and I don't care what kind of money goes through here. I'm looking for a killer. And if I have to kick over a couple of apple carts in here, I will . . . I want you to know that going in. I've got a job to do. I want you to know, for you personally, that I want you out of the way if that happens. I owe you for some things."

"I always remember that, Detective Martaine. I'll keep your comments in mind."

"I'll be back to talk some more."

"I look forward to it."

Bobby Lee left the club, and stood outside for a moment, blinking in the bright daylight, before he got into his car and drove into Uptown. He parked across the street from the Calhoun Square shopping center in a red NO PARKING zone, and waved a greeting to one of the uniformed officers on foot patrol outside Calhoun Square.

"Hey, Spike!" he called to the young rookie, who he remembered from a class he'd taught at the Academy. "Where's the coffee shop in here?" he said, pointing at the two-story shopping complex.

"There's a couple, Detective," the rookie said. He lifted his hat and ran his hands through his crew-cut blond hair. "There's one just inside each of the main entrance doors on the first floor, then there's a diner upstairs, and you can get coffee in Figlio's restaurant there."

"You know a girl named Josie works in one of them?"

"Oh, yeah." The blond rookie grinned. "Used to be a stripper, works down in Coffee Express on the other end of the ground floor. Real looker, but bent, you know how strippers get."

"Thanks," Bobby Lee said.

"She into something we should know about?" the young officer said.

"No, I just need to talk to her about one of her 'dates,'" Bobby Lee said.

"I'd like one of those dates."

"I'd think a young stud like you would get all the dates he'd want without having to pay for it."

"Oh," the rookie said. "That kind of date."

"Yeah," Bobby Lee said. "Later."

He went into the mall and as always was struck by the combination of hip and bizarre that was Uptown street life: a herd of young kids in the long dark coats and black clothing of the Goths hanging around outside the body-piercing shop; several young execubabes in their tight-fitting short black skirt suits; two baggy shorts-wearing skateboarders getting a lecture from a hugely muscled black security guard. All the diversity that made Uptown the crossroads of the hip, the young, and occasionally the lost. Back when he was in patrol, he'd worked on a number of runaway cases. They always seemed to gravitate toward Uptown with its plethora of restaurants whose Dumpsters they could dive for food and its serious drug and prostitution subculture that carried out its business in plain sight, yet unseen by the straight passerby.

He walked through the mall to the far side where the Coffee Express counter was located across from the bookstore. A pale white girl in her mid-to-late twenties, dressed in a long black clinging dress and the black lipstick and heavy mascara of a Goth, made an espresso drink for a young man who looked like an ad executive on a break.

Bobby Lee waited until she was through and she said, "What can I get for you?"

"What time does Josie come on?"

"She doesn't come on till three—she should be here in about ten minutes."

"You are?"

"The barista," she said, bristling. "What do you want?"

"I meant your name."

"I know what you meant. Just because I serve you coffee doesn't mean I have to talk to you or tell you my name. If you don't order something, I'll have the security guard move you out."

"Nice attitude," Bobby Lee said. He took out his badge case and showed her his ID.

"So?" she said. "What do you want?"

"A cappuccino, small," Bobby Lee said.

"That I can do."

She made him the drink. While she was busy at the espresso machine, he looked at the clipboard leaning against the cash register. A work schedule was sketched out on the first page and the name for this block of time was Susan.

She handed him the cappuccino and he said, "Thanks, Susan."

Susan looked at him for a moment, then at the work schedule clipboard. She reached out and turned the clipboard facedown.

"That's $2.10," she said.

He slid three ones across the counter and said, "Keep the change."

"Big spender."

"You disrespect cops because you don't like them, or is it to prove a point to somebody?"

"I don't know anything."

MARCUS WYNNE

"You don't know anything?"

A tall blond girl dressed completely in black from head to toe—black Levi's, a tight black T-shirt, big black Doc Martens, and a black leather jacket—came to the counter and paused at the sight of Bobby Lee. She was beautiful, with a heart-shaped face drawn into hard, severe lines. While she was probably no more than twenty-four, she carried herself as though older.

"Are you Josie?" Bobby Lee said.

"He's a cop, coming around asking for Josie," Susan said.

"Nice try," Bobby Lee said. "It was great not talking with you." He turned to the blond girl and toasted her with his coffee cup. "Hello, Josie. You got a good friend here."

"Hey, Josie, do you want me to stay?" Susan said.

"No, thanks, Susan," the blond girl said.

"I'm meeting Alfie at the Uptown for a drink. If there's a problem, call me on my cell. You sure you're okay? You want me to stay?" Susan said.

"I'm fine, go ahead, tell Alfie I said hi," the blond girl said.

"Yeah," Bobby Lee said. "Tell Alfie I said hi."

"Later," Susan said to Josie, ignoring Bobby Lee. She took up her purse and swept out. Bobby Lee watched her cross the street where she went up to a big half black man with a mane of hair pulled back in a ponytail sitting on a motorcycle. Something about the guy reminded Bobby Lee of something, but then Josie spoke to him.

"What do you want?" she said. She had the cooperative stance and tone of someone who had experience dealing with the questions of police officers. "Am I in trouble?"

"No trouble. I just need to ask you about some of your old customers from the club."

"People I danced for, I don't see them anymore."

"You saw some of them outside the club for some personal business, didn't you?"

Josie went behind the counter and began straightening up the work area. While she was tidying, two customers came to the counter.

"I'll help you if I can, Officer. But I don't need any reminders of that place. I put that part of my life behind me," she said. She turned to the two customers. "What can I get you?"

Bobby Lee waited until they had their coffees and left.

"I want to know about the cops you used to date and a young Australian guy who came in there. You know who I'm talking about?"

She had the resigned and hopeless look of someone at the end of something, Bobby Lee thought. She turned away from him and began wiping at the counter furiously.

"I don't suppose it will do me any good to say I don't know anything?" she said.

"Look, this can be easy . . ."

Several more customers came to the counter. She turned to face him and said, "Look, I really need this job and I'm here by myself. Can you come by later and I'll talk to you then? I'll tell you all I know, it'll take a while. I need this job and I can't talk to you and serve customers at the same time."

"That sounds reasonable," Bobby Lee said, relenting. "What time do you get off?"

"I close at midnight."

"I'll be by before then unless I get caught up in something. You wait for me if I run a little late," he said.

"Cops always tell me that," she said.

"That's something you're going to tell me about," Bobby Lee said. "Sorry."

Lieutenant Simon Oberstar sat in the small office accorded to an officer of his rank and looked at his walls and the mementos there. Like many other police administrators, his walls were covered with cheaply framed certificates—from the FBI National Academy, the American Society for Law Enforcement Trainers, and other organizations—and lots of photographs. Here was one of him as a member of the motorcycle squad back in the sixties, here was one when he was on the very first Emergency Response Unit squad, the first SWAT cops ever in the Twin Cities; here was another taken on the day he'd gotten his detective's shield. He looked smaller in that photo, with his close-cropped hair and big jug ears, and a much leaner body.

He'd been young, then.

The walls belonged to the department and the job; everything up there had to do with his identity as a long-time hard street cop. But the desk was his personal territory and the pictures there were of his wife and his kids. Two great kids, Marge and Roger, both in good colleges with all the concomitant expenses. He made sure they lacked for nothing: new cars when they graduated high school to see them through college and on their way in the world; tuition bills paid promptly, and plenty of pocket money for the clothes and the other things a college student needed. He didn't want them to work, though both of them held part-time jobs and told him it was more for the social aspect than for the money. He'd worked his way through school and he knew just how hard that could be.

Alone on one corner of his desk, where it occupied the biggest part of his vision, was a portrait of his wife Angie. Angel, he used to call her. She was the sweetest, kindest woman and the best person he'd ever known. They'd met at a church service not long after he'd started with the police department. He'd grown tired of the loneliness he felt, even with the company of other single cops; he was tired of the endless rounds of drinking and casual sex with the cop groupies that swarmed the young single officers. His partner, Bill Dillon, had invited him home several times for supper. Simon had bloomed in the comfortable house and with the great meals his partner's wife put into him.

Bill's wife Maureen had told him that if he wanted to meet nice girls he had to go to church. He took her at her word and had gone to mass with the Dillons. He signed up for the young Catholic singles group that met one Saturday a month for socializing. He'd met Angie at his very first meeting there and it was as though they had known each other forever. They laughed at the same things, and she knew just how to draw out his funny insights and quirky character from beneath the hard shell he maintained for the job.

They had almost twenty good years together, the kids only eighteen months apart. She'd been the perfect policeman's wife. Then the sickness came, and it ate away at her so fast it seemed like a wildfire raged inside her, shriveling her, but at the same time illuminating her from within with a fierce white light. He remembered sitting beside her bed, stroking her hand, her thin face framed by the beautiful Hermes scarf he had spent most of a paycheck on after she'd lost her hair. She was still so beautiful to him. He watched her go that day, watched how she smiled at him before she closed her eyes, and minute by minute, hour by hour, she faded like a candle flickering its last in a puddle of wax. She went the way she wanted, surrounded by her two children and her husband who loved her more than anything in the world.

A part of him died that day and would never be reborn. The rest of him was injured so profoundly that his entire view of the world changed. The only things that mattered to him anymore were his two children, and even to them he became removed and reserved. He out at home for Max and Bobby; he hoped it wasn't causing them too much stress. He knew this was a big one for Bobby Lee, not just a big one but *the* big one that every ambitious detective hopes for, the front-page case that builds a career while getting him the attention and the accolades that were so few and far between in the jungle on the street. Bobby Lee was working night and day on the case and he knew Bobby had the right instincts; he was going to run down those leads to their source and that meant repercussions within the department. He had to think about how to handle that, because graft and corruption were one thing, complicity in murder another. Neither was good, but the two of them together were devastating.

He had to think that through.

His phone rang, a second line he maintained for private calls.

"Hello?" he said.

"Simon? It's Josie. I have to talk to you about this cop that came to see me today."

couldn't bear to tell them that he wanted to cling close to them; he couldn't bear the pressure it would put on them.

So he threw himself into his work to the point where the chief had finally taken him aside and told him he was working to self-destruction. The chief asked him to take over the Special Investigations Unit, and handle the delicate cases by bringing his expertise inside and devoting it to bringing up the young detectives.

That worked.

The chief's intervention had channeled all Simon's grief and loss into something constructive, something he loved, and that was mentoring young police officers. That saved him. The respect and affection of the younger detectives, who called him Obi-Wan, brought a second springtime into his life.

Or so it felt.

This case that Bobby Lee, the sharpest of his detectives, was working on . . . there were complications there. He'd made Bobby Lee for a comer when he first saw him in uniform, doing a street interview with a witness. Bobby Lee had all the right instincts, all the right moves, knew how to jolly an answer out of someone and leave them with their self-respect, keep somebody on his side or at least neutral out there in the arena they called the street. He'd put a word in for Bobby Lee when he tested for detective and snagged him as one of his own when he came into the Detective Division.

He'd grown close to Bobby Lee, but it was hard for him to socialize with Bobby and his family. Bobby's wife Maxine reminded Oberstar of Angie—painfully so. While Angie had been short and plump, Maxine was tall and thin, but both of them had the same warm and loving nature and a great gift for making their men feel safe and at home in the circle of their family and their friends. If he was honest with himself, he'd admit that there were times when he was envious, maybe even a little jealous of Bobby Lee and Maxine and their close-knit family. Like Angie, Max was the perfect police wife. Or so it seemed.

He wondered how the cannibal killer investigation was playing

Charley drank his wretched home-brewed coffee and stared at the image of Anurra on his wall. He tried the name out loud.

"Anuuuura."

It sounded better when rolled out long. He'd said it so many times the sound was familiar on his tongue.

He picked up his cordless phone and dialed Kativa Patel's office. The secretary told him she was out to lunch and could she take a message?

"No," Charley said. "I'll call her back later."

He dialed Mara, only to get four rings and the answering machine with its cool message: "No one's answering the phone right now. Please leave a message and we'll get back to you as soon as we can."

He hung up and looked out his narrow window onto the street. It was cold and wet and gray, all the reasons not to live in Minneapolis during the cold time, which was half the year. But the cold time had its own beauty, especially during the fall and the still bitter silence of midwinter. He went to his nightstand and took out his spotless Glock pistol.

He knew an excellent way to blow off steam, since it seemed that sex wasn't going to be on his agenda for today. He took out a Kydex inside the waistband holster, and snapped it onto his thick belt, then took out a matching double magazine holder and snapped it on the off side. He took the full spare magazine and slid it into the pistol, then pulled back the slide and chambered a round, press-checked the Glock for a glimpse of bright brass, then holstered the pistol. He took out his weapons bag from the storage chest where he kept it and his other gun paraphernalia, and loaded up another spare magazine and put it into the double pouch. Then he threw two boxes of practice .45 ammo into the bag along with his hearing protection headset and some amber shooting glasses.

A little violent exercise would help clear his head.

It was only a short drive to the Edina Shooting Range, a small indoor/outdoor facility in the western suburb of Edina. During the day it was mostly empty, with only a few off-duty police or security guards practicing. Occasionally there would be a class from the Edina Police Department, who shared responsibility for the range with the city.

Charley nodded to Lyle, the range manager, who raised his hand, checked a clipboard inside his office, and said, "Pick a lane, any lane. Don't expect much today in the way of traffic. You need some targets?"

"Let me have two combat silhouettes," Charley said.

Lyle handed him two of the big B-27 targets of a black human figure superimposed on a white background. Charley went into the range and hung his target on a hanger, then hit the button and slid the target a measured seven yards from him. He drew the pistol and ejected the full magazine and the chambered round. He put an empty magazine in place, slid the slide back a fraction to cock the Glock, then holstered it.

Starting with his hands relaxed at his side, Charley drew the pistol slowly and smoothly, lifting his sweatshirt over the concealed pistol, acquiring the grip and then drawing the pistol in one smooth motion, the off hand meeting the gun hand in the center of his belly on the way up to line up on the plane of his eye. When the front sight was lined up on the target he pressed the trigger with just the tip of his finger and broke it without a wobble. He felt, rather than heard, the faint click of the falling internal hammer that drove the firing pin home.

He dry-fired several more times before he put in a loaded magazine and racked the slide to chamber a round, then pressed the slide back just slightly to visually confirm a chambered round.

Time for rock and roll.

He holstered the pistol and stood relaxed before the target, then he smoothly lifted his shirt with his left hand while simultaneously gripping the pistol butt with his right hand, pulling it with one smooth continuous motion, the left hand meeting the pistol midline on his body, wrapping around the right hand and locking the pistol solid as it came up into the plane of his vision, his finger on the trigger now that the front sight was on the target and as it came into the final focus of the front sight the trigger's remaining slack was pressed out and the weapon bucked in his hand and a neat hole appeared directly in the center of the face of the silhouette, precisely where the bridge of a man's nose would be.

He held his position for a moment, covering the target while he assessed his hit, then lowered the weapon to a low ready, then reholstered. He repeated the routine time and again, single shots till he'd run through all ten of the rounds, then when the slide locked back he did a smooth reload from the waist pouch, slamming the magazine home and remembering to keep his pinky finger out of the way as the magazine went into the shortened grip of the Glock 30. The magazine locked home, he let the slide go forward, his finger on the trigger and pressing the slack out as the weapon closed in on the visual plane between his eye and the target and another hit in the small ragged hole the size of a quarter in the center of the silhouette's head.

"You're averaging 1.6 seconds," Lyle said from behind. He was holding a Pact Timer in his hand.

"You checking up on me?" Charley said without looking around.

"Oh, yeah. Got to keep an eye on you, mister. Anybody that shoots that good I got to keep an eye on. Nobody else that comes in here shoots that good."

"Probably 'cause they take lessons from you," Charley said. He took two fresh fully loaded magazines from his range bag, put one in the smoking pistol and another into his magazine pouch.

Lyle laughed. "I never teach anybody to shoot as good as me, you never know who might come gunning for you."

"Ain't that the truth."

"You ought to come down, teach a class. Make a little bit of money to keep you in ammunition."

"I don't have the patience for teaching," Charley said. "I got my hands full with other things."

"Think about it, anyway," Lyle urged. "I could get you a bunch of people to take private lessons."

"These days I just like to shoot, Lyle." Charley turned his attention back to the silhouette, brought it back to the shooter's box, and taped over the ragged hole in the head of the target.

"That son of a bitch has got a headache," Lyle said.

"Kill the head and the body will follow."

"Remind me never to piss you off."

Lyle went back out into the commons area with his timer, leaving Charley to look at his target. Charley backed the target out to seven yards. Next was double taps. He'd put a 3×5 card on the chest of the silhouette. From the holster he presented his weapon and fired two rapid shots, one right on top of the other, at the 3×5 card. Two holes a little over an inch apart appeared in the card.

The more he shot, the more he was reminded how much he loved the ritual of shooting. There was so much in common with photography—having the right equipment set up the right way, seeing and visualizing the shot before you even began to put it into motion, letting the thinking mind set aside any other thought other than the mantra of front sight, press, front sight, press, just like with the camera—viewfinder, press, viewfinder, press. He lost himself in both of those rituals, in the seamless flow of decisive moments.

He missed this, he knew, and he was amused by his own obstinacy in refusing to fall back into the weekly practice that had been one of the defining anchors of his previous life, his life with the shooters and the looters, the gunfighters and street operators of the Special Activities Staff. He wondered for a moment, with an emotion quickly quashed, just what sort of operation his old crew was running. But he didn't really want to know that now. Those days and those activities were behind him. He was a photographer and shooting was a hobby, not an essential survival skill in his job.

But why did he feel the need to work on it so hard today?

2.17

Maureen DiMeola had been the second shift desk manager at the Days Inn–Airport for ten years. She'd developed a keen sense for all the different types of customers she saw, and this one felt like trouble. He was a light-skinned black man dressed all in black, with his ears and his nose pierced. The nose bothered her, he had a small piece of bone or wood completely through his septum.

Just disgusting.

It wasn't a good sign that he was carrying a guitar case. So many of these so-called musicians felt they had to trash a room to prove they were real rock and rollers. Maureen liked music but disliked musicians as a consequence of dealing with too many obnoxious ones over the years.

And this one wanted a particular room as well.

"Room 314, mate," the black man said. "The back corner room there on the third floor. I stayed there once before, it's me lucky room. How about it?"

His driver's license said Albert Williams, but he didn't look like an Albert Williams. That didn't sound like an Australian name and he had the same accent as the guy in the car commercials. But she couldn't very well refuse him; it was the middle of the week and most of the rooms were empty. Like any good desk manager, she kept the let rooms together so the maids could get them cleaned up more efficiently in the morning.

But she didn't feel like arguing with this man; something about him put her off.

"All right," she said. "Here you go. If you intend to play that, please remember that other guests have a right to quiet."

"I'm the quiet sort myself," the man said. "I'll keep it down."

Alfie took the key and hefted his guitar case in the other hand and went up in the elevator to the third floor. He'd picked out room 314 during an early reconnaissance. The room was on the outside of the building, directly beside a stairwell that led to the parking lot. A roof access stairway was blocked with a single hanging chain. The room was in the back of the building, away from the reservations desk and the heavily trafficked area around the weight room, indoor pool, and breakfast dining area. Since it was the middle of the week, the rooms on either side, as well as above and below, were vacant. He'd checked for himself before he went to the front desk.

He wanted to ensure his privacy.

He went into the room and drew the curtains tight. He set his guitar case down on the nearest bed and opened the case and took out several small safety pins he used to secure the gap between the curtains. He hung the DO NOT DISTURB sign on the outside knob, then closed and locked the door. He took a rubber door stop wedge out of the case and kicked it firmly into place at the base of the door, then turned to take stock of the room: two twin beds, a single big mirror over the simple dresser, a television set on top of the dresser, an open closet, and a bathroom with a small tub and shower.

Everything he needed for the night.

He took a CD player with two small detached speakers out of the case and arranged them on top of the dresser. Then he took out his nulla-nulla, the club's blunt head still matted with hair and tissue visible through the plastic bag he'd wrapped neatly around the end of the stick. When he removed the plastic bag, an awful reek of rot puffed out. His nostrils flared at the scent.

Then Alfie stripped naked, rolling his clothes into a neat bundle and placing them inside a small rucksack he took from the guitar case. He set out his Emerson fighting knife and a H&K USP Compact .45

automatic pistol where he could get at them easily. If he was interrupted or attacked, he had everything set for a quick getaway.

The last thing he took from the guitar case was a bag of paints and a candle.

Alfie turned on the CD player and the low rhythmic drone of the didgeridoo began to fill the room. He eased the volume down: he didn't need it loud, he needed it clear. He undid the tie that held his mane of kinky hair back in a ponytail and shook out his hair, combing his fingers through it, forcing it up and out, framing his face in a halo of black curls. Then he pushed the beds far apart, up against each wall, making a larger space in the middle of the room. He set the candle, unlit, in the middle of the space he made.

Time now for the paints.

He laid out the pouch that held small tubes of paint and sat cross-legged in front of it. Dissatisfied with the light, he got up and turned off the room lights and was pleased to see how the pinned curtains held out the fading daylight from outside. He lit the candle, and it seemed then that the room filled with shadows, dark shadows hovering at the perimeter of light the candle threw into the dark room. He sat cross-legged once again, taking a deep even breath to calm and center himself, his nostrils flaring wide to take in the scent of rotten blood and flesh from the nulla-nulla laid alongside his other weapons.

White paint on his face first, a base pattern across the broad forehead and nose and cheekbones down to his jaw. Then a series of small yellow dots across his brow and down the bridge of his nose, trailing off the nose into squared dots on each cheekbone. He highlighted his ears in white with a yellow daub on each earlobe. He stood, then, and admired his face in the mirror. In the flickering candlelight, it seemed as though his face floated in the darkness on the smooth surface of the mirror, his naked body a sexless shadow.

He ran white up and down the limbs of his body to meet in the center, white as a base and red ochre, the special paint that had the reek of his club in it, in squares on his chest. Carefully, he drew the small stick figures that represented those he carried within himself. His nostrils flared again and deep in the back of his throat he tasted old blood.

He stood naked before the mirror with the old symbols across his flesh.

He took a leather loincloth from his bag. The skin was smooth from age and long wear. He'd made it from the hide of the first man he'd killed on the puri-puri apprentice's path. He thought of that day, so many years ago, and his shaman mentor Ralph, who had taken another name he was not allowed to say. That name had passed to Alfie when he killed Ralph. Alfie still thought of his mentor and almost regretted killing him, though both of them knew it was coming and that it was necessary for the transference of what they both carried, the dark spirit presence of the Imjin Quinkin. Alfie remembered Ralph's head bowing in submission to the blow of the nulla-nulla, and afterward, the ceremonial meal. Alfie had sung the song that celebrated the passing of his mentor and the taking of Ralph into himself. And then he went alone into the foothills around Jowalbinna to the initiation cave in the dark of night. He'd twisted through the narrow passageways and left bloody scrapings of himself on the sharp-edged stones, and when he'd finally worked his way into the inner chamber, he vomited, leaving both bits of himself and of Ralph there in the dust of the final cave.

That was the first step on the dark path he took alone as a vehicle for Anurra.

Or was he a gateway?

He didn't know. All he knew was that something dark moved through him and that dark thing demanded certain things and in return he felt the presence expanding him, like a dark cloud expands before it bursts into thunder and lightning.

The drone of the didgeridoo seemed louder and the candle began to smoke, leaving faint tendrils of gray in the deep shadows of the darkened room. Alfie looked up at the smoke detector, stood on a chair and removed the battery, setting it on the dresser. Then he stood and swayed, slowly at first, letting the sound of the didgeridoo fill his head and vibrate his very bones with the steady drone that rose and fell in time to his small twitchings, and the first small steps, then the regular stepping in and stepping out, circling the candle, a microcosm of the flames he'd danced around before, shuffling his feet, raising his knees for every other step, slapping his side, knocking his knees at the appropriate place in the ancient rhythms . . .

. . . he was a gateway, and he began to drone under his breath, a tune that had no tune, a melody with no melody, a song with no words, just an attunement of the vehicle his body was with the sound of the didgeridoo and the rhythmic claps on the CD matched the rhythmic stomp of his own feet, and the images in his mind seemed material in the gathering smoke in the room, there the twisting of the Rainbow Serpent as it strained to give birth to man and all the other animals, there an emu, then the death adder and the dingo, there the spirit ancestors, the hated Timara and the sacred Imjin, the clan of the Imjin to which he was sworn, man hunters, man eaters, bearers of the blood club that he now raised in his hand and swung through all the angles of attack, the heavy club flickering in his hand from all the angles it could sweep across, down, up, forward, the nulla-nulla live in his hand as he smote his clan's enemies and the enemies of the others he had taken money for to strike . . .

His vision blurred even more, or else perhaps the smoke from the flickering candle clouded his eyes, and it was as though he was in the cave again, the ancient initiation cave, having crawled through in the dark of night, man brain in his belly and his shaman-mentor's blood on his hand and his club, seeking the vision of his ancestor and Anurra had come to him, Anurra who rode him when he needed expression in the world of man and must cross the line between the man's world and the Dreamtime.

A story unfolded in front of his eyes like the reel of a movie: Anurra hunting, hunting, killing and eating and killing and eating; behind him came a Timara and there was a man and a woman with the Timara and they tracked Anurra to the cave. They stood outside in the daylight, because Anurra couldn't bear the light of day, and threw rocks into his cave to drive him out. So Anurra began to sing a love magic song to the woman, and the woman came to him and he held her before him as a shield against the angry man and the Timara who stood behind him, long-limbed like the shadow of a kouri tree.

And when the angry man came . . .

KNOCK, KNOCK, KNOCK.

The heavy knocking at the door jarred Alfie from his vision. He cursed softly, his vision blurred, disoriented by his abrupt departure from his dream state.

"What is it?" he said.

A harsh male voice replied, "Police. Open the door."

Alfie took a deep breath to quell the sudden knot in his belly, and took a moment to remove himself completely from his vision. He looked around the room. There would be no explaining this.

"Just a minute, mate!" he called. "I'm on the toilet, be there in just a jiff."

"Open up!" the police officer said again.

Alfie heard the click of a key being inserted into the lock and then the door opened up a few inches, only to be brought up short by the rubber door stop and the door chain. Alfie allowed himself a brief flash of regret and thought that there was nothing else to be done now. He snatched up the rucksack with his clothing in it and threw it on his back, clipped the fighting knife to the string holding his loincloth in place, took the nulla-nulla in one hand and the H&K USP .45 in the other, then slammed his body against the door, forcing back the police officer trying to enter. Then he kicked the door stop free and threw back the chain. When the policeman threw himself against the door again, Alfie flung the door wide open so the officer's rush carried him into the room. Alfie stepped nimbly to one side and brought the nulla-nulla down in a flashing arc to impact on the greater peroneal nerve complex on the outside of the policeman's thigh.

"Ah, Christ!" the policeman shouted, clutching at his leg as he fell.

Alfie kept the stick in motion and gave Maureen the desk clerk, who stood there, eyes wide at the vision that confronted her, a sharp poke in the belly that doubled her over. He shoved past her and ran down the stairwell into the parking lot where his motorcycle was parked beside a lamp that illuminated the lot. At the bottom of the stairs he bumped into a man beside the soft drink machine and knocked him down. The man pushed himself up on his arms, gaping at the apparition of an Aborigine in full paint and loincloth brandishing a club in one hand and a pistol in the other.

"Stop!" the policeman shouted from upstairs.

Alfie snatched a glance over his shoulder and saw the policeman limping down the stairwell with his pistol in hand. Damn. Alfie began to mount his bike, but paused as the policeman came clear of the ground-floor stairwell and limped around the corner of the building.

It was time for something more modern with a little more reach. Alfie stuck the nulla-nulla under the rucksack straps across his chest. The H&K pistol fit his hand like a glove and he threw the pistol up and when the sights were roughly aligned he pressed the trigger twice.

Crack, crack!

Two fast shots at the policeman, one went wide and whanged off the concrete wall of the stairwell, the other clipping the officer low on the torso and spinning him so that he stumbled over his own feet and fell. The officer caught himself on his hands, the Beretta he held going off as he involuntarily squeezed the trigger. Alfie slowed himself down and put two fast rounds in the officer's torso, then threw his leg over his bike, the seat hard against his naked bottom, and inserted the ignition keys.

A bullet hit the front headlight, splintering it in a shower of glass and metal. Alfie jumped and saw the wounded officer rolling over and over, his pistol in both hands outstretched and shooting. Alfie levered the H&K into a strong Weaver stance and emptied the remaining rounds in the weapon at, around, and into the police officer who rolled behind a car, huddling behind a wheel well as the heavy .45 slugs dug divots out of the parking lot and exploded sparks off the sheet metal of the cars around him. Alfie stuck the blisteringly hot pistol beneath a shoulder strap and kicked his bike into life, pushing it off with both bare feet. The cop was still alive and trying to get a shot angle on him as Alfie tore out of the parking lot on his motorcycle, and accelerated away into the night.

2.18

Bobby Lee took the call about the motel shooting from a patrolman who'd been on the Simmons crime scene.

"Hey, Detective?" the patrolman said. "You're going to want to come out to the Days Inn by the airport. We had a guy dressed up like an Indian shoot a cop."

"Shot a cop?"

"Bloomington PD. Took four hits on the vest and one clipped his ear, but he's going to be okay. He emptied his Beretta on the guy, thinks he hit him. Witnesses say it was like the OK Corral out here."

"What do I got to do with an Indian?" Bobby Lee said.

"This guy had a war club he hit the cop with, fucked his leg all up," the patrolman said. "This guy was painted up like the painting on the wall at the Simmons house. I remembered you said the perp used a club on Simmons."

"What's your name again?"

"Tim Chance."

"Tim Chance, you're going to make a fine detective someday. Stay right there, I'm on my way."

"Will do, Detective."

Bobby Lee grabbed his jacket and paused only long enough to grab an extra box of .45 ammo for his Smith & Wesson from the storage room. He took an unmarked squad out of the motor pool and burned rubber into the street, the back window light bar flashing blue and red, just like when he was on patrol in a marked squad, one of the street animals out there running it down, and for a few minutes it was just that simple. This was something he could deal with: a suspect, a sighting, a shooting. This was a starting point. He still had to interview Josie when she got off work and that would eventually lead him someplace, but this might get him where he wanted to be much sooner.

It took almost half an hour with the late rush-hour traffic to get out to the airport and the Days Inn. Marked squads blocked the parking-lot entrance; both Bloomington and Minneapolis PD were well represented. The Days Inn sat right on the border of the two municipalities, but when a cop got shot, nobody paid attention to jurisdiction—you just went. That was the rule. If one in blue goes down, everyone in blue goes out. Period.

Bobby Lee pulled up beside a Minneapolis squad where he saw the patrolman Chance talking with a Bloomington plainclothes. Bobby Lee got out and said, "Hey, Chance!"

Chance waved him over and shook Bobby Lee's hand, then said to the Bloomington plainclothes, "Detective Morrow, this is Detective Martaine from Minneapolis. He might have an interest in this guy we're all looking for."

Morrow was a burly Norwegian with a furrowed face and unusually fat cheeks, which made him look like a sullen chipmunk.

"Hey, Martaine," he said. "You looking for a nut dresses up like an Indian?"

"Run it down for me, will you?" Bobby Lee said. "I just got here, I don't know about any Indian."

"Sure," Morrow said. "Our patrolman answers a complaint from the night manager, she's over there with EMS, took a bad whack in the belly from our bad guy. She tells a story of some weird-looking guy, maybe half Indian, maybe half black, bone in his nose and all kinds of ear piercings, a musician, shows up and wants a room. The guy pays cash. She lets him have the room, then comes up later and smells smoke, hears some weird music. She figures him for a doper maybe setting up to make a deal out of the room, they do that sometimes here."

Bobby Lee nodded and grinned. "Do tell. I was here a couple of years ago, on that takedown with the Jamaicans."

"No kidding?" Morrow said. "I was still in the bag then. Was off that day, but I heard about it."

"So this maybe doper . . . ?" Bobby Lee urged.

"Right. She backs off and calls in a unit. Our guy, Billy Williams, he comes in, she gives him the rundown, he goes up to have a look. Smells smoke, hears the music, bangs on the door. The guy inside has a funny accent, right? Not Indian, Billy thinks maybe English or something, might be an India Indian instead of a Minneapolis Indian, but they don't exchange but a couple of words. Guy won't come out, so Billy uses the access key the manager gives him, then this guy comes busting out. This is where it gets weird. The guy is naked except for a whattaya call them, a lion cloth . . ."

"A loincloth?" Bobby Lee said.

"Whatever," Morrow said, irritated. "Like a fucking thong for men. He's wearing a backpack and he's got a fucking pistol in one hand and a nightstick in the other. He lays into Williams like a pro, takes out his leg and limps him up bad, pokes the broad from the desk in the gut and drops her, then bolts down the stairs and gets on a motorcycle. He and Williams exchange shots. Williams thinks he got a few into the guy and his motorcycle. The naked Indian gets a couple more off, then rides off like, what was the fucking Lone Ranger's sidekick . . . Tonto?"

Bobby Lee laughed. "Jesus, that's one for the books."

"You got that right," Morrow said. "Now where do you figure in?"

"I'm looking for a guy who might be some kind of Australian native. Kills people with a club."

"The cannibal killer thing?"

"That's my baby."

"I don't envy you one bit," Morrow said. "Let's go up, have a look in the hotel room. Forensics is working the scene up there now. I got all kinds of extra bodies working this parking lot. Man, I hate a shooting in a parking lot. That's what I tell all my rookies: you want to murder someone and get away with it, kill them in a parking lot. Trace evidence gets blown all over the place, you can't find anything . . . I hate it."

"We didn't make this guy for a shooter."

"Oh, he's a shooter all right. Forty-five, too, and handy with it. You see some of these dirtbags, they favor the nine. I don't like running into a guy who favors a forty-five and can shoot it."

"I know what you mean," Bobby Lee said.

He followed Morrow up the stairwell to the hotel room, and showed his identification to the patrolman outside the door jotting down the names of each officer who entered the scene.

Morrow pointed to the items the forensic team had carefully bagged.

"We got some good things," he said. "Little CD stereo system, his guitar case. We'll get some prints, there. Guy was toting all his worldly goods in that guitar case like some kind of movie bandit."

Morrow took a pen from his pocket and lifted a loop of a soft roll cloth that held tubes of paint and a wide mouth jar.

"He painted himself up with this stuff," he said. "Didn't do anything on the wall, but maybe we got to him before he did that."

"This connects," Bobby Lee said. "We got paint like that in the two homicides we got him for."

"I can help you out on that," Morrow said. "We're booking it into evidence for our lab, but have your guys bring your samples down and we'll rush it, look for matches."

"I owe you big, Morrow."

"Buy me lunch sometime, you big city detective. Then we'll call it even."

Bobby Lee did a careful interview with the wounded police officer, and an even longer and more thorough one with Maureen DiMeola, the front desk clerk. She had a sharp eye and was very specific in her description. She figured him for light-skinned black or mulatto and she stuck to her conviction that he was some kind of musician. Between the detailed description of the subject and his motorcycle, some fingerprints and the paints, Bobby Lee finally had a real case going. Now it was time for street police work. He had to get a description out to every patrolman and every snitch in town. It was premature to go to the press, but that was a final option. This guy was a real looker and it shouldn't be too hard to find him if he was still in the Cities, especially since he was sporting an Australian accent. Most people had seen enough Crocodile Dundee commercials to place the accent.

And if someone spotted him, Bobby Lee could catch him. And if he caught him, he could grill him and put the pieces of this bizarre puzzle together.

He got back downtown quickly, winding his way through the light post rush-hour traffic. Back at the office, he hurried through the milling detectives changing the guard for shift change and barricaded himself behind the phone in his cubicle. First he called Oberstar, who was out, then the state Bureau of Criminal Apprehension crime lab technician who was working on a match between the paints found in the hotel room and the paint samples taken from the walls at the Simmons and Nyquist homes. After his flurry of calls, he sat back in his chair. Now he had to wait. The lab would be working overtime to make the paint match, but that was still going to take some time, so he'd just sit here and wait. He still had the midnight appointment with Josie to think about. He was tempted to blow off their appointment and catch her another time, but the discipline of a good investigator asserted itself. He'd make that appointment. He picked up the still warm phone and called home.

"Hello?" Maxine said.

"It's me," Bobby Lee said. "We got some big breaks going here, I got a solid lead on the guy. I got to work late tonight, won't be home till after midnight."

"I married the midnight rambler," Max said lightly. "Did you get something to eat?"

"I'll order in a sandwich or maybe Obi and I will split a pizza."

"Make sure you eat something, you always forget to eat when you're excited. You got time to say hi to Nick?"

"Yeah, put him on."

There was a sharp click as Nicky picked up the extension phone. "Hi, Daddy!"

"Hey, buddy," Bobby Lee said. "What are you doing?"

"Playing Nintendo."

"Are you winning?"

"Yeah."

"I'm going to be late tonight."

"Okay. See you later," Nick said. He hung up.

"He sounds sooooo excited," Maxine said.

"Hard to compete with Nintendo," Bobby Lee said. "I got to go. If I get some slack time I'll call you before you go to bed."

"Oh, I almost forgot," Maxine said. "Obi called for you around three."

"I left a message on his machine when I got here. Did he say what he wanted?"

"Just that he had to talk to you."

"I'll find him," Bobby Lee said. "Love you."

"Love you, too. Be careful and remember to eat."

She hung up first. Bobby Lee slowly replaced his phone, then went down the hall to Oberstar's office. The lights were off and Obi's coat was gone. Bobby Lee went back to his desk and phoned Obi's pager, entered in his desk phone number, then sat and worked on his notes from the hotel shooting. It was good to have some solid leads to dig into. Time passed. He looked at his phone and wondered where Obi was. He paged him again, and this time only a few minutes passed before Obi called him back.

"Where you at?" Bobby Lee said.

"You alone there?" Obi said.

"Mullins and Carruthers are here. You need help on something?"

"What you got going?"

Bobby Lee filled him in on the motel shooting and said, "I got great leads on this guy, Obi. I got this son of a bitch, I know I do. Got a good description, witnesses, paint samples. The BCA lab is doing a rush job to match the paint to Simmons and Nyquist. Don't know why he was dressed that way in a motel, but we got him shooting a cop."

"Jesus," Oberstar said. "Is the cop okay?"

"His vest took most of it. He got a good look at the doer, but the motel manager got a memory like a video camera."

MARCUS WYNNE

"You got a sketch?"

"Bloomington is working one up. We'll get a good one, the Bloomington detective is all right."

"What's his name?"

"Morrow, he's an old hand."

"I heard of him. What about the financial end of things, you sniff anything out on that?"

"Nothing other than what I told you, you were looking more into that. What do you got?"

"I got a few things," Oberstar said. "It sounds like you're right on the doer. What about this meeting you got for tonight?"

"The hooker? At midnight, when she gets off work at the coffee shop."

"Where are you meeting her?"

"At the coffee shop."

Oberstar paused for a moment, then said, "All right. You going to have enough time to get this motel stuff done?"

"I'll get it taken care of."

"I'll talk to you later," Oberstar said.

"You coming back here?"

"No . . . I'm working on some other things at home."

"Okay, Obi-Wan. Don't work too hard."

Bobby Lee hung up the phone and realized he hadn't eaten since noon. He looked at the clock and figured he could make a drive through for fast food on his way down to the coffee shop.

Everything else was in motion.

2.19

Jay Burrell paced back and forth on the weathered deck overlooking the waves lapping the beach and fought the urge to throw his phone out into the ocean.

"This is a major mess," he said to his caller. "I'm getting him out of there, but I need to know that you can sweep up, after. We can't have any comeback from this."

"What do you expect me to do?" the caller said. "I can't stop the description from going out. Your man won't be able to hide out once we get the description out."

"Do what you can," Jay said. "I'll see to the other and get him out."

"I . . ."

"Do what you can!"

Jay hit the END button and took a few breaths to calm himself, then dialed in another long-distance number, this one to a plane charter operation in the States.

"It's Jay," he said to the man who answered the phone. "Is the charter ready?"

"Sure thing, no worries."

"It's going to be soon. How long before you can get it on station?"

"Pilot's there now, got a flight plan pre-filed for the weekend, but the aircraft's fueled up and the pilot's at a hotel right near there. I can get him on his mobile anytime."

"Have him stand by that phone and you stand by yours. My cargo is coming out sooner than I thought."

"No worries. We'll be there."

Jay hung up the phone and glared out at the ocean. He'd planned on surfing again this afternoon, but the crisis in Minneapolis demanded attention and he knew there would be more phone calls.

He didn't have to wait long.

"We've got a bit of a bollocks here," Alfie said without preamble. His voice sounded tinny over the line.

"I've already heard," Jay said. "What is in your mind?"

"Don't go that way, mate, I'm in no mood to hear it. Have you got my ride out sorted?"

Jay stifled the urge to shout. "Yes. Eden Prairie Airport just outside of Minneapolis. The charter is waiting for you there. How long before you can get there?"

"I can be there in just a jiff, mate."

"There's some cleaning up to do. Are you up to it?"

Alfie paused before answering. "That depends. I don't have much time."

"Can you check your e-mail?"

"Yes."

"There will be some details in there for you. I need you to take care of the two most pressing loose ends..."

"Send me what you like, mate, but I sort my messes out my own way. I'll see what you've got. Have the aircraft standing by, and I mean standing by ready to fly, four hours from now. That's two A.M. my time."

"Four hours?"

"That's what the man said. Have him there, ready to go. Alfie out."

There was the click of the phone hanging up on the other end.

"But..." Jay began. "Son of a bitch."

He dialed the charter operator again and gave him his instructions, then finally gave in to his frustration and threw his portable phone out into the surf.

"SON OF A BITCH!"

MARCUS WYNNE

Alfie was furious with himself. He'd gotten well away from the motel before he pulled behind an empty garage and put his clothes on over the paint and loincloth. He'd wiped his face clean with his T-shirt and kept his helmet in place as he rode to Susan's place, where he cleaned himself up, leaving smears of dirt and paint in Susan's shower. He cleaned up his clothes as best he could and then walked to a nearby Internet café where he called up his e-mail. He read the e-mail carefully, committing it to memory before deleting it.

He didn't have much time to get this last job done. It would be better just to fade away and let the locals spin their wheels trying to find him . . . he'd be half a world away and they'd never find him there. Killing the lead investigator wasn't the best way to go, in his opinion. It wouldn't stop the investigation; all it would do would be to stir the cops up even more. But it was too late to question why.

He wouldn't have time for the ritual with this one.

187

Charley was in his apartment talking to Maxine on the phone.

"Do you want to come by and have a beer?" she said. "Bobby Lee is going to be back late tonight, probably after midnight."

"How late are you going to be up?"

"Oh, you know I'm always up late when he's not home."

Charley pictured her standing in her kitchen, twisting the phone cord around one finger as he'd seen her do so many times before.

"I could come by," he said. "I've got some things to do, but I want to talk to Bobby Lee. I could come by before you go to bed."

"I won't tell Nicky, I'd never get him down for bed then. Just come by, I'll be up."

"It's a date, baby," Charley said. "Should I wear my lucky boxers?"

"You couldn't handle it, fool. Wear them if you like, though."

"See you later, Max."

"Night. Be careful!"

Charley put down the phone and sat down in his armchair. Something was bothering him and he didn't know what. He kept looking at the photograph of Anurra on his wall. He stood up and went to his nightstand table, opened the drawer and took out his pistol, press-checked it to make sure it was loaded, and checked the spare magazine. He took out two additional magazines and a box of Remington Golden Saber hollow points and loaded the two extra magazines, then slipped them into a Cordura pouch. Then he took a few minutes and set up his gun belt as though he were still working: the thick inch-and-a-half-wide belt held the waist holster right behind his right hip inside his Levi's, the Kydex magazine pouch on the left side with the double Cordura carrier behind it. With his knife clipped in his pants pocket, that gave him a pistol, a knife, and counting the ammo in the pistol, forty-one rounds of .45 ammo.

He was loaded for bear.

Why? Because it felt right and he'd learned in the hardest of schools that all he needed to know was to trust himself first and foremost and to be ready when his inner voice told him to be ready.

There was violence in the air tonight.

Charley went and stared out his window, pulling his shirttail over his armament. The cold had begun to settle in as late fall dropped into winter. No snow yet, but there had been early morning frosts and the snow would not be far behind. Across the street in the ice cream café they'd even stopped putting out the tables in the tree-shaded courtyard once it got dark. Only a few diehard customers carefully bundled against the cold would sit out once the sun fell away.

He let his hand fall absently to the pistol holstered at his side. It'd been a long time since he'd worn his workbelt set up like this. The last job he'd done on the Special Activities Staff was provide security for a couple of Technical Services Division technicians who'd been setting up an electronic listening post for a domestic operation; one of the few sanctioned operations on U.S. soil, it was aimed at a suspected domestic terrorist with ties to Middle Eastern terrorists.

He didn't like to think of those days. He'd had a great job, doing important things, working with people he honestly thought were the best and the brightest the U.S. could field. But he couldn't put aside his bitterness at the stupidity with which they were deployed by a contradictory administration that couldn't decide what its policy was when it came to covert operations.

That cost lives.

He checked the position of his weapon with his elbow and thought that he was ready. But for what? He felt stupid standing there, armed to the teeth, not an operator but a photographer, a police photographer with a fine arts business that barely paid for film. He turned away from the window and pulled on his leather jacket, leaving his shirttails hanging out over his weapons. He didn't think much about having two layers over his weapons . . . after all, he wasn't going to use them anyway.

He'd go for a drive, smoke a cigar, think for a while, then go over to Bobby Lee's and keep Max company until Bobby Lee got home.

After driving round the Lakes and aimlessly through the streets, he found himself parked just outside Mara's building. She was home; he could tell by the lights that went on, then off through the windows. Mara was so free and easy in some things, but she was astonishingly thrifty when it came to other things, and she always turned off the lights when she left a room, even if only for a moment. Charley smiled. It was a thing that amused him and endeared her to him at the same time.

She wasn't alone. There was someone else in the apartment. He saw a shape pass before the windows a couple of times before he saw a man with a goatee stand against the window and look out, much as Charley did when he was there. He'd deliberately not called her, and it was for that reason that he sat alone with his feelings—which weren't anger or jealousy. Instead he felt almost relieved, certainly not surprised . . . and that was surprising. He pulled away from the curb and a few blocks away pulled into a convenience store and used the pay telephone to call her.

"Mara? It's Charley."

"Hello, Charley. Where are you?"

"Would you give me Kativa's home number? I need to ask her something about those pictures."

There was a long silence, then a slight, knowing laugh. "Of course," she said. "Just a minute."

She set the phone down, then came back in a moment and said, "Here . . . it's 920-4988. Is that all you need?"

"Who's your friend?" Charley said.

There was another longish pause, then laughter.

"Oh, Charley," she said. "Are you spying on me?"

"Just curious."

"You're not lurking outside, are you?"

"Down the street."

"So that's why you called."

"I needed the number."

"You've got her number all right, Charley. And mine, too, I suppose. I think you should make it a new habit to call me before you come over."

"If you want that."

"Yes."

"You're important to me..."

"Never mind. Go well and tell Kativa I said it was fine. I'll talk to you sometime soon. Good night."

She hung up the phone, leaving Charley staring out into space, the phone still screwed tight into his ear. He thought for a moment about calling her back, but decided not to. He laughed out loud for a moment, genuine laughter at his confused state and contradictory impulses, then held the hook down till he got a dial tone and put another thirty-five cents in and dialed Kativa's number. The phone rang four times, then the answering machine came on with a synthesized computer voice that said, "Please leave your message at the beep."

Charley said, "Kativa, this is Charley Payne. I wanted to talk to you..."

The phone beeped as Kativa picked it up. "Hello, Charley?"

"Screening your phone calls?" Charley said. "Are you sorting through all your date offers tonight?"

"Yes, it's a difficult thing to be so much in demand. What are you doing? Where are you calling from? It sounds as though you're outside."

"I'm at a phone booth. I was wondering...could I stop by for a few minutes? I've had some thoughts about this Anurra Quinkin thing..."

"Of course you can. Do you know where Java Jack's Coffee Shop is?"

"Sure. You didn't tell me you lived so close by."

"I didn't want to give you any ideas," she said.

"I have lots of ideas."

"Are you working on that case tonight?"

"That's what I'm telling myself. You?"

"I'm just staying at home doing girl stuff. Come by. I live across the street from Java Jack's in the corner apartment building, apartment 214. Ring the buzzer and I'll let you in."

"I'll be there shortly."

Charley hung up the phone. He still felt confused. He was armed to the teeth, driving around aimlessly, and he had a date with a beautiful woman. He laughed and wondered what Bobby Lee would make of all this. That reminded him of his promise to Maxine to stop by and see her and Bobby Lee. He checked his watch. He had time enough to stop off and see Kativa and still make the run over to Bobby Lee's house and catch Max before she went to bed.

It was good to have friends, he thought. It was good to have places you could go where they would always take you in no matter how late it was.

193

2.21

Bobby Lee parked his squad in front of Calhoun Square on the Hennepin side. He slid out from behind the wheel and stretched his back to get the kinks out, then went into the shopping mall entrance and turned left to the coffee shop. Josie's friend Susan was wiping down the counter.

"Where's Josie?" Bobby Lee said.

Susan didn't look at him. She just continued wiping the counter, then turned to wipe down the espresso maker and said, "She went home early."

"How long ago?"

"About an hour. She didn't feel good."

"So you just showed up to take her shift, huh?"

"That's right," Susan said. "That's what friends do. You know anything about that?"

"Was she alone?"

"I don't remember."

"Don't fuck me around here or I'll go out of my way to make your life miserable. Where and when did she go?"

"I'm making a complaint on you."

"Was she alone?"

"I said I don't know."

Bobby Lee turned away and said over his shoulder as he went for his car, "You and me, Susan, we're not through yet. I'll be back to see you."

He got back in the car and accelerated away. Josie lived in the Lake/Lyndale neighborhood, only a short drive away. He motored down the streets till he found the address he was looking for, right off of Lyndale. It was a borderline neighborhood, with a few dealers in nearby Powderhorn Park that could make a squad, unmarked or not, from a block away. He didn't bother looking for a parking spot; he just pulled up in the space beside a fire hydrant and got out to walk the three houses down to the address. He saw her name on the buzzer for the fourth apartment, which made it one of the top two apartments. He hit the buzzer and leaned on it. He heard footsteps upstairs and he saw through the glass of the front door that Josie was standing at the top of the stairwell, looking down at him. She hesitated for a long moment, then came down and opened the door.

"It's a wonder you still have glass in the door, what with this neighborhood," Bobby Lee said. "Did you forget about our little appointment?"

"No," Josie said. There was resignation and something else in her voice. "I didn't forget."

"Your friend didn't pass on your message. If you left one."

"Don't get her in trouble, she's not any part of this."

"Let's go upstairs and talk."

Josie led the way up the stairs, her arms still tightly crossed on her chest as though she were clinging to herself. She stopped before the apartment door, the tarnished brass 4 slightly askew.

"Go ahead," she said. "He's been waiting for you."

"He?" Bobby Lee said, instantly alert. "Who?"

She pushed the door open and stood to one side.

"Him."

Bobby Lee peered cautiously around the door, one hand on his holstered pistol. Simon Oberstar sat in a battered old armchair facing the door, his coat open and his tie angled across his big belly.

"Come in, Bobby Lee. We've got a lot to talk about."

"What are you doing here?" Bobby Lee said.

"Waiting for you," Oberstar said. "Come in and shut the door."

Bobby Lee came in, cautious as a cat, one hand hovering near his weapon, and Josie shut the door behind him and quietly turned the lock.

"Josie," Oberstar said. "Go in the bedroom and wait for me there."

Josie hurried through the front room, not looking at either of the men, into a back room. She shut the door lightly behind her as though she didn't want to draw any attention to herself.

"We've got a problem, Bobby," Oberstar said.

"What is going on here, Obi?"

"Think it through, Bobby Lee. I know you know."

"A piece of ass is one thing. This is another."

"What do you know?"

"Just what got me here, Obi. What's going on?"

"I love her, Bobby. I can't let you do anything that will hurt her."

It suddenly became clear to Bobby Lee and it was as though someone had lowered a clear glass jar over him, neatly cutting him off from the rest of the world but preserving his vision.

"Obi," he said softly. "Obi, what are you into?"

"It's the money, Bobby. That's what it was always about. Money. I needed some, so did the others. You know how hard it is, to spend for private schools for your kids because their mother is gone? To put kids through college today? You don't know yet, but you will. Nicky is a smart kid and you're going to want the best for him. And you'll find a way to get it for him because that's what fathers do for their children, they find a way to make the best for them."

Oberstar's eyes gleamed and filled. He brushed at his face.

"I'm ashamed, Bobby," he said. "Of what I've done and what I let happen. There's no excuse for it and I know it now, knew it all along. But I can't let it go on any longer, I can't let Josie get caught up in this too."

"Simon, listen to me," Bobby Lee said. "This isn't about her, never was about her. You need to tell me what you've done. What do you have to do with the killings? I don't care about the money, I don't care about that, what I want is the killer. Tell me you're not part of that. Tell me you don't know who the guy is, Obi."

"I don't know who it is, Bobby . . . what are you going to do?"

Bobby Lee felt as though someone had cut him open and his feelings and thoughts were running out to spill at his feet.

"I don't know what to do," he said. "I don't know what to say."

"We can find this guy together, you and me," Oberstar said, hope in his voice. "But we got to make sure he doesn't talk . . . you and me, we can finish it on the street, we won't have to hurt other cops, we can leave me and Josie out of it. That's what you want, that's what I want, right? We want the killer, everything else, I swear to you on my wife's grave, I can stop it and clean it all up. But we got to do this together, Bobby. Please, for me. For all I've done and been for you these years, help me with this. I can get through it if you'll only help me."

For Bobby Lee it was as if a movie were playing pictures from the past over the shattered visage of his friend and mentor: Bobby graduating from the academy with a first in pistol shooting, Oberstar, his proud instructor, beside him; walking a beat on the North Side with Oberstar; Obi pinning Bobby's detective shield on; Angie's funeral, where Bobby had held his friend close while he wept and wept . . . and over all of that the image of Madison Simmons hung like a butchered deer in season.

"Tell me what happened, Obi," Bobby Lee said. Resignation and sadness thickened his voice. "Tell me how we got to this place."

"You know how I got here," Oberstar said, self-disgust and anger in his voice. "I got kids to look out for. They weren't selling anything here, they were just washing the money. I had to take out a second and then a third mortgage for the kids . . . I got in over my head, I could of lost my house, the kids would have had to drop out. You got a child, you know what that's like . . . you do what you got to do to make sure they're taken care of. They offered me a great consolidation mortgage and I took it."

Oberstar sighed heavily and fell in on himself, diminished in the armchair.

"That's how they set the hook," he said. "They get you with something easy, then they start asking your advice about things, then they ask for some little favor like hey, would I talk to Vice for them, lighten up the enforcement at the club, or did I know somebody who could put in a word with the Liquor Board. That's how it starts."

He looked back through the apartment to the closed door where Josie waited in silence.

"And this is how it ends. Do I got to eat my gun here to make this go away? Are you going to do that to me?"

"No," Bobby Lee said. "I'm not going to do that to you. But you're going to tell me what I want to know. Everything. And then I'm taking down the killer. Then you and I are going to figure out where else we go with this."

"Bobby . . ."

"Tell me," Bobby Lee said. There was no mercy in his voice. He settled himself on the thin-cushioned couch and put his notebook on his knee. "Tell me the story."

It was well past midnight when Oberstar finished and Bobby put away his notes. He was heartsick. Oberstar had broken down several times, wept out loud in braying cries that brought Josie rushing out of the bedroom to him. Each time he sent her back into the bedroom and kept up the story. Bobby Lee didn't know what to do. He tried to force his brain to work, but he kept turning over images from the past in his mind over and over again. Oberstar crying had torn a hole in him and all the images of his past seemed tainted by this mockery of the man he loved and respected.

Oberstar sat, broken, in the chair, his big shoulders slumping forward, his back curved like a question mark. He wouldn't look at Bobby.

Bobby wanted to be home in bed with his wife, to hear the soft breathing of his child safe in his bed, to be in the embrace of everything he called family.

That's what he wanted now.

But he couldn't leave Oberstar alone like this.

"Let's go, Simon," he said softly. "You can come home with me."

"I can't," Oberstar said in a broken voice.

"Just come on," Bobby Lee said. He stood and took his friend by the arm, pulled him unwillingly to his feet. "I don't want you to stay here tonight. Come home with me, Simon."

"I don't want Max to see me like this," Oberstar said.

"She'll be asleep," Bobby Lee said. "Tomorrow we'll work things out. I don't want you to stay here."

"I'll be fine with Josie."

"Please, Simon. Just come with me."

Oberstar's head drooped and he looked only at his feet. He turned away and went back to the bedroom where Josie was, and they exchanged a few words. Bobby Lee heard her asking "Why?" and Simon's muttered response. Then Oberstar came back and said, "Okay, Bobby. We can go now."

Oberstar followed Bobby out to the car like an obedient child and waited for Bobby to open the car door and then close it after him. Bobby Lee got in and started the car, then pulled away from the curb and began to carefully navigate the dark streets. The two men drove in silence. It seemed as though there was a great fog in front of Bobby's eyes and he found himself crying silently in the car, tears rolling down his face and he couldn't make them stop. No time at all seemed to pass as he rolled through the night, and still there wasn't a word passed between the two men, each trapped in a vision of the past and the harsh reality of the present. Soon he was in his driveway, turning off the lights and coasting the car into place as was his habit when he came home late, so as not to wake Max and Nicky with the lights and engine.

The house was dark except for the porch light; Max always kept the light on for him.

"It's my job," she said. "To keep the lights on for you."

The two of them got out of the car and Oberstar fell in behind Bobby Lee as they walked to the door. Bobby Lee unlocked the front door and led the two of them into the warmth of the house. He stood there for a moment, then touched the front room light switch. The light came on and illuminated Alfie Woodard sitting in Bobby's big armchair.

"Cheers, mate," Alfie said.

Bobby Lee froze and Oberstar stood there with his mouth gaped wide.

"Max! Nicky!" Bobby Lee shouted.

"Sorry, mate," Alfie said. "It was only business."

Bobby went for his gun the same instant Alfie raised his.

MARCUS WYNNE

He hadn't expected to end up bedding Kativa, but like so many other things in Charley's life, events came to a conclusion that surprised him. She was waiting for him in her warm, lavishly decorated apartment. Soft jazz played, a Coltrane retrospective, and she handed him a glass of white South African wine.

"From Cape Town," she said. "Where my family is from."

It took only a few minutes of stilted conversation before they set aside their nervous babble and reached for each other. She took him by the hand and led him into the bedroom and the big bed that filled the room.

The first time was frantic and urgent.

"That one was for me," Charley said. The next time he went slower and concentrated only on pleasing her. After, she lay curled in the crook of his arm, her arm thrown across his chest, her hair in a pretty disarray across his arm and the pillow.

"So much for not poaching my friend's boyfriend," she said.

Charley shifted uncomfortably. "Mara never claimed exclusive rights. Let's not talk about that."

"As you like," Kativa said lightly. "Would you like another glass of the Zinfandel?"

"Yes," Charley said. "I would."

She slipped out from beneath his arm and pulled on a silk robe that clung to the curves of her body and went out of the bedroom. She returned with the wine bottle and both glasses. She filled one glass and handed it to him.

"Here we are," she said.

"Thank you."

"The pleasure is all mine," she said, smiling.

She let the robe fall and then slipped back into bed, holding her wineglass with two fingers. They drank the icy Zinfandel in silence.

"Have you thought of anything else about those pictures?" he said.

Kativa looked startled. "That's a funny question for now," she said. "Or are you just using my body to see if you get better answers?"

"Yes, and yes," Charley said, grinning into his wineglass.

Kativa laughed. "Oh, you are a hateful man. No, I haven't thought much about it."

"I can't get it out of my mind. Even when I close my eyes, I see that image. I even dream about it."

"You're not thinking of it now, are you?"

Charley shifted again. "Yes, I was. Some."

Kativa untangled herself and sat with her back up against the headboard. "That could be a source of worry for you," she said.

"Why?"

"When I was in Quinkin country I asked a lot of questions about the magic. It's hard to get answers, but I did get some good stories. One of the signs that a sorcerer is working on you is obsessive thoughts and dreams. You see, the sorcerer doesn't want you to know you're being spelled until it's too late to do anything about it. But it's always a symptom, having the same images and recurrent thoughts in your dreams."

Charley looked at her with amazement. "You mean to tell me you think I'm the target of a spell?"

"Not necessarily you in particular," Kativa said seriously. "But anytime you look at those images, you could be inviting Anurra into the place of your spirit. That's what Aboriginal magic is about: putting influence from one powerful person into another person."

"I don't think that's it," Charley said. "I'm just puzzling out what would make a man act in such a fashion."

"That's your civilized mind, Charley. There's a part of your brain that's not so civilized that doesn't agree."

Charley shifted to one side to look at her.

"That's an unusual thing to say," he said.

"Why?" she said. "You know that it's true."

"I do wonder about it . . ."

Kativa settled back and toyed with her wineglass.

"Tell me what your dreams are like," she said.

"There's one in particular I've had," he said. "I'm in the dark, it's night, and I'm in a hilly country with thick shrub brush. I'm climbing a hill, and there are big slabs of stone fallen all around making crevices and caves. I'm chasing Anurra, but somehow he gets behind me and then he's chasing me . . . I'm alone, but sometimes there are shadows around me, and some of them are speaking to me, and others are talking about me, and most of them are trying to help me but some are trying to trick me into listening to them. I always get the sense that there are many, many others just watching to see what happens.

"I'm in this rock depression, so deep it's like a big bowl or the Coliseum in Rome. The seats are filled with dark spirits watching me and Anurra fight with each other, and some of the spirits are cheering for him and some of them are cheering for me and some are just cheering because they love to watch the fight."

Kativa's eyes were large and round, liquid in the dim light. "How do your dreams end?"

Charley shrugged. "I always wake up," he said. "It feels like I miss the ending. Each time it seems that the figure of Anurra gets bigger and stronger . . . but so do I."

"A bush doctor would say that both of you are going to meet someday."

"Maybe."

"Is that why you're wearing a gun? You said you weren't a police officer . . ."

"I'm not," Charley said. "I don't know why I put it on tonight . . . I just felt as though I should be prepared."

"Do you have to go?"

"Yes."

"Where are you going?"

"I need to talk to my friend, he's the lead investigator. I told him I'd come by. I wasn't counting on this."

She laughed. "On this? Either was I. But I won't keep you. Will your friend still be up?"

Charley glanced at the clock. It was after midnight.

"I'll drive by and see if the lights are on," he said. "I was supposed to be there earlier and visit with his wife, she stays up late. Bobby Lee is probably still up."

"Do you want to call?"

"No, his son will be asleep and I don't want to wake him. I'll just drive by."

Charley slipped out of bed and picked up his clothes from the floor. He quickly dressed, taking a few extra moments to properly seat and position his holster before dropping his shirttails over it and shrugging into his bomber jacket.

"The well-dressed gunman," Kativa said. "I must say the ensemble suits you."

"I'll call you tomorrow," Charley said.

"Please do," she said. She slipped on her robe and walked him to the front door. They lingered in a good-bye kiss, and then she said, "Be careful."

Charley left the building and stood outside for a moment. He stared up at the night sky and listened to the hum of traffic, the chirp of crickets, the single solitary slam of a car door somewhere down the street.

He felt as though he needed to hurry.

Alfie stood over the two downed men. The big older one was done for, but the other still struggled for breath and stretched out one hand to claw for the big stainless-steel automatic he'd dropped. A tough fighter, this one, still able to draw after taking two rounds to the chest. Someone to respect.

MARCUS WYNNE

Alfie looked at the wall clock and calculated time and distance to the airport. He didn't have time for the ritual. At least not the full ceremony.

"Well, what do you think, mate?" Alfie said to the dying man on the floor. "Should I take a little time with you?"

Charley got into his car, backed out of the parking spot carefully, then drove down Forty-third Street to the parkway and followed it around toward his apartment. He'd meant to stop and pick up his folder of notes, but instead he drove right past. It wasn't a long drive to Bobby Lee's, but Charley felt as though there was an elastic band stretched between him and Bobby Lee, and that the band was stretched to its limit and was just now rebounding and pulling him forward with ever-increasing speed. At each stoplight and stop sign, he weighed the chance of getting caught against just running the light. He couldn't calm himself down.

Something was wrong.

Alfie dragged Bobby Lee by his heels a short distance away from the body of Simon Oberstar.

"Just a little bit," Alfie said. "You deserve that."

Bobby Lee spat up blood as he struggled to speak. He flailed feebly with one hand.

"Take it easy, mate," Alfie said. "It'll be all over in just a tick."

Charley turned down Hilow Road. Bobby Lee's house sat in the end cul-de-sac of Hilow Court. He saw Bobby Lee's squad in the driveway. The porch and front room lights were on.

Why was he rushing?

He turned off his headlights and eased his car to the curb one house short of Bobby Lee's, even though there was plenty of space in the driveway. He squeezed out of the car quickly to minimize the momentary flare from the interior light, then stood in the street and tasted the night air, sniffing for trouble.

Something compelled him forward, the Glock in his hand without even thinking about it, not even pausing to call for help because he knew and felt the urgency of need, right now, and the door was there and he didn't try the handle he just kicked hard and came to a bone-jarring stop at the heavy reinforced door, so he turned the handle and entered violently, button hooking through the doorway and around the open door, quick scanning over the sights of his pistol as he had done so many times in the killing house at Harvey's Point, so strange to be doing it in his friend's front room, and he saw Simon Oberstar lying on his back, two holes in his chest, and Bobby Lee struggling under the foot of a dark-skinned man in biker leathers and Charley put his sights on the black leather and pressed the trigger twice quickly, throwing two rounds at the figure who wasn't there anymore...

Where?

"Oi, mate!" the dark man shouted. Charley was already rolling forward, catching himself as he tripped over Bobby Lee, turning his fall into a forward shoulder roll that took him across the floor and the minimal cover of the heavy oak dining-room table. He kicked hard and knocked the table over, taking momentary cover behind it.

Crack!

The table split as heavy caliber bullets bit into it. Then there was the pause Charley was waiting for as his opponent stopped to reload his pistol. Charley inched out from behind the table and saw one knee and booted foot protruding from the edge of the dining-room doorway, just beyond where Bobby Lee lay. Charley aligned his sights with all the speed he could muster and fired two quick shots and was rewarded with a loud "Fuck!" and the sound of scrambling and falling.

That was his cue.

He speedloaded the Glock, letting the nearly empty magazine fall to the floor while he slapped another ten rounds in, then he stood up and ran toward the dining-room doorway, every step a shot in cadence, chewing up the edge of the doorwell as he shot through the wall at his opponent. He moved cautiously around the corner, exposing only his pistol muzzle and his eye as he worked around the corner and saw a blood trail that led farther back into the house.

"Maxine! Nicky! It's Charley!" he shouted.

MARCUS WYNNE

206

There was only the ringing in his ears.

He knelt beside the still figure of Bobby Lee. Blood pooled beneath him. Charley touched his neck and felt a faint and thready beat. Charley picked up Bobby's pistol and stuck it in the back of his pants as a spare and reloaded the Glock again.

"Hang on, bud," he said softly.

He inched down the hallway toward the back of the house. His every sense was carefully attuned to the nuance of movement in the house: faint breezes, the hum of the furnace, the smell of blood and gunsmoke, the tears welling in his eyes as he fought back the urge to run back to his friend's side, his jaw tense as he bit down the urge to run madly through the house and find the dark man.

To kill the dark man.

That's what was important and he needed to move slowly to do that.

Charley paused beside the half-opened door to the room that doubled as a study and a media room, a haven for Bobby Lee's big-screen television and little Nicky's Nintendo system. Never leave an uncleared room behind you; that rule was cast in stone. Charley nudged the door open farther with his foot and inched around, his weapon extended, staying well back from the open door as he slowly cleared the dimly lit room. The door opened another foot and then stopped. Charley looked down and saw the slim, delicate fingers of Maxine's hand curled limply, as though she were cupping something that had flown away.

Charley fought harder than he had ever fought before to control the feelings that roared up in him. He compressed them all into a tight little ball and then put the ball in a box and put the box on a shelf in his head. He entered the room violently, button hooking again, and clearing the room.

Maxine must have been sitting in the big armchair, now tipped over on its back. The television was still on, with the sound off. She had fought; Charley saw the bloody streaks on one hand. Little Nicky was half under her, boneless and limp, almost as if he were sleeping, and thankfully Charley couldn't see the boy's face, pressed up against his dead mother's body.

"Oh, no," Charley keened. "Oh, no."

He put it away, and forced himself to kneel and touch each of the thin necks even though he knew what he would find. Nothing, not even a stirring, though they were both still warm.

He stood up and stepped away from them, something dead inside him and something else springing to life, something he had never felt before, a pure clean surge of hot hatred, a dark brightness at his center focused on one thing and one thing only: killing the man who'd done this.

Where was he?

Charley went back into the hallway and listened carefully. His hearing was returning after the crash and bang of shots from earlier. His vision seemed even more acute than usual. Everything he looked at was recorded like a snapshot, framed in the viewfinder of his mind, never to be forgotten. At the end of the hallway was a door that led to the garage and then the last door, which opened into the backyard. The blood trail went that way.

Charley felt a sudden foreboding and he ran forward recklessly, his pistol extended, to the door that opened out into the yard. He quick peeked out the door, exited violently, and took cover behind the old unused propane tank beside the back steps.

Nothing.

He came out in the hunt, his pistol extended, its muzzle tracking wherever his eyes went.

Nothing beside the garage.

Nothing beside the big tree.

From a few houses away, he heard a motorcycle kick into life. And over it, a loud sound: "Wonk! Wonk!" and then the sound of the motorcycle revving into the distance.

Charley ran back into the house, picked up the phone.
Dead.

He ran back to the front room, knelt beside Bobby Lee.
Dead.

His pistol dangling limp in his hand, he heard the sound of sirens far off and growing, and he went outside to meet them.

MARCUS WYNNE

PART 3

Charley sat slumped on the rear bumper of a squad car and watched the bodies being carried out now that the Forensics Unit had completed the crime scene survey. Tears welled in his eyes when he saw the final gurney come out, the one with a small body hidden by the big black bag, so tiny a shape. He spent more hours being interviewed by the other detectives, their intensity masking the rage they all felt at having two of their own go down. He had to give up his Glock and spare magazines to the investigators. But finally they let him go, and he got into his car.

He drove carefully, just under the speed limit, all the way to his apartment. It was almost dawn, and the light was glimmering in the east and thinning the dark that hung over the city. There was a faint fog in Linden Hills, and the streetlamps seemed to flicker and glow like candles in the damp haze. It reminded him of stories he'd read about old London, with the lamplighters and the foggy streets barely lit by the candle lamps.

He parked in the lot behind the building and slowly made his way up the stairs, the sound of his footsteps an indictment, and he was careful not to let any of the night's images come up from where he had carefully put them away. He didn't want to see those images anymore.

Charley let himself quietly into his apartment and locked the door behind him, then went into the kitchen and took down a bottle of Bushmill's Irish whiskey that Bobby Lee had bought him as a birthday present a few months back. They'd barely tapped it, and it became a joke between them as they laughed, remembering the time in their youth when they'd gone through a bottle of Bush a night.

They'd only shared a few drinks out of it that night, and none since then.

Charley took a tumbler and filled it with ice, blinking in the sudden harsh light of the refrigerator as he filled the tumbler to the brim with whiskey. He sat in his armchair, the bottle close at hand, and took a long hard swallow that burned its way into his gut. He concentrated on that feeling and nothing else, as though the fire of the whiskey would wash something clean inside him.

But he'd need more than whiskey for that. Charley took careful stock of himself, noting his huge anger, carefully banked, and just touched on the terrible sense of loss and sadness that lurked behind the anger. Anger was best put to use, and he'd have to think clearly how to put his to use. The dark man had gotten away for now.

But only for now.

Charley sat in his chair and drank himself to sleep as the early morning light burned away the lingering fog outside and cast long shadows in the street.

Deep in a whiskey sleep, Charley dreamed:

. . . walking, walking, in hilly country where the hills were the color of tan, marked out with dark barked trees whose branches reached like thin fingers toward the blue expanse of sky . . . the tan of the ground knife-edged dry grasses, the bark of the trees, close up, gnarled and worn like the skin of an old woman's breast and the trees evenly spaced like the ranks of a hidden army.

Charley walking, looking, but not alone . . . Kativa is with him, magnificent in her nakedness, her full breasts bouncing with each stride and Charley seized by a sudden pang of lust and an embarrassing erection that poked the front of his loincloth. He's carrying a spear in one hand, and they are hunting . . .

Hunting . . .

They are walking toward the hills where sandstone escarpments have tumbled like children's blocks and lay jumbled like small sticks after a storm.

The crevices and caves between the rocks look small from a distance but they steadily grow larger as the two of them travel toward it, the silence between them seems natural, as though they are connected in some silent way.

There is a clearing where the trees don't go, and there are many chest-high pillars of mud, the nests of termites caulked and grown almost to the height of a man. One of them is directly in front of Charley and he is drawn toward it, stands before it. Slowly, bits of baked clay flake from the top of the termite's hill. Charley raised his spear, but not in fear—in recognition.

The clay flakes away and a big portion of the mound cracks in two and falls, one piece forward to land at Charley's feet, the other falling back behind the mound. The piece at Charley's feet looks like a mask, and when Charley looks up he sees Bobby Lee, his head and face covered with matted dried clay, his eyes closed . . .

But now they open, and they are black, blacker than the black of embalmed eyes, but Charley knows that he can see, his friend is dreaming on the other side of the Dreamtime and this is the message:

"He's here, Charley," Bobby Lee's voice whispers in Charley's head. The dead lips don't move, but the dead eyes seem to gleam as though something were inhabiting them. "In these hills in the Quinkin country. She can take you to them."

Charley is silent as he looks at Kativa, who stands with her back to the mound, shivering in fear.

"The two of you together," Bobby Lee's voice said. "Then you can kill him, Charley, strike him down. Strike him down first and you will save her and revenge me. Kill him for all of us."

There were two smaller mounds nearby. Both of them flaked and broke open and one was Maxine and the other was Nicky. Maxine's eyes opened and she said, "I always loved you, Charley." Little Nicky's eyes rolled open and he said, "Please, Uncle Charley, I'm so cold . . . take me with you, I don't want to stay here . . ."

"This is where we are, Charley," Bobby Lee said. "Until you've killed the Quinkin."

Charley awoke with a shout, reaching for where his pistol would have been holstered, fumbling for a long moment until he remembered where he was and that his pistol was in the evidence locker downtown at Police Headquarters.

"God," he said. His voice trembled.

The whiskey bottle was almost done, and he had the foggiest of hangovers to deal with right now. He went into the bathroom and washed his face, brushed his teeth and gargled, then picked up the phone and called Kativa as he stared out the window at the busy street below.

"Hello?" Kativa said.

"It's Charley," he said. "You heard about last night?"

"It was on the news this morning," she said. "I'm so sorry, Charley. I tried calling but there was no answer and the machine didn't pick up."

"I didn't get in till about four this morning."

"Have you eaten?"

"No."

"Would you like me to bring something over?"

"That would be good," Charley said. "I need to talk to you."

"I can come right over."

"Do that. Maybe you could stop and pick up some sandwiches. Is your passport current?"

"Yes, why?"

"That's something I need to talk to you about."

"I'll be right over."

Charley hung up the phone, then went to the table that served as his desk and took out a battered address book. He flipped through several pages till he found the name he was looking for. He let his finger rest on the name for a moment, then picked up the phone and dialed a number in northern Virginia. The phone rang twice and then was answered by a cool male voice that said, "Extension 3067."

"Is Walker there?" Charley said.

"Yes. May I tell him who's calling?"

"Charley Payne."

"One moment, Mr. Payne."

There was a long pause on hold, then the phone clicked and the slight southern drawl of Terry Walker's voice came through.

"This is Walker."

"Terry? It's Charley Payne."

"That's what I heard, Charley Payne, the one and only major pain himself. How you doing, Charley? Still in Minneapolis, I see."

"That's where I be, brother."

"So what's up? Come to your senses? Ready to return to the job you were born to do? Or you just want to borrow some money for more film?"

"I need a favor, Terry. A big one."

The other man's voice dropped a tone. "What are you talking about, Charley? You in some trouble?"

"No. I'm not. But I need help on something. Can you talk?"

"Sure, that's the advantage of being a big muckety muck. I can do whatever I want."

"I need a check on all noncommercial aircraft that departed from Minneapolis and any other airport within a fifty-mile radius. Private aircraft with a capability for transoceanic travel. Manifests, times of departure."

"That is a big favor, Charley. What do you need it for?"

"You remember my friend Bobby Lee?"

"Sure, the super-duper paratrooper you ran with. Good guy, we had beers together in Tyson's Corner once when he was out, remember?"

"Somebody murdered him and his family last night," Charley said. He cleared his throat. "That somebody is an Australian Aborigine with some operator training. I think he flew out of here last night. There's no way for a guy as distinctive-looking as this one to have slipped away unless he flew out."

There was a long silence on the other end of the line.

"You say he's an Australian Aborigine," Walker said. "Trained as an operator, working in Minneapolis? How do you know all this?"

"I got some lead into him last night."

Another long silence and then Walker said, "Charley, I can see we need to talk. Stay at the phone you're at and I'll call you back shortly."

"Roger that, Terry."

"I'll be back to you in just a minute."

Charley replaced the phone in its cradle. Fifteen minutes passed and then the phone rang.

"Okay, Charles, listen up," Terry Walker said. "You're into something bigger than you may realize. What did your friend have to do with this Australian?"

"He was investigating the Australian as the prime suspect in a series of murders here . . . nutcase murders. The guy was eating people."

"Jesus, that's an MO you'll never forget. It fits into something else. You're not inside, Charley, and I can't give you all that I've got. But I'll tell you if you get anything on this guy, we'd be interested in what you have to say."

"I'm not going to be run, Terry. I told you what I need. If you can't do it, then don't jerk me around."

"I'm not jerking you around. It will take me a little longer to get that info for you. I'll tell you this, if he got to a plane, he'll be heading back down under, in Queensland."

"In the Laura bush country?"

Terry Walker said calmly, "You knew that?"

"I had a hunch."

"That's a damn sight more than a hunch. Who do I talk to about the investigation out there?"

Charley told him and Walker said, "I'll be talking to him. You still a contract photographer?"

"You're current on me, Terry. What are you not telling me?"

"I'm not telling you that we've had a long-time interest in a guy who fits your description and that it has to do with some controlled substances. I'm also not telling you that we have no record of him working in the States, but we've seen that unmistakable signature of his in some incidents overseas. And I'll tell you, straight out, that you're better off staying way the hell away from this character."

"The plane information?"

"I'm working on it with FAA."

"If I were to find something, say overseas, who would I call?"

"Call this number: 1-888-555-3214 and ask for me by name. That's good from overseas, night or day. All you got to do is ask for me by name."

"Thanks, Terry."

"I owe you for this one, Charley. Big time. Stay in touch and call me if you get anything. I'll have that FAA information for you shortly. Will you be at this number?"

"Standing by."

"I worry when you start in on that old military jargon, Charles. Means you're slipping on your game face. Don't try to run this alone— stay out of it. We've got people looking into it and you'll be contacted if you can help. You're not that far outside. You could probably use the money, right?"

"I'm through there and you know it," Charley said gently. "And I'd rather take pictures. Thanks for the brief, Terry. I'll wait for your call."

"I'm sorry about Bobby Lee, Charley."

"Thanks, Terry."

Charley replaced the telephone and settled back to wait.

217

3.2

Alfie Woodard and Jay Burrell sat out on the wooden deck that ringed Burrell's house on the beach in Cairns. The tropical sun lay heavy on the water; even in the shade it was in the high eighties and muggy. Both men wore oversized aloha shirts and baggy shorts that reached to their knees. Alfie's lower left leg was heavily bandaged.

Burrell pointed at Alfie's bandages and said, "That was a serious mistake."

"No arguing that, mate," Alfie said. "Balls up all round. Nothing to be done about it now."

"Your leg?"

"Better. The lad that came in after me, he was a serious sort. Professional. Didn't expect the likes of him coming in after me."

"It won't hurt for you to drop out of sight for a while. I assume you're going up to Laura?"

"Be the best thing for me to go bush for a while and that's what I need to do."

"I need to have a way to get hold of you if things happen."

Alfie laughed. "You still don't have it sorted, do you, mate? It's just like the bloody pop tune. Just call my name and I'll be there."

Burrell regarded him for a long moment, then shrugged. "I'll call and leave a message with your friend at the Laura bar. You'll check in there from time to time?"

"That'll work, mate. Me pal Peter will take notes."

"I know."

"Right then."

Alfie stood up and stretched, favoring his injured leg. A big heavily muscled white man in his early twenties came out the sliding-glass door behind the two men.

"Heya, mate," Alfie said to the man, who ignored him and said to Burrell, "You got something for me, boss?"

"Not yet, young Tim," Burrell said. "You'll have to wait your turn. Alfie here has everything sorted, so you won't be making any trips to the States soon."

"That's not what I heard," Tim said, still deliberately ignoring Alfie and speaking only to Burrell. "Heard it was a proper cock-up."

Alfie laughed out loud and said, "Where do you find these arseholes, Jay? The local pub?"

Tim turned and flexed in Alfie's direction. "I'd mind yourself, blackie."

Alfie brushed past Tim to get into the house. "Blackie?" he said, laughing. "See you later, china plate."

"I hate that black bastard," Tim said.

"I wouldn't muck about with him," Burrell said. "Alfie's got a bit more blood on his hands than you. Don't let that Abo bush doctor bit fool you—he's as good as it gets."

"I wouldn't have made the mess he made."

"What's done is done. You'll get your chance." Burrell paused. "Did you go over the figures on the latest shipments?"

"Right, then."

"What's it look like?"

"The U.S. interdiction effort is focused on the south borders. Our operations in Aruba are under heavy surveillance and we've lost several shipments to the Coast Guard. I think the idea of moving the product way north and then into the States through Canada and down will be the best way to go. Minneapolis would have been a good place if it hadn't been so mucked up by your friend. We can bring product into the smaller uncontrolled airfields, disguise some shipments as small hunting charters. If we keep shipping it up and off-loading it in Canada and then taking it down, we can minimize our losses."

MARCUS WYNNE

Burrell yawned and hid it behind one hand. "You're a quick study, Tim. Keep up the good. I'm going to check out the surf."

"Right, boss." Tim watched Burrell walk down to the beach, then went into the house. He stood at the front door and watched Alfie walk away toward town.

"Bloody bastard," Tim said softly. "I'll see to you one day."

Alfie walked up to the side of a hulking four-ton, six-wheeled all-terrain vehicle parked outside a grocery store. A logo of a mountain with an all-terrain vehicle superimposed was stenciled on the side, just above the words "Adventure Company." The Adventure Company ran a series of tours and four-wheel drive expeditions into the northernmost parts of Queensland and the Cape York Peninsula. The big truck made a weekly trip up to the Jowalbinna bush camp in the foothills of the Laura River country where Alfie came from. Catching a ride with the driver was the best way to get deep into the country and the driver stopped off in Laura, where Alfie lived in the hills outside the town limits.

Alfie thumped the side of the Oka truck and greeted the driver, a young, lean, and wiry white man whose cotton shirt and shorts hung on him like oversized flags, "We ready to go, mate?"

"Just a tick, mate. Then we'll go," the driver said. "You in a hurry to go bush, are you?"

"Just to get the hell out of Cairns."

"It's changed, hasn't it?"

"Not the place it used to be."

"You that old? You look younger."

"It's clean living, the proper diet, and enough beer, mate."

The two men laughed. Now that he was heading back to his country, Alfie's look had changed. He'd swapped out his motorcycle leathers for battered khaki shirt and pants, light boots and a bush hat. With his faded and frayed canvas carryall, he looked like any other Aboriginal on the streets of Cairns. Coming back required a change in his attitude, something he reflected in his posture, which drooped as he drew into himself. There was still plenty of prejudice against the Aborigines in town, some overt, most covert unless he wandered by one of the bars when a group of workingmen were drinking. Then Alfie slipped into a long familiar state as effortlessly as stepping into his pants in the morning, a state where the words and the looks slid off an invisible sphere he kept round himself. It was something he'd learned early on, and his experiments in puri-puri had taught him how to fine-tune the art of psychic self-defense. He visualized a sphere around himself and it was as though his hearing was turned down, and he held the power he possessed in check so as not to lash out at the ignorant around him. He just turned away inward from the external fray and let himself settle in the light trance of Dreamtime wandering and let his mind go where it would.

"Let's hit the frog and toad, mate," the driver said, bringing Alfie up out of his reverie. Alfie climbed into the back of the vehicle and the driver's assistant, a quiet young girl, got into the front passenger seat beside the driver. Alfie was grateful for the din and grind of the engine and the two whites' disinclination to speak. It gave him the opportunity to drop into a light trance and begin again the communion he felt with the ancestor spirits who guided him. The outer world seemed dimmer and dimmer as they drove through the outskirts of Cairns and followed the highway north to Port Douglas, where they picked up a small family doing the Jowalbinna tour, and continued on through Mossman and up the long highway to Laura.

When they picked up the family, Alfie moved to the back of the vehicle and became even quieter, smiling and nodding at the nervous American family's attempt to make conversation. It suited him to do so, for each mile north and closer to his home and his ancestral lands caused him to shed the layers of acculturation he wore like too many layers of clothes. When he was at home, it was as though he were several people. One part of him was the experienced special operator, who read the lines of the land like a schematic for a gunfight; another part was the young Aboriginal boy who'd wandered in these hills in a time he couldn't consciously remember; another was the dark puri-puri master who looked for the slanted escarpments where the magic images could be drawn, and yet another part, a part that rarely surfaced, was the quiet Alfie Woodard who enjoyed the sense of coming home. The role he played for Jay Burrell, that of the cocky Aussie who looked like a rock musician, that part disappeared when he went home. It was a mask he wore to hide his secret self away. The principle of multiple layers the SAS had taught him, to disguise real purpose within layer upon layer of deception, seemed so natural to him since he'd applied it to all the aspects of his life.

They drove along the winding highway that followed the coastline and then headed inland before they came to the dusty little town of Laura and its single long street dominated by the Quinkin Bar and Hotel. Alfie got out of the vehicle, nodding his thanks to the driver, hoisted his battered canvas carryall, and walked away. He stopped in the bar and nodded to the big, quiet white man behind the bar.

"G'day, Peter," Alfie said. "Got any mail for me?"

"Not a thing," Peter said.

"Thanks, then."

"Ta."

Alfie stepped out onto the porch. The sun blazed, a weight on his hat and shoulders. Alfie took off his shoes and stepped down into the dirt and wiggled his toes.

He was almost home.

He walked alongside the road for a while, enjoying the feel of dirt beneath his feet, then followed a dirt track that branched off from the main road. There were some manufactured homes where members of the Ang-Gnarra tribal group still lived. He passed small black children playing in the dust, and fat tired women who sat idly on the steps and watched him. Several of them called to their children when they saw him coming and took the children inside. There was one group of men he passed, a few elders and some younger men. He recognized several of them as Law Men who kept tabs on the younger men and punished them when necessary. He'd taken a spear in the leg from one of them himself when he'd come back here on leave and gotten himself good and drunk. It was an old punishment, but a good one. No more humbug out of him after that.

They all knew him for what he was, which was why no one spoke to him or greeted him after his periodic absences. They'd never mention it to a white man and they discussed it only among themselves. No one approached him for help with love magic or improvement spells, no one asked him to prognosticate for them, few of them dared to acknowledge him.

Sometimes Alfie wished they would.

It was a dark and lonely path he'd chosen, and here, in the place he most wished to be accepted, it was the one path that led him far away from everyone.

But what was he missing? Drunken camaraderie with other drunks? A fat and miserable wife, squalling children? He'd chosen a path to power and that was important to remember. He walked through the settlement and let their gazes beat on his dusty shirt like silent blows. He left the homes behind and, after another mile, the dirt track began to fade out as he climbed the hills, watching for snakes as he set his hardened feet carefully among the stones. He walked through a natural amphitheater, a strange circular place where the trees would not grow. There were many termite hills there, many of them the height of a man's chest. In the old times, a dead Aborigine would be put into the termite mounds until only his bones remained. Then the bones would be laid to rest in his ancestral home.

Alfie had put his mentor Ralph into one, then collected his bones at the end of the dry season and kept them in the cave he called home. This was his songline, his walkabout path, and he came this way every time he returned from a job. The walking, the sun, the dust beneath his feet, the rough sandstone that ground beneath the calluses of his feet, they all seemed to wash something out of him, leaving him feeling free and clear.

Free and clear of everything but his ancestral spirit, the dangerous Anurra.

Alfie climbed the hills, following a game trail that might be over ten thousand years old, working his way through the boulders and fallen sandstone escarpments till he came to a bluff that seemed to rise directly out of the ground. He walked around to the far side of the bluff, where a narrow chimney gave the strong and flexible an avenue to lever oneself up the face of the bluff to an underhang. Alfie braced his back against the stone and worked his way up, pushing with his legs.

There was a natural cave there, sheltered from wind and rain, deep and dry, and it had been the home to the Ang-Gnarra shaman for tens of thousands of years.

It was where he lived. The shaman was home.

In one corner of the large frontal cave was the neat stack of bones of the man who'd made Alfie, Ralph the old shaman who'd been shunned by the other Aboriginals because of his explorations into the dark path of puri-puri, who died at the hand of his young apprentice as his own mentor had died at his hand.

The walls and ceiling of the cave were covered with images, some of them tens of thousands of years old; others as fresh as Alfie could make them. There were new symbols, symbols from the Dreamtime walkabout that Alfie made going out into the white man's world and making his way back, taking his pay in the white man's world, which gave him the total freedom and autonomy to do exactly as he wished to do in his world, the world of this cave.

He stripped himself naked and set his clothes and his satchel in a small narrow natural alcove. Then he stretched out on his back, the stone cool and rough against his back and naked buttocks as he stretched out to his full length and stared up at the ceiling, lit by the slanting sunlight from outside, as though he were staring up at the stars of a summer night.

Charley was unsteady on his feet in his apartment; the floor seemed to swell beneath him like the deck of a small boat on rough water. His head was muddled with fatigue, sorrow, and a raging hangover. But when Kativa came into the apartment, he drew himself up, bracing himself with his feet wide apart. She set down a paper bag with food in it on his coffee table, then came to him for a silent, long hug.

"Eat," she said.

Charley sat down and ate his sandwich in silence, carefully chewing each bite and forcing himself not to bolt his food down. Kativa sat on a kitchen chair, her knees pressed tight together, and hunched forward to rest her elbows on her knees. She said nothing while Charley ate. The silence grew thick till Charley set down the crust of his sandwich and said, "Thank you for the food."

"You're welcome. How are you doing now?"

"I need you to go to Australia with me."

"What?"

"I need you to go to Australia with me," Charley said in a measured voice. "I need your help."

"Help with what, Charley? I can't just take off and go to Australia. Why are you going? What are you going to do?"

"The man who has done all this, the man who killed my friend, he's in Australia."

"How do you know that?"

"I have friends in the business who keep track of men like this."

"Then you need to tell the authorities what you know and let them sort it out, that's what they do."

"Kativa, there is more to this than meets the eye. There's something strange going on, something you know about . . . all this stuff about the way Aborigines think about magic and the Laura bush country. I had a dream, a terrible dream this morning while I slept. It was like the dream you told me you'd had when you were in Australia, except that when I was dreaming it was like Bobby was talking to me. It was a place like you described to me, in a clearing with these mounds of clay, and you were there with me. I know this sounds insane, but I think it's a message to me: you and I are to go to Australia together and find this man."

"And what? Kill him? Turn him in to the police? Charley, this doesn't sound insane, it is insane."

"You told me about your dreams. You told me that the rules of every day don't apply to the Aborigines and their magic. You've felt it yourself, you said, and you told me about my own dreams. Kat, I'm tired beyond tired, but I know something as sure as I know anything, and that is the man who killed my friends is in Australia and somehow there's a connection between you and me and him. We are meant to do something about it."

"I can't be of any help," she said, standing and crossing her arms tightly across her chest. "I don't know anything about this sort of police work."

"What about the dreams, Kativa? What about those? You know the truth in those. I'm getting them now. I'm putting aside all my rules for living in this world so I can understand the rules this man lives by—and I'm getting it now. Will you help me?"

"I can't just go, I . . ."

"I need you to go with me," Charley said. He stood and turned her to face him, tilted her chin up. "You know the area, you know how it all works. The Laura bush country, that's where he is now. I need you to believe in me right now, I need you to believe in what you already know. For some reason we're all connected in this. You know the area and you'll know what to ask people. We can find this guy together."

MARCUS WYNNE

228

"What will you do when you find him?"

"What needs to be done," Charley said in a flat, final voice.

Kativa shrugged off his hands and went to the window, her arms still tightly crossed on her chest, hugging herself fiercely.

"I'm frightened by this," she said. "I'm not like you. I'm sorry for your friends, but I can't just go off with you, chasing something from a dream."

"You know better than that, Kat. You've felt something happening as well. Don't deny it, you know it. You're part of this whether you like it or not. If I'm with you, I can protect you. But we have to follow him to end this. Do you believe your dreams will get any better if you stay here and pretend that there's nothing you can do?"

Charley looked at her back, at the ridge of tension in her shoulders, and he lowered his voice, not quite pleading. "I can't do this without you, Kativa. Please."

She lowered her head, chin to her chest, uncrossed her arms, and wiped her palms on her slacks.

"I'll need to tell them something, at the museum . . ." she said.

"Tell them you have a family emergency."

"I'll need to pack some things . . ."

"We'll go to your apartment."

Within two hours they were at the Northwest Airlines ticket counter, where Charley paid full fare coach for a round trip to Australia, nearly maxing out his credit card. They would fly from Minneapolis to Los Angeles, then connect onto Cairns, the gateway city to the Great Barrier Reef and the Laura bush country. It was a four-hour flight to Los Angeles, a two-hour layover, and then eighteen grueling hours on a 747 packed with pasty pale vacationers looking for sun and fun down under. They were unable to get seats beside each other because of their late booking, so they sat alone with their thoughts, and dozed, and turned with uneasy dreams.

They went quickly through Customs in Cairns since they only held carry-ons with a change of clothing and some toiletry essentials. Outside of Customs in the public area a big sunburned blond man in

shorts, flip-flop sandals, and a ragged T-shirt held a sign that said
CHARLES PAYNE.

"That would be me," Charley said to the big man, who held out
his hand and said, "G'day, mate. I'm Fredo. Here to give you a lift to
the hotel. You'll be wanting a washup and some shut-eye, eh?"

"Thanks, Fredo," Charley said. "This is Kativa Patel."

"G'day, Kativa," Fredo said. He pointed at their carry-ons. "Is this
all your kit?"

"Yes," Charley said.

"Right then," Fredo said. "Let's hit the road."

They followed the big blond man out into the parking lot.

"I didn't know you had friends here," Kativa said.

"Friends of my friends are my friends," Charley said. He was
slightly dizzy from jet lag and the sudden change from the chill of fall
in Minneapolis to the blistering heat of the tropical summer sun down
under.

They stopped before a battered four-wheel drive Toyota truck.

"You'll have to squeeze in, or she'll ride on your lap, mate," Fredo
said. "I got to have room for the stick shift." They managed to all get
into the cramped cab of the truck.

"I booked you in at the Radisson," Fredo said. "Nice American
hotel right on the water. Nice view, decent enough place. You can walk
right out the door and out onto the beach, go for a stroll and get some
good tucker in the town."

"Thanks again, Fredo," Charley said. "You got something else for
me?"

"Oi, mate, just a tick?" the blond man said. "Let's wait till we're
away from the airport and the coppers here."

Fredo gunned the truck to life, leaving a blue-gray cloud of smoke
behind him. He pulled away and drove for a few minutes on the exit
road from the airport. He pulled over to the side of the road, carefully
checking his mirrors.

"Here you are," he said, pulling an oily bundle from beneath the
driver's seat. "Check it out, but keep it low, eh?"

Charley unfolded the bundle. Inside was a battered Browning

High Power semiautomatic pistol and three magazines, two of the standard thirteen-round magazines that fit flush in the magazine well, and one of the extended twenty-round magazines that protruded from the butt of the pistol. Charley kept the weapon in his lap, his elbow squeezing Kativa over into Fredo's bulk. Charley quickly stripped the pistol, examining the works and checking the firing pin, then reassembled the oily weapon and worked the action several times.

"Ammo?" Charley said.

"Ah, right. Kept that separate," Fredo said. "Here you are."

He handed Charley a small rag that tinkled and a plain small cardboard box. The cardboard box held 9mm full metal jacket NATO ball rounds and the small rag held ten Winchester Silvertip hollow points.

"Best I can do at short notice, mate," Fredo said. "The shooter's worn but it works just fine. Feeds ball no problem and it feeds those Silvertips just the same. Goes right to point of aim at seven yards and fifteen, so if you're doing your job it'll do. Don't get caught with it. It's cold and won't come back to me, but you will be in for a long cooling."

"I got that. Thanks, Fredo," Charley said.

"Look in the glove box there," Fredo said, pulling the truck back onto the road. "That manila folder? That's the other stuff you'll want."

"I appreciate it," Charley said, slipping the folder into his carry-on bag.

"No worries, mate. All part of the service."

They drove in silence for a time, then Fredo pulled up in front of a big hotel and stopped short of the entrance. He turned off the truck, then handed the keys to Charley.

"You can drive a manual, right?" he said.

"Sure can," Charley said. "Everything okay on the truck? Anything I need to know?"

The big man scratched at his face and said, "Check the oil once in a while, feed her good gas, she'll take care of you. You'll need it if you're going bush. There's spares in the bed and toolbox, complete set of tools. There's a false bottom in the toolbox and a twelve-gauge shotgun with a box of 00 buckshot in there. That's legal, but barely. You won't run into any problems if you've got it handy in the bush, but keep it low around here."

"I'll do that, Fredo."

"My number's in the folder," Fredo said. He got out of the truck. "Cheers, mate, miss. See you."

Fredo lumbered off, his hands buried in his pockets as though he were only out for a stroll. Kativa watched him go and said, "Who is that man? And why the gun?"

"He's a friend of a friend, Kat, like I said. And the gun . . . I need to be able to defend us if we run into this guy."

Kativa shook her head and combed her fingers through her hair. "I can't make any sense of this," she said. "I'm too tired, I need to sleep."

"We'll take care of that," Charley said. He reinserted the ignition key and started the truck and drove into the self-park garage beside the hotel. They took their bags and walked through the garage into the hotel lobby, decorated in a faux tropical motif complete with a trickling stream and artificial trees holding a variety of stuffed birds. After they checked in, Kativa led the way straight to the room without saying another word. She ignored Charley while she stripped down and went into the shower.

While she was in the bathroom, Charley flipped through the manila folder Fredo had left with him. Fatigue weighed heavy on him and he fought the droop of his eyelids. He pulled out a thin sheet of onionskin typing paper and read the short note:

This is who we're looking for. We've been looking for him for the same reasons. We're interested in what you find. I know you're not on board, but consider it favors in the favor bank. You can call us for a bailout and we'll take care of the sweeping after. Try to keep things clean and hand it off to us. The other guy is his boss. We'd like to have a long chat with him as well. See you when you get back. Good hunting.

T.

Charley pulled out the first of two 8×10 photographs. This one was grainy black and white, but despite the slight blurring there was no mistaking the face: this was the man who had been standing over Bobby Lee's body. At the bottom of the photograph was written "Alfred 'Alfie' Woodard." The shot was of a man, dressed in a black leather motorcycle jacket and dark pants, coming out of a storefront. His hair was pulled back in a ponytail and his face partially obscured by sunglasses. But the face was the face in the image Charley pulled up effortlessly from his photographer's memory.

The other photograph was of a handsome, sunburned man, barechested and dressed in baggy surfer's shorts and holding a short surfboard. At the bottom of that photograph was the name Jay Burrell and a local Cairns address. Charley studied the man's face and memorized the round, smooth face that was younger than the eyes. Jay Burrell. He'd need to get a street map, get oriented, and then pay a visit to Mr. Burrell.

Behind him, Kativa came out of the shower, wrapped in a long towel.

"It's free," she said. She slipped beneath the covers in the bed and turned her back to him.

Charley looked at her reflection in the mirror, then slid the photographs back into the envelope. He undressed quietly, turning the lights down, then showered, letting the heavy beat of hot water wash some of his tiredness away. After, he slipped into the bed where Kativa slept heavily, and carefully wrapped himself around her, and slipped into a dreamless sleep.

Jay Burrell listened to the edge of fear that had come into his caller's voice; that was something he hadn't heard in this man's voice before.

"We don't know where he is," the caller said. "He's a material witness for the police and he's dropped off the face of the earth, nobody can find him anywhere. He might be off looking for you, unless you decided to disappear him and not tell me, like you didn't tell me a damn thing about this whole mess."

"He's not going to come here," Jay said.

"He was that cop's best friend," the caller said. "He's a forensic photographer for the police but he's not a cop. He was some kind of intelligence officer for the Army, so maybe he has some way of sussing you out."

"What makes you think that?"

"Don't ask me to do another thing . . . I'm done with all this," the caller said.

"You're done when I tell you you're done," Jay said. "Things got out of hand," he conceded.

"You don't know how much," the caller said, his voice breathy. "All this wasn't necessary—you should know better that I would never do anything against you. I had no part in anything those two had going. But the FBI is here now, looking into things . . ."

"There's nothing more for them to find. There's no track, no trail. It all ends there," Jay said. "You just need to stay cool, keep your mouth shut, and monitor the situation. I've arranged for additional payment to cover your difficulties. And then you can just go back to your life because, like you said, things got out of hand. I won't be doing any more business in Minneapolis."

"I want to be through with this."

"Pretty soon," Jay said with certainty. "Pretty soon."

He hung up the phone and stared out at the ocean through the big glass-sliding door, his hands locked behind his back. After a long while, he picked up the phone and entered the long-distance number for the Quinkin Bar in Laura.

"Hullo, Quinkin Bar and Hotel," a male voice answered.

"Yes," Jay said. "I'd like to leave a message for Alfie Woodard."

"He won't be in for a few days, is it urgent?"

"Not particularly. Would you have him call Jay when he comes round?"

"No worries, mate. Call Jay. That's easy enough."

"Right then, ta."

"Ta."

Jay studied the surf and the cut of the waves and thought of getting his board out again. He surfed every morning. That was his favorite way to start the day, rolling out of bed and getting his board into the water first thing. It was a heaven he'd made for himself, starting first in Humboldt County in California growing marijuana, then moving down the coast to Huntington Beach outside of Los Angeles till the law enforcement heat got to be too much. His dope-financed surfing vacations provided him with plenty of good places to go. Australia was perfect for his operational headquarters because he moved no drugs in or out of the country; all he moved was money and information. His aircraft were headquartered in Mexico; his major finances in Caracas, Venezuela, and Oranjestad, Aruba; his trucking operation in Arizona, and his domestic money laundering operations in Minneapolis and Dayton, Ohio. Now he'd have to divest himself of the properties he managed in Minneapolis, carefully but quickly, and expand his operations in Dayton. He didn't want to pump that up too much, but it would have to do until he found a new opportunity in the Midwest.

So much to do.

MARCUS WYNNE

Jay Burrell knew he sat at the top of the food chain when it came to narcotics trafficking. And no one had gotten close to him, not one of the government organizations like DEA or CIA. He knew he was watched with sharklike keenness by those organizations, but he was smart, cunning, and careful, and able to afford the very best legal and accounting help. To anyone who cared to look closely at him, he would appear to be a very successful real estate trader who'd made good investments and gotten good return, enough to finance his love of surfing and his modest expatriate lifestyle in Cairns. He traveled a lot, but there was nothing illegal about that.

He had some odd acquaintances, but there was nothing illegal about that, either.

He decided to surf, then go into town for a late lunch. A little diversion and socializing would do him good. He didn't want to think through, at least not yet, what he might have to do if someone had connected him to Alfie, and Alfie to the Minneapolis killings. He didn't believe any of his people were up to the task and he surely didn't want to take Alfie on his own. So he made himself a mental note to go to one of his many paid contacts in the Australian government and have a search run on Charley Payne of Minneapolis, Minnesota, and see just what kind of man *might* be tracking him.

237

Alfie Woodard lay in that dreamy state between wakefulness and sleep, the place where the body can be sound asleep and the mind awake and alive with visions. In the cave he called home, he often spent hours in that state, dreaming, feeling the images come up from within him as well as from the very stone around him. When the dreaming took him, he would lie there for days, coming out only to relieve himself, drink some water and take a light meal, and then lie back down to follow the dreamline wherever it led him.

This was the world of his real self: to walk in his mind among the spirits of his ancestors and to confer with the other members of the ancient and malevolent Imjin tribe. There was a particular voice that spoke to him, a haunting voice that directed him, the voice of Anurra:

Timara is coming . . . Timara is coming with the woman and there is danger for you. Prepare, prepare, for the hunter is coming for you . . .

He had been chosen for a task. Chosen for what, he wasn't sure yet, at least not consciously, but that was unimportant. But the path he'd been on continued to unfold in front of him. It had seemed so easy, those years past, when Jay Burrell had first sought him out and asked him to do a job. Jay had said, in his disarmingly frank manner, "Would you kill a man for me?"

Alfie had barely paused to answer. It was as though he'd known the question was coming before it was uttered. He said, "Sure, mate. I can use the money. But it won't be cheap."

The killing began exactly when he needed to take his study of puri-puri to the next level. Each killing was a ritual and each time the ritual became more focused and his dreaming more intense as he took the very substance of his victims into himself. Each time the mask he wore in the outer world became easier to discard, and each time the return to his cave became more important, till he was increasingly reluctant to leave. Here was where his real work was to be done.

A swirling montage of images began to form in his mind: a woman, her face hidden, lit from behind with brilliant light outlining her in a bright nimbus but leaving her features in shadow; the tall thin blond man who'd fought so well in the policeman's house; Alfie limping toward the aircraft that waited for him.

There was meaning and connection to all of this, but he wasn't fully aware of all of it yet. He was confident that understanding would rise up in him when it was the right time. He only knew that, for now, he needed to prepare and for that he needed to tend to the needs of his body: exercise, eating, sleeping.

He woke himself slowly and opened his eyes. Daylight slanted into the cave, the razor edge of it stopping at the shadow cast in the back of the cave where Alfie lay. He got up and retrieved the small roll of paints he'd assembled to replace the one lost in Minneapolis. He stretched himself out on his back in the shadowed rear of the cave and turned his attention to a bare space on the wall, close to where it sloped into the floor.

He began to draw.

A woman's figure first, small breasts poking straight out in the vigor and firmness of youth, with a smooth and rounded belly, her legs splayed wide and one arm crooked invitingly across her belly. He sketched quickly and confidently, the image growing larger in his mind. He sang as he sketched, a soft hum like that of the didgeridoo, singing love magic to the image and reaching with his mind to the woman in the Dreamtime, a woman he felt he'd met somewhere, a woman he felt coming to him soon.

She would be with the hunter the Timara favored.

Alfie let the dark spirit move through him and his hands went to another blank spot on the wall, near the woman's love magic image, and he began to sketch quick harsh lines, an image of a man upside down, a tall thin figure etched in black with a white line down the middle, each hand clutching a weapon, dangling limp and useless. Alfie outlined the image in red and a dark song whose words he could not utter rang loud in his head.

Death magic to this man.

Kativa tossed and turned in her sleep as something dark reached out to enter her dreams...

...She was walking toward dun-colored hills covered with thin trees with branches that looked like arms reaching to the sky, the fallen slabs of sandstone that covered the hill hiding caves and crevices between. She was naked, enjoying the sense of sun on her breasts, the cool breeze across her thighs, a loincloth concealing her womanhood but her breasts proudly on display. She felt a warmth between her legs, a delicious teasing, perhaps from the heat and moisture that built there as she walked, the exercise warming her like a lover stroking her breasts and back. She was in the moment and the moment was delightful.

She wasn't alone.

Behind her came a tall thin man, his stride the length of a tree trunk, slipping from tree to tree to come up behind her, hiding for a moment, and peering out between the branches, his slim limbs hidden by the limbs of the trees. She felt him looking at her with lust and she enjoyed that, enjoyed the thought that he was looking at her bare buttocks and back gleaming with sweat in the midday sun.

Ahead of her, someone faintly called out her name. She couldn't make out the voice, so low it was almost below the threshold of her hearing, but she felt it like a pressure in her head. It drove her forward, urging her toward the caves she saw ahead of her. She couldn't see who was calling; he was hiding in the rocks ahead of her, calling to her, just ahead of her. It was singing she heard, in the space before hearing, sweet on the surface but somehow rough and discordant just beneath, calling her forward now as she stood in the shadow of a great hill, looking for a way up. There was a path, a narrow path so old that it looked worn into the stone, and beside the path was a human skull, and its jaws clattered together and said, "Welcome, woman. Bring us your flesh so we may walk again."

Kativa sat bolt upright in the bed, tangled in the sheets. She was streaming sweat. Her sudden waking roused Charley, who sat up groggily and said, "What is it?"

"...I was dreaming."

That brought Charley into full wakefulness. "Are you all right?" he said.

"It was a horrid dream."

Kativa got out of bed and went into the bathroom, shutting the door behind her. "I need a shower," she said through the door.

"Right," Charley said.

Kativa stood in the shower stall and let the steaming water roll over her, heating her throughout and relaxing the tension she felt in her neck, back, and pelvis. The dream images lingered and the memories of her nakedness in the sun bothered her. She scrubbed at herself fiercely, as though she could wash the memory of that voice out of her self. Then she dried herself with the big rough terry-cloth towels and wrapped one around herself and came out into the room.

"Would you like to shower?" she said to Charley. "There's plenty of hot water."

Charley was sitting cross-legged in the middle of the bed, clad only in boxer shorts. "Yeah," he said. "I would."

He stood up and paused before her, one hand resting tentatively on her shoulder. "Your dream?" he said.

Kativa shook her head no. "I don't want to talk about it," she said. "It's just more of the same. Take a shower and we can eat."

Charley nodded, then went into the bathroom and showered while Kativa changed into khaki trousers, a light linen short-sleeved shirt, and sturdy walking shoes. Charley came out of the bathroom and changed in silence. Then the two of them went downstairs to the lavish breakfast buffet. After eating and many cups of coffee, Kativa said, "Now what are we to do?"

Charley nodded, sensing a change in her. He sipped from his coffee, then said, "There's a man, a local, I have to take a look at. The man we're looking for, he's been seen with this guy. How well do you know this town?"

Kativa shrugged and shivered as though she had a sudden chill. "Fairly well."

Charley handed her a slip of paper with Jay Burrell's address on it. "Can you get us here? Do you know where this is?"

She studied the address for a moment. "Yes," she said. "It's a street that parallels the main beach, right outside of town. It's a long walk, or we could drive by there."

Charley nodded. "We'll want to drive by first, get a feel for the area."

"Do you know who you're looking for?"

"I'll know him when I see him."

They left the restaurant and went through the lobby to the adjacent parking garage where they'd left the pickup truck. Charley walked completely around the truck, then knelt and looked quickly into each wheel well and under the carriage of the truck.

"What are you looking for?" Kativa said.

"Nasty surprises."

"You've done this sort of thing before."

"What's that?"

"This sort of thing . . . looking for people."

"Yep."

"Are you going to tell me about it?" Kativa said, heat in her voice. "Or am I to guess, like I have with so much of what you do?"

Charley got in and started the truck, and swung the passenger door open.

"Get in," he said.

Kativa got in and slammed the door with more violence than was necessary.

"I'm not a child," she said. "And I'm already in this with you. I have a right to know if you know what you're doing. I still don't even know why I'm here."

Charley thought for a moment, then turned the truck off.

"Fair enough," he said. "I know what I'm doing. Before I was a photographer, I worked for our CIA. I was a street operator."

"What's a street operator?"

Charley laughed and said, "It's somebody who operates on the street. I've done this sort of thing all over the world. Some other time I could give you a long précis on what I've done and how I've been trained, but we don't have time for that now. I think you've seen enough to understand that I know what I'm doing. It's no longer my first choice for a profession, but it's how I made my living for a long time. Why are you here? There's not a logical answer to that question, but then there's nothing logical about this whole Quinkin angle. That's why you're here. The truth is, Kativa, everything important about this guy came from you. I need you here to help me sort out what I may find and to help me get what I need to take this guy."

"To take him?"

"That's right."

"You mean to the law?"

"Don't be naïve."

"There's more than one kind of law here, Charley. That's something you should know."

"We're operating on my law right now."

"The Aborigines have their own law and it would certainly pertain to this."

"What do you mean?"

"In each tribe, there's a council of older men, the elders. Within that council is a group called the Law Men. Their job is to enforce the taboos and the tribal laws—and that includes the practice of magic. If we found what tribe this Quinkin belongs to, we'd have allies in the Law Men. They would want to put a stop to him."

"So what, they'd try him in some kind of court?"

"Not exactly. They'd decide among themselves what needed to be done—and then they'd do it. It might be something like a beating for a small transgression, or a ceremonial wounding of the leg with a spear for a young man who got drunk and caused trouble. It can go all the way to the killing of a dark sorcerer if it calls for it."

"We don't have time for that," Charley said. "I don't know if this guy is going to stick around or not. We need to find him and fix him right now."

Charley started the engine and backed the truck out of the parking spot.

Kativa turned away and looked out the side window.

"Is that what the gun is for?" she said.

"It could be."

Kativa wrapped her arms across her chest, hugging herself.

"Kativa?" Charley said. "I need directions."

She steered him through the town with brief, succinct phrases. They found the street, a winding narrow two-lane that passed in front of many large houses that backed onto the beach.

"It's that house on the crest of the hill," she said.

Charley shifted into low gear and slowed as the truck sputtered to the crest of the hill. The front of the house and the yard was set off by a low wall and a wrought-iron barrier gate that led to the sidewalk. The house was L-shaped, with the short base of the L pointing down a short slope directly to the sea.

"Nice," Charley said.

He paid close attention to the layout of the house, noting how the wall and the iron gate blocked off the front but that the driveway and rear of the house were open to the beach, with nothing to interfere with the view from the big windows at the rear of the house. It would be best to approach from the sea and he saw how it could be done: he could walk in from a vantage point down the road and right up into the back of the house. There were lights on the back deck facing the ocean, but they all seemed to point in rather than out. That augured well for a night approach. There was no one outside, but he caught a glimpse of someone moving inside the house, past a front window and then disappearing into the depths of the house.

Charley put the truck back into gear, drove to the end of the road and turned around, then drove slowly past the house once again. As they passed the house for a second time, there was a big man, heavily muscled and dressed in a singlet and shorts, standing on the porch. The big man raised his hand to wave as they passed. Kativa and Charley both waved and continued on without stopping.

"So what now?" Kativa said.

"We go back to the hotel and wait awhile. Then maybe we'll take a walk on the beach."

"And then?"

"We're going to find some maps of the Laura country and we'll talk about our trip up there."

"Who was it, Tim?" Jay Burrell said.

"Some bloke and his girlfriend. Probably looking for a way down to the beach."

"Are they gone?"

"Just turned round and went."

"Fine then. I want you to go into town and wait for the bus with our friend Alfie on it."

"I hate that bloody bastard."

"Put it away and save it for another day, Timmy. You'll get your chance. I may end up putting you with Alfie on this next thing anyway."

The big man lurched off, leaving Jay studying his fingertips steepled in front of his face.

Alfie was disturbed by the summons back to Cairns. He'd just begun to renew his routine in the cave: eating, sleeping, walking in the hills, and spending more and more hours communing with the spirits that filled the air of the dark hills. A young Aborigine boy, dressed in tattered shorts and T-shirt, had come to the foot of the cave and shouted the message up to him before turning away and running as fast as he could. Alfie took his time walking into town to check his message at the bar. He leaned on the bar and made his phone call to Jay Burrell and listened to the tension in the man's voice.

Something was bothering him.

He didn't bother going back to the cave; all he had with him was the clothes on his back and that was enough. He kept a room well stocked with clothes and other accoutrements of the outside world in Jay Burrell's sprawling house. So he caught a ride back down to Cairns on the daily bus.

Jay had sent his buffoon Tim to pick him up at the bus stop. Alfie saw him well before the burly white man saw him, and reminded himself to steer clear of any provocation.

Tim pulled the sedan close to the curb when he finally saw Alfie standing patiently in front of the Cairns bus station.

"Get in, blackie," Tim said. "I don't have all day."

Alfie got in the left-side passenger door and sat beside Tim without a word.

"You got nothing to say?" Tim blustered, unnerved by the slow look Alfie gave him.

Alfie ignored him, and drew inward in silence, still making the transition from the man who lived in a cave to the Alfie Woodard of the outside world. He wasn't going to let the juvenile maundering of the young man interfere with him. He didn't say a word to Tim, even after they arrived at Jay's beach house. Alfie remained silent until he went into Jay Burrell's office.

"What's so important that you need me back here?" he said.

"There's a man maybe come looking for you," Jay said.

"How do you know?"

"A contact in Minneapolis tells me he dropped out of sight suddenlike after you left. I checked up on him. He's a serious fella, this one."

"What do you know of him?"

Jay handed him a manila folder.

"Have a look," he said. "This is the guy you left standing on your trail."

Alfie sat in an armchair, crossed one leg over the other, and began to flip through the sheets in the folder. One piece of paper had the Central Intelligence Agency letterhead, but the bulk of the file was information retyped by someone who had read the original file.

"Ex-CIA Special Operations?" Alfie said, amused. "What a world we live in."

He pulled out a photograph of Charley Payne, the name written on the bottom of the 5×7, and studied the face.

"Too right, that's him," Alfie said. "He was a good fighter, this one."

He gathered the thin sheaf of papers together, spending a moment lingering over the photograph, then tapped the papers together into a neat and orderly pile and set it on the edge of Jay's desk. He leaned back in his chair and interlaced his fingers across his belly.

"So what do you want me to do?" he said.

"What do you think?" Jay said. "This has to be sorted."

MARCUS WYNNE

"Fine," Alfie said in a calm, almost bored voice. "I'll kill him once he gets here. How is he supposed to find me?"

"This one has got connections. They could be pointing him right at me. You've developed a reputation and an unmistakable calling card, my friend. Those jobs in Paris, Amsterdam, Bangkok, and Caracas... your ritual draws a lot of attention."

"You wanted attention, attention you got. You've always wanted to send a message. I don't think the message was ambiguous. Do you?"

"You may have to change the way you do business."

"I think it may be better if we ended things."

Jay stood up, alarmed. "What do you mean?"

"It's the end of things, Jay. With me. This last thing... I've been getting a feeling. Getting me own kind of messages. It's the end of things. I don't want to do this anymore."

Jay sat on the edge of his desk and swung one leg back and forth nervously.

"Don't tell me that the famous Alfie Woodard is getting cold feet on me," he said.

"Nothing to do with it, mate. It's just time for me to stop and turn my attention to other things. I've got another life that needs tending to. I've done enough for both of us."

"I need you, Alfie."

"You need what I can do... and you've been grooming muscle-head over there to take my place in any event. Give him a chance to stretch his wings a bit, maybe he'll surprise you. He's got potential, if he'd learned to shut his mouth and get on with it."

Tim, who'd been standing in a sullen silence by the door, opened his mouth, then shut it.

"Like that," Alfie said.

"Piss off," Tim said.

Jay spoke quickly. "I need you to sort this out. After you get this cleaned up you can go back to your cave in Laura and do whatever it is you do there. But this is your mess and it's followed you home. You need to sort it out."

Alfie nodded in amiable agreement. "No arguing with that, mate. I need to get it sorted. But there's something about this, something I've felt coming for a while. This man, he won't walk away."

"You think he'll be working with the cops on this?" Jay said.

"Not his way," Alfie said with assurance. "He won't want police, but he might bring some of his spooky friends. He'll need someone to help. He won't know the ground here."

"I can pay to have the airport watched, but he could be flying into Brisbane and making his way up here by bus."

Alfie leaned back in the chair, closed his eyes. For a moment he felt the pull of his dreamy state and he fought that off for the moment. "No need, Jay. He's probably already here, maybe even had a look at you, if it's you that he's tracking. All we need to do is keep our eyes open and he'll come right to us. Maybe we'll dangle me."

"Dangle?"

"He may know something about you, but he's seen me. If he sees me again, he'll recognize me. Count on that."

Jay gestured at Alfie's beat-up bush khakis. "Even like that?"

"Even like this."

Tim snorted in disdain. Alfie looked over his shoulder at the big man and grinned.

"You'll never amount to anything till you learn some things, Timmy my lad," Alfie said. "You think everything is just as it appears at the moment you look at it. You never bother to think that maybe, just maybe, things and people are not always what they appear to be. When you start to understand that, you'll know something. Then you might really be dangerous."

"Piss off, Alfie," Tim said defiantly. The absence of censure from Jay emboldened him. "You and your bloody bush doctor bullshit. If you hadn't been playing that game in the States we wouldn't have this problem now."

Alfie laughed and shook his head. He put his bush hat on and slid it forward so that it shaded his eyes and relaxed back into the armchair.

"You'll get your chance, Timmy," he said.

MARCUS WYNNE

3.8

In their hotel room, Kativa sat across from Charley, the small table between them. She sat on the edge of her seat, in marked contrast to Charley, who slouched in his chair with the easy insouciance of a well-fed cat.

"So what now?" Kativa said.

Charley sat forward and flipped open a large-scale road map on the table.

"There's not much to Laura," he said.

"It's not much more than a stopping-off place for people on their way up to the Cape," Kativa said. "There is a settlement there, but it's not in the main town on the road, it's off behind it in the foothills. That's the Ang-Gnarra tribal lands."

"You know your way around up there?"

"Yes," Kativa said. "I spent a lot of time there. There will be people we can ask about this man."

"They'll speak to you, then."

"I hope so. If he's up there, you better believe the natives will know all about him. You said you had a photograph?"

"He's hard to forget," Charley said. He took out the 8×10 black-and-white and handed it to Kativa. "Here."

Kativa slowly studied the photograph. "He looks familiar, somehow," she said. "He certainly won't be hard to find if he dresses like that."

"I don't think that will be the case."

Kativa nodded. "I think you're right. We can go to Laura, show that photograph. Someone will recognize his face."

"How far is Laura from here?"

"It's the better part of a day's drive, much of it over dirt track, but that truck should handle it just fine."

"How are your contacts there?"

"I know a few people there. Peter, who owns the bar, he knows everyone in the area. He often holds mail and takes phone calls for people. If anyone would know, Peter would."

"Then let's go talk to Peter," Charley said. He gathered up the stray papers and replaced them into the folder. "Let's hit the road."

The road to Laura was long, bumpy, and dusty. When they arrived, they got out of the truck and Kativa looked around while Charley stretched the kinks out of his back. Laura was the same as she had left it: sleepy, dusty, almost ominously quiet in a midday silence under the somnolent heat of the tropical sun. There wasn't much to the town: a battered collection of peeling white-painted buildings, the centerpiece a two-story building with a sign out front that said QUINKIN BAR AND HOTEL. A dusty semitrailer was parked directly across the street from the bar. Kativa led Charley into the cool dimness of the bar. It was a small place, dominated by the battered wooden bar with a tarnished brass foot rail, a few scattered tables, and a stairwell that led upstairs. A young Aboriginal girl tended the bar where a dusty man in a bush hat and khakis, a driver by the looks of him, nursed a beer. In a corner of the bar was a table where two ancient, wrinkle-faced Aboriginal men sat together and watched Charley and Kativa with interest. The bar was otherwise empty.

"Here now," the truck driver said. "Fresh company."

"G'day," the bartender said. "Get you something to drink?"

"Two Castle lagers," Kativa said. "As cold as you've got them."

"Can do, mate," the bartender said. She produced two icy bottles from the cooler behind the bar and set out two frosted mugs. "Fancy, eh?"

Kativa and Charley poured their beer into the mugs and drew gratefully from them.

"Is Peter about?" Kativa said.

"No," the bartender said. "He's off today. Can I help you?"

Charley took the 8×10 photograph out of his bag and slid it onto the bar. "Do you know this man?"

It was apparent from the look on her face that she did. She straightened up from her friendly lean across the bar and stepped back.

"I know of that fella," she said. "He won't like you showing that picture around."

"You know him?" Kativa said.

"I know *of* him," the bartender corrected. "Precious little and that bit more than I want to. That's Alfie Woodard, that's the name he goes by. He stays up in the hills. You want to know more about him, ask them fellas there." She pointed at the two old Aboriginal men sitting at the table in the corner, their faces puffy and folded with age, framed with bushy white hair. "You ask them fellas what they know about Alfie Woodard."

"Thank you," Kativa said.

"Don't be thanking me," the bartender said, her arms crossed tightly across her chest. "I'll thank you never to mention it to Alfie Woodard."

Charley and Kativa looked at each other for a full moment, then Charley shrugged and went over to the table where the two old men sat.

"Excuse me," he said, holding the photo out. "Do either of you know this man?"

The old man closest to him turned rheumy eyes, the whites a faint yellow, at Charley and appraised him slowly. Then he looked at the photograph for a full minute.

Then he laughed.

"That fella won't like that you have a picture of him, no he won't," the old man said.

"You know him?" Charley said.

"I know that man, and I knew the boy before he got took away."

"Took away?"

"Government took him, put him with white people because he had a white father that ran off. Did something bad to him, all that did."

"Do you know where he is?" Charley said.

"He stays in the hills."

"Where in the hills?"

"White fellas better off not going in these hills looking for this fella. This man do something bad to you, he know you looking for him, carrying a picture of him."

Charley eased into an empty chair at the table. The other old man nodded and grinned as Charley sat, Kativa standing by his shoulder.

"I need to talk to this man," Charley said. "Can you help me find him?"

The old man who'd done all the talking looked into Charley's eyes, a direct and knowing gaze Charley found unsettling.

"My name is Robert Kramer," the old man said. "That's the white man's name I was given. You didn't come here to talk to this man."

Charley bit the inside of his cheek, took a long slow breath, and said, "I just need to talk to this man."

The other old man laughed.

Robert Kramer drew himself up and said sternly, "Best not to lie to a Man of the Law, fella. Not your Law, not your concern, but not good to be lying. You come to kill this man, it's all over you. We can see it, any of us who walk the Dream."

Charley glanced over at the bar to see whether the bartender had heard any of that. It seemed as though the bar had shrunk around him into the narrow view of a telescope: Charley, Kativa, the two old men, the bartender whispering something to the truck driver. Charley heard a hum, a deep background hum just barely over the threshold of his hearing, and he had a little fugue where it seemed as though he were dreaming with his eyes open and it was as though he'd been here before when he said, "You're right, Robert Kramer. I've come to kill this man because he's a bad man and I want you to tell me where he is."

MARCUS WYNNE

Both old men laughed at that, a deep rich sound that caused the bartender to look over, and then quickly away.

"You're in Quinkin country now, white fella . . ."

"My name is Charley Payne, and . . ."

"It's not your name in the Dream, Charley Payne," Robert said. "We've seen you coming. That's why we're sitting here today, me and my mate. We've been waiting for you."

The other old man nodded and smiled. There was a big gap in his smile where several teeth were missing. "Waiting for you," he said. "We sure have."

"Maybe we shouldn't talk in here," Charley said.

"Nobody's listening to us," Robert said. "The girl at the bar, she knows better, that trucker is too pissed to pay attention to anything that's not in his face."

"We just want to find . . ." Kativa said.

The old man cut her off with a glare. "I know who you are, girl, and I know the part you're to play. This is men's work, you best sit somewhere and let the man listen and talk." He turned to Charley and said, "You have to listen to make sense of the Dream, and you're here to learn about that."

Kativa nodded in agreement, touched Charley on the arm, then went to the far end of the bar where she sat and ordered another beer.

"She's in this with me," Charley said.

"This is men's work, Charley Payne," Robert said. "Tell us about the Dream that brought you here to us today."

"How do you know about my Dream?"

"We dreamed the same Dream, Charley Payne. We saw you coming. You've been here before, in your Dreaming."

"What did you dream of?" Charley said.

"Timara," Robert said. "Been dreaming of Timara Quinkin, come to hunt the Imjin in his home. That's who travels with you, Charley Payne."

"That's right," the other old man said. "We've been dreaming of you hunting. Not today, who you're looking for. He's not here today, mate. He's down in Cairns, looking for you."

"How do you know this?" Charley said.

Robert Kramer spoke slowly and deliberately.

"We had a mate," he said. "Another Man of the Law. Tribal elder, his name was Ralph. Good mate, but he liked to look too long in the Dream, looked down ways it was best to leave alone. This was not that long ago. He was one of the strongest of us in the Dream, and people would come to him for help, good magic and spells to help them. But he started to think of himself as being something he wasn't, no, Ralph wasn't what he began to think he was. Started looking down the dark ways."

"Yes, he did," the other old man said. "Looked down the dark ways."

"He went down that path alone," Robert said. "We tried to warn him, but he was a Man of the Law, saw things his own way. Went way down that path alone, then he found this fella Alfie. A young man with money enough he didn't need to do anything but follow old Ralph around."

"Ralph liked that, you see," the other old man said. "He liked having company on that dark walkabout."

"Alfie learned all he could," Robert said. "He was a good student. Too good a student. And then one day, Ralph stopped coming around. No one saw him, knew where he went. Some folks say that the Quinkin took him for dabbling in what he did. But we Men of the Law knew better. Something took him all right, something that worked through that boy Alfie. Alfie, he's not a boy anymore, not easy for the Law Men to counsel. He went his own way, and we didn't have any more disappearances here. But in the Dream, we could see what happened each time he went away. That's how we know about you, Charley Payne. You were meant to come here. That's why we've been waiting for you, to help you put things right in a way we can't."

Charley sat rock still for a long moment, then finally nodded his head in acceptance.

"Okay," he said. "Maybe I'm crazy. But I've been dreaming, too . . ."

Robert laughed. "Crazy enough to fly halfway round the world because of a dream? That's crazy, all right." The old man leaned across the table and stabbed his finger forcefully onto the tabletop. "But here you are."

"So what are you going to do?" Charley said.

"That's not the way of the Dream, Charley Payne. We see you having a meeting with this man. And we have a way of seeing..." Robert said.

"If he's not there now..." Charley said. "I need to see where he lives."

The two old men looked at each other, then Robert said, "Knew you'd say that, mate."

"So you'll help me?" Charley said.

The two old men looked at each other, then back at Charley. They both nodded, then pushed their empty glasses away, stood up and pulled on their battered bush hats and left the bar, pushing through the door into the bright light outside. Charley followed them.

"Will you show me?" he said.

"Leave the girl here," Robert said. "We'll take a long walk. She'll be fine here."

Kativa had followed as far as the doorway. "It's okay," she said to Charley. "I'll be fine. I'll wait right here."

Charley tossed her the keys to the truck. "I'll be back in a while."

"Longish walk, mate," the gap-toothed elder said. "You'll want a hat and some water."

Kativa went back inside and returned with a liter plastic bottle of drinking water she handed to Charley. "Your hat is behind the seat in the truck," she said.

Charley went to the truck and got out the hat and seated the battered drover's hat on his head. Holding the bottle of water in his hands, he set off after the two old men. They were deceptively fast; their boneless shuffle in the dusty side of the road ate up distance faster than it seemed. Charley had to hurry to catch up to them as they turned off the main road onto a dirt track that led through a small cluster of manufactured homes and trailers, the yards littered with garbage and rusted automobiles. It didn't take long before they were walking up into

WARRIOR IN THE SHADOWS

the hills past the settlement. The old men were silent, only exchanging the occasional look with Charley. They wound their way up into the first sandstone escarpments of the foothills and Charley saw his first rock painting, of an emu and a dingo, on the walls of the artificial cave created by a fallen sandstone slab.

"Who drew these?" he asked the old men.

"Ancestors," Robert said. "Long time ago, during the Dreaming."

Charley followed them up the narrow path. He read the land with the eyes of an infantryman. When they paused while picking their way carefully up the slopes, Charley looked back and fixed landmarks in his mind. This was good country for the defender and tough country for an attacker. Kativa had told him that the old Aboriginal camp sites were situated in the hills with overwatch positions so that lookouts would have plenty of opportunity to see any approaching enemy making their way up the slopes. It would be a tough battle coming up these hills against an opponent who knew you were coming and was prepared for the fight. The terrain was perfect for ambushes, with many switchbacks on the trail overlooked by rock ledges, where an attacker could lurk and bring fire—or arrows, or stones—down on your head and still have plenty of cover.

Tough terrain to hunt in. And who would live out this far? Alfie Woodard. Charley was glad to have the man's name. Alfie Woodard was a man of the city, an urban warrior who dressed like a rock musician . . . what was he doing living out here so far away from anything resembling the civilization he so obviously relished? Charley didn't understand that, but then he didn't understand any of what was happening to him right now. A part of him watched himself in bemusement, wondering at how he had in a matter of minutes accepted that two old men in a bar had been waiting for him to arrive so they could show him the lair of the man he hunted—all because they had dreamed of it.

Just as he had dreamed of it.

Robert stopped at the foot of a sheer rock face that shot straight up and then broke into what was obviously a small cave entrance about forty feet up.

"Here's the place," Robert said. "This is where he lives."

MARCUS WYNNE

"How does he get up there?" Charley said.

"Climbs, mate. He's a young man, like you. He can climb right up there," the gap-toothed other elder said. He pointed at a narrow chimney that led to the cave entrance.

Charley saw how it could be done; if he levered himself into the chimney, he could push with his feet and inch his way up with his back wedged against the opposing wall.

"You say he's not here?" Charley said.

"I told you, mate," Robert said. "This man is in Cairns, looking for you."

"All right," Charley said. He studied the cliff face and the chimney. "I'm going up there."

"Wouldn't do that, mate," Robert said. "Bad magic in that place, all this place, but worst up there. That cave is as old as the ancestors. That cave is where the black comes from."

"The black comes from?" Charley said.

"You know what we're talking about, Charley Payne," Robert said testily. "The black magic, mate. Alfie Woodard is the blackest of the black and that's why that little girl back at the bar won't speak of him. She's afraid of him, just like everyone else. He's a bad one, and in the Dreamtime he's something else. He gave up something a long time ago for that power he's got and something got inside him. That something is old and black and lives in this cave . . . lives in this cave even though Alfie's not here. He goes by another name when he's alone here. He's like many people in one skin, this fella. He's one man when he comes here, he don't look nothing like your photograph of him. But when he's in that cave, something else is him, not him being something else. That's what you need to know about Alfie. We can't help you in here with him, but we've been doing a Dreaming, had a talk with the other elders and we'll do what we can, do a ceremony to help you and maybe light your way. But what's between you two is between you two and it's been that way forever."

The two old men exchanged glances once more.

"No laughing here, mate," the gap-toothed elder said. "Feel the air here? Everything's dark even in the bright light of the day. Imagine what it will be like here in the middle of the night, in the darkest time of the night. That's what you need to know. That's when you and this one will meet. In the dark of the night. And only one of you will walk away from here."

"Time we be heading back," Robert said. The shadows had grown appreciably longer as the day had gone on.

"Is there another way to the top?" Charley asked.

"There's another way to the top, but then you have to figure out how to get down," Robert said. "You follow along this little game path here, this way," he said, pointing to a footpath about as wide as two human feet pressed together. "Along the side of the hill and it comes to a little boulder field. You climb that up to the top, puts you right above the cave, some little old gnarled kouri trees there. You hang over the top and you can see your way in. But there's no climbing down that, the cliff faces in. No, you won't be getting in that way."

Charley looked up the cliff face. There would be no getting to that cave, if it were occupied, by working your way up the chimney. All the occupant had to do was lean out and drop a rock on your head and you were done for. And there was no burning anyone out of a dry cave. He stepped back and studied the hill, saw the gnarled trees at the

top and had a glimmer of an idea.

"I want to look in the cave," Charley said.

"He'd have been on us if he was here," Robert said. "He won't be back for days now. You'd be taking a risk even in the light of day. But you go ahead if you must . . . take a look if you think you have to."

Charley felt a deep cold sense of foreboding in his belly. For a moment, as he studied the cliff face and then the dark faces of the two elders, he thought about how easy it would be to just walk away from all this, to go back to the tavern and collect Kativa, go back to Cairns and get on a plane and leave all this madness behind, forget about the deep fear and worry that rose in him now. But an image rose up in him, an image of Bobby Lee, Max, and Nicky as they were wheeled out of their home, huddled shapes on metal gurneys, and it was as though a switch were flipped inside him, transmuting his raw fear into raw anger, something primal that heated him from head to toe in one hot flash of barely controlled rage.

"Wait here," he said to the elders. "I only want a quick look."

He went to the rock face and raised one hand, tentatively, as though to stroke the surface and get a feel of it. Then he levered his back against one side of the chimney and walked his feet up, leaving him in an L-shaped position in the narrow deformity. He began to walk his way up the cliff face. It was harder work than it looked; he had to keep steady pressure even though the chimney widened in a few places, and he had no rope or safety devices to catch him if he fell. It took twenty long minutes to work his way up to the cave entrance, and then he realized that he'd have to lunge for the ledge outside the cave in order to get out of the chimney. He stayed braced, his legs trembling with the effort, and visualized the entire sequence of moves he'd have to make in order to catch the little rock outcropping that afforded the only handhold on the small ledge that jutted out from the cave's mouth. He took a deep breath, then another, then lunged and caught the rock outcropping with his left hand, then his right, then pulled himself the rest of the way onto the narrow ledge. Now he could stand erect, the big muscles of his legs trembling with the effort, his back and buttocks raw under his khakis. He waved to the two old men below, who pointed back at him and waved.

Then he turned to the cave.

It was larger and deeper than it appeared from the ground. Charley ducked his head and went in, but the entrance soon shot high into a ceiling that left plenty of room for his head. The ceiling and walls were covered with images and what looked to be the remains of a stalagmite on the floor was intricately carved and etched. It was dim, but there was light from the cave's mouth and another source from farther back in the cave. He could reach up and touch the ceiling with one hand, but still had plenty of room to stand. The cave was at least twenty by twenty feet, a good size, and in the back of the cave there was another narrow opening, an extension of the cave itself. Charley knelt and peered through and saw more skylight filtering down from above, and another narrow passageway that led farther into the bowels of the hill.

There were obviously other chambers back there, but this was where the cave's occupant spent his time. There was a rush mat against one wall, a rumpled sleeping bag laid out on it, a set of candles in the wall niches, a flashlight beside the sleeping bag. A small ledge held two leather bags. There was nothing else in the cave, but Charley could feel the sense of occupation. The rocks themselves seemed as though they were about to press in on him, and the images on the walls and ceiling seemed to move with the shadows cast by the sharp-edged sun falling into the mouth of the cave. There was a distinct boundary between the dark and the light at the front of the cave, and it seemed as though the images and pictures—of the Quinkins he recognized and other strange shapes—were still and lifeless in the light. But in the shadows, and especially in the boundary area between dark and light, the images seemed to have a life of their own, a life that stirred them and urged them away from the light and into the dark that lurked in the back of the cave. There was light there, too, a sign that some kind of passageway led to the top of the cave and let sun shine in, but he didn't want to go back there. He had the sense of something watching him—and he didn't know if it were the images or something else entirely.

He only knew he wanted badly to get out of there. His legs trembled, and he fought the urge to urinate. He took the time to look in the small leather bags on the ledge and he found that they contained tiny pots of paint and colored dirt for the images. There was a fresh image not far from the sleeping bag, fresh in its colors, but there were many others that had been added, in some instances right over an older image. The image was of a woman, naked and light-skinned and full-breasted, running toward the image of Anurra, his knobbed penis held high like a massive club. Beneath that was the image of a pale thin man, like a Quinkin, one of the Timara, held upside down and a stone knife wielded by an invisible hand sawing at the throat, spilling blood like that of an animal trussed upside down for the slaughter. Charley reached out as though to wipe the image, but something stopped

MARCUS WYNNE

him . . . he couldn't bring himself to touch that image, fresh as it was. And he knew who that image represented.

He stepped back into the light and felt the warmth of the sun across the back of his legs, still trembling from the effort of his climb. Charley backed out of the cave slowly, crouching to exit the cave mouth and stand on the small ledge. The two elders stood below watching him. Charley studied the cliff face above the cave's entrance. The rock was solid and it would take more explosive than he could carry, assuming he could get some, to close it off. No, there wouldn't be any closing this off. There was no way to climb higher than the cave mouth from here, not without climbing aids and ropes.

Charley stepped delicately and levered himself back into the chimney crack, and came down more quickly than he'd gone up, leaving raw spots on his hands, back, and buttocks where the harsh rock scraped against him. The two elders helped him out of his forced contortion to stand. They brushed dirt from him. His shirt and pants clung to him in places, lightly pink with seeping blood from the scraped places on his back and legs.

"He's having a taste of you," Robert said. "That bad fella, he don't like to have you right away. Wants you tender like a roo after it's been run for a while. But he'll have a taste for you now, you've spilt your blood in his home."

"I'm all right," Charley said.

"What did you see?" the gap-toothed elder said.

"There's not much up there," Charley said. "He sleeps there, though."

"He does more than that there," Robert said. "But it's not anything you'd see quick. Did you go into the deep of the cave?"

"No."

"Felt something, did you?"

"Yes."

"Been a long time since I was in that cave," Robert said. "Back in the thirties, before the war, I went into that cave. I was a young boy then and full of myself."

The gap-toothed elder said, "We were all young boys once, and full of ourselves."

"The man who slept in that cave was away, and we dared each other to go up into the cave," Robert said. "That was a bad thing, and if the Law Men had caught us, we'd of taken a spear in the leg for sure, no doubt about it. But we went, and we looked, and I crawled back through that passageway."

"What did you see?" Charley said.

"That's old Anurra's place. You go into that back chamber his image is right up on the wall with all kinds of old puri-puri paintings. It's a bad place, that place. There's some light that comes down from a crack in the rocks above, I don't know if it's big enough for a man to get through, but it's big enough to light the back chamber. There's a natural spring in the back of that cave that gives good fresh water. If you were up there with some food you'd have everything you need. But this Alfie, the one Anurra rides now, he likes to come out, he likes to live in several dreams at once. He goes away, that's one Dreaming, he comes back, that's another. But the real Dreaming for him is in that cave and what he does up there."

"What does he do up there?" Charley said.

"Dreams, mate," the gap-toothed elder said. "Dreams dark things till they happen. And that's where you're already fighting him, in his dreams."

"There was a new image up there..." Charley said.

"We know about that," Robert said. "Before you come back here, we'll draw an image someplace else. You won't be able to see it, but it'll help you if we can."

"What else can you tell me?" Charley said.

"We've done what we can, mate. It's up to you, now," Robert said.

With that the two elders turned and began to walk down the trail. Charley followed them and the three men made their way down from the hills in total silence, each alone with his thoughts. Back in the Quinkin Bar, Kativa sat waiting.

"What have you found?" she asked.

"What I need," Charley said. "Are you ready to go?"

MARCUS WYNNE

"Are you all right?" Kativa said with some concern. "You'd better drink some water. You look dehydrated."

Robert laughed. "He's dried out some. Been out in the sun for a good long while, he was."

Charley bought and drained two one-liter bottles of water, one right after another, barely pausing between them.

"That's better," he said. "Are you ready to go?"

"Yes," Kativa said.

She paid her bar bill and followed Charley out of the dim bar into the heavy light of day outside. The two elders followed them out and stood in the shade of the awning outside.

"Thank you," Charley said to them. "How will I find you when I come back?"

"Whether we're here or not, you know what needs to be done," said the gap-toothed elder.

Robert nodded in agreement and said, "G'day, mate. Good hunting to you."

The two old men went back into the bar.

"What was that all about?" Kativa said.

"I'll tell you all about it on the way back," Charley said. "We know where he lives. But if he's down there looking for us, we need to do a few things."

He got in the truck and started the engine. "Let's go," he said.

Once Kativa shut the door, he turned the truck around in the direction of Cairns and accelerated away, eager to meet the dark man of his dreams.

Alfie Woodard catnapped in the room Jay Burrell kept for him in his house. It was a spartan room with minimal furnishings: a comfortable bed, a few dressers and foot chests. The closet held clothing, and not just the baggy dusty khakis he preferred when he was home, but some of the denim and leather he wore when he was away in the world outside. A small box held a variety of decorative metal piercings that went into place only when he went away. Another larger locked box held a variety of firearms. While he arranged for weapons when he traveled, as any professional would, he liked having the tools of his trade handy when he was back and they were safer and easier to maintain here.

He woke from a strange and disturbing dream. It bothered him that he couldn't recall the specific details; long years of training and experience had given him the ability to recall his dreams in detail so as to re-create the tapestry of his night journeys. But he couldn't recall anything now, and all he awoke with was a profound sense of unease. He sat up, then went to unlock the box and inspect his personal weapons. He took out an old U.S. Government issue .45 automatic, lovingly maintained and fully loaded with magazines he rotated to preserve the springs. The pistol had been lightly customized by a gunsmith in the States, the barrel and feed ramp throated and polished so as to easily feed the Federal Hydra-Shok hollow points he favored, the extraction port widened and beveled, the trigger tuned and low profile Novak sights. It was simple but effective, which reflected Alfie's credo when it came to weapons.

Then he took out his nulla-nulla. When he was with the Special Air Service in East Timor on a job, he'd used a nulla-nulla to take out sentries instead of his silenced MP-5 submachine gun, much to the amusement of the senior operators, who let him do as he pleased once he'd shown he could do the job.

The experience had stood him in good stead.

He wrapped his hand around the worn grip of the nulla-nulla. The striking head was still sheathed in plastic. There was a faint reek of rotten blood from the club, matted beneath the plastic in head, brain, and hair. His two targets from Minneapolis were still with him. He hadn't done the two policemen and the family that way; there hadn't been time and it had been a rush job anyway. He'd done them quickly and efficiently.

Maybe he would tell Charley Payne that before he took him down.

There was a sudden stirring in his memory when he thought of Charley Payne; he had a brief image of a tall blond man, a figure stick thin and tall in the background . . . the background of what? He couldn't recall and that bothered him.

He put away his weapons and went out of the room, dressed only in his beat-up khaki trousers, bare-chested with his array of scars on show. His torso was coursed with gunshot and knife wounds and the whorls of ritual scarification. He nodded to one of the hanger-ons that Jay called his staff as he went into the kitchen. Tim sat at the kitchen counter eating a huge sandwich.

Alfie ignored the big man, who visibly bristled as he looked at Alfie's scars. Alfie went into the refrigerator and took out some luncheon cuts to make himself a sandwich.

"Put a shirt on, blackie," Tim said. "You're turning my stomach. I'm trying to eat my lunch."

The other bodyguard got up and left the room.

Alfie took out some sliced ham and cheese and piled it onto a slab of white bread.

"Did you hear me?" Tim said, pushing. "I said put a shirt on."

MARCUS WYNNE

Alfie took a butcher knife from the wooden block near the sink and began to slice fresh tomatoes into thin slices that he arrayed on his sandwich.

"Where's the mayonnaise, Tim boy?" he asked.

"Piss off," Tim said. Alfie reached across the counter for the pot of mayonnaise where it sat in front of Tim. Tim struck Alfie's hand away, and as he did, Alfie moved quickly and neatly slashed the back of Tim's hand with the butcher knife.

"Fucking hell!" Tim shouted. He slapped one hand on the butcher-block counter as he began to rise to his feet and Alfie slammed the butcher knife point first through the back of Tim's hand and pinned him to the counter.

Tim screamed. Jay came running into the kitchen from his study.

"What the hell do you think you're doing?" Jay shouted. "Roy! Get in here!" he called to the other bodyguard, who came in and visibly paled at the sight of Alfie sitting down to eat, gazing mildly at Tim, who writhed in pain, pinned to the counter with a knife through the back of his hand.

"I'm eating me sandwich," Alfie said. "Bread's a bit off, though."

"I'm going to kill you!" Tim shouted. Tears of pain ran down his face and he twisted on his stool, trying to find a position that eased the shocking pain.

"You've got the talking bit done, mate," Alfie said, picking up his plate. "Best you clean yourself up before you put me off my lunch."

He walked through the kitchen, brushing past Roy, and disappeared into the study, where he sat down in a chair facing the big windows that looked out over the ocean. He settled into the chair and finished his sandwich. Jay came into the study and stood behind him, fists on hips. Alfie studied Jay's reflection in the window in front of him, raised one hand, and gave Jay a little wave.

"He's going to be useless, now," Jay said.

"He's always been useless except for kissing your arse," Alfie said mildly.

"This gets the rest of the staff upset."

"Need to get better staff, mate."

"I've been thinking of that."

"Need better than that to take my place. Have some pride in your operation. Like the Yanks say, you want someone who'll be all that he can be. Something like that. Good ham, by the way. Where did you get it, in town?"

"I've got people looking for this American," Jay said.

"You mean Charley Payne," Alfie said. "Ex-CIA, one of the wonder boys from the Special Activities Staff, who are bad news when you put them out in the field. Para with the 82d Airborne Division, saw action in the Gulf, and then went into the CIA paramilitary program where he got poached for the SAS. He was with them the same time I was with our SAS. Got a good reputation in the field, but considered hard to manage by his superiors."

"You've been reading up," Jay said. He dragged over another chair and set it facing out the window beside Alfie and sat down.

"You've got good connections," Alfie said. "Read mine in a while?"

"Paid good money to disappear it not long after you went off the reservation for me."

"Interesting psychological brief, what?"

"What are you going to do?" Jay said.

"Wait for him to show up. It won't be long."

"How do you know?"

"I just know," Alfie said, twisting restlessly in the chair. "You know better than to keep asking me that."

"In case you haven't noticed, this puts a real strain on our operation. This needs to be put to bed."

"Put to bed?" Alfie said, amused. "That's an interesting term you Americans use. Put to bed. What does that mean, really?"

"I have people checking the hotels in Cairns and in Brisbane for recent arrivals. It'll take a while, but it's getting done. I want you to take him someplace away from here. We don't need the attention."

"Jay?" Roy, the bodyguard, called from the door behind them. "I'm going to have to take him into hospital, he's bloody well fucked up."

"Do what you have to," Jay said.

MARCUS WYNNE

"Right then, I'm off," Roy said.

Alfie looked at Roy's reflection in the glass and said, "Don't let the door hit you in the ass."

"Piss off," Roy said as he left.

"You may need their help, you know," Jay said.

"They're not going to be any help to me. And if this American is half as good as he is on paper, they're not going to be much good with him either."

"What are you going to do."

Alfie leaned back, and let the images of his home rise up in his mind.

"Wait," he said. "Dream a little dream."

On the long ride down from Laura, Charley told Kativa the story of the cave and the two old Law Men and what he'd felt there in the cave, deep in the heart of Quinkin country.

"It was like being in a spotlight of darkness in the light of day," he said.

"We're in a world where the normal rules don't apply," Kativa said.

"I know he bleeds," Charley said. "And as long as that rule applies, that's all I care about."

"All this feels so out of control . . . I don't know what to do and yet I feel as though I'm doing something I'm supposed to be doing, like I'm part of a plan . . ." Kativa began.

"I know exactly what you mean," Charley said. "I know exactly what you mean."

When they arrived at the hotel, Kativa went straight to the room. Charley spent a few minutes with the concierge and then went to a builder's supply house with the directions from the concierge. He bought a seventy-five-foot coil of rope and some carabiners and some lengths of strapping and returned to place it all in the locked tool locker in the bed of the pickup truck. In the cab, after a careful look around, he took out the Browning High Power and checked the chamber to make sure there was a round in place, then dropped the magazine and tested the strength of the spring with his thumb.

All was well.

He drove back to the hotel, then went up to the room, where Kativa sat on the edge of the bed, combing out her hair.

"I need a shower," he said.

"I left you plenty of hot water," she said.

Charley stripped and showered, the hot water stinging the fresh abrasions on his back, buttocks, and shoulder blades. He let the hot water beat on him till it began to run cold, then he turned off the water, his skin tingling, and dried himself with the heavy terry-cloth towels. He studied himself in the mirror. There were bags under his eyes and he hadn't shaved. He used the soap and the provided razor and scraped his face clean as best he could. Then he came out and quietly slipped into fresh shorts so as not to wake Kativa, curled into a loose ball on the still made bed. Charley stood there for a moment and looked at her, and a fierce wave of some emotion akin to affection and protectiveness rose up in him. He watched her breathing easily, then slipped into clean blue jeans and a T-shirt and let himself out, the ice bucket in hand. He padded barefoot down the hallway to the ice machine, noting and nodding to the burly man he passed in the hallway who was studying the key in his hand and the room numbers. After Charley brushed by him, the big man turned and watched him go into the alcove where the ice machine was. When he heard the rattle of ice cubes, he continued down the hall to the elevators and returned to the lobby. The big man stopped and said to the bell captain, "Which room did you say my mate Charley was in?"

"Room 304," the bell captain said.

"I knocked and there wasn't any answer."

"I could ring up for you?"

"No," the big man said. He handed the man a twenty-dollar note. "I'll drop by for him later. Thanks for your help."

"No worries, mate."

The big man went out the lobby door into the long driveway and took out his cell phone. "I've got him in the Radisson downtown, boss. Saw him myself in the hallway. It's the American for sure."

"Good work, Roy," Jay Burrell said. "What about Tim?"

"They're keeping him in hospital overnight; one of his ligaments is severed and he's going to have to have surgery to reattach it. Couldn't get him in today, so it will be first thing in the morning."

"You hang tight there," Jay said. "Get you a room there."

"As long as you're paying, boss."

"Stick close and keep an eye on the American. Find out what he's driving. We'll send someone else along to lend you a hand."

"Just don't send that bloody Abo, boss. That fella gives me the creeps and I won't put up with this bit about Tim."

"That's my worry to sort that out, Roy. Are you heeled?"

"Too right, boss."

"Don't take matters into your own hands, Roy. Wait for help. Just wait for help. Understand?"

"Got ya, boss."

"We'll speak soon," Jay said. He hung up first.

Roy went back into the hotel, nodding to the bell captain, and said, "Don't mention it to me mate if you see him, will ya? I want to surprise him."

Then he went to the check-in counter and asked the girl, "Got any rooms left?"

Alfie double-tied the laces of his low-cut chukka boots and tugged his socks up. He replaced his shirt with one the same color of his battered and worn khaki pants. A light bush jacket went over the shirt. Then Alfie opened up his weapons locker and took a look at what he had handy. He took up, then replaced a H&K PDW with a suppressor, then took it out again and laid it on the bed. He took out two magazines and several boxes of 9mm ammunition, and loaded the magazines with twenty-nine rounds each, pressing down on the last round to check the springs. He quickly stripped down the miniscule submachine gun and checked the parts, lightly oiling them with Break Free before reassembling the weapon. He took out a canvas sling for the weapon and attached it, then removed it and replaced it with a simple bungee cord. With his Leatherman tool, he crimped the ends of the bungee cord fitting round the folded stock of the weapon and the forearm grip. He took a roll of black gaffer tape and carefully wrapped the metal fittings where the bungee cord was attached and made sure that when it flexed and moved it made no noise with the metal parts all covered in layers of black tape.

That would do as his main arm.

One last thing was needed before the weapon was ready. He took a brass catcher bag fitted with a metal frame that held the bag close, but not too close, to the ejection port of the submachine gun. It would catch all the ejected cases and not leave anything for the cops to work with other than the hollow points in his target. The customized attachments with the silencer made the miniscule submachine gun a bit awkward to carry with the stock folded, but when the stock was extended it was a handy weapon for an assassination.

Which was the whole purpose of this night's operation.

He took out a .38 caliber revolver, a four-inch Smith & Wesson, and loaded it with fresh shells. That he tucked into his waistband, with two speed loaders bristling with hollow point Federal Nyclad bullets tucked into the strong side pocket of his bush jacket. In the front right pocket of his pants he clipped an Emerson Commander, the big folding fighter he favored over most other knives, and in his left pocket he shoved the Leatherman tool.

Alfie stood in front of the mirror in his bathroom and inspected himself. He flexed up and down on the balls of his feet, listening to see if any of the metal on him clicked or made noise. He was satisfied that he was dressed for silence. He took a moment, and let his brain settle and sort out the quiet in the house. He could hear stirrings in the next room, the metallic clack of a bolt being retracted and then let forward on a firearm, murmuring voices. Jay was sending one other man with Alfie to deal with the American. The other man was to be the wheelman on a Toyota minivan. The minivan reminded Alfie of the matutu buses in Africa, except this one had no windows.

There was a tap at the door.

"Come," Alfie said.

Jay opened the door and stuck only his head into the room. "You ready to go?"

"Yes," Alfie said. "I am. Who's the driver?"

"Stevie. He'll keep his mouth shut and do what you tell him."

"That will be something to see."

"If you can do it elsewhere than the hotel, that would be good."

"I don't like working with someone else."

"If you and Roy can get him into the van, take him away out bush. That would be best."

"I'll have a look around, see what we can do."

"Don't look around. Get the job done."

Alfie tugged gently on the door handle, pulling Jay slowly into the room. "Don't use that tone with me, Jay. I told you, I'll take care of it. And this is the last time. No more of this. I don't need it."

Jay stepped back into the hall. "You like the money too much."

"Not this much," Alfie said. He stepped into the hallway and brushed past Jay. "Let's go."

A short, squat, and heavily muscled man with sandy blond hair came into the hallway from the room next door to Alfie's. He had on a long black leather car coat that came to his fingertips, a white T-shirt and black Levi's and heavy boots.

Alfie looked him up and down.

"Nice outfit," he said. "What are you carrying?"

The blond man held open his jacket. Slung round his shoulder beneath the coat was a sawed-off Remington 1100 automatic shotgun. The barrel had been removed forward of the tubular magazine and the butt of the shotgun was missing after the pistol grip. Tucked into the right side of his waistband was some kind of large caliber revolver.

"Got the Remy for heavy and the Python for light," Stevie said.

"Nice," Alfie said. "Did you wipe off the brass in the Remy before you loaded it?"

Stevie looked chagrined. "No, mate, I didn't."

Alfie grinned at Jay and said, "Well, get to it, Stevie my lad, because we don't want to leave the hallways littered with shotgun shells with your prints on them, now do we?"

Alfie watched the other shooter empty the magazine of the shotgun, carefully working the action, then put on thin surgical gloves and wipe each brass shell with a handkerchief before reinserting them into the magazine.

"That's better, isn't it?" Alfie said. "Now we can go, Stevie."

Alfie brushed past his big backup and led the way toward the minivan parked outside the kitchen door. Stevie followed in his wake.

"Do as he says," Jay said to Stevie's back.

Stevie turned back and dropped a wink to Jay as Alfie went out the kitchen door.

"I got it all covered," Stevie said.

"We'll see," Jay said.

He watched the two men get into the van, Stevie in the driver's seat, and he hoped that Stevie did have it all covered. He didn't want any comeback from this, and he hoped the shotgun and the element of surprise would be enough to take Alfie off the books forever.

3.12

It was late, and Charley, lying beside Kativa in the big bed, felt restless. He'd lain down beside her to rest but couldn't sleep. Kativa stirred, then turned away from him, one hand flung over her head. She'd been sleeping since they'd returned while Charley, still abuzz with his emotions since his exploration of the cave, hadn't slept at all. He slipped out of the bed, careful not to wake her. He stood in the moonlight filtering in through the curtains and let the air-conditioning raise goose pimples on him. Outside he saw boats harbored in the hotel marina and watched the running lights of boats come and go in the harbor. Charley quietly lifted an armchair into place before the window and sat in it, propping his feet up on the windowsill. He wished for a cigar, or even a cigarette, and settled for a small bottle of Courvoisier cognac from the minibar poured into a water glass. He enjoyed the drink; it served to put his mind at rest for a short time and let his unconscious sort through his options and formulate some kind of plan.

The glowing face of the clock radio showed it to be almost 11:00 P.M.

He set his empty glass down and enjoyed the mild buzz he got from drinking on an empty stomach. He looked at Kativa, still deep in sleep, and considered calling room service but decided to wait despite the pang in his stomach. From the hallway outside his door he heard the rattle of a trolley cart. He got up and went to the door and opened it and saw a maid pushing a cart down the hall.

"Excuse me," he said. "Is room service still working?"

"Yes, sir," she said. "All night. The menu changes at eleven, though. You can get sandwiches and salads all night. There's a menu in your dresser drawer. Would you like me to..."

"No, thank you," Charley said. "I'll take a look at it. Thanks."

She smiled and nodded and continued pushing her cart down the hallway. Charley shut the door and went into the bathroom. He studied his face in the mirror. There were new lines there. He sluiced cold water from the sink over his face till he lifted the fog in his mind.

There was a knock at the door.

Charley reached for a towel and ran it quickly over his face and hands. "Just a minute," he called from the bathroom.

They entered hard. A sharp kick to the door, just under the doorknob, cracked and shattered the doorjamb and a heavy shoulder crashed the door open. The point man entered, stumbling, his short shotgun caught for just an instant on a piece of the broken jamb.

That was all Charley needed.

He let his startled jump of surprise transmute itself into a leap of anger, and he went for the shotgun, gripping the barrel and the pistol grip and levering it up toward the ceiling, tying the first man up with his own weapon. The shotgun went off as the muzzle went past Charley's head and blew a sizable hole in the ceiling, dazzling Charley with the flash and the sound. Plaster descended like fog. There was another figure behind the point man and Charley continued to maneuver the first man's body so that he was between the second man and Charley.

Charley drove a bare foot hard against the first man's lead knee, buckling his stance, and then drove his own knee hard into the man's groin and midsection, driving and driving with the knee to get him to loosen one hand. When the attacker's hand came off the forearm of the shotgun, Charley levered it round on the short strap so it was pointed backward at the head of the attacker, who saw what was coming and began to strike with his free hand at Charley. Charley struggled to put the shotgun muzzle onto the big man's body. The man was strong; he pushed as though in a rugby scrum and drove Charley back into the room. The second attacker was nowhere to be seen. For an instant the muzzle crossed the big man's shoulder and that was close enough for

MARCUS WYNNE

Charley; he pressed the trigger and a charge of buckshot tore a massive wound into the man's shoulder. The point man screamed and bucked away, pulling the shotgun with him. Charley levered the shotgun into the soft part of the man's throat and pulled the trigger. The shot blew the front of the man's skull away, and he dropped cross-legged in a heap on the floor.

Kativa screamed as the nearly headless man dropped near the bed where she sat bolt upright. Charley spun around, shotgun at the ready, expecting the second man. There was no one at the door. Charley went to the broken door and chanced a quick peek out, shotgun at the ready. There was no one there.

"Get up!" he snapped at Kativa.

He heard voices in the hallway and when he peeked out again he saw other guests peering cautiously from their doors.

"Call the police!" Charley shouted. "There's been a robbery and one of them is still loose."

"Too right," came a shout from down the hall. "We've just called."

Charley backed away from the door and stepped sockless into his shoes, leaving the short laces untied. He shouted out the door, "Everyone stay in your room! One of those men is still running around with a gun!"

He heard doors slamming shut. Then he grabbed Kativa's hand and tugged her quickly from the room and down the hallway to the exit at the end, one hand holding the sawed-off shotgun. At the end of the hallway, Charley peeked quickly into the stairwell, then pushed Kativa inside and eased the door shut behind them.

"What are we doing?" Kativa said.

"We need to be clear of that room," Charley said. "There's one more around here. I don't know if he's run off . . . he could be waiting for us. If we meet the police down here that should put him off. I'm not letting go of this gun till that happens."

They went down two flights of stairs, their footsteps soft and cautious as Charley led the way, carefully working each corner in the turning stairs till they came to the ground floor. He paused for a moment, listening. In the distance he could hear the distinctive rise and fall of the police sirens. He pressed the door open and looked out into the parking garage where the pickup truck sat.

No one there.

He took Kativa's hand and led her quickly across the open space of the driveway to the cover of the rows of parked cars. He began to stalk cautiously toward the pickup, his eyes scanning every shadow and niche in the parking lot.

"Wonk! Wonk!"

Charley froze at the strange sound. He kept the sawed-off shotgun at the ready. He pushed Kativa down behind a car as he crouched, searching for the source of the sound.

"Wonk! Wonk!"

The echoes of the sound whispered back and forth in the confusing acoustics of the garage. Charley hesitated, then led Kativa forward again quickly, closing the gap to the truck.

"Wonk! Wonk!"

Charley stopped between two cars and slid prone, looking beneath the row of cars they were in. He saw no feet, no signs of anyone crouching behind a car. He stood up carefully, took Kativa's hand, and they rushed the short distance to the cover of the truck.

"What do you want me to do?" Kativa said.

"Be quiet," Charley whispered. He slowly opened the driver's side door, peered inside, then told Kativa, "Get in. Slide all the way over."

She got in and stayed crouched below the level of the window. Charley slid in behind the wheel with the shotgun resting on the right-hand window.

Ting! A single bullet cracked the windshield.

A silenced weapon.

"Stay down!" Charley said, turning the ignition key. The truck rumbled into life and Charley worked the clutch and gearshift with his free hand, steadying the wheel with his knee, then gripping the wheel with his left hand and steering it sharply out of the parking space. He hit the gas and the truck sputtered as it accelerated.

He had only an instant to glimpse the figure that sprang from

MARCUS WYNNE

between two cars and landed on the truck's running board before he felt the hot silencer, still smoking from the last shot, dig into the soft skin behind the hinge of his jaw.

"Hey, mate," Alfie said. "Let up the gas, will you?"

The shotgun was forward of Alfie in the window; Charley couldn't lever it back to bring it to bear on him. So he eased up on the gas, slowing the truck. Everything seemed unnaturally slow and his consciousness shrank to a tight focus on the pressure of the hot muzzle against his neck and nothing else.

"Take it easy," Charley said. Kativa shrank against her door in fear.

Charley eased up on the gas even more, then pulled the shotgun trigger at the same time he stomped the brake. The blast of the shotgun at the same instant of the sudden stop caused Alfie to pull the muzzle of his machine pistol off line and his resulting shot creased Charley's jaw instead of burying itself in his neck. Alfie scrabbled on the running board for balance, then fell off, rolling neatly in a judo roll and coming up with his weapon leveled at the truck. The back window and right-hand mirror shattered in a spray of suppressed fire, the only sounds the shattering of glass and the faint *click click click* of the silenced submachine gun.

Charley felt another round crease his shoulder, another pluck at the hair on the side of his head. He kept the truck going fast, and took the first sharp curve on the exit ramp without touching the brakes. The truck teetered and sideswiped the wall, breaking off the other exterior mirror. Charley chanced a quick look back and saw nothing. He raced the truck through the next level of the parking garage to the street level. The attendant booth was empty but the crossbar was down. It was a heavy metal-reinforced job and Charley didn't think he could drive through it. He stomped on the brakes, looked round quickly, and then leaped from the truck and ran for the attendant's booth.

"Stop right there!" someone shouted.

Charley whirled around and saw two police officers aiming their pistols at him. He froze, slowly lifted his hands with the shotgun still in his right hand, and said, "There's another one here in the parking garage. He's armed with a silenced machine gun and he's coming this way."

"You're the man with the gun, mate. Down to your knees," the taller of the two policemen said. "Don't you do anything with that shotgun or I'll shoot you."

The other officer moved forward and Charley saw the sudden hole that appeared in his forehead, first black, then red as he stopped and fell forward with a look of utter surprise. Charley threw himself to one side and smashed the door of the attendant's booth open with his shoulder. He hit the lever that controlled the access arm. There were more shots; the other police officer was emptying his revolver.

Then there was silence.

Charley rolled forward out the door and came up behind the concrete pillar that held the parking arm motor and counterweight. The other police officer was down; he had a neat array of red and bleeding holes in his chest. He wore no protective vest.

Kativa sat behind the wheel in the truck. Standing on the driver's side running board and peering out from behind her, Alfie held the muzzle of his machine pistol firm against her head.

"Stay where you are, Charley," he said.

Charley pointed the shotgun at the two of them. From where he stood it was ten yards and he was on the left side of the truck; the two of them were pressed against the driver's side of the right-hand drive pickup truck.

"I know what you're thinking, Charley," Alfie said. "There's no way you're going to get a shot with that shotgun. You only have a few left . . . you're not going to try for a head shot with a sawed-off shotgun, are you? Be real, mate."

"Let her go," Charley said.

"Oh, that would be smart, wouldn't it?" Alfie said. "Just like in the bloody movies. Let the girl go, do the chivalric thing."

"If you hurt her, I'll kill you," Charley said.

"Oh, I think you'd kill me no matter what I did," Alfie said. "Where you going to go, SAS man? If you move out from cover I'll tag you and you can't hit me from there. If I move from my lovely cover here, you'll tag me. And I haven't grown old in this skin by being stupid. We'll meet again soon, Charley, and in the meantime this lovely lady will be going with me. Maybe you can catch me before I do something reprehensible, eh, mate? You know how I like to work, don't you, Charley? A little of this, a little of that, a little bit of her body fat? You know where the best parts are on a woman's body? Hips and breasts, Charley. Hips and breasts."

"Leave her be!" Charley shouted. His very being trembled with the desire to dash forward and empty his shotgun into the man taunting him from behind Kativa's fearful face.

"Not today, Charley . . . not unless you move fast. We're driving away, Charley," Alfie said.

The vehicle inched forward, Kativa working the clutch with her foot. Charley trembled with rage from behind the pillar, unable to move. The killer's words almost had the desired effect; he almost lurched out from behind cover to strike Alfie down.

"Not tonight!" Alfie shouted as the distance between them grew. "Not tonight!"

The truck turned into the street and Charley saw Alfie push Kativa over into the passenger side of the cab and take over the wheel. The truck accelerated away.

Charley had no chance of hitting him with the shotgun at thirty yards; no chance without endangering Kativa. He heard more sirens coming and knew that in moments the garage and the surrounding streets would be swarming with police. He had no time to waste explaining his circumstances. He knelt over the dead police officer and took his revolver and two reloads from his belt. He tucked the revolver inside his waistband and held the shotgun close beneath his jacket. He checked the chamber. Two shells left. Everything else had gone with the truck.

He needed a vehicle and he was going to have to get one soon. Alfie Woodard wouldn't go far in that truck and the closest place that might offer him shelter was Jay Burrell's home on the outskirts of Cairns.

WARRIOR IN THE SHADOWS

3.13

Alfie took the truck for a few blocks, neatly avoiding the arriving police, then abandoned it where he and Stevie had left the Toyota minivan. He forced Kativa into the vehicle and then drove the short distance to Jay Burrell's house.

Jay sat in his front room, his bathrobe open over bare chest and boxers, when Alfie forced Kativa into the room and down into a couch.

"What are you doing?" Jay said. "Why did you bring her here?"

"We're not staying long," Alfie said. "Her fella will be along shortly to try and collect her."

"What am I supposed to do?" Jay said. "He'll bring the cops right to my door."

"Not this bloke. He wants me for himself, doesn't he, dear?" Alfie said to Kativa.

"Now she knows me," Jay said.

"Don't matter, mate," Alfie said cheerfully. "She's going north with me."

"Don't hurt me," Kativa said.

"Wouldn't let it happen, dearie," Alfie said. "You wouldn't hurt the lady, would you, Jay?"

"Get her out of here and tell me what you expect to do about Payne."

"I'll let you work that out, mate," Alfie said. "Since our working agreement is over. That was a nasty little surprise you set up with our boy Stevie, who unfortunately didn't last the night. Not much on the uptake, that one . . . he seemed a little too eager to show me up a bit . . . before he blasted my head off."

Jay stood there for a moment, then edged slowly toward the end table beside the couch.

"I don't know what you're talking about," he said.

"Sure you do," Alfie said. "You had it all thought out. Me and Stevie do these two, then Stevie does me. Leave all three of us there for the coppers to find, makes a nice neat ending to a proper puzzle here and in the States."

Alfie's eyes gleamed as though he were suppressing laughter; he looked as though he was enjoying himself.

"Not nice, Jaybird, not nice at all," he said. "A bad way to end our relationship, mutually beneficial as it has been all these years. And it reeks of amateur hour as well. Did you think I'd let that lad backshoot me?"

Jay made the move Alfie had anticipated: a sudden lunge for the end table and the gun hidden in the drawer there. The suppressed machine pistol made a barely audible pop and the subsonic 9mm round took out Jay's knee, punching a smooth white hole that became bright red and left a massive exit wound in the soft flesh back of his knee. Jay toppled to the floor, clutching his ruined knee, his mouth open in a soundless scream of pain.

"I expect you and Charley Payne would have a lot to talk about, mate," Alfie said. "You could tell him all about what's been done and what's not. A real good heart-to-heart chat."

He stepped over Jay, paused for a moment, then put a bullet in his head.

"Wouldn't want you to have any ideas about comeback, mate," Alfie said in a gentle tone. "Sorry about the chat. I do know how you looked forward to that. Ta, mate."

Alfie pulled Kativa, shocked into silence and submission, along with him out to the garage.

The abandoned pickup truck was empty and worse than useless; the bullet-shattered windows and perforated body had drawn a crowd of gawkers and then finally the police, who swarmed the area like angry wasps whose nest has been disturbed; two dead officers left them angry and intense. Charley stood on the edge of the crowd. He'd dumped the shotgun in a trash bin and took stock of what he did have: the policeman's .38 revolver and two reloads stuck in the back of his pants beneath his shirt, a folding Emerson fighting knife in his right front pants pocket. That was the total stock of his armament. He was dressed and in shoes but his wallet with all his spare cash was on the floor of the shot-up truck and being busily gone through by responding police, one of whom came through the crowd, holding the illegal High Power between two fingers as though he were carrying a turd.

Not good.

He stepped into a fish and chips shop, well away from the crowd, and asked to use the telephone for a local call.

"No worries, Yank," the grease-spattered cook said. "Right there behind the counter."

Charley dialed Fredo's contact number from memory. The phone rang for a long time before Fredo answered it.

"Hello?"

"Fredo, it's Charley."

"Wondered when I'd be hearing from you. I've been watching the telly; they broke in special with news of that mess down your way."

"Things aren't great."

"What do you need?"

"Transport."

"Mate, we've got to be careful. I've got my directions here, too."

"I need a vehicle right now, Fredo."

There was a long sigh from the Australian.

"Right then," he said. "I saw your small friend being taken away by the police; I suppose you'll need another?"

"If you've got one to spare I won't say no."

"Where are you now?"

Charley got directions from the chip cook.

"In half an hour, be in the parking lot behind Milly's bar, just down from where you're at," Fredo said. "I'll pull up and leave the keys in the car. I'll be in the bar having a few till closing, then I'll take a taxi. When I wake up tomorrow, I'll be looking for my car. Will that work?"

"It'll do, Fredo. Thanks."

"Remember to look under the seat before you drive off. There will be a little package there for you. If anything comes back to me, I'm saying it was all stolen—you're on your own with this, mate. Sorry, but that's how it goes."

"Understood. Thanks again. I'll be there."

"Auto break down?" the chip cook said.

"Right," Charley said. "Somebody lifted my wallet as well."

"Bloody hell, probably the fucking backpackers."

"Would you advance me some chips?"

"No worries, mate."

The cook pulled fresh hot french fries from the deep fat fryer, tossed them in a bin with salt, and then scooped them up into a cone made of newspaper.

"Hot and fresh and on the house, mate."

"Thanks, friend. Appreciate the use of the phone."

"No worries. Come back by when you've found your wallet, Yank."

"I'll do that," Charley said.

MARCUS WYNNE

He went back out into the street, munching the french fries, grateful for the carbohydrates and the quick energy they represented. He stood outside Milly's bar, a lively place where a number of patrons stood out in the street and watched the crush of police cars heading for the Radisson.

It was almost exactly a half an hour to the minute when he saw Fredo pull into the unmanned parking lot in a battered old Subaru station wagon. Fredo saw him, nodded, then scanned the parking lot for any witnesses. He turned off the engine, shut off the headlights, and levered his big frame out of the small station wagon. He came up to Charley and said, "Here's your ride, mate. Remember what I said."

"Do you have any money, Fredo?"

"Wondered if you'd ask that. Look in the package. This is my personal car, so mind it. Plenty of spares and a full tank, should get you where you need to go. Doesn't eat much gas, burns a little oil. There's spare of that, too. Anything else?"

Charley held out his hand. The big man hesitated, then shook it.

"Luck, mate," Fredo said. "I got the feeling you're going to need it. And I've got quite a bit of cleaning up to do."

"I'm sorry for that. Couldn't be helped. Let our mutual friend know I'm sorry and I'll be talking to him soon."

"I'll do that, mate. Good hunting."

The big man went into the bar. Charley watched him go, then got into the station wagon and pulled out into the crowded street.

WARRIOR IN THE SHADOWS

Alfie forced Kativa into the trunk of a battered Alfa Romeo sedan. She tried to resist, but Alfie stunned her with a single vicious slap across her face, then shoved her in beside the spare tire and some loose tools.

"Be real careful now, woman," Alfie said. "We've got a long way to go at a hard drive. If you're not cooperative, you could end up at the bottom of the Laura or the Mossman River. The crocs will make a fine meal on you. Of course, you'll be drowned anyway, so that won't matter, will it?"

Kativa turned her head away as he shut the trunk closed over her, the last glimpse of his face shaded under his bush hat, his dark brown eyes, flecked with yellow in the faint light, gleaming like a feral cat's in the dark.

She was jostled and bounced as the car took off; the bad springs in the suspension gave her no rest. The smoother stretches of paved highway eventually gave way to the grind and dust of a gravel road and she knew now where he was taking her: she was on the road to Laura.

Huddled in a ball, she fought her fear. In the dark, phosphenes swam before her eyes like little dots of light. They were like the fireflies she'd seen when she visited a friend in Indiana and watched when the children gathered them up into jars and took them into the darkened houses to light up their play. After a time she began to hallucinate; stress, fear, a blow to the head, and the darkness conspired to create a series of images before her eyes: the picture of Anurra drawn in blood in the crime scene photographs; herself as a child playing in the walled-in yard of their home outside Johannesburg; the face of Charley Payne and then the figure of Alfie Woodard, the quiet figure in dusty khakis who was so very dangerous.

Dreaming, Kativa, you're dreaming now, a voice came into her head. *Dreaming of what once was and what will be again. The Laura country, the hills dotted with trees, color of sand and brown and faded green dancing in the heat of the midday sun, the feel of dry grass and dirt beneath her bare feet, and if she kept it a dream she'd walk away from this like a dream . . . she is walking through the thin forest of tall trees that give way suddenly to a clearing where the trees have shriveled down to bare broken stubs grasping like bony fingers at the sky, row upon row of clay termite mounds, each as tall as a man, and she is being prodded from behind, but each time she turns her head she can't see anything but a glimmer of something dark at the corner of her eyes, something that stays behind her with malevolent ease and glee, always behind her, prodding her forward with something large and hard and with a sudden stab of fear she realizes it's a gigantic penis, erect and hard, prodding her like a spear from behind.*

She moves forward reluctantly, the sweat of her body trickling to pool in the liquid heat that grows in her womanhood, sweat mingling with something else, a dim-edged vision of lust, Charley over her in the hotel, easing himself into her and rocking himself into a frantic eye closed and gasping orgasm, her grasping at him and feeling his body and Charley's face changing even as she came beneath him, transforming into the shadowed face of Alfie Woodard, his eyes gleaming with lust and a dark malevolent glee.

"That's right, my lovely," he said. "That's how I want you to be."

She turns to push away the hard prodding from behind, but now there's nothing there, only malevolent laughter and then the sharp Wonk! Wonk! she remembers from the parking lot, so she runs and stumbles before a termite mound. Before her eyes the mound top begins to stir, long rivulets of dirt breaking free, a small cloud of dust and then a big chunk of the mound breaks away and exposes the face of Charley Payne, his eyes black and the flesh of his face swarming with termites that take sudden wing, filling her eyes, her nose, and her mouth with the stale bitter tang of rotten flesh and she cries out "No! No!" and behind her the prodding becomes more insistent

MARCUS WYNNE

and she is forced forward over the mound, her naked breasts pushed against the rotting face of Charley and then she's entered from behind with something unbelievably large and painful and it feels as though she is being split wide open and she cries out "No! No!"

And the trunk opens and in the dim glimmer of the earliest light of the day she sees the face of Alfie Woodard looking down on her and saying, "Cheerio, Kativa. Time to get home and soon to bed, I think."

3.16

Charley drove fast and hard, racing through red lights after stopping only long enough to ensure there was no other traffic coming. The events at the Radisson had drawn every patrol officer downtown and left none on the outskirts of the city. No cops between him and Jay Burrell; nothing but road between him and Kativa and Alfie Woodard. He forced himself to mind his driving and pay attention to the road.

The small friend Fredo had given him was small indeed: a customized Walther PPK .380 automatic with a AWS suppressor on it, a quality assassination piece that would put him in prison forever if possession of a slain police officer's revolver didn't. The suppressor would give him a tactical advantage if he could take Alfie by stealth, but he had only two magazines of eight rounds each to do what he needed to do. He didn't want a gunfight; what he had in mind was a straight-up and simple execution. All he had to do was get close enough. But first he had to get through whatever security Jay Burrell had round his house.

He drove down Burrell's street and as he approached the house he dimmed his headlights and cruised by slowly. The lights were on in the house. He drove to the end of the street, where the beach parking started, and stopped the Subaru. He slid out and chambered a round in the tiny Walther. The suppressor was longer than the pistol, but when firmly gripped it balanced in a decent enough fashion. Charley held it in his hand low at his side, and walked along the beach toward the brightly lit house. From the beach, he looked into the living room and kitchen; the rest of the house was hidden from his viewpoint. He decided on fast and hard from his options; he didn't have time for stealth. He walked from the beach directly to the kitchen door and tried the handle.

Unlocked.

He eased open the door, the Walther held ready. Once inside, he left the door slightly ajar, brought the weapon up at the ready and inched through the kitchen, the sights of the silenced weapon tracking wherever his eyes went. His ears strained for any sound, his eyes preternaturally keen, even his sense of smell was heightened. There was a scent of something... what was it?

Blood and urine.

He eased around the corner into the living room and saw the body of Jay Burrell curled on the floor. There was no doubt he was dead; he could see the open cavity of his skull from where he stood. There was a massive wound on the dead man's knee; Alfie had crippled him before he killed him. Charley cleared the room as he came in. No one else was there, at least no one still living. The room didn't look as though there had been a struggle.

Charley went through the front room into the study that opened out onto the ocean. There was a big desk there. Charley looked into the drawers, starting with the bottom one first. He found a .32 Colt automatic, one of the old ones, and replaced it in the drawer. There were some surfer magazines, some correspondence, financial statements and spreadsheets. In the top drawer, as if hastily put away, was a box of Zip disks. Charley looked at the unlabeled disks, then at the expensive Macintosh PowerMac G-3 with a big Studio Display monitor set up on a separate table beside the desk. There was a Zip drive in that machine. He set the Zip disks on top of the table and thought about Terry Walker and the help he'd given him.

Time for that later.

He went quietly out of the studio and went quickly and efficiently through the rest of the house. There was no one there.

That told him exactly where Alfie Woodard would be.

He stood in what was Alfie's room and wondered at the difference

MARCUS WYNNE

between this room and the bare cave in the Laura foothills. This was a way station for a man between two worlds. A closet held motorcycle leathers, a variety of stylish shirts and leather pants, heavy black boots. On one side, segregated by bare space on the hanger bars, were two sets of identical khaki clothing, battered and worn and slightly frayed, shirts and matching pants with beat-up chukka boots beneath them. He found a battered canvas carryall in the back of the closet and took it with him. In the washroom he found a flashlight that still gleamed bright, the batteries still fresh, that and a coil of rope went into the bag. He looked around in the other rooms and grinned fiercely at his good luck when he found a Mossberg 590 Police/Military shotgun and two boxes of buckshot. Now he could reach out a little farther.

He went back to Jay's office and looked at the computer. He shoved the Zip disks into the carryall, then took down the side of the mini tower computer's main compartment. It only took a few minutes with a screwdriver to remove the hard drive and stash it in the carryall. Then he spilled a few buckshot shells out and loaded the shotgun with nine rounds in the tubular magazine and six on the sidecar ammo holder. He took three of the six rounds and carefully scored around the plastic hull of the shell a quarter inch above the brass base. Those he set in the last three slots of the ammo sidecar. Then he filled the pockets of his coat with spare shells.

Properly geared up, he looked outside to make sure no one was watching, then he took a set of car keys from the rack beside the back door and went to the car parked outside. This one had only half a tank of gas, but there was a space in the garage where a car had been recently parked. Charley went out and got back in his Subaru and drove it in and parked next to the remaining car. He cut a length of garden hose and siphoned gas from Jay's car into the Subaru. Topped off and properly gunned up, he was ready to go north.

Charley drove fast and skillfully. He'd done the route once in the light of day and he had a Queensland map book in the car. He made good time. There was a long stretch of coastal highway, and he looked out at the ocean glimmering off to his right, the hint of waves, the distant lights stretching across the water. In another time, he would have liked to have stopped the car and waded out into those waters for a quick swim to wash away his tensions and his worry and all the things he kept bottled up inside him.

But that would have to be for another time.

He made the turnoff from the paved highway to the gravel that led toward Laura and the shaman's cave. In the dizzying fatigue he carried with him, it seemed as though images rose up spontaneously, like a movie beamed into his head:

Kativa bent forward over a termite mound, savagely mounted by a squat, dark man; Charley struggling from within a termite mound, his mouth full of dirt and gasping for air as light disappeared as though he were being buried alive; maniacal laughter around him, in him, through him, permeating his head and punctuated by a rhythmic Wonk! Wonk! Wonk! Like the ringing of a great bell only inches from his head; Charley floating above Upton Street, looking in the window of his tiny apartment and seeing Mara lying alone in his bed, looking at the walls with tears in her eyes; Bobby Lee and Max and Nicky, all holding hands and Bobby Lee waving frantically at him, Nicky jumping up and down and Max holding her hands to her mouth as though to hold back a cry; and it seemed as though Bobby Lee was coming to him and he was there and he said, "Partner, slow down. He wants you to drive fast in the dark and hit something, get bogged down or killed, that would make it easy for him, you've got to slow down and take it easy, you'll get there in the daylight and that's what he's worried about. If he goes to ground and you're around in the day. If you damage your vehicle you won't get to the cave until dark and that's his country out there, he wants you on foot and alone out there in the dark with him . . . slow it down and you'll make better time, drive through the night and get there in the day and you'll be able to take him, you'll be able to find him . . . slow down, Charley, slow down . . ."

Charley shook his head violently to clear it and looked down at the speedometer. He was going too fast, driving faster than the reach of his headlights on the gravel roadway. He eased off the gas and brought the car down to something that felt like forty-five miles an hour; he was too tired and too rattled to try to translate the kilometers on the odometer to miles.

MARCUS WYNNE

In the farthest reaches of his headlights there was something in the road.

Charley pressed on the brakes, lightly at first and then harder as the Subaru swayed from side to side as it slowed. Two kangaroos stood in the middle of the road, fixed in his headlamps, staring as if fascinated by the sight of the car bearing down on them out of the dark. Even after Charley came to a complete halt, the two kangaroos stood there. They were big, at least up to his chest in height. If he'd hit them at speed, it would have been like hitting two big deer at seventy miles an hour. He'd have had them through the windshield and trashed the engine compartment for sure. He inched the Subaru forward, almost touching them before they moved in long bounds out of his way to the side of the road. They stood there and looked back at him. One lingered and stared with eyes that gleamed red in the light of the headlamps. He could swear he heard something that sounded like a faint wonk, wonk, in the distance.

He continued on more slowly and the hours slipped by in a slow, steady stream. There were more animals he slowed for, dim figures at the side of the road or hurrying across the middle, but none that stopped and stared at him as the two kangaroos had. There were many gleaming eyes on the side of the road, feral red and some of them nearly at the height of a man. This wasn't his country he moved through, this landscape of night, and he felt some hostile presence lingering, as though he were watched every inch of the way.

He continued to make good time. The pale fingers of dawn light wrinkled the night sky. It wasn't long before he drove in full light, and it seemed as though he were waking from a dream when he pulled into Laura and parked the Subaru across the street from the Quinkin Hotel and Bar. Charley sat there for a moment. His forearms trembled from holding the wheel for six hours on gravel roads and the sudden silence made him aware of a faint humming inside his head.

It was early in Laura. No one was up and about. A black dog crossed the road and went right down the center of it. Birds made an intermittent cacophony, punctuated by stretches of silence.

Everything was very still.

Charley got out of the car, stretched his back muscles, and leaned against the car while he worked the kinks out of his legs and lower back, finally putting his hands on his hips and rotating them with a series of satisfying clicks until his vertebrae settled in place. When he felt ready, he took out the canvas carryall. The shotgun would be a problem till he got out of town. He solved that by wrapping it up in a nylon tarp he found in the tire boot of the station wagon. The shotgun made a neat bundle and the carryall was slung across his back.

Then he set off.

The black dog watched him with curiosity. Nothing else stirred in the town. He stepped off quickly, walking past the old buildings and making his way up toward the foothills, following the old dirt road that passed the shanties and battered trailers of the Aboriginal settlement. Birds seemed to herald his coming, passing along a series of cries as he went past the trees where they flocked.

It took him over an hour to get to where the dirt track narrowed into the footpath that wound up into the sandstone hills. He wondered briefly if he should have brought the car this far, but coming on foot seemed more flexible; at least this way he could see and hear better. Despite his fatigue, he felt switched on. The walk had done him good. His blood was pumping and his chest rising in a steady rhythm of strong breathing. He judged himself to be far enough away to break out the shotgun. He unwrapped the weapon and chambered a round, then tucked the tarp into the carryall. He continued on, the weapon carried loosely in one hand. The hills slowly grew as he got closer. Soon he would go off the trail to parallel the path while taking advantage of the concealment of the trees and bush. He had to balance his need for speed against concealment.

Charley found his thoughts going in all directions from fatigue. It wasn't the same as last night, in the dark, when he felt as though he'd been the unwilling star in some malevolent movie. The track he walked on seemed more familiar than it should, and that thought nagged at him, the sense that he'd been here before. Of course he had been with the two Aboriginal elders, but since then he'd been plagued with sudden visions, little remembered insights that guided his feet exactly where

MARCUS WYNNE

they needed to go, guided his vision to exactly what he needed to see.

He looked ahead and saw small in the distance the sandstone outcropping and the hill where Alfie and Kativa would be. He knew that they were there right now, he could sense them in some way that he couldn't explain but just had to accept. Just as he had to accept his sudden knowing that he wasn't alone.

Around a turn in the trail, standing beside a tall tree that provided shade against the brutal heat, were Robert and his gap-toothed companion. Both men were nearly naked, dressed only in loincloth and with paint daubed and drawn on their skin, both leaning on short spears with wicked metal points. Robert held a broad-brimmed bush hat in one hand.

"G'day, mate," he said to Charley.

"What are you doing here?" Charley said, wiping perspiration from his head onto his sleeve.

"Put this on before you bake your brain," Robert said, handing Charley the old hat. "You know better than to be walking out here without cover for your head."

Charley put the hat on. "How long have you been waiting?"

"Long enough to see you," the gap-toothed elder said. He seemed taller in the light. "Saw you coming in the Dreaming last night, been waiting for you to show up. Walking our songline we been, singing the song of you and this Quinkin."

"Have you seen them?" Charley said.

"They're here in the cave, where you were before," Robert said.

"You've seen them?" Charley said.

"You still don't see things even though they're right in front of your eyes, do you now, white man with a Quinkin soul," the gap-toothed elder said. "You see some strange things on the road last night? Maybe two kangaroos looking at you? Maybe that was us or maybe it was something else, but how'd we know about it? You tell us? You're in the Dreaming now, Charley Payne. You're in Quinkin country."

"I don't have time for games," Charley said. "If you've got nothing of use to tell me, then get out of my way."

"We're here to help you, Charley," Robert said. "We've been helping you all along, ever since last night. We were out here singing the song that kept you safe on the highway, see, while that black fella up in those rocks with your woman was singing a song to kill you on your way. We've been waiting here for you because we saw you in the Dreaming, yes, the Dreaming, and we saw you coming this way. Not the same way you came before, but you already knew this way, didn't you?"

"Yes," Charley said. "I knew."

"So here's the things we brought for you," the gap-toothed elder said. "A hat for your white man's head, to keep it from burning off. And this, to keep the black fella's spell off you till you get close enough to use that shotgun." He handed Charley a rock quartz crystal the size of a walnut.

"And then this," Robert said. He handed Charley a thin bone about three inches long. "This is for the woman."

"What is this?" Charley said.

"You give it to her when you find her, when you get away. When you and the black fella fight, she'll be able to help you better with this than with any gun. You tell her to point it at him."

"Point the bone at him?" Charley said.

"Yes," the two men said as one. "Point the bone at him. The bone is for who is in the flesh with that man up there. Your shotgun will do for the man. But you need to do for both if you're going to fight Anurra in the Dreaming or out."

"Will you come with me?" Charley said.

"Not in the song," the gap-toothed elder said. "Though I'd like to see his death myself. You're meant to go alone up there and we can't see how it will go. But you have everything you need to see it through, Charley Payne."

"Everything you need," Robert affirmed. "Time for you to go. You want to meet him in daylight and you're coming up here in the middle of the day. You want to have it all sorted before dark. You don't want to be out here after dark. If we see you coming, we'll fetch you out, but you have to have it all sorted by then. Do you understand? By the light of day some things need be done. Come dark it's a different set of rules and you'll be running hard if it's not sorted by then."

The gap-toothed elder cackled with laughter. "You'll be running hard either way, Charley Payne. There's a lot of dark things up in those hills and not all of them care for Anurra, but you'd be alone on foot in dark country and you don't want that. No, you don't want that."

"Thank you," Charley said. He put the crystal in his left front pants pocket and tucked the bone in beside it.

"That's good," the gap-toothed elder said. "Keep those things close to you, we know where you are and what you're doing."

"Do you know how I can get up there any quicker?" Charley said.

"Follow your instincts and your training, Charley Payne," Robert said. "A man with your background knows how to fight from the land. Use all your skills and knowledge to see you through. You'll be all right as long as you listen to yourself and not to him."

"He's been talking to you," the gap-toothed elder said. "Ever since last night. He's got something of yours in the woman, he's been calling to her, and now he knows you, he can see you in the Dreaming."

"What can he see?" Charley said.

"Only through a fog," Robert said. "We're helping you there. He knows we're out here, he knows who we are. He and us, we've got a long history. He'd probably try to kill us off right now if he weren't so worried about you."

"We've got as much to lose as you do, Charley Payne," the gap-toothed elder said. "You're not in this alone, though you'll feel alone. You're not alone. We'll help you best we can. Remember that if it comes to fighting . . . no fighting if you can avoid it. Just kill him, quick and clean, don't mess about. Kill him quickly and you and the woman get clear of here by nightfall. We'll take care of the rest of things, things you don't need to know about."

"I'll remember," Charley said. "I didn't see any weapons in his cave. Is he armed?"

The two elders looked at each other and laughed.

"Someday you'll understand better," Robert said. "He's got all kinds of weapons, just not the kind you're used to seeing. But yes, he's got the weapons he started with last night because he knows he has to fight you on this side of the Dreaming. You're too hard to fight only in the Dream."

The other elder looked up at the sun, then back at Charley. "Go, Charley Payne. We'll be waiting for you."

They stood there as though to see him off. Charley screwed the hat down firmly on his head and strode off, his attention now on the hills ahead, his vision probing beneath the trees and the turning path in front of him. He didn't know what was happening. He had only his deepest instincts to rely on and they told him this: something larger than himself was moving through him, something that was a force for the good, and that would sustain him in the fight ahead. He kept his eyes fixed on the hill that grew steadily in his vision and he strained to see the mouth of the cave where the shadows slanted across to hide it.

There it was, a darker place in the shadows. Up there Kativa and something that went by the name of Alfie Woodard waited for him.

3.17

They had a harrowing climb up the rock face. Alfie had untied her wrists and wedged her into the crack of the rock chimney, then wedged himself beneath her and forced her up with thrusts from his hips in a frightening parody of sex. He literally threw her from the chimney into the cave, his strength seemingly superhuman. Then he came in behind her and retied her wrists.

"Do you know this country?" he asked her.

"A little bit," Kativa said.

"More than that, I think, love," Alfie said. "I know lots of things about people I take an interest in."

". . . I studied here . . ."

"Based out of Jowalbinna, weren't you? Bit farther from here. Could walk there in a day, though."

"Yes," Kativa said, "I was in Jowalbinna."

They were in the back chamber of the cave, where dim sunlight filtered down from a crevice far above. A small stream of water sprang from the wall and made a tiny, still pool against the wall before it disappeared again into the rock. Alfie sat down, his back against the wall.

"That's fresh water, there," he said, pointing to the spring. "Can you reach it all right?"

"I can't drink with my hands tied," Kativa said.

"Sure you can," he said. "Just lie on your side and your mouth will be right there, you can lap it up as nice as can be."

"What are you going to do with me?"

"Ah, that's the question, isn't it?" Alfie said.

Kativa couldn't see his face clearly in the shadows, but his eyes were wide and staring in a strange way and gleamed with feral light from beneath the hat he kept on his head. She turned away from his gaze and looked around her. This chamber didn't have the walls covered with images as did the outer chamber, but the single largest image on these walls, the centerpiece for all the others, was the large ochre image of Anurra. This was his home, his base, and all the smaller images round it told a story of conquest and killing, of men suspended upside down, of crying women, of children twisting in the gnarled hands of the Quinkin.

This was his home.

"What will I do with you, Kativa Patel?" Alfie said, more to himself than to her. "I could keep you for a while, work love magic on you, I could kill you, I could let you go. But there's that man out there . . . he's a strong one, your Charley Payne. He's a tough old bird and he won't just go away if I let you go, no, he's got blood on his mind."

"You killed his friends," Kativa said.

"Yes, I did. Purely business, though I might have used them if there had been more time. You don't know much about your friend Charley Payne, do you, Kativa?"

"I know that however long it takes, he'll get to you."

"He has a reputation for that. Did you know he was a killer, too?"

Kativa didn't rise to the bait. She felt a little bit of slack in her bonds and looked at the walls while she worked at her wrists.

"Oh, he's a killer all right," Alfie went on. "One of the best, supposedly, till he grew a conscience and got tired of being used. He and I, we're a lot alike, me and Charley Payne. Reading his file was like reading my own. We both got tired of killing for other people—even though we're quite good at it. That happens to men like us, you know . . . we reach a time in our life when it doesn't seem important anymore, the jobs, the missions—and we want to change our lives, do something different with our time. But we have all this time invested in being something that the regular world just doesn't really understand.

MARCUS WYNNE

Doesn't really want to understand. We're killers, and the truth is, at one time, we liked it. But I've grown tired of it, had enough a long time ago. What I do for myself is to help something else, to make a power grow. You felt that, didn't you?"

"I don't know what you mean," Kativa said.

"Don't pretend," Alfie said. "Your life hangs by the sheerest thread right now. You're a woman involved in men's magic and you know what happens there, don't you? What's your role in all this? How do you think you came into play?"

"I helped him find you."

"Yes, you did. That was fine work, too. Who'd of thought there was an expert on the Laura rock art working in Minneapolis?"

Alfie laughed.

"You've seen me in two of my faces," he said. "You've seen the face I wear when I go out into the world, where being an Aborigine isn't necessarily a cross to bear. That Alfie, he's a card, isn't he? I made him up from here in the cave, a man with a pleasant face who does my work for me . . . and there's this other Alfie, the one who comes and goes unnoticed, just another Aborigine in his bush clothes, probably just another drunk Abo . . . and then there's another Alfie, and it may be that he's the truest one of all. He's the one those old souls in Minneapolis saw before they died."

Kativa shrank as far as she could, the man's gaze on her like a weapon.

"It's not what you think," he said. "I'm not a rapist. I don't require you in that way. I used to have needs like that, but it's easy enough to tend to. That's something I save for my time outside. No white Australian woman would be involved with an Aborigine, and Aboriginal women . . ." He laughed. "They sense something going on with me. Real drag, that.

"You know about the Dreaming," he said. "You know about the demands of witchcraft, you know how all that works. These people, they're tools, a means to an end, to brighten the flame that surrounds me in the Dreaming. You've seen that in your own Dreaming. We're all there, you, me, Charley Payne, even the twisted little souls I gobbled up . . . they're all here. This is where they all come to. This is just one in a long series of battles that have gone on since the Dreaming. You, me, Charley—that triangle goes back.

"Look, here," he said, pointing to an image on the wall. A thin black Timara Quinkin fought with a miniscule Imjin Quinkin. The Imjin had four smaller Imjin painted inside his belly. In the background was a stick-thin female Timara Quinkin, with long pendulous breasts, hiding herself behind a rock.

"That's us there," he said. "Or so I was told by someone. Do you know how old that image is? Over fifty thousand years old, the scientists would say. Whether you believe or not is irrelevant, Kativa. Because what's true will be true whether you believe in it or not."

Alfie stood up. He studied her from beneath the down-turned rim of his bush hat. He went into the front chamber of the cave, then returned and sat cross-legged across from her, his back to the wall. In one hand he held a nut-brown human skull, in the other his submachine pistol, which he set carefully beside him.

"This man told me," he said, holding the skull balanced in the palm of his hand. "Me mate and fine teacher, Ralph. Ralph, meet Kativa, Kativa, Ralph."

He held the skull out toward Kativa and grinned at how she shied back against the wall.

"Don't worry, girl. He won't bite. Good man he was," Alfie said. He set the skull down and picked up the submachine pistol, which he stripped and began to clean with a small cleaning kit in a round metal tin. He seemed satisfied to work in silence while Kativa watched him. He quickly reassembled the weapon, working the slide back and forth. Then he inserted a magazine and chambered a round.

"There, that's ready," he said.

Then he stood up and stripped off his clothes, standing naked in front of Kativa, who stared at the scarification that striped his body. He look a loincloth and wrapped it around himself, then took his cloth roll of paints and began to hum as he painted himself. It didn't take long. He took a long bone from a stone shelf and put it through his pierced septum, then took out his partial plate and exposed his knocked-out teeth. When he was through, he took the skull in one hand and weighed it.

"We'll be busy in the front cave for a while," he said. "You'll be quiet or else I'll gag you. There's no toilet arrangements for you, so you'll have to hold it or do it in your pants. You may as well spend some time in the Dreaming yourself. You've been doing that a lot lately, haven't you?

"Right, then, Ralph?" Alfie said to the skull he held in one hand. He went into the outer chamber of the cave and left Kativa alone. The slanting light that filtered down into the back chamber seemed dull, and the day's passage somehow quicker. From the outer chamber came the droning hum of a didgeridoo, not loud, but steady and insistent, just above the threshold of her hearing.

His caution had cost him a lot of time, but at last Charley stood at the foot of the chimney beneath the shaman's cave. He'd hidden nearby for an hour, carefully watching the cave mouth, and he'd seen nothing. But he'd heard things, words carried on the hot still air, and then the drone of a didgeridoo. Charley felt the pressure of time now. It was late in the afternoon and he had a long hike to get up the back way above the cave mouth. The elder's insistence that he do what needed to be done in the light of day nagged at him. He would prefer to strike at night, take Alfie out fast and hard in the dark when he would be most tired, then take his time getting out of the area—or even stay the night till light filled the sky again.

But that thought chilled him more than the prospect of the fight to come.

He turned and moved along the face of the cliff, away from the chimney, and found the narrow footpath that led up and around the hill. The trail petered out quickly and he picked a course through the shattered fallen sandstone slabs and the boulders that dotted the hillsides like granite eggs. The ground was rough, and there were numerous holes. Water seeping from the incessant rains of the wet season had worn holes in the softer stone to make caverns beneath. Somewhere among the holes was one that opened into the shaman's cave, but he didn't want to go that way. The best way was the hard way: straight down the rock face and into the cavern.

He was nearly to the top when he saw the snake. It was as thick as his wrist, winding vigorously toward him, and it seemed as though it were coming right for him, the forked tongue probing the air, tasting for scent. Charley stepped back to avoid the snake and stepped into a sandstone hole that seemed to suck his foot down and hold it fast while he fell backward. There was a wet pop and a sudden sharp hot pain in his ankle and he knew he was in trouble now. The snake paused for a moment, as though to survey the scene, then coiled for a strike at his leg. Charley struck at it with the shotgun butt again and again. The snake struck at the stock, leaving little wet spots where it spilled venom. Charley couldn't free his leg, but he pinned the snake down with the butt of the shotgun even as it wormed closer to him, then took out his Commander knife and stabbed it right through the skull, pinning it to the ground. The snake thrashed back and forth, trying to lift its head.

Charley eased his foot out of the hole, limped back a few steps, and sat on a boulder to assess the damage. The ankle was already swollen and discolored; he had a significant sprain at the very least. He couldn't tell if it was broken, but it hurt like hell and every time he put weight on it, pain flared as though his ankle were on fire.

He was in trouble.

He looked at the snake slowly thrashing, then at the hilltop above him. No other choice, no other option. He had to go forward as best he could. He picked up a heavy stone, then limped back to the snake and thoroughly crushed its head before he took the knife out. He flicked the still twisting snake away with the butt of the Mossberg. Using the shotgun as a cane, he limped back to the boulder. He wiped the knife off in the grass, then cut a long continuous strip of cloth from his jacket. He wrapped the ankle tightly, then relaced his boot carefully over the swollen ankle, then added another length of fabric tied over the boot, doubling his support. He stood and gingerly put weight on the foot. It still hurt, but the support made it tolerable for now. He looked up the crest of the hill at the falling shadows and grimaced. He'd be lucky if he made it to the top and then the ledge that overlooked the cave's mouth in two hours.

MARCUS WYNNE

He didn't want to fight in the dark, but it looked as though he had no choice.

He toiled his way up through the boulders, biting back a scream when he banged his ankle against a rock. He used the shotgun as a cane, the duffel bag a sweaty nuisance across his back, and it was as though he could hear the two elders speaking to him.

We told you, Charley. He's slowing you down. Come full dark, that's how he wants it, you in the dark. You've got to hurry, Charley Payne, no matter how it hurts, because come full dark, if you haven't engaged him, it will be too late. Keep going and don't stop, it's not only your life in this life but in the Dreaming that counts . . .

"Son of a bitch," Charley said to himself. He chanted an old army marching song to distract himself from the pain. "C-130 rolling down the strip, Airborne Rangers on a one-way trip, stand up, hook up, shuffle to the door, stand right up and jump some more . . ."

He couldn't help but be aware of the slanting sun. The sun that had weighed so heavily on his head slanted across his shoulders now; it had fallen a measurable distance since he'd left the foot of the cliff. But he was almost to the top of the hill, and then he had only to make his way around to the front of it, where he'd surveyed the tree before. He struggled through the brush as the climb grew steeper. He grasped at heavy stones to pull himself along, and pushed with the shotgun. The butt of the shotgun grew dusty and scarred, but that was the nice thing about a pump-action shotgun, it would function no matter how dirty it got.

At the top of the hill he rested. His lungs gasped for air, and his whole body trembled with the effort it had taken. His foot throbbed angrily and the pain seemed to echo in every fiber of his being. He felt nearly done and he hadn't even started yet. He limped slowly and cautiously through the boulder field atop the hill, pausing from time to time to force his heart rate down and to look and listen for any watchers. Finally, he stood beside the big tree that marked the point above the cave's mouth. He set all his gear down and stretched out on his belly, then inched slowly along to the edge of the cliff. He listened for a few moments, then carefully poked his head out to take a look.

Nothing. No sound. Just the twenty feet or so to the ledge outside the cave, and then the long distance below to the ground.

Charley pulled back and rolled on his back. He slowed his breathing to center himself. Above him, the sky was beginning to dull with the creeping approach of sunset. He had very little time left if he wanted to get out of Quinkin country before dark.

He opened up the duffel bag and took out the length of rope. After carefully examining the length of it, he made a firm coil and then knotted one end of the rope around the base of the big tree. He lay flat on his back and tugged and tugged at the rope and studied how the tree supported it. No problem there.

He checked his knife, the blade's finish dull with the blood of the snake. The edge was still good though the tip had smashed flat on a stone; it scraped as he folded it back into its handle. The shotgun was in good shape. He slowly and quietly worked the action to be sure, then emptied the rounds from the magazine and replaced the first three with the scored rounds he'd made earlier. One scored round in the chamber, two to back it up. He didn't want to use buckshot in the cave. The silenced Walther went into the breast pocket of his shirt after he poked a hole in the bottom of the pocket for the suppressor to go through. It made for a crude but efficient holster, especially after he buttoned the flap round the grip of the pistol. The two reloads for the revolver went in his right back pants pocket, and the policeman's revolver was crammed in tight in the front of his pants. He cut another length of rope and made a crude sling for the shotgun. He hung it around his neck and thrust his right arm through the loop so that he could throw the shotgun over his back.

He was ready.

He checked the position of the sun in the sky. Long thin shadows seemed to creep from the trees. For a moment, he gave himself over to despair at his injury, the lateness of the day, being alone.

He was alone at the end of the day.

So he slung his shotgun, checked the position of his other weapons, then backed toward the cliff, making sure that when the rope coil fell, it fell to one side and not across the cave's mouth. In a good tight position, he stepped backward and began the short rappel to the cave's mouth.

Alfie crouched across from Kativa, his back to the wall, his painted body and face seeming to emerge from the images on the wall behind him. Inconstant shadows came and went from the candles he set out to augment the fading light from above.

"He's coming," Alfie said. "He's close by, but I can't see him. The old-timers, they're helping him. They can't get me themselves, though they'd love to try. The song doesn't go like that. Has to be the white man that does it now."

Kativa was silent. She stared at the man who crouched across from her. He seemed as though he had stepped straight off the wall from the images there, straight from some dark dream where he pranced and capered over her bound body.

"Charley Payne," Alfie said thoughtfully. "I've seen him in the Dreaming, just like I've seen you. He's a man of two faces. Every man has a hidden face, but Charley Payne, he knows how to go between the hidden face and the face we show everyone else. That was what he learned when he was a CIA man: how to be something and appear to be something else. That's what the Dreaming is. You see one thing, but the reality of it is something else instead. The reality is hidden, the face that shows is false. That's something your Charley knows well. That's why he's such a good hunter; he can sniff out the prey, find the ones who can guide him like you, the elders. Everything comes to him when he needs it. You've seen both sides in him, and that's part of what draws you, because you're just like us."

"I'm nothing like you," Kativa said.

"Not like me in the sense you're thinking, girl. Though I could make it be that way if I chose. You're two things in one body as well. You're not conscious of it, at least not yet. But before the night is through you'll know."

"What are you going to do to me?"

Alfie went on as though he hadn't heard her.

"You're two beings in one body," he said. "The face you show right now hides the face inside, the face so secret you don't even know what it is. That's the face I see, it's the face Charley Payne felt underneath. It's what draws you together. Look here."

He pointed one finger at an image on the wall beside Kativa.

She shifted to look at the rock painting. There was a stick figure of a woman with pendulous breasts and broad hips. On the right side of the image was another Quinkin stick figure carrying a long spear, on the left side a drawing of a smaller Imjin Quinkin wielding a four-headed club.

"It's an old fight. Do you know how old that painting is?" Alfie said. "At least fifty thousand years old. Fifty thousand years ago, a shaman in this cave looked into the fire and then at the wall and drew an image of a contest he saw in his mind. And tonight, fifty thousand years later, we'll have this contest. You've been dreaming about it, haven't you? Seen the images, felt the chase, seen the fight as it unrolls just like across a movie screen in your mind? You're a player in a much larger game. We're all pawns of something bigger, right here, and to-night something greater than us moves through the three of us, you, me, and Charley Payne."

He paused a moment as though listening.

"And I think he's here," he said. He listened intently, his head cocked to one side, and then shouted, "Hoo roo! Charley! We're back here, mate!"

3.20

Charley inched his way down the cliff until he was level with and to one side of the ledge that fronted the cave's mouth. So far he'd been as silent as possible. Braced in an L-shaped body position, his brake hand blistering from friction, he paused to listen. He heard the murmur of words coming from the cave's mouth.

This would be close work, pistol work.

He eased the revolver out of his pants with his right hand and let himself hang in the air, then quickly he pushed himself off the rock face and let the momentum carry him right onto the rock ledge. He landed on both feet, the momentum making him stumble slightly, his right hand outstretched and the front sight of the revolver aligned with his eyes. No one in the spacious front chamber, but in the back he heard the murmur of Alfie Woodard. He quickly settled himself and un-wrapped the rope from around him, looping the loose rope around a rock outcropping. He hesitated a moment, and then the voice came, a challenge from inside, "Hoo roo, Charley! We're back here, mate!"

Kativa saw Charley first. "Charley, look out! He's . . ."

Alfie catapulted across the chamber at her and struck her with a backhand while shoving her to the floor.

"Shut up," he hissed.

Kativa threw her legs against his and caused him to stumble. Charley rushed into the second chamber just as Alfie fell backward, fumbling with his machine pistol. Charley fired once, twice, three times as he came and Alfie got off a short burst. One of the rounds glanced alongside Charley's head, making him stumble backward to land with a solid thump on his buttocks, shocking his spine. He dropped the revolver and swung the slung shotgun awkwardly around. Alfie rolled backward and began to come to his feet as Charley leveled the shotgun, thumbed off the safety, and pulled the trigger. The scored slug broke off neatly at the scoring and escaped from the muzzle as one solid block of wadding, plastic hull, and buckshot, leaving only the brass head cap and a shred of plastic in the chamber. The hasty slug continued on in one solid mass. If it had impacted squarely on Alfie's shoulder, it would have blown it completely off and out of his body, but instead it hit the deltoid muscle and tore it clean off, exposing the pink bone and flesh and the yellow body fat before it dotted over with red.

"Ah, fuck!" Alfie cried, falling backward.

Charley racked the slide once again, but the shell lifter stopped on the remains of the hasty slug in the chamber. He drew out the Walther and fired as Alfie scuttled through the low opening into the farther chambers that led deep into the cave. The low *phfft* of the pistol contrasted with the whine of the ricocheting bullet as it bounced around the interior of the cave. Charley saw Alfie wriggling into the back chambers of the cave like a snake leaving a trail of blood. Charley scrambled forward but Alfie was already through into the next chamber. Holding the Walther on the passageway to cover it, Charley took out his knife and cut Kativa's bonds with one hand, then closed the blade and tucked it away.

326

"We have to get out of here," he said.

He tugged her into the front chamber, crouching low to make sure he still had a line of sight on the back chamber and the narrow entrance to the rest of the cave where Alfie had disappeared. He showed her the rope and said, "Can you let yourself down? It's not far. Wrap the rope around yourself once and walk backward till you hit the bottom, then wait for me."

"Don't go back in there," Kativa said. "He wants you to go in there after him."

Alfie called to him. "Charley Payne! You got me a good one, first blood to you, mate! Good one! C'mon back, I'll tell you how your friend died."

"Go," Charley said. He helped her with the rope and said, "If you can't stand straight back, just shinny down and keep yourself off the rocks. I have to cover you from here."

"Don't go in there, please, Charley, he wants you to go in there."

"Just go, Kativa. Now."

She let herself down and Charley watched her shinny herself down the rope, bouncing off the cliff face in several places, but she got down quickly.

"Remember the little boy?" Alfie called. "You know how he died, Charley? You know how he died? He was trying to protect his mother. You know who he called for before he bled out? He was calling for you, Charley Payne. He was calling for you to help him."

Charley turned and screamed, "Fuck you!" He worked the action and got the short bit of shotgun hull out and racked another round into the chamber. He held the gold bead sight steady on the hole, irregularly shaped like a cancerous mole, in the back wall of the second chamber where Alfie had disappeared. Then he fired another hasty slug straight into the center of the hole, racked the slide back and shook the loose bit of shell out, then fired again and shook the loose bit of shell out, then chambered one of the rounds of buckshot from the magazine and fired it into the hole, then another, then another, then another.

The cave filled with blue gun smoke, and his hearing was gone, his shouts like murmurs in his ears beneath the ringing from the concussion of the shots; his vision was blurred by drifting smoke and tears of rage and the bright muzzle flash of the shotgun.

"That's for them!" he shouted.

There was no response.

"Charley! Come down! Don't go back in there!" Kativa called up to him.

Charley backed away slowly and looked down from the ledge. Kativa stood below and waved at him, urging him down.

"I need to make sure," he said.

"It's getting dark, we have to go!" Kativa said.

He looked at the sky and the dwindling light. The cave was silent. But to clear it, he'd have to go back in and crawl headfirst through that narrow passageway. If Alfie was still alive, he'd be waiting until Charley did that and shoot him helpless in the hole.

Outside, it was growing dark.

He looked at the hole. But he had to leave. He looped the loose rope around himself and did an easy body rappel down to where Kativa waited for him.

"Let's go," he said. "As fast as we can."

Alfie Woodard wormed through the narrow passageway like a furious wounded snake. Besides the bloody wound to his shoulder, chips and rock fragments peppered his skin, and several buckshot pellets were lodged in his legs. But Alfie felt no pain now, and the blood leaking from a dozen places on him served as a lubricant as he wormed through the stone, following a narrow tunnel just barely big enough for his body. The tunnel had made a sharp turn that had saved him from the worst of the gunfire, but ricocheting pellets had struck him. The tunnel sloped upward in the depths of the hill, and after a long climb in which the rocks began to scrape his ragged flesh, he came into a chamber barely big enough to stand in.

He stood there, body trembling with exertion and something else, his body paint smeared with blood, and he threw his head back, eyes rolled back to the whites, and began to sing a song of vengeance, a song that might be fifty thousand years old. He turned off the part of himself that still felt pain and planted his back against the wall of the chamber and his feet against the opposite wall and began to climb up the narrow passageway. At the very top, like a tiny silver dime held at arm's length, was a sliver of sky, growing dull with darkness. He droned in his chest in a deep imitation of a didgeridoo, and the image in his mind was of him becoming stronger, of the weak vessel of his wounded flesh filling with strength that ignored the loss of blood, ignored the pain, ignored everything except the task at hand of getting up and out of the hole.

Images rose in his mind, released by the old song he sang: a boy, playing with sticks, dimly seen parents laughing; his foster homes; himself standing over the body of Mr. Edwards; his first parachute jump, dangling in the harness and whooping with joy, to the amusement of the Airborne instructors who'd expected him to fail; his first talk with his mentor Ralph, and the day that he had killed him; the look of resignation and acceptance in Ralph's face as he had bowed his head to accept the blow of the nulla-nulla war club; the long line of killings he'd done for Jay Burrell and how his power had grown in the quiet times after, when he'd lain here in the cave and explored it all thoroughly, all against the contingency he felt coming out on the horizon. The mission, the problem, the solution to everything that was here tonight, this was what he'd been born to do, this was why the Dreamtime ancestors had chosen him, guided him to Ralph who had taught him the way of puri-puri as best he could and then died as a willing sacrifice to propel his best and only student forward. All of this had been dreamed before, and only the end of the dream wasn't clear because that hadn't yet been decided—and that's why he had to get out of the cave.

There was a hard part in the passageway where it was too narrow for him to lever up with back and leg, so he inched his way up, callused toes gripping tiny holds and his fingers clawing for purchase on the battered stone. At the top, the narrow passage required him to turn his head so that his head went through, then one shoulder, and then the rest of his body squeezing over the agonizing wound in his other shoulder, the bloody matter spreading around the hole in the rock, and Alfie Woodard was no more, it was Anurra who stood with trembling legs beside the hole of his birth, ready for his final initiations, an initiation that required the blood of his old enemy and the woman.

He stood there and let darkness fall around him, then knelt and picked up the nulla-nulla club he'd lain there against this contingency so long ago. No more guns. This would be settled with club and knife. He looked more carefully and found the weathered plastic pouch, weighted with a stone, and took out the Emerson CQC-7, its blade still slick with the Break Free lubricant he'd sprayed on it when he'd cached it there. He clipped the knife to the front of his loincloth, took the

MARCUS WYNNE

nulla-nulla in his hand, and then limped to the edge of the cliff.

It was almost full dark, well into the gloaming of dusk. He came to the tree where Charley had rappelled from, and he laughed.

"Good one, mate," he said. He tested the rope. It still held, so he took the rope in his hand and stood there, then threw back his head and shouted out, "Wonk! Wonk!" The cry of the Quinkin hunter rang through the darkening hills. Then he wrapped the rope around him in a hasty rappel and made his way down the cliff. At the foot of the cliff he took a moment to get low to the ground and pick up their sign. Like he thought, they were wounded and slow. An Aborigine SAS trooper who'd been the best tracker in the unit knew just how to utilize that to his advantage.

"Wonk! Wonk!"

Anurra was on the hunt.

WARRIOR IN THE SHADOWS

Kativa and Charley were running through the thick brush. In the dark they had lost the thin trail and so they oriented as best they could, using the big hill and the cave as a landmark. The thorny brush tore at their clothes and skin, leaving bits of cloth clinging to branches, and Charley wished for the time to clean up their back trail. That wasn't going to happen. All they had now was speed and a good head start and the hope that their pursuer was badly wounded.

"I know I got into him," Charley said half to himself. "It will slow him down."

"He wants it this way," Kativa said, her voice full of fear. "He wants to fight you in the dark."

"What did he tell you?"

"He said that this was all foretold, that the three of us were in this together in some way."

In the distance, they heard, "Wonk! Wonk!"

The mocking cry sounded closer, or it could have been a trick of the night air, clear and cold, carrying the sound farther. Kativa stumbled and fell; Charley picked her up and urged her forward.

This is what he wants, Charley thought. *He wants us to rush blindly, and then he'll get close and bound around us, count on us being so scared we'll only look back, herded like crazed animals wild with fear.*

Charley knew how to fight that. He looked over his shoulder as he ran, calculated time and distance, read the terrain. They ran past a rock outcropping that would be perfect, on the edge of a clearing. He slowed to a stop, holding his hand up to silence Kativa's question.

He recognized this place.

In the wide clearing were long uneven rows of chest-high termite mounds, daubed clay that in the dim starlight looked like crouching humans.

"I've seen this place before," Kativa said.

"Yeah," Charley said. "We've both been here before."

He took her hand and led her back to the rock outcropping that hulked on the edge of the clearing. It was twice the height of a man, and the top was worn like an old molar, with a declivity in the center and sides that made a ragged ring around the top. He stooped, looped his hands, and hefted Kativa up on the top of the rocks. Then he held the shotgun up and said, "Take this end and pull."

With her help he pulled himself up. From the top they had a good vantage point; he could see almost a hundred yards to their rear in the dim light. He looked back over the field of termite mounds and felt a cold emptiness in the pit of his belly.

Yes, he'd seen this place before.

In the dim starlight it seemed as though everything rippled for a moment, like the still water of a pond ripples under a faint breeze. He heard the voice of Robert the Aboriginal elder saying, "You've been to this place before ... now you'll see it through."

"Did you hear something?" Charlie said to Kativa.

She paused, listening. "No," she said. "Did you?"

"I can't tell," Charley said. "I don't know anymore."

Charley counted his shotgun shells. Four shells remained in the magazine and he had two loose ones in his pocket. He thumbed those two into the magazine. That gave him six rounds of buckshot. He took the magazine out of the silenced Walther and counted four rounds in there with one spare magazine of eight rounds. He'd lost the policeman's revolver in the mad scramble in the cave. The Aborigine's machine pistol would be effective at close range, but Charley could reach out farther with the shotgun. Alfie would know that to use his weapon to maximum advantage, he'd have to get in close. Charley meant to deny him that opportunity. He'd keep him out farther with the ambush he was preparing, where he could punish the hunter with the heavy fire-power from the shotgun. Then he could move in close and finish him with the Walther.

Right here was where it would finish.

There were several other rock outcroppings he could have chosen, but this one, while not the most desirable, would work. Alfie had been a ground fighter, an infantry man, who knew how to read the terrain and he would be watching the most favorable bits for an ambush. Charley hoped to stay one move ahead of him by picking a bit that wasn't as choice but would still serve.

"Wonk! Wonk!"

He was closer still.

RANGER OF THE STARS

3.23

It surprised Alfie that they made no attempt to clear their trail. Someone with Payne's background would at least try, not that it made much difference to a tracker of Alfie's skill. But maybe the time spent as a photographer had dulled Charley Payne's operator instincts. He was limping badly and he had the woman with him, and both were slowing him down. He would be burdened with the fear of anything happening to her and that was a significant handicap. They would be somewhere just ahead, he knew. The place of their final confrontation was as well known to him as the cave he'd wormed out of. Like Kativa and Charley, his Dreaming had led him to that place before.

Up ahead was the field of rock outcroppings that surrounded the clearing where the termite mounds waited in long rows. If they were going to strike back, they'd pick a place like that. Alfie slowed and let his senses, enhanced by his altered state, probe slowly forward. There was something . . . he crouched low in the dim light and looked closely at their trail. He saw sign: a rock tipped up, exposing the dark side still matted with dirt, a single thread hanging from a thorn, the compressed dirt where a man's heavy weight and booted feet had been. He was still on track. Charley Payne was angry and alive and still mobile and he had that shotgun. For a moment, the old SAS trooper in Alfie was angry for bringing a knife to a gunfight, but then he squelched the thought: that's not how it was meant to be.

He inched forward, every sense alert, aided by his vision that seemed preternaturally keen, which limned each rock with a little nimbus of light like an aura. Each tree branch seemed to speak to him in the movement made by the breeze. He sniffed for scent that spoke to him, the smell of sweaty humans and a trace of the scented deodorant that Kativa wore.

They were close. Very close.

Charley saw the dim figure moving from rock to rock. The Aborigine sensed an ambush, but he moved forward carefully and well. There was only a hint of a hitch in his stride to indicate he'd been wounded; the man still moved with the supple flow of a healthy animal. Charley watched him with dread. The hunter was cutting their sign and like a good soldier, he was looking ahead for possible ambush sites. He'd slowed, and it seemed to Charley that their hunter was sniffing the air as though he could scent them.

The gold aiming bead on the muzzle of the Mossberg shotgun shivered a bit as Charley eased the long gun into a braced position on the rock. A hundred yards was too far for buckshot and he didn't want to mess about working with another hasty slug. He had to wait until Alfie was close enough to get most of the buckshot into him and that meant twenty-five yards. The Aborigine was carrying something in his hand that wasn't a submachine gun; it looked like a longish club.

The hunter slowed to a stalk; there was no doubt that he sensed something. He came forward, foot by cautious foot, as though he expected them to spring from the bushes. But his attention was on the rock outcroppings. As Charley hoped, Alfie needed to follow their trail into the rocks and that would bring him in close enough for the shotgun to be the decisive factor.

He hoped.

Alfie saw that the trail led into the rock. It looked as if they had slowed before they got there. Were they cautious entering the boulder field, as he was, or had they been surveying for a likely ambush site? Charley would want to fight. He would have circled back on this trail before now but for the woman. From the look of her tracks, she was nearly exhausted, dragging her feet, and Alfie knew that her long night of fear had nearly broken her. That was one of the things Alfie was counting on: the white man was tired, in country he didn't know, and he had someone else to tend to. Alfie could get close to them, run them ragged, then circle around in front and take them at close range.

But there was something in these rocks.

Be careful, a voice in his head said. *The man is close.* Alfie nodded in agreement, and then other voices rose within him.

Anurra, it's time. All this is over for you, Anurra, go back to the cave if you want to live. Anurra, look over there, what is that? Anurra, look over here, what is that? Are we out here, too, Anurra? Old Men of the Law, the Law Men, remember us, Anurra? We're here now to see you. No more humbug, no more evil from the thing that used to be Alfie Woodard. He'd been a good boy before you, but that is done and now you, Anurra, you have to go. The Old Men are watching you and we will see you die.

Alfie stayed frozen in place as those voices came and went in his head. He paused to listen, and he thought he heard the far off drone of a didgeridoo and voices raised together in a song that was singing his death. He skinned his teeth back and said, "Not tonight, Old Men. Not tonight, with your feeble songs."

He forced himself to concentrate on the trail in front of him. He picked up his pace and turned his anger into immediate action. The wound in his shoulder burned as though someone had thrust a burning ember into it and twisted it clockwise, just as the spear heated hot had burned in his leg when the Law Men wounded him as a boy.

"Piss off," Alfie said loudly, as though the voices in his head could hear him.

He stalked closer to what waited for him in the rocks ahead.

MARCUS WYNNE

3.26

Charley watched the Aborigine hunter shake his head as though deviled by insects; he stumbled forward and touched his wounded shoulder as he slowed his pace. Then he seemed to recover himself and he came toward the rocks that concealed Charley and Kativa. Charley held the gold bead sight of his shotgun on the growing figure and counted off the paces as the hunter came straight on, the caution in his pace changing to hurry. Something was bothering him, perhaps the wound or else the time he'd already spent cautiously stalking them. Alfie glided smooth and dark, part of the night, and he looked like one of the figures from the cave wall come to life, a long shadow striding between shadows coming for them.

He was almost there. A few more steps and the ambush would work. Charley guessed him to be twenty yards away and then saw that what the hunter carried for a weapon was a long ornate club. Alfie's eyes gleamed fiercely in the dark, his hair matted with sweat and blood, his body covered with smeared paints, the wound in his shoulder massive and black, still running blood. The club was firm in his hand and there was something clipped in the string of his loincloth as well.

He was close enough.

Charley held the gold bead on the Aborigine's midsection and clicked the safety off the shotgun.

Alfie threw himself to one side in a long roll that took him behind a rock even as the shotgun blasted a long tongue of flame at the rock. Charley cursed and racked the shotgun again and again, filling the night with the sing and whine of ricocheting buckshot pellets. Six rounds and the shotgun clicked empty and still he wasn't sure, though he knew he had the hunter in his sights. They had to move fast. He abandoned the shotgun and grabbed Kativa's hand. He pulled her up and they leaped from the top of the boulder and fell the six feet to the ground. When they crumpled to the ground, Charley's ankle collapsed beneath him.

"Damn!" he said.

Kativa shouted, "Charley!"

A club came whistling out of the dark to strike him solidly on the shoulder.

The click of the safety had warned him to leap for cover. The first two rounds had sent pellets biting into his right side as they glanced off the rocks. Those new wounds had slowed him even more as he blinked to restore his night vision shattered by the muzzle blast of the shotgun, and then he saw them stand and leap from the boulder. He rushed them as they landed, his club held high, and he stumbled just a bit and his blow missed the blond head and hit the shoulder . . .

Charley took the blow and spun to face his attacker. He pushed Kativa behind him. She stumbled and fell and Charley bulled forward, tying up Alfie's arms with his, pushing them both back.

"Run!" Charley shouted.

Kativa ran. Charley pushed Alfie back to create distance and fumbled for the Walther stuck down inside his shirt as Alfie swung the nulla-nulla at him again. Charley clawed the pistol out as he stumbled backward to give himself room.

But then Alfie turned away and ran after Kativa.

Kativa ran. Her fatigue and muscular soreness fell away with the rush of adrenaline her fear used to propel her forward. She looked over her shoulder and saw the face and figure of Alfie Woodard looming up behind her, one hand reaching for her and the other with the club poised high.

———

Charley was right behind them and he saw Alfie take her, the quick flash of the club, and then Alfie spun, with Kativa in front of him.

Alfie held the club across Kativa's thin neck, one end levered into his other arm in a modified figure four choke hold.

"What now, white man?" he said. "Think you can kill me before I snap her pretty little neck?"

He torqued the stick and Kativa choked, her frail hands tugging at the club.

"Put the gun down, Charley Payne. Then we'll settle this proper," Alfie said.

Charley held the weapon out in front of him. His hands trembled as he aligned the sights and kept the suppressor aimed at Alfie. He kept coming forward, but stopped when Alfie torqued the stick tighter and Kativa began to struggle for air.

"Okay," Charley said. He kept the gun aligned on Alfie. "Let her go, Woodard."

"My name's not Woodard anymore, white man. Woodard, that's a white man's name."

"Anurra, then," Charley said.

Alfie laughed. "Not bad, white man." He eased up on the stick and Kativa's breath came in short, rasping chokes.

"Here's what I propose, white man," he said. "You and me, we've men's business to see to. Old men's business, too. Not just the Old Men, but old in time. Don't you feel it? Look around you, at all those watching."

He nodded his head at the termite mounds that surrounded them.

"They're all watching. You know that? The ancestors, they'd take a body and put it in a mound, let the termites eat off all the meat, come back at the end of the season and break it open and take out the bones. They were easier to carry that way, see, and then they'd bring them back to the ancestral grounds. Very important, that. Now my ancestral grounds are run by the white man, my ancestors . . . I don't even know their names. But I have an adopted family, Charley Payne, a whole slew of adopted ancestors to call on."

Alfie threw his head back, his eyes rolling white in his head, and laughed a guttural laugh. "I've been adopted every which way you can, Charley Payne. Drop your gun. We'll finish this the way it was meant to be. You can't kill me with that .380 before I kill the woman."

Charley hesitated, then a strange certainty rose in him. He lowered the pistol and tossed it aside.

Alfie let the stick down from Kativa's neck, pushed her away, and then brought the club whirling down into a cruel blow on the outside of her leg that collapsed her in a heap, clutching at her numb and useless leg.

"Just to keep her from the gun, mate," Alfie said. He raised his club and charged forward.

Charley went for the CQC-7 knife he kept clipped in his right front pocket. He'd trained and practiced for years and he could draw, open, and slash with that knife in 1.2 seconds. He got the blade open and slashed across Alfie's stomach as he blocked the stick with his other hand. Alfie locked up with him hand to hand, his painted face only inches from Charley's, his breath hot on Charley's face, the Aborigine's face drawn in a rictus of rage, teeth skinned back and something not human glaring out of his eyes. The two men rocked back and forth, then Charley drove a knee hard into Alfie's inner thigh, causing him to stumble enough for Charley to break free and push him back with a front kick.

Alfie sprang backward and thumbed open the knife he drew from his loincloth. He lunged forward swiping with the knife and then brought the club into play, swinging it in a wide figure eight while he advanced on Charley, the club providing a shield while he looked for an opening to cut.

Charley ducked back, then lunged forward, cutting at Alfie's club hand and yanking his knife back before it was struck away. He tripped over a low rock and fell on his back, kicking out to keep Alfie away and catching an agonizing blow on his leg. He rolled to his feet and flung a hand-sized stone at Alfie, catching him in the chest. Alfie sprang forward, chopping down with his stick. Charley leaped out of range and swiped wildly with his knife to keep the Aborigine at bay.

MARCUS WYNNE

3.28

It was biting cold in Minneapolis, with a crystal-clear sky and the sharp edge of bright light on the snow piled on the streets and sidewalks. It was too cold to be sitting outside, but Charley bundled up and sat at a lone table and chair outside the Linden Hills Café. Inside, Kativa waited for their coffee and rolls. Charley took out the crystal from the left side pants pocket where he kept it. He held it up to his eyes and studied the world through it. Everything looked so normal in the light of day.

Kativa brought out coffee and croissants.

"What are you doing?" she said.

Charley wrapped his fingers around the crystal and put it away.

"Nothing," he said. "Just remembering how some things end."

"Pretty handy with that, white man," Alfie said. "Used it before. I'll take it with me to use on the woman, later."

Alfie lunged forward, poking with the stick and caught Charley a sharp, breaking blow in his ribs. As they circled, Kativa crawled for the Walther. Charley cried out, "No!" as Alfie swung and struck her across the back of her head, laying her out prone on her belly.

"Bastard," Charley hissed.

"She'll come to when I'm snacking on you," Alfie said.

Charley held a rock in one hand and his knife in the other. He feinted as though to throw the stone, then suddenly rushed in and struck Alfie hard on the wounded shoulder. Alfie screamed then, a thin high shriek like a rabbit in a snare. He dropped his club and Charley entered slashing, kicking the club away. Alfie took two long hard cuts on his left arm, but got Charley with a long gouging cut across his pectoral muscles before they both sprang back to create distance and circle once more. The two men circled each other and for each of them it seemed as though the termite mounds around them began to shimmer.

Charley saw a flash of doubt cross Alfie's face and in that moment he knew something was speaking to the hunter. He lunged forward, his knife extended like a fencer's foil, and he buried the blade in Alfie's throat, right in the hollow between the collarbones, and he twisted his knife to cut out and at the same moment felt the cold penetration of Alfie's knife deep in his belly, cold, then hot hot hot, and pushed Alfie away and saw the Aborigine bring both his hands to the terrible wound in his throat as he stumbled and then fell back.

Charley fell onto his back, pressing his hand to his belly and feeling the greasy coil of exposed intestines. Alfie's last cut had opened him, and even in the depth of deepening shock he knew to hold himself together, to hold himself hard. He lay there on his back, knife still clutched in his fist, feeling his blood pulse over his hands. He seemed to lay there for a long time, listening to his breathing and feeling himself grow cold. Then faces came into his shrinking field of vision, Kativa's and someone else. Sudden fear gripped him as he saw the painted face of an Aborigine peering over her shoulder, but then he heard the voice of Robert, the Law Man, "We've come to take you back."

Then it was as though he was borne by many hands through the bush while a song sung by many voices played in his head as he was carried to a place where the blue lights of an ambulance flashed like so many winking eyes.

MARCUS WYNNE

The surgery took weeks to recover from. Multiple cuts and blood loss and a major abdominal wound had led to a serious infection, and Charley spent long days in a dreamy haze fostered by painkillers and fatigue. But he healed well. Kativa stayed at the hospital when she could and at Fredo's when she couldn't. The police had left him alone after long questioning, even though they were barely satisfied with the story of him being set upon by drunken Aborigines who'd robbed and nearly killed him. Kativa had given Fredo the Zip disks and the hard drive Charley had taken from Jay Burrell's computer; that went a long way to making amends. Charley had gotten a bouquet of flowers, with the strong hand of Terry Walker's handwriting on the card: "With Thanks from the Christians in Action."

That told him what he needed to know.

It was toward the end of his hospital stay that Robert the Law Man came to see him.

"You're looking better, mate," the Law Man said.

"Thank you for your help," Charley said.

"It's us that should be thanking you," Robert said. "You saw it through."

Charley reached slowly and carefully into the drawer of his night-stand. He took out the small bone and the quartz crystal.

"I think you should have these back," he said. "I didn't get a chance to use them."

"Oh, you used them all right," Robert said. "I'll take the one back."

He took the small bone and tucked it into the breast pocket of his khaki shirt.

"You keep the other. A memento."

Charley held the quartz crystal in his hand, wrapped his fingers around it.

"I'll do that, Robert."